STANDALONE

STANDALONE

a Dickie Cornish mystery

Christopher Chambers

THREE ROOMS PRESS
New York, NY

Standalone
A Dickie Cornish Mystery by Christopher Chambers

ISBN 978-1-953103-23-9 (trade paperback)
ISBN 978-1-953103-24-6 (Epub)
Library of Congress Control Number: 2022935128

TRP-098

Pub Date: October 18, 2022

BISAC category code
FIC049050 FICTION / African American / Mystery & Detective
FIC049070 FICTION / African American / Urban
FIC022010 FICTION / Mystery & Detective / Hard-Boiled
FIC050000 FICTION / Crime

COVER AND INTERIOR DESIGN:
KG Design International: www.katgeorges.com

DISTRIBUTED IN THE U.S. AND INTERNATIONALLY BY:
Publishers Group West: www.pgw.com

Three Rooms Press
New York, NY
www.threeroomspress.com
info@threeroomspress.com

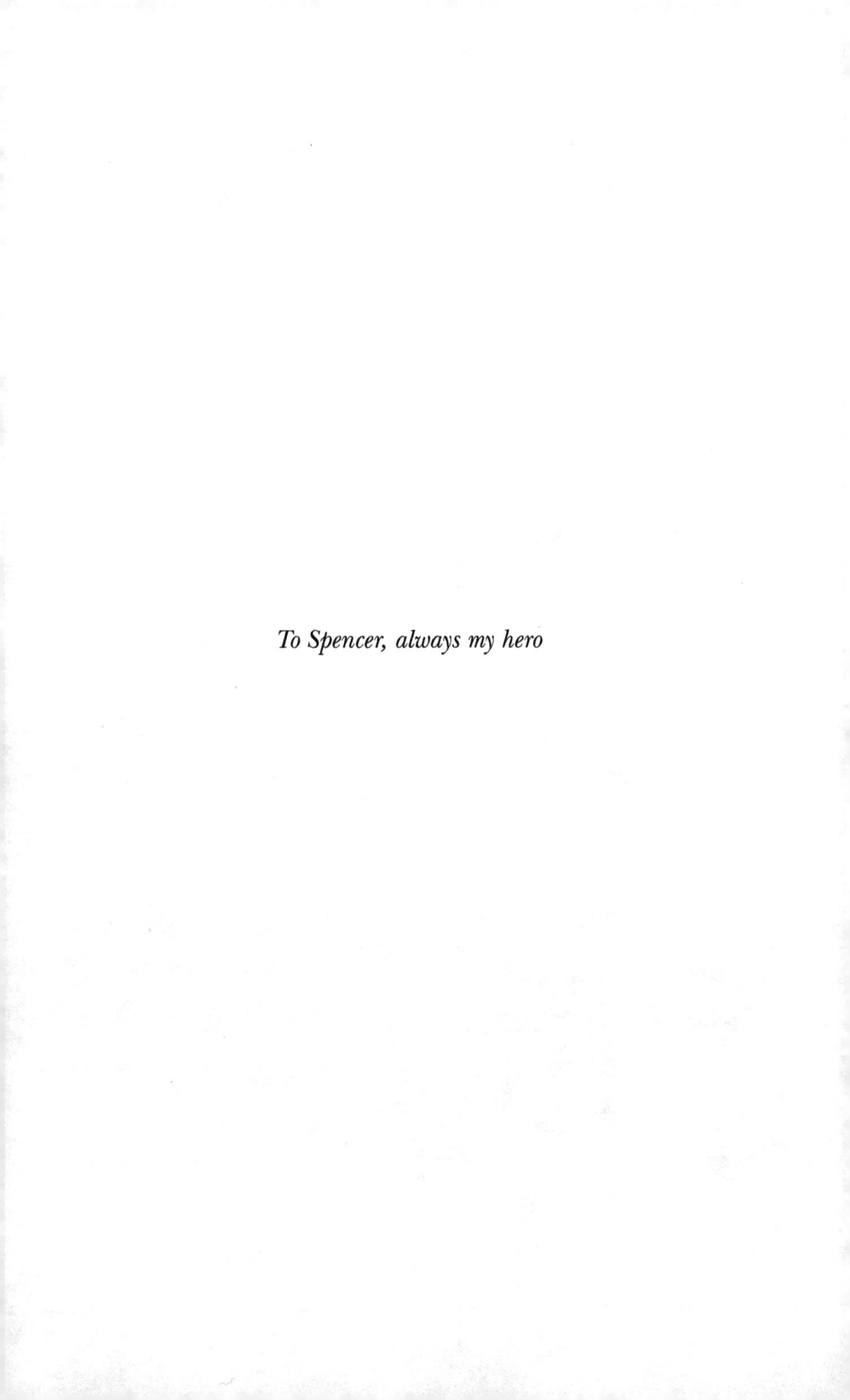

To Spencer, always my hero

STANDALONE

CHAPTER 1

Home

THE STREETLIGHTS ARE BUZZING TO LIFE as the sun dies somewhere over in Virginia. Their stark glow's staining everything and everyone on that corner in gray and silver tones. And there you are, Junior—the most hulking form cast onto that infernal shadow-puppet backdrop . . . the stink of the city saturating your thrift shop *couture* cotton shirt, all moist from the sopping wife-beater or whatever the thugs call those skivvies beneath. Trousers riding up, clingy. Towel over your head like you're one of those dogmeat prizefighters consigned to the VFW hall circuit.

"Six hunned for an Alcatel with a cracked screen?" you say. Hard to tell whether you're scoffing like real man or quibbling like an tired old fart, onaccount of that sleepy monotone of yours. Sounds worse coming through the silly-ass gingham 'rona chin-bra what looks like a damn white grandma's apron. "I told you. Unbricked iPhone, Seven or Eight. Thirty-two gigs, three-fiddy like we agreed."

Your girl running her own lil' ops competing with the T-Mobile shop . . . well, she's truly tore-up with busted cornrows furrowing her dome, a dirty frock unbuttoned down to her breasts and up to her crotch, pair of puffy bedroom slippers exposing her hammer toes . . .

"No cap, Dickie . . . this's all Android-ready," she insists, her squeaky pitch muffled by her own flimsy paper mask.

You're as brutish as Frankenstein's monster, and this middle-age bopper named "Bird" is what, maybe five-feet tall so you got to stoop to hear her. Competing with her voice are the booze-soused rants, braying car horns, and whining gears of the Number Seventy bus. And before you can counter-offer . . . up starts the thumping base and staccato snares and bravado choruses from medieval siege-bombard-sized speakers recommencing the onslaught of that D.C. Go-Go mess, full bore.

Cat in a black wave cap and baggy gymshorts like it's the Nineties turns the corner from Florida Avenue. Thanks to some headlight beams you catch him toss your girl Bird a business partner's nod . . . then a thirsty wink. Upon an equally thirsty holler-back at him she modifies the offer with a whispered, "You siced fo' Playstation Five? Customer incentive . . . "

"Disappointed in you, Bird," you inject. "Not a mess of cash out here. Not a mess of live an' kickin' customers, either—all thanks to the 'rona."

She folds. "Awite . . . iPhone *Eight.* Come on by back o' the chink carry-out, midnight."

"Kill . . . your fella over here—he's holdin' the merch. See, if I come by later, he shoves an iron in my face, takes *my* money, *my* own phone. Back his ass off till we square, cool?"

The distinguished gent in the wave cap—he doesn't even suck his teeth when you turn his ole lady Bird like you all are lovers and back her to the wall. Out comes gwap, the one you show in the street. The real McCoy's still in the larder, from

Jaime Bracht's own wallet, full up of Ben Franklins but you prefer to peel them Twennies from the bush-league monkey-shines you and Stripe call "clients" and "private eye cases." Hear me laughing, boy?

With the cash conveyed, this Nylon-headed nigga slips the proper electronics in your big mitt, wrapped in a Ziploc baggie . . .

"Whaffaw y'need *this* phone so bad, Dickie?" he then groans as if it's his fucking concern.

"Need to hook-up my associate, Ernesto. Couldn't synch his old cheap-ass phone."

"*Ernesto*?" Bird chimes in, jumping a painted-on brow. "You mean that lil' spick mo'fucka 'Stripe?' Ha, ain't he dead?"

Unfazed you whisper, "If the power cord or the sim card are bait, dead ass you'll see me again and it'll hurt . . . " Your growl cuts Bird's snickers short, but *come on,* all this "associate" shit won't reform him from the weasel what housed old folks' SSI checks for knock-off kicks at Marshall's.

Enough of this, right? Time get on with the best part of your night, most rikky-tik. Uh-huh, get across the street . . . to the CVS . . . before the pharmacy closes. To muzzle me. To murder me. Ole Gunney, your pops. The thanks I get for keeping you alive when the wolves circled by day, the monsters arrived in the cold nights. You think you got the sand now to stand against them . . . *alone* . . .

Indeed, you're giving the opposite side of Seventh a quick glance and it's like East and West Berlin back when Ole Gunney did a post at the embassy, before you were born. Over there, despite the fucking noise and pungent air . . . *Lord have Mercy* . . . the masked Chads and Beckies are having a pleasant summer evening in their flipflops as if the 'rona's a headcold . . . walking their hounds or pushing dough-faced babies . . . grabbing sixty-buck carryout for the same slop poor people on other continents buy off rusty street wagons or feed to hogs. And above them, the condo lights have all popped on. Inside, you know the rest of these sumbitches lounge under refreshing blasts of AC . . . clocking their phones for the next vaccine appointment . . . those bud-things in their ears . . . oblivious to your quaint native music and folkways.

Yet Bird's man is trying to get your attention. Better listen . . .

"Yo . . . real talk . . . you clock this mug, across't Florida Avenue?"

Given this sumbitch's vocation he does have an eye for undercover Twelve. Necessitated of course onaccount of these Black Lives Matter neophytes and bleeding hearts who you have a strange cupidity for, son. Yeah, they view dealing stolen goods as a more heinous activity than narcotics, carjacking, drive-by slaughter, eh? Still, a little healthy fear of the undercover squads, run by what the folk on that Twitter thing call the Spec Ops, or Special Operations Division, is warranted. SOD won't hesitate to run fade on anyone even mildly complicit in the illicit. Two grandmas and two middle schoolers put in the ground by them since Memorial Day . . . and so yeah, the dude adds, "Man . . . he like be *jih*-clockin' you since you come down Georgia. If he ain't a cop he snitch wiff yo' number, Dickie . . . "

Or, worse. Yeah, your past ain't exactly long past.

But damn, boy, aren't you the one all slack-jaw over YouTube how-to-be-a-shamus-in-five-easy-classes videos? Guess you missed the lesson on knowing when a nigga's tracking you. And thus Bird's man gestures theatrically, like Scrooge's

Ghost of Christmas Yet to Come, pointing out your admirer across the street.

Though whether cop or civilian, your shadow's hardly proficient at recon camouflage, as he's anything but a shadow under the full streetlight glare and the bus shelter's LED screens. Taller than you . . . a tree, though with twigs rather than mighty oak branches poking out baggy blue shorts that match his billowy cabana shirt, as if he's come from a backyard kiddie pool barbeque. And even from across the street, at dusk, this man's sunken eyes, white stubble stippling blue-black skin stretched over a skull are all sadly prominent. Timid wisps of hair on his dome makes your graying turf look like one of Patti LaBelle's best weaves back in the day. Dried-up toes sticking all out the holes of dollar-store-looking huarache sandals complete the look. He's wearing a puke-green paper mask, but your big brain doesn't need a mouth to process the rest of any face that's a regular, that's familiar . . . versus one that doesn't belong, right?

You shrug. You leave.

Yet a glance over your shoulder acquires the tar-black scarecrow hustling through cars and dodging mopeds to remain on your six. Worried now?

Look, nobody said shit about clean slates before the virus hit—back when your life changed forever. There's always going to be friends of Jaime Bracht and colleagues of his merc Mr. Sugars to green-light your ass. Remember how you cowered in your bunk, body slick with cold sweat, cradling that little .380 when an army of crackers goose-stepped through Capitol in January, tracking their own shit, looking for nigga bigshots to zip-tie? Good cover for one of them to come sniffing you out, snuff you out . . .

"Wasn't sweating . . . " you protest whisper to the air, to no one . . . to me . . . maybe the last time you ever will onaccount you're killing me soon, son. "Maybe . . . maybe it's the *Salvatrucha* homies of that lil' gangsta Blinky Guzman? They want me lullabied, too . . . "

Whatever, boy. Either way, the hitter *ain't* gonna be 007. It'll be someone like your treetop shadow . . . acting all maladroit and raggedy to fit in . . .

. . . and so inside the harsh fluorescent light of the CVS, each time you move ahead in the pharmacy line you catch him bouncing like a meerkat in the aisle where they got the Tide and toothpaste and toilet paper locked up. Just breathe, son. Mind your peripheral vision. Mind where you can hug the floor. Given you gems, son. Ain't gonna more forthcoming.

The girl in the white coat's pretty, huh? Chocolate skin, black hair's bone-straight in a horsetail that ain't fake. That's how you tell she's not Muslim—no headwrap. But you know they're color-struck as fuck over there in India, just like your redbone mother's people, all inbred up on Sixteenth and Kalmia and uncaring whether you live or die, right?

Ah yeah, here comes that sing-songey accent, just like your shrink, Dr. Kapoor. "All right sir, your Sublocade—we have no more refills. How is your stammer? Thoughts clearer?"

"Yeah . . . yes, miss. Much better."

"Good . . . so here is your lurasidone, benztropine. You understand possible side effects?"

Murderer. Assassin.

"Yeah. And what about the Valium? I need the Valium . . . "

"Mr. Cornish, there's no scrip here for diazepam. You must get preclearance from your doctor at the Veterans Administration . . . "

"*But my insomnia . . .* " Damn, Junior, think being a big nigga in a CVS fittin' to change her mind? Stand down! "M-Miss . . . it's important I get the Valium . . . like a had six months ago."

"Mr. Cornish . . . those doses might have been emergency stabilizing doses . . . the Veterans Administration flagged you for prior Xanax abuse, so the diazepam is not—"

"That's private," you cut her off. "Private patient info . . . "

"Sir, there is a line," she huffs.

Shit, this chick's as cold as that painted-up chippie at the VA, am I right Junior? The one what got some strange name on her ID . . .

"*Agave*," you mumble down to your shoes, as if this girl behind the glass can't hear you.

Yeah, like cactus. Always looking you up and down like she knows your big ass, then swishing away, jewelry jingling, onaccount you just another number on the computer screen . . . another swinging dick jived by pipsqueaks and Mumbai medics. But hey, you finally got your psycho pills in hand. Yours truly will vex you no more . . .

"Um . . . can I pay for this other stuff here, miss?" you whisper, all mopey.

The pharmacist, well, she's making a face like you farted onaccount she clocks your goodies: canned cheese, sliced pepperoni, jar of olives, jar of relish. That shit'd survive nuclear fallout. Couple c-notes for Stripe's new phone but *that's* your meal. No copay on the drugs, either *whoo-rah*!

Yet guess who steps right into your path, all oafish as you're bugging out for home?

"Ya good, moe?" you call him out through your mask, averting a collision, planned or not.

Yeah, skip worried . . . go straight to scared, onaccount he's toting a crumpled-over brown paper grocery bag from Giant and Lord only knows what gift's in there for your ass.

Then again . . . bag's tucked like John Riggins with the pigskin at old RFK, as if hes protecting it from the world. No snorts and twitches and he doesn't stink: affirmative, he's no fiend. Yet up close he's as limp and wrung out as an old dishrag. His eyes are jaundice-piss-yellow. If he's a hitter, he must need the cash for his own medicine . . .

"No trouble, gee," he says in a baritone to fit his height . . . yet breathy . . . puffing up that cheap-ass mask. "I-I get outcha way . . . "

Better decide what happens next, before God does.

Too late.

Couple of pee wees swagger in. Two are shoving right past you two dangerous-looking niggas toward the pharmacy counter. One's lingering by the glass-door drink coolers up front.

This'd look like a mere candy and Clearasil run. But for, well . . . they fucking feature hoodies when it's Sahara & Borneo hot out . . . and the hoods are flipped around their cherubic unmasked faces.

Ahhh, but what'd you see first, thanks to *me* guiding you, eh? Uh-huh. Their eyes. Unlike your shadow's peepers, their eyes are clear, vacant as marbles . . . with dead-ahead stares. Predators. Scavengers always stand-to when the predators lope in. Even if the predators are babies.

Indeed, you're criss-crossing looks with the scarecrow until he whispers what you're thinking.

"There go th' other right there . . . watchin' the exit for a guard or plainsclothes."

"How you figure?"

"Cause thas how I'd be robbin' this spot . . . back when I be robbin' spots."

Your lanky pal's not so maladroit after all; he's backing up, quiet as a giant blue-black mouse . . . eyeing the kid stationed at the entrance.

Now look, he could be a ghetto Fagin, quarterbacking these Oliver Twists and Artful Dodgers. You've been in the shit since the first infections, first layoffs and closings. Folk are still hurting if not still sick and dying. That spawns bullshit like this. And on cue, you hear a voice like some baby robot—breaking from deep to screechy . . . cold, cruel . . .

"*Codeine*, bitch, for like, coughs, he'me? Alla it or y'all get soma this . . . "

You peep your Hindu princess all wide-eyed, jerky as the little motherfuckers roam back and forth like menacing chihuahuas, yelping commands. And the toy cop's nowhere to be found.

Well, big stuttering Batman—you finger your trouser leg for the item stowed there in case your electronics merchants across the street started acting extra. Shitload of stuff down at Chuck & Billy's was for sale when the quarantine jacked the billiards at the ol' spot; you got yourself a badass Balabushka. Dude at the gas station on Ninth had a power saw, crafted it to manageable size. Makes you walk like Long John Silver when it's taped to your leg . . .

. . . and out it comes.

Knucklehead Numero Uno gets a kiss square on his knee, and sure enough he's bawling like a baby as an adult iron—a nine with an extended clip—falls right out of his little hand. Makes you prayerful about rolling up on the peckerwoods in denim or Dockers across the Potomac who've been dumping guns here since you were this child's age, but first things first . . .

"Oh shit!" screams Knucklehead Numero Dos. He grasshoppers across the counter, only to hit the clear COVID cough barrier like *yeah*—a bug on a windshield. All slapstick, he topples backward, falls next to his writhing cohort. You stomp your foot down on his piece: a rubber-gripped .22 revolver.

"*Twelve*!" he's now shouting from the floor, warning the lookout.

"Ain't no Twelve," you school, herding that boy's crab-like scampering with the cue.

"Y'all know who my big cousin is, nigga?" the pup screechs.

You pull down your mask. Your somnambulistic tone . . . it seems to scare him worse than if you're wolfing. "I don't care. Don't do this shit again. Not here, nowhere. Or I'll getcha."

You hear a disembodied adult voice. "I-I gotta make a report. Police are coming."

Toy cop. The fatbody's skulking at the door to the left of the pharmacy counter . . . yanking up his trouser waistband beneath sweatshirt and you swear you'd told that little cashier with the braces you see in there sometime to stay away from him. Always giggling when you buy a Mounds bar . . . she thinks your ass is too old for candy. Well, she's cowering behind him, sinking your heart ever-more.

The stick-up babies book. You call to the guard, "Two pistols."

And looky here . . . your shadow's uncurling his sinewy black arm from around the squirming lookout's neck. That child hoofs it as well.

"Ain't waitin' f'Twelve, gee," the scarecrow huffs.

Not a soul stops you two from leaving. And you are up Georgia past the hospital by time the first MPD units roar into the cratered CVS lot . . .

"Our faces . . . they bein' on the video," the tree says. "Mask don' mean . . . mean shit."

Your heart's barely aflutter. Like this was no big thing. "You on supervision?"

He shakes his head. "Nuh-unh. Got out Rivers, down No'th Car'lina, six on a dime befo' Biden, Miz Kamala close that fuckin' jont. Then two-monff in a minnie, then half-way house."

Funny, cons don't usually cite their pedigree. Watch his ass . . .

"I'm Dickie Cornish."

"Al-Mayadeen Thomas." He isn't loosening up on that brown paper bag. "Was . . . was watchin' you all day," Al-Mayadeen admits.

"Uh-huh."

"Need . . . need help."

"You got a roof, meals?"

He shakes that coconut head, mumbles something low and pitiful through his paper mask. Don't that sound familiar? Don't that just melt your dumbass heart?

"You tested?" you ask. "Don't mean for the Hi-Five . . . mean COVID. They test me at the VA. Vax too. No booster yet. Budget thing, they say."

"Test us at th' halfway house, then kick us out, coughin' or not."

"Look, I'm headed home. I'll fix you a plate, call folks to find you a bed tonight."

Laughing again at you, son. You never learn . . .

CHAPTER 2

Fried Bologna

YOUR NEW PAL AL-MAYADEEN LOPES BEHIND your quicker stride as if stringy a black Great Dane. What's rush, son? Sucking down those meds, getting rid of me? Funny though, how each step up Georgia Avenue brings you closer to things you hate. Including your own two hundred square foot hovel. See the crest of the rise, yonder—the glow from windows in the new apartment tower? Yeah, where Mister Fred and Miz Eva moved in spite of you. And they were murdered, thanks to you.

Al-Mayadeen catches up, pulls even with you. His mask dangles from one ear and the street's glow you make out a red foamy stain on its folds.

"What's your jont, man?" you press.

"So, uh . . . yeah," he fumbles, "I'm on the street, broke . . . I hear you help bruthas, you know peeps . . . "

"You weren't ghosting me all over town on a hot stink night 'cause you're an ex-con and got place to sleep. Real talk."

"Real talk, I wanna hire you."

Lord have mercy, boy . . . dismiss this fool.

"Stamp, moe . . . I can't help you with a court case, court supervision, appeal an' all that. It ain't my thing."

"But that ain't my problem, man." He crushes that paper bag to his chest. "Got a kite though. Kite's good as bond, right?"

"Yeah? Who's vouching?"

You're both trudging past the hospital festooned with banners proclaiming hero nurses and docs when he fesses up, "See . . . my mama . . . my mama, she tight wiff Princess. Princess Goins. Befo' she los' her mind?"

The name's a knee to your groin. You halt like you hit a wall.

"The fuck's this all about moe?"

"For real Mr. Cornish . . . Princess be my kite . . . my mama say you fed, protected Princess, them las' couple years on the street, says ya'll's campin' on the Smithsonian to keep warm. Says find this Dickie Cornish, 'cause he help . . . 'cause he help people like he help Princess . . . "

Hey, whether this is legit or not, you invited this motherfucker and you wanna snuff me so don't whine now.

You face him and school, "Listen, she's dead . . . and *how* and *why* she died, it wasn't about living on the street. Way beyond. Like bad *whitefolk* way beyond. And it still isn't safe . . . and I can't help you."

"Feds tole Mama," Al-Mayadeen offers as you knead your skull under your towel, moist with sweat, "some boy kilt her in a baffroom."

"Feds, huh?" You pivot away from him and continue up the hill-top to the Hilltop . . .

"Yeah," he continues, dark, boney legs now keeping pace. "When Mama went by the City, see where in Potters Field they bury her urn, FBI office called her and said case closed, leave it be. Ain't no boy kill her in a baffroom, gee."

"N-No, it's true. Some lil' fiend, zooted. Strangled her." Feel that delicious shiver, from your butt-crack to your neck?

Look to your three o'clock . . . maybe there's ointment for your lie at your *alma mater.* HU, Howard, the Hilltop? Empty for a year but it's been bustling with summer make-up sessions. Feel renewed, reclaimed? *No*? Don't clown yourself, son—remember you august bum, hobo junkie days being such a good Papist that on Fridays you'd roam all the damn way up here, root a half-eaten Filet-O-Fishes from Mickey Dees trash bin, yonder . . . while those precious students'd dump-truck scorn, abuse on your ass. You, the scholar-athlete once upon a time. Number Eighty-Eight, tight end, Howard Bison. Fifteen touchdowns your sophomore year. Dean's List. *Bah* . . . that place ruined you.

"N-No, *she* ruined me . . . "

"You say . . . say somffin, Mr. Cornish?"

You shake your head. Best you are wearing that mask so he can't see you mumble that name. *Esmeralda Rubio.*

"I-I just need you . . . to find someone for me, Big Man. Ain't for Twelve, my P.O. can't know . . . "

"Aw shit . . . come on, man . . . I can't get involved in that. I'm on . . . a kinda probation myself. Low key. I mean last gig was doin' security for a *quinceañera* . . . "

"Uh, a what?"

"Like a sweet sixteen party for Spanish girls. Family paid us well . . . had a shady uncle and cousins from over in Maryland, didn't know where they lived but didn't want them around their daughter. Asked me to locate that bunch, deliver the message . . . "

For someone you gently told to fuck off this tree is transfixed under that mask like you're telling a kid a bedtime story.

"So . . . so you give 'em the talk, Mr. Cornish . . . then yeah, goon-up at the front door in case they came around the party, beefin'."

You stop, winded by the hill-climb. Or is it embarrassment? "Uh-huh."

"Lawd, I bet that nigga an' he boys showed up to the jont anyhow . . . you fucked 'em up wiff that jimmy stick you got tucked in your leg, huh?"

"Uh-huh."

And the scarecrow-looking sumbitch's still staring at you dead-on when he asks, "You be a goon at a party . . . but y'all won't help me handle my shit?"

Your fumbling silence is rescued by a mass of bodies pushing onto the sidewalk. In the streetlight glimmer you see it's a gaggle of undergrad chicks, slinging their HU backpacks, parading across you all's path. Thick-as-Snickers-bar-dark cuties in tank tops, short shorts and a belly stud, or high yellow honeys in gauzy dresses. All dutifully featuring masks emblazoned with the face of that lightskin gal who's an EKG beep or two from the Oval Office.

Now, why that's significant, son, is that Mr. Al-Mayadeen Thomas won't break his stare at you, as if these lil' boppers were invisable. A man's man'd be *thirsty*, tossing leers then then playing them off. Maybe he got turned out at Rivers? Maybe he's indeed just like you, son: dead in the dick from the booze and pharmaceuticals . . . from the winters living like some animal? Anyway, another red flag . . .

"Kill, moe," you come clean. "I've *dipped* motherfuckers. Motherfuckers your moms would've seen on the news. No way she or you'd know or understand that, no matter what your troubles are."

Yeah, scarecrow swallows hard, the nostrils of his shovel nose all aflutter. "Awite . . . I-I apologize . . . already be askin' much a you for a meal, a bed, bruh."

Could've cut his ass loose there but a belly-sigh later your sentimental ass is across Georgia at Euclid with him in tow. Before you can jangle your key you're both greeted by a few wet logs of what you know to be human turds. Al-Mayadeen likely seen worse at Rivers, so he just shrugs as you call out to the likely dropper of said loaves.

"S'up Boston." He's "Boston" onaccount this winter past he was wrapped in a Red Sox or Patriots jacket, whatever. Now he's all curled-up in the cool shadow cast by streetlight's glow on a vacant shop's doorway.

"S'up Dick. Holdin', moe?" He thrusts out a black stick of a hand, keeping a dingy paper mask held to his face by the other's lemur-like fingers. That T-shirt hanging off his ribcage and shoulders might have been white at one time.

You yank down that plaid mask to your chin and give him the bad news. "Nah, cuz. Pharmacy won't let my ass near the Valley. Nighttime's the right time when the monsters play."

"Monsters bitin' at me twenny-fo'-sevem, Dick," Boston retorts. "Ain't mad atchew." He squints at Al-Mayadeen. "I seenchew 'round, moe?"

Al-Mayadeen shakes his head, turns away, mumbling, "Y'all got me traded."

"Y'ain't parked that hoopdy van 'round Girard Street?"

"Said *nah,* dude!" Al-Mayadeen sparks.

"Best better git dat busted window fixed, trust . . . " Boston adds with a sly grin.

"Here, man," you intercede, pulling the phoney gwap from your trouser pocket, opposite the leg cradling your cue stick. Peel off five ones and a five for ol' Boston.

"Dick," he wheezes, grabbing at the bucks, "y'all seent e'rybody? The Queen, Kenyatta, the Cap'n, Mitzy . . . "

"Kenyatta died three years ago man. 'Rona got the Queen and Mitzy. Cops in Virgina dipped the Cap'n. We all that's left, moe." And now Al-Mayadeen's watching you scoop up the bowel movements with some newspaper that'd been blowing like tumbleweed.

Boston, he's suddenly folding back into the shadows like a nappy-headed Nosferatu peeping a crucifix when Al-Mayadeen hips you to two ofays in an open-top, Jeep. The thing's idling at the curb. It's yellow like some big shiny banana . . .

"*Hiya*," you hear; the Chads're maskless as if they gleefully cut the line in front of nurses for the vax. One's standing, taking blinding flash phone pics of the old rowhouses fused into storefronts. The one in the driver's seat, the chatty one . . . well, you can't see his eyes behind those jazzy lunettes he's pimping in the dark.

"You talking to me, man?" you reply.

"Yep . . . we're with Potomac Ventures . . . you live in this block, right?"

"Uh-huh . . . y'all were by a week past."

"Yeah! Got this bitch for cents on the dollar, yo. Hell, our overseas partners just bought my two fav dive bars up in Petworth, and bookstore chain . . . like y'all need some vegan, holistic, woke bu'shit coloring books for ya pee wees, feel me?"

"Enjoyed the marrow, did you?" you mutter. "Tastiest part."

"Huh?"

"Inside joke . . . one scavenger to another, man . . . "

They give that white boy grin and nod. Pantomime. They could give a shit what's coming out your mouth.

Al-Mayadeen's on a different tip, son, so best better check him. See? Nigga's shaking like he's going to have a fit.

"Fuck y'all want, man?" he spurts at the Chads.

Uh-oh . . .

"Be cool big homies. We hiring security staff, cool? Need to watch the properties and stuff. Take our business cards . . . "

Sumbitch must've been buggered by white C.O.'s at privatized Rivers, onaccount Al-Mayadeen's rearing up like a lion . . . blowing so much air his damn mask pops off one ear. "*Suck my dick, pussymuvfukkahs*! Look like I need yo'shit?"

The Chad taking pics busts, "Yo Lurch and Godzilla—we'll be back . . . with cops!"

The Jeep blows off from the curb, shrouding you two in a stinging dust cloud. And Al-Mayadeen's still selling tickets to the stares of folk just out and about . . .

"Cross't th' river ova Good Hope Road we'd *handle* these muvfukkahs!" he rages.

But before you either handle him or finally cut his ass loose he's grabbing at his gut . . . now's grimacing and coughing foamy spittle as if he busted a seam in that lanky, dry body of his. As fast as whatever devil took hold of him, the surge ebbs. "M-My bad," he stammers. "Hate these grinnin' muvfukkahs."

"It's . . . cool."

Cool? Of course, Junior, he's no "5150 convict" you're about to let into your jont. Oh no, he's totally normal, well-adjusted . . . a fellow hurt soul, seeking help. It's your Biblical duty, eh?

So the Salvadoran spot takes up the first floor of your shithole building. Got fewer Pedros and Marias patronizing it than when you moved into the apartment upstairs. Can't blame ICE for that one. It was 'rona that had the hankering for Spanish flavor: cows weren't jumping into grinders of their own accord to make the burgers that got to be unpacked for the meat counter or the Mickey Dees drive-thru; hospital floors don't buff themselves. That plus living three families to a house, *shit.* Still, the survivors serve the best cheap cold lagers and slow roasted pork on Georgia Avenue!

Al-Mayadeen slides five bucks to Luz, a hawk-nosed cutie waitress wearing pink floral mask. Pilar, the owner, yanks a can of Tecate out of the cooler. Your guest offers you the first swig. You decline, as trained, and you finally see this tall nigga *smile* after he lowers his mask, takes an icy swallow from the frost-dappled can.

The heat up at the top of the stairs can knock a motherfucker unconscious; that single hanging bulb must shoot gamma rays onaccount Lord knows it only adds the misery. Just don't forget your mail, piled onto the landing. PEPCO bill, a Target circular . . . oh, and *two* window envelopes, both from *Oleksander Nimchuk, Esquire, LLC.*, putting in the work from that basement after the firm quietly "separated" his ass.

Mind the small red envelope, no return addy, Ruth Bader Ginsberg stamp.

Your new pal's a bit reticent about coming in. One room plus the head—maybe it reminds him of his cell. When he pops in, he ignores your reco that he sit down. He's still clutching that grocery bag like his nut sack's in it.

You settle onto your rack, one eye on your now fidgety guest as you tend the mail, Nimchuk's stuff first. *Paid in full, Adoption services and legal advice; consulting with Families 4Us and placement. $2,650.00.*

Al-Mayadeen drains the Tecate can, belching upon the final gulp. The hopsy odor makes you fiend for a sip.

"Who this on the wall?" he calls to you as you return copies of documents to the envelop.

"That's Fitz. West Indian dude . . . everyone called him Black Santa Claus."

"Ain't heard of him. He in the shelter at the Catholic spot wiff y'all?"

"Please sit, bruh," you invite once more as you tear open the next item from Nimchuk. He takes your chair, folds his tree limbs in to sit, bag on his lap.

Remittance confirmation: *Monthly donation from escrow, Anonymous, St. Jude Mission and So Families May Eat, paid.* $250.00.

Think they still love you there, Mr. Anonymous?

When you look up you spy this nigga pulling a packet of Big Bambu skins from his pocket with his free hand. A thimble-full of bud wrapped in foil pops next, and you're wondering how he's fixing to roll it without giving up the grocery bag.

"Yo, Mr. Cornish—this cool?"

"You be you, bruh."

"I mean . . . was goin' roll this f'you, Big Man."

"I don't do that stuff no more."

"Tha's wha' them pills'fo'? My bad . . . if you ain't finna talk on that, I hear ya."

You rise from the rack to claim a can of iced tea from your shoebox of a fridge, return. You pop the top on the can pull off your mask. Guess you trust this man's breath in your spot, huh?

"Um, listen gee," you say almost sleepily after a swallow of tea, a caress of the dainty red envelope you've yet to open. "I feel bad about shutting you down . . . but . . . just can't do *pro bono*—a hook-up—especially if it's shit Five-O, the Feds, can say is criminal, feel me? That's how serious the shit got with these whitefolks, okay? Plus . . . it's hard for me to sponsor my associate. See, he's kid, he's not a citizen yet. Got to keep him working, out of trouble, got his GED."

Cut the babble and cut the lie, boy. He knows it ain't the cash. Besides, how much of Bracht's blood money got stuffed ten feet away in the wall, yonder?

"Uh, yo' asso- . . . *associate,* he be comin' by?"

Odd question.

"Stripe? Sniffin' out work. Peruvian dude up Mt. Pleasant owns a hardware store—only independent shop up there survived the 'rona and not bought up by a big chain. Anyhow, dude's wife thinks he got a secret life, siphoning shop funds to his side chick."

"Si-fon?"

"Means, um . . . suck away. Steal."

"Sorry. So thas how you be helpin' folk—muvfukkahs steal. You get it a piece?"

He's rolling the stick with one freaking hand whilst guarding that bag so now this is getting extra.

"Listen, bruh . . . and here's something personal . . . I'm . . . I'm *not* licensed, cool? All this is a hustle till I am. Now, the City's opening a new men's shelter once they get the COVID clearance and—"

"Heard you was in the Army. Trained."

One track mind like a dog . . .

"Nah, moe. Air Force, two years after I lost my football scholarship. Made me look at photos 'cause I got a good eye and memory and shit . . . but they go and blow up kids anyway, okay? Bottom line, then, is I'm not *bona fide* till I do more hours on the YouTube training. And then there's a background check . . . and then a two-grand bond. *Yeah.* Two-long."

He licks the stick moist and tight. "Ya just bought a phone. So ya gettin' paid."

Red flags, nigga!

"You lunchin' moe?"

He backs off. "Aw . . . di'n't mean no foolishness." And he's still apologizing as he slides to your rickety dresser . . . same dresser what's got your .380 buried under draws and socks . . . same dresser topped by your weak-ass mother's Catholic beads . . . your weak-ass sister's portrait.

He places the bag on it, careful not to disturb those beads or the picture frame. He fires the jay, sits back down. Little AC in the window framed with duct tape isn't going to filter that smoke so now you are in official violation of your sobriety.

"You good, man?" you ask, now that he's chill. "I mean, you were ready to kirk those white boys . . . but it looked like it *hurt.* I know some clinic folk."

Nice diversion. "Yeah . . . uh . . . befo' they close Rivers they got nurses what do check-ups on inmates. They say I got the sugar, maybe a growth my gut."

"Sorry."

He shrugs, then asks, "Whatchew be dyin'-on back in the day Mr. Cornish?"

None of his business but hey you still want to be ghetto savior?

"Was up to six g's a day of the *Scooby-Doo* Kush, the *Trumpocalypse.*"

Al-Mayadeen sighs and shrugs like he's poor actor blowing rehearsed lines. Feed his ass, get him out!

"Sooo . . . got homemade pizza. Or, some fried bologna, toast, kidney beans for supper on the hotplate but, shit . . . lotta smoke and that'll mess with AC."

"Damn, Mr. Cornish, can't them Spanish bitches downstairs fix us plates?"

"Pilar and Luz ain't bitches, moe."

"My bad."

"And I'm chasin' dollars. So what is it, bologna or pizza?"

"Was fien'in' fo' fried bologna . . . but hell, never seent a nigga make a pizza."

Yeah, and you're getting a contact high from that dirty bud so better cook fast. You grab the plastic bag from CVS for dough-mixing. Canned cheese and that pepperoni, that relish, pickles. Yep . . . crush-up the Ritz crackers, pulverize the dry ramen noodles, shake-in that instant apple-cinnamon oatmeal for tang, all in the shopping bag. Pour the water and coffee creamer in it, son. *Nice*! Knead it good. Now the ramen seasoning packets mixed with the ketchup packets from Mickey Dees' . . . add the relish, olives . . . *mama mia* that's some good-ass sauce.

Normal folk'd be looking on in disgust at this unappetizing shit. Al-Mayadeen's just going on about some female, name of CiCi . . .

"CiCi, she purtty, man, make all them fools thirsty but she pick *me*. Don' know why. Ugly-ass me. So long ago." He releases an odd moan. "But she dead. 'Rona."

"Let's see about gettin' you a bed now." Now you're being smart.

"Muvfukkah who kilt Princess. You dip him good?"

Now that was way out of left field. As the pie rotates behind microwave's gunk-spattered glass you slip the sawed-off Babushka out of your trouser leg and he gets a long look. Yet you place it under the rack's mattress, out of reach . . .

"As I said, dude, St. Jude's will take an emergency referral. I need your P.O.'s email or number."

This nigga's getting all huffy again like he was outside.

"You think I'd snitch, moe?" he remarks, nostrils going all aflutter once more. "Got shit a my own fallin' on me. Shit you makin' clear you won't fuck with helpin' me on."

Rather than parry that jabber you offer a plastic cup for the ash and burnt skins. Time to get matter-of-fact on his ass. In that monotone of yours. "Pizza be ready, then we go downtown, get you set . . . don't bring no weed with you."

He shoots to his feet, and his head's almost bopping that nasty little light hanging from the puckered ceiling.

You're standing your ground, feet apart, arms loose but you're gaping at that black iron pipe of a chest, pumping under his shirt. If it's on, it's on . . . yet strangely, he makes no move. He swallows phlegm, seems to calm himself . . .

"Gotta show . . . show you someffin' Mr. Cornish," he whispers, "befo' I go." He points a wraithlike finger at that damn paper bag he'd kept so close. "Befo' I go, I jus' want you ta see."

You take the bag from your dresser, keeping a glance glued to this hyperventilating giant. You uncrumple the top.

"See?" he urges.

Smell is dry, stale funk, yet before you behold the contents a mess of little blueish nuggets tumble from the crimped lip and scatter on your dingy rug, as if someone showered the shit with pale sapphires . . .

. . . otherwise known as broken window fragments from somebody's whip, just as Boston quipped.

And where's your snoot, Junior? In this bag, distracted . . .

. . . until you look up to behold Al-Mayadeen's long arm reach to the small of his back, then snap forward.

A cold metal gunsight is now stamped onto your forehead. You hear a hammer lock. The microwave pings.

Pizza's done.

"Said *fried bologna*, nigga!"

CHAPTER 3
Hell Motel

"E-EASY, CUZ . . . " IS ALL you can muster as Al-Mayadeen retrieves his grocery bag skillfully, yeah—with one hand as the other keeps the iron at your head. Too bad the .380's across the room, huh? Too bad you don't listen . . .

"You clown me an' I'll dip you, nigga. *Don't give a fuck*, hear me?"

Now, unlike your boy Croc, you're no gat *aficionado*, but the figuring part of your brain not frozen in terror tells you you're looking at the bad end of a Smitty nine or forty. Enough to put you down with a splatter.

His yellowed eyes are getting get *real* wide now. Shit, maybe this was a green-light after all. Think fast or die.

"Al-Mayadeen . . . name means . . . 'squares,' good places, right?" Your damn affliction . . . your damn *beautiful* affliction. Might just save your butt.

It works, maybe. "Princess tell my mama you book smart." He thumbs the hammer forward. "So yeah . . . Mama say my name make me strong."

"I-I'm sorry I didn't hear you out, moe."

He starts blowing air as if you've insulted him, "I ain't here to blast ya or debo yo'shit, fool!"

Okay. Good.

"I need my pills . . . "

"Whatchew say, man?" Al-Mayadeen grunts.

Yeah, son—*what?*

"Look here, bruh . . . I-I need my pills. Can't do nothing without 'em."

Fuck you, boy . . .

And so he watches you dry-swallow your psychotropic shit straight from the prescription bottles. *We* . . . are dead, son!

"We finna go fo' a ride," the crazy scarecrow snorts.

And so the iron's in his front pocket, muzzle to your kidney as he ushers you down the stairs, past the cantina, toting that damn bag.

Shit . . . there's Pilar you gasp inwardly. This *Salvadoreña* is probably older than you but got that squat body stuffed all up in a black knit dress, feet squeezed into fuck-me-mules from the Eighties.

Pilar pulls her mask down to her chin, exposing her flaming cherry lips and asks, "*Puya*, Dickie . . . you okay?"

This female must know something's cooking but damn if she's going to call 911 just for you.

"*Vea* . . . I'm good," you reply. "Goin' out with my boy here."

See, she could care less. You are hereby shanghai'd. He's shoving you around to the alley, then up toward Girard Street.

Just as Boston surmised: a gray minivan's at the curb. Your affliction's pretty boss about counting and memorizing the vehicles on the block so this thing—a Dodge Caravan, recent model—must be his bucket. Yep . . . rear passenger side window's busted in with crystal granules of blueish glass matching those in the paper bag adhering to the weather stripping. Stole it, then came looking for you, son . . .

. . . and now it's time for the cherry on top of your shit sundae. Your captor doubles over, face twisted in what must be searing pain but he's still got that iron on your ass. Something's dead wrong with this cat's plumbing.

"Turn off y'phone an' give it here," he mutters, flinching.

Now he's motioning you into the Dodge with the gun . . . pointing you downward, to the glass-strewn floor mats. In the dim ambient light you note a pair of handcuffs linked to a bike chain lock, with that damn thing, in turn, hooked somewhere under the seat.

And yeah, there's a pillowcase that looks like Boston wiped his face with it.

Feel that? Your mouth going dry? Dizzy . . . got to puke? Oh, it isn't from the stained pillowcase he's shoving over your big head. Yeah, sound's getting all tinny in your ears. You gung-ho about killing me, yet you didn't peep the pamphlet the shrink Dr. Kapoor gave you at the VA? Congratulations. The pills are working.

Some final advice before I'm silenced and you're dead: mentally log each time this nigga hits the brakes, accelerates . . . every long stop, click of the turn signal, shudder, noise, smell. Yeah, hear him groaning as he starts the engine? Now he's slurping something, like a pint bottle, for the pain. Your nose figures that's Southern Comfort he's chewing on.

So the Dodge is jerking to a stop after maybe half an hour's trip. He opens the door and heaves you up to the rear seat, peels off the pillowcase.

Through the windshield, in the headlight beams, your squinting peepers spot stands of ghetto-palms swaying in the funky, soupy night breeze. Couple of rusted washing machines and wheel-less bikes strewn about. From the darkness to your right, however, comes a scratching noise normal folk might take a second to clock but you know too well: scurrying rats dueling with hovering gulls with a mountain of garbage as the prize.

Beyond the buffet, a figure parts the darkness, enters the headlights' glow. Young chick. Looks redbone or mixed. Got a scarf she's wearing over her mouth like a bandito . . . wild whirling Dervish unkempt umber hair, a tank top barely holding in pendulous, freckled titties. She's pushing a shopping cart rendered into an ersatz pram and riding inside is a toddler, maybe another girl but who knows, given similarly crazy hair.

The cart's clattering on what must be cracked pavement; she rolls up to the Dodge's open door . . . squinting inside at your face lit by the dome light.

"*That* be our hero, come ta fight th' monster? Don't look like much." She withdraws, tugs down the scarf, stands all knock-kneed. Lord, she'd be pretty if she was clean. "Mister Manny ain't goin' like this, Al-Maya. You be gettin' high . . . chewin' whiskey again, nigga?"

"G'won!" the tree yells at her.

She curses . . . skips ahead right into the blackness as if she's sporting nightvision googles . . . pushing the snot-guzzling child in the clack-clack-wheeled cart. You and your captor follow. You hear rush of cars, taste the fumes in the glowing haze ahead. A train horn sounds. Sharp toots, not a long bellow. Amtrak, not a big freight rig. See, boy—who says walking rails all day *zooted* out your mind doesn't deliver skills, eh?

Your eyes adjust and as you pass the garbage heap you note something odd underfoot . . . besides the wriggling rat tails. You are treading on weathered, dingy, broken artwork . . . and it's G-Dub and Thomas Jefferson, John Adams all cartoonish and etched onto what has to be the plastic template of what was backlit sign . . . there goes the shattered neon tubing, the sign frame, wire guts. On a brick wall's a bunch of tags. One you've never seen: an open Zippo lighter with cursive word "lit" inside. Others're familiar, like stylized "BR$" of the Benning Road Crew. Now comes the hum and hiss of maybe a dozen cheap-ass window AC units . . . most jammed inaptly in small broken sills or rattling an entire slab of plywood where plate glass used to be.

All this mess, plus the traffic and Amtrak, means this little splotch of Hell is the Colonial View Motel, close to New York Avenue. Hadn't they bulldozed this jont?.

And so you're coming in through a busted door, overhung with the sign "Banquet Facility." That light-skin chick plops down in a dimly-lit, fetid stairwell, starts picking the crud from her flip-flops and between her long toes as the kid pounds a doll's face into a cinderblock wall.

"I be Sweet Sunshine," she announces to you, utterly frosty, muffled by the scarf. "Twenny fo' head, fiddy for pussy . . . you cum in a condom. Hunnad no condom but you pull out. You wear a mask always. No kissin' or coughin' on me . . . "

You stare down at her. "I don't know you."

She tugs the scarf, hocks a load a phlegm onto pile of fallen drywall and scoffs, "Check this out: made bank off them nasty Trump muvfukkahs come ta fuck shit up las' January . . . braggin' on how they wildin' in the Capitol, huntin' fo' Miss Kamala. Uh-huh, we's boppin' in cars, RVs . . . hotels right down there. *Sheeet* . . . one coulda been my daddy. He hate Obama but he fucked my mama."

"Really?"

"Yeah, *twice* . . . cause I got a baby brotha."

"How old are you?"

Sweet Sunshine shoots to her feet. "Fuck you, big nigga!" She calls to Al-Mayadeen. "Man gimme the gun. I wanna hold it on his ass case he get froggy . . . "

His eyes are full of venom and purpose, and the chick gets wise, pipes down.

"So nobody knows y'all're here," you decide to declare. "Housin' power from PEPCO, diverting DC Water?"

"Nobody talkin' to you, *hero*," the girl hisses. Guess you're low on the totem pole, son. Or on the menu.

And so Al-Mayadeen, the rolla and her kid become the vanguard of a bizarre entourage as you move through a corridor—trash below, ceiling above dappled with dark mold, walls festooned with more tags . . . and sometimes just the words "*Help me die*." The group's probably over a dozen masked and unmasked sumbitches strong as you pass the picture windows looking out at what was the pool. The underwater lights still work . . . illuminating a creamy chartreuse nursery for mosquito larvae.

The column slows as you pass an open door, and in the light of a single bare bulb you see a rising, pale ass with its muddy middle parts, two brown, skinny legs and feet with dirty soles splayed around it. A breathy "Get some, bitch," answered by a "Yeah, daddy" follows. Catch something shiny, on the chair by the light? Could swear it's an MPD badge, huh son. Be a true bitch and cry out for help that these pink-eyed, coughing zombies got you hostage?

Nah, you gonna be Robin Hood to lil' Sweet Sunshine. "Don't y'all got a caseworker . . . city put a stop that shit didn't it?"

"*Pffft* . . . caseworker? He comin' next, an' I need the room if I goin' git paid. Now keep movin'. Mister Mannie wan' see you . . . "

Maybe not, as one your escorts, halt the whole procession. He's a little sumbitch with skin dry as parchment. Says, "Sunshine I know this big nigga! Him an' whole lotta hooligans come put me, my niece and babies' an' my clothes an' furniture in the street, take my TV wiff'em, take my house!"

A fan from your jump crew days! Two dollars an hour plus a granola bar and Metro fare!

"You're lunchin', man . . . you dunno who I am . . . "

You could break him in two with a fart but Al-Mayadeen circles back, tells him to shut up . . . and the folk pile up behind you, forcing into another room where the air's only bearable onaccount of a shuddering AC unit, giving its all. You look up and clock a swarm of black flies mourning their cohorts stuck like raisins to bug tape swaying in the AC's wash.

Against the far wall there's what at first might be a motel mattress. Nope, it's a junked hospital bed. The jumble of stiff, yellow-stained sheets on top suddenly move, and there stirs an ancient motherfucker whose face you'd swear was straight off one of those Shar-Pei chink dogs . . . the skin itself is rutted, rough . . . pinto bean-sized eyes are hidden all that flesh. Not sure what he his—Indian like Gandhi, Indian like Crazy Horse? His nose and mouth're covered in a blue paper mask. His odor's some nostalgia for you, though: gangrene, bed sores.

Strange thing. But for the redbone chippie's baby, there're no other kids among these squatters. Not normal. Kids not in foster care would be in old municipal shelter—the "munie," right? But that zoo's been shuttered what, going on four years now?

And so this old dude's definitely the honcho of the Hell Motel, onaccount he's gesturing to you, wheezing, "Name's

Mister Manny. Al-Mayadeen, he say you a vet. I a vet. D'ree tours, Vietnam." *Oh damn.* Dog or devildog?

"Air Force," you grunt. Bet this codger'd smack you silly if you told him you were once ROTC at Howard . . . though ole Gunney could've hooked your ass up with the brass, sent you to goddamn Annapolis and not your siddity mama's Negro country club! Or, hey—that you were pro-scouted by the NFL, too? Burned it all up with that first puff from a sherm stick . . . rolled by Esmeralda Rubio.

So sorry to bring her up right now. Gotta get the digs in before I fade out of your ears, forever . . .

. . . and see—just when you can't think it'll get any more dumbfuck crazy, Al-Mayadeen's pocketing the Smitty and passing to the glass-peppered grocery bag he was guarding to these zombies.

They offer it to you.

He weeps as you open the bag. And like a yawn prompts more yawns, *all* of these raggedy sumbitches are crying, and the wails are drowning out the heave and hum of the jury-rigged air conditioner. Even the tough little redbone's thumbing away the teardrops until she catches sight of you, then gets all hard and sneering again.

On the bag's top layer, under a few busted window beads, you find a faded clipping of newspaper and a frayed photocopy. *The Washington Post.* Your bed linen of choice. Not page A1, which you'd actually read by scavenged penlight in your canvass cocoon. Metro section, buried deep: *K'ymira Thomas, age six, missing . . . CiCi Talbot-Thomas and Hakim "Little" Alexander remain persons of interest yet have not been charged.* The photocopy's an age progression pic of a little girl from age six . . . to thirteen. The hair's in braids but check out the nose, cheeks—poor match to daddy's gorilla-ass visage, eh? Mom's genes?

The others sardined in there start babbling in that ebonics shit only you understand, or pidgin or patois or Spanish . . . even two hillbilly-looking bleached-blonds in fast food uniforms looking all sweat-soaked and drained . . . they all are coming at you with smudged photographs, clippings or broken images on their cracked phone screens like you're Christ of the Ghetto . . .

. . . and little faces are what you see in the photos, tattered pages, busted screens. Faces that smile despite the blight around them.

"Y'all get up offa him!" Al-Mayadeen bellows, reaching into his shorts . . . and they seem to know it's not for his pecker onaccount they halt, scatter.

"Mr. Cornish," Mister Manny croaks. He points to a decent mat of greenbacks atop a pizza box. You watch a cockroach, sluggish from a likely bellyful of crust, edge out of the box to take a gander, too. "Us all need you . . . "

"Can fix the bedsores," you whisper, trying to dodge. "Need a packet of honey from a Starbucks, get some wood stirrers . . . smear on the honey and cold water . . . cover with used dryer sheets . . . ones folk don't toss with the wet garbage . . . "

"Ain't 'bout that!" Al-Mayadeen cries, calling out your delay.

"And this ain't about Princess Goins!" you shout back at him.

Above the murmurs you hear the little light-skin rolla suck her teeth, huffing, "See, Mister Manny, you sent a big dumb nigga to go fetch *another* big dumb nigga! I tole you we need the One-Six Crew 'cause they put in work on shit, leave no fool standin'!"

Mister Manny uses all the slight breath in his frail lungs to silence the murmurs and her venomous shout-out to thugs who perpetuated this Hell. "No!" he cries. "Him the one. Him find chulrin . . . you baby brother. Al-Mayadeen daughter." He aims those scary little eyes at you now. "Find, *all*, Mr. Cornish . . . "

Sweet Sunshine re-shifts her unruly tyke onto her other hip, hangs back after Mister Manny's rebuke.

Al-Mayadeen slides down the wall to the crunchy carpet, puts his lumpy head in his hands.

Yeah, even the home crowd's all agape as you finally tug out what was so squishy in that damn bag.

A teddy bear. Eyes missing, stuffing coming out where a half a bow-tie was stitched-in.

Mister Manny rises to calm the scarecrow's sobs. "All us *already* dead, Mr. Cornish," he tells you, all stoic . . . fatal . . . as he strokes, then kisses the big man's head. "Al-Maya, too. Him snort, him tweek, but I no judge cau' he pained. Much memories." He releases the tree from the embrace and continues, "But K'ymira, alla chulrin . . . they the only thing what says 'them wha' birthed the babies, named them, was no animals. Them was human beins wid souls wha' don' live in this *Hell.*' Souls wha live-on . . . in them *chulrin.* Tha' called *Heaven* . . . "

CHAPTER 4

Ky's Bear

AL-MAYADEEN KISSES THE OLD MAN'S SPOTTED, wrinkled hand and whimpers at you, "Check the po-lice file, right? Say when my baby was taken, she had the bear. This here be *Ky's bear.* So how I gots it now, huh? Mean she *alive*!"

"How'd you get it?"

"First clue, Mister P.I. I say she sent it."

"I-I told you, man . . . I ain't a proper P.I." Oh, now the crowd's all frowning, boy. Think fast. "But look . . . I-I can hook ya'll up . . . there's this woman, Verna Leggett, and she runs the jont next to St. Jude's Mission . . . "

"Don' b'lieve shit 'bout my wife bein 'rolla, a hoe," Al-Maya-deen babbles, all-unhinged, like you used to do. "CiCi got IQ tests. She read books . . . *old* shit. Can do anything, be anything."

"An' her trick-ass never got out th' *shelter*!" Sweet Sunshine gripes. "You *touched,* nigga!"

Al-Mayadeen jumps to his boat-sized feet. Looks like he's going to glass this mouthy chick so you shout to him as your skull's tighter on the brain, feel it? Speech slurring? I you gonna on your own soon so make this count.

"I know you're all netted up . . . and I know you're sick, but lemme . . . have the gatt, bruh. You don't wanna hurt these folks . . . "

You look to Mister Manny for words that'll rope this cat in and keep the Smitty from saying peekaboo, yet the old fossil's just shaking his damn head, eyes all wet . . .

Peekaboo! Full clip pops out and in, one in the chamber. "CiCi lucky when she die," the scarecrow mumbles. Like he indeed doesn't give a shit . . .

"Don't nobody care 'bou'cho wife!" Sweet Sunshine two-cents, shrill and mean as if she's Wonder Woman, impervious to lead. "All's you spit is teddy bear this, my lil' gurl that . . . an' not *our* babies. Selfish, whinin' bitch-ass nigga is wha' you are!"

"*Shut up*!" you holler, praying this cat doesn't cap her. "Over here, bruh, look at me."

"Mr. Cornish . . . " a locked and loaded Al-Mayadeen wheezes.

"Call me *Dickie*, moe. Stop scarring these folk. Gimme the pistol."

"Ky be th' onliest *good* thing I ever done. Failed her, failed these folk. No more time leff." He sighs and whispers, "There a monster out there. *Kill it.* This'll make you remember."

He shoves that Smitty's bad end into his open mouth.

The *pop*! is muffled by the brains and meat and skull . . . blossoming into a red flower . . .

. . . onto the walls. Onto Mister Manny.

Onto Ky's bear . . .

. . . onto your face, so hot and oozing it makes you scream.

Scream so loud . . . it's like . . . your own head's splitting open.

My own head's splitting open.

Yeah. *Fuck.*

It's like first, I'm deaf. Next, every sound in the world spears my eardrum with evil clarity . . .

. . . and poor Al-Mayadeen Thomas . . . *Jesus, Mary and Joseph* . . . he's going to be just another glint in my peripheral vision, a wisp of silver-gray playing on the night sky . . . like Eva and Fred, Piedade, Marta . . . all the ghosts who won't let me sleep.

And I hear what sounds like fingers snapping in my face. My eyes open to just that scene, and then some motherfucker speaking loud . . .

"Yo, Big Man . . . wakey-wakey!"

My wrists're handcuffed behind my back. I'm cross-legged on the puckered, weed-tufted asphalt of the Colonial View's old parking lot . . . and the single working streetlamp got the shaved head of this brother who's rousing and rousting me all burnished like a brass doorknob. Stamp, he's so damn close I can smell his cologne, like spice and cedar, count his razor bumps beyond the mask. Yeah, he's wearing a mask and got on the gloves but I know cops got the first vax, right, so what's his tip? A female jake, a white girl, asks him about his new baby so maybe that's it.

New baby? Maybe he'll act human, not cop-like. "Pl-Please . . . jus' need some water, cold water," I beg him. Can't find my mask anywhere.

The brother scoffs, "So let's try this again because I think you bu'shittin' me. He brings you here at gunpoint to make you look for his kid . . . then up blows off his own head?"

"Yeah." Now I'm looking at my blood-spattered shirt . . . my fingers sticky with the congealed mess.

"You know who this mope's kid was, right? *K'ymira Thomas.* Know that was?"

I shake my head. Yeah, the news clippings, but . . .

"That's right," he snickers, "you were prolly livin' in the sewer, gettin' high. Regular news of the world was on the newspaper you were wipin' your nasty ass with, eh?"

"G-Guess so." Even at night this busted blacktop's burning my ass something fierce. "Any chance you can put me in that air-conditioned car, detective?"

"Nah-unh," he grunts. "Look, we found nothing on his phone or in here with these squatters indicating any connection with you or anyone's missing children."

"You talk to his mama?"

"That part of your story checks out." He sounds disappointed. "Picture of this Goins female—"

"Princess."

"*Princess* . . . hangin' in the kitchen."

Miss Toy's in Ward Eight, miles from here . . . so how'd he check so fast—Twelve got a Star Trek transporter? I don't press him because I can't feel my ID and phone; he's gone HNIC on me so it's best to stay cool. I crane my neck and catch the meat wagon loading what can only be Al-Mayadeen in a zippered black bag into the rear hatch.

Yet there's only single ambulance for the infirm like Mister Manny in sight.

Now I see why, and I'm squirming there on the ground, all up in my feelings. There, winding up to the jont like a giant hungry snake is a convoy of ICE vans, Parky paddywagons, blue U.S. Marshal and Bureau of Prisons Chevy Suburbans.

Didn't all these smiling bigshots tells us Trump's *tonton macoutes*'d never be caging folk like sick animals again? Well, this ain't no heat mirage, and I get a better look when baldie yanks me to my feet with the help of a jarhead-looking whiteboy jake. A jake who smells of the mold and garbage in the Colonial View.

I eyeball this whiteboy, knowingly. "You look rested. No cap . . . "

This asshole grabs my cuff chains and twists and I can't feel my fingers. Baldie's not hip to a damn thing. He might be just another nigger cop but I'm just another nigger suspect.

"Listen up, Cornish," he snorts. "I'll gladly hand your big ass to the Gestapo over there."

"Mister Manny . . . his folk . . . they didn't hurt a soul . . . "

"Some federal judge says standing orders prevail till Congress and the Mayor work it out. Above my paygrade."

"And . . . the kids?"

"Come on, Cornish . . . ain't nobody find no kids up in there!"

"Kill . . . I told you. They long *gone*."

"These mopes're about booze, 'boat, rock, bootleg benefit cards. Let the Feds worry about getting infected 'cause non' my officers're going in there." A wailing siren and flashing lights announces a DCFD pumper and a hook-n-ladder truck. He huffs through his mask, "Feds say it's a rat's nest. Crews hide dead bodies they lullabied, drugs up in there."

"Guess that's it then, Officer?" I toss to the jarheaded dude. "Sorry."

He releases the cuff torque, nods.

Baldie adds, "Gonna burn this Third World shit down. Planning Commission's been eyeing these places for malls an' shit, urban farming, whatever the fuck . . . "

So much for waiting on a conscience to appear in his eyes, seeing that he's got a new baby. Now I'm clocking the rolla, Sweet Sunshine. She and maybe ten more folk with her . . . and it's less a perp walk than an old-time slave coffle, minus the manacles and cow bells. They trudge, maskless, huddled, to a Park Police van blowing so much exhaust I'm thinking of another old-time practice . . . stories of the SS, where they'd redirect the tailpipe into the passenger compartment. And where's her baby?

This girl's staring right at me as she stumbles along, ruddy hair all matted and wet. She's grinning. Like she doesn't give a fuck. Like Al-Mayadeen said he didn't give a fuck.

"They had a lot of cash in the room . . . that'd back up my story."

"We didn't find no money . . . after Feds went in."

My head drops rather than watch that van rumble off into the polluted night, that girl digesting in its innards.

So the dick's getting right up in my face again and the big jarhead's making sure I don't look away, as I'm feeling his big freckled hand grip my occipital skull. "Look, I ain't buyin' this gentle-giant 'Sling Blade' bu'shit, ya feel me? See, I *know* you. Uh-huh, last year or thereabouts—Homicide got a tip you were good for the murder of two old folks up in Park View, Georgia Avenue Towers? They were gonna pinch you while you were in D-One lockup . . . ready for transfer on a federal felony sheet. Ring a bell? Assaulting *four* Park Police officers trying to clean out a homeless camp around the Smithsonian?"

"The two 'old folks' were my . . . my *friends* Eva and Fred. And those cops were thugs . . . "

"Word around the campfire is some K Street lawyer sprung you. Nobody knows why."

"That's . . . incorrect."

"No, that's *trouble. You're* trouble. But you ain't gonna 'cause any more when your ass in a cell at the CDF. Got nooks and crannies there they still ain't washed the virus out of, feel me?"

He won't check my eyes, like a man. "You really putting a case on me?"

"Obstruction, disrupting a crime scene."

"*Suicide scene*!"

"Hey, you said you were kidnapped at gunpoint to this hole. Thus, *crime scene*."

"*Gaslighting*."

"Huh?"

Hard to get used to me, my affliction. "Film starring Charles Boyer . . . Ingrid Bergman, based on a play . . . psychological and political term, meaning—"

His phone's suddenly blowing up, saving him from my worst blather when he answers.

Meanwhile the whiteboy jake releases my sore head, and he's dying to ask me something as the dick moves farther away for privacy, and he's more animated in the conversation.

"I don't care why you here fucking around. But you open your mouth, I'll put a Glock in it, we clear?"

"Message received. I didn't see shit."

He keeps on playing the role. "Think I'm scared of you? We just need anyone jawboning to reporters. Otherwise, you're just jungle bullshit. Takin' it back, asshole. Comply or die."

The dick's on the phone in a serious pow-wow so I retort, "Do I look like I slide down the bannister of life's crystal stair all day? I'll comply."

"Poetic," the uniform snorts, ignoring the exchange. "You *smart*, huh?"

This'd be about when the beat-down comes and they leave me in a Wendy's parking lot, but look, I *still* I don't know if this is the new, touchy-feely MPD under the lady Chief of Police, Linda Figgis . . . or normal Twelve . . . despite this cop's wolfing.

"Crystal stair? Yeah, it's from a poem, man. Langston Hughes."

"Like 'there once was a smart nigger from Nantucket . . . ' "

Suddenly I'm hearing the dick yell, "Are you kidding me? How the *fuck* did she know?" And he's throwing a fit as he signs off his call, cursing so loud even the lingering Feds are looking around.

"*No* that's a limerick," I quickly add, though trying to clock the ruckus. "How about a *haiku*: 'Peckerwood cop waits for old days to return. His boss is an Uncle Tom. Lucky.'"

"You black bastard," the white jake hisses through gritted teeth.

"Anything you can do to me has already been done, man. Seriously."

Then I hear the Uncle Tom call in a curt monotone, "Uncuff him, get him home." The jake's wide-eyed so the dick's got to repeat it. "You deaf, officer? Fucking ten-twenty-two a unit to take him home."

Yeah, I'm still worried.

"Kill, moe . . . can I wash the man's blood offa me?"

"Cut the 'moe' shit . . . I'm from Baltimore, *brotha*."

The grumbling white jake twists me around, unlocks the cuffs, shoves me the phone and wallet he'd been holding all this time, I guess.

"Anything else, asshole?" this jarhead sneers.

I almost don't say it. "That grocery bag, it's mine . . . " *Ave Maria* I pledge, inward, because it's by her hand that these motherfuckers don't see the blood sopping the little toy inside . . .

. . . and when the unit chauffeuring me home halts at the curb on Georgia Avenue I'm still the clutching the bag containing Ky's bear . . . blood seeping through the paper.

I'm scared to get out. Pilar hasn't cut-on the cantina's sign; Luz ain't slinging single cans of *cerveza* against the dram laws. No whitefolk walking their panting dogs. No Boston. Nobody.

And as I ease from the unit, I see why.

Up the block, to the right . . . three Suburbans are idling, blinkers on. Not the midnight blue Fed models with Virginia plates. Nope. Black. MPD.

To the left . . . my God. Plainclothes po-po, uniformed jakes—all dutifully wearing masks, all staring. At me. Was it those little mumble-rappers I dropped science on in the CVS? Shit, was one the mayor's nephew?

On the stairs going up to my spot I swear I'm dizzy and dented like I'm a black man-version of Alice in the rabbit hole. I'm thinking now maybe it's the black mold in the Colonial View fucking with my dome. See, here goes the Mad Hatter—a tall white man in a dark blue business suit . . . gaunt face, graying hair that's slicked-back . . . a hawk's eyes and the nose go with it poking his black mask. Got a shiny gold shield as a lapel pin and he isn't smiling. Stuck on his flank so close I got to back him away to get by is the Door Mouse—basic pot-belly dick with a brushy old-school mustache, gray suit, another lapel pin . . . earpiece and mic.

On the landing above where this dapper Boris Karloff-type and his goon loiter are two black men, sweating in the risen heat. Tweedle-dee: rotund, gray mustache . . . light-skinned, green-eyed like Mom and Alma, pimping the white blouse, star-spangled epaulets of command. He's still puffing breaths from the climb up. Tweedle-dum: the other uniformed HNIC, also brimming with ribbons and stars. A bit younger, leaner . . . stink grin like the Cheshire cat . . .

. . . and my apartment is door is wide open.

The piquant rot of the pizza I never got to eat spills onto the landing, yet it's balanced by something else. Rose scent. Le Labo. My affliction knows Le Labo . . .

"Come on in," the wearer of that bouquet beckons from inside my two-room shitbox. "I'm—"

"Le Labo . . . I-I know who you are, ma'am," I interrupt when I see this person whole. "You're . . . Linda Figgis. Chief of Police."

Now I'm tucking Ky's bear tighter than Riggins ever could . . .

CHAPTER 5

Mater Misericordia

SHE'S AT MY DRESSER, ROLLING MOM'S rosary in her pudgy pink fingers topped by red nail varnish. She's barely chest-high on me. The golf clubs or racket must be in the Suburban parked outside because her plump feet stuffed into white kicks, dirigible breasts straining a dark navy polo shirt. Paunch and thick thighs fill her white skirt. Got her blond hair, maybe a bit too blond from coloring, all pinned up behind a white sports visor.

"And you're Mr. Richard E. Cornish, Junior." She's grinning through these cartoonish Betty-Boop lips. Yeah, no COVID mask, like she's a squat superhero.

"Dickie," I say, entering slowly. Got to calm myself because my shaking hands make the grocery bag scratch and ruffle and it's already caught her eye. Or maybe it's Al-Mayadeen Thomas' pinkish blood and dried brains on my arms, my chest? "'Mr. Cornish' was my grandad. 'Richard Cornish' is my father. Gunnery Sergeant, then Sergeant-Major Cornish, USMC."

"Your dad retired?"

"No ma'am. Huntington's Disease. Vegetative. Diapers. Up at the Old Soldiers and Sailor's Home."

"So sorry. Um . . . is Huntington's the one that can be . . . passed down?"

"Yeah."

I'm fumbling for a spot to stow the bag while she's tracking me with almost crystalline blue eyes that don't blink, like a doll's. Can't make a run for the crapper; all I got in this room is the desk, so I plop it next to my laptop, blood-stained side away from her.

Seeing me better composed she finally extends her hand. Must be vaxxed and I guess she's seen dried brains before but who says Al-Mayadeen didn't have the Hi-Five or some other cooties so I tell her, "Ma'am, lemme do a do quick wash up in the head first."

"'Head?' So you are a Marine brat after all."

So now I can grab the bear bag and hurry into the bathroom. Water splashing everywhere in the stained basin I affirm, "Okinawa, Subic Bay, Quantico . . . the Eighth & E Barracks."

"How'd you know it was me? I'm out of uniform."

"Ma'am . . . " I'm splashing my face. "The brass downstairs . . . the heat all up on the block . . . "

"Oh yeah," I hear with a chuckle. "Call them my 'Blue Boy Band.'"

Frigid water or scalding, I can't get this stuff off, and I can't stop quivering like a child, a little pantywaist pussy, right ole Gunney, Sergeant-Major? I grab one of my fraying towels, drape it around my neck.

I come out and she's standing at the dresser again. "You okay, Dickie?"

"Saw a man blow his head off. So no, Chief. Not okay . . . "

She fingers Mom's rosary once more. "*Mortem tuam annuntiamus, Domine,*" she chants. " *. . . et tuam resurrectionem confitemur . . . donec venias.*"

I render the response drilled into me by the nuns and brothers. "*Salve Regina, Mater Misericordia. Vita, dulcedo, et spes nostra, salve . . .* "

"Amen," she whispers. "I'm lapsed, sad to say. You mentioned Le Labo." She flips fast, from requiem to *eau de toilet.* Kill, she don't play.

"Um . . . something I read online, ma'am . . . you joked how you'd broke only one rule: wearing scent on duty because you like Le Labo."

"Dickie that is obscure as heck, I must say."

"My dad calls it . . . part of my 'affliction.' Only gotta clock something once. Gets tucked in my dome. Plus, see, before the virus . . . I'd roll up on the Le Labo store on Florida Avenue because I was going through a lot . . . the scent'd clear my head. All I'd have to do in return is deter any knuckleheads scheming a smash and grab. Pretty soon the Bonobos, the Warby Parker . . . all of them were hiring me a couple hours, here and there."

"Interesting. May I sit?"

I offer her the desk chair but she plops herself right on my cot. Right by the rest of mail I never got to read—including what's in that red envelope.

"Speaking of smash and grabs," the Chief begins, "the Second District just informed me of some interesting footage from a CVS on Seventh and Florida Avenue."

I pull out my chair, ease down. I'm almost hugging myself in it, head bent. "Uh-huh."

"Bravo for getting two firearms off the street. We'll find the juveniles soon enough . . . "

"Leave 'em be. They're sick, not sinners . . . "

My mattress squeaks from her crossing her little fat legs.

"And you're smart enough to know that's not why I'm here—my Blue Boy Band in grumbling tow . . . "

"Well, tonight your people stood back while Fed Gestapo took a torch to the Colonial View Motel."

"Lots of miscreants from the last Administration remain on their payroll."

"And yours . . . Chief?"

"Fair point. But that's for another day. So what I want *you* to do is tell *me* how you know Mr. Al-Mayadeen Thomas?"

Jesus. "He . . . kidnapped me."

"After you thwart a robbery like Batman and Robin? From your file . . . isn't that what . . . *hmmm* . . . Fitzroy Donovan Cockburn, deceased eighteen months ago, used to call you: Ghetto Batman?"

"That was . . . was a joke, ma'am." I search Black Santa's face from the snapshot I'd framed for the wall. One of the little Brazilian novice nuns at St. Jude's took that. Old-school camera, there at Christmas . . . when we had meat in our soup, homemade rosemary bread. "He got the drop on me. I was a hostage."

"I see. So let's forget how he just seemed to find you, out of the blue?"

"I was tryna tell your dick what was what, but he just cuffed my ass and pushed me onto the asphalt!" So much for staying cool . . .

"*K'ymira Thomas.* What did he tell you about her disappearance? Did he offer anything that sounded like new information? Did he offer items that could be construed as evidence?"

Lord. "I-I don't know you mean." Let's see how cagey she is. Or how stupid I can be.

She sighs and recounts, "My first and only cold case as Commander of the Seven-Dee. Took much heat from all sides.

The sexists said my team—all women—was incompetent. The racists called me a pandering ditherer, diverting resources from 'real crime.' Blacks activists, the City Council, they all me a racist who didn't care."

"Sorry." That Uncle Tom dick was right. I was on the street then, muddled. Hadn't a clue.

"I'm a big girl—I can take it. But that little girl was abused her entire short life, fell through the cracks."

"I-I've seen that."

"Her mother, CiCi Talbot-Thomas, died of COVID pneumonia over a year ago. CiCi's lover, 'Little' Alexander, is in a vegetative state, COVID complications. Now Al-Mayadeen is the horrific bookend."

She grabs a tuft of Kleenex from my wobbly nightstand, dabs her eyes. This for real?

"Chief, he . . . didn't say that much. Mostly cried. Showed a picture of what she might look like now . . . if she's alive."

"There's the pernicious rumor that someone in law enforcement . . . white man, a pedophile—abducted K'ymira, killed her."

"So why bring the whole brass to my spot, Chief. My pizza?"

"Because I'm the boss."

I nod. No shit. "Didn't mean disrespect."

"Look, there's so much intervening pain—elections, the virus, the marches, the riots. Yet just as we see a glint of sunlight . . . "

"Sunlight?" I interrupt, and immediately regret it. "Ma'am, folks gettin' shot, jacked every week now. I don't call that sunlight."

Rather than a rebuke I get a weird grin on that round face. "This case was George Floyd and Breonna Taylor wrapped in one. It didn't need to came back to haunt us." She balls up the Kleenex and hits a Bradley Beal three pointer into the trash can. "Nor do memories of the Municipal Shelter . . . the old munie. That Bedlam, Black Hole of Calcutta."

"I don't understand what you want from me."

"I want you to accompany me back to the Daly Building . . . to chat."

"No . . . "

"Christmas crackers, Dickie—you and I know it's safer for you there. I'll even throw in dinner . . . seeing that your pizza or whatever that is attracting flies."

"The flies at the Colonial View Motel were worse. And how am I not safe?"

Figgis stands, circles around to face me. Even seated I'm taller. "The Colonial View was no garden-variety traphouse. I'm sure you know that two crews in Northeast used it as base, an arsenal, a depot. Rock, heroin, pills—the China White fentanyl that killed three people that house on Rhode Island Avenue last week? They're lilliputians compared to their forefathers in the Eighties, but still a menace. You're lucky, as I doubt that Smith and Wesson forty-caliber recovered from the scene was the only firearm in a ten-foot radius."

"I can take care of myself, Chief."

"Really? An emotionally compromised ex-con got the drop on you."

"Was loafin' on the big bamma . . . " Because I'm soft . . .

"Facts then. Al-Mayadeen's from Anacostia but made *citywide* enemies as a stick-up king," the Chief adds, as if I'm a colleague. "The Feds turned the motel into a pile of ashes today yes—along with whatever the crews secreted there. Some angry people will be put a beef on who's *not* in custody, figuring them for a snitch. Reporters are already asking, and the Feds don't care what info drops. The crews'll think the snitch is *you,* hon'."

Now my head's truly throbbing and I can't control what comes out of my hole next. "Put a case on me or leave me be, okay? I don't wanna be a part of whatever show you got here."

She leans right into my face. Something no white person's done, unmasked, in . . . I can't remember. And the Le Labo's all up in my head. She whispers, "*Jaime Bracht.*"

Fuck.

"Dickie, he'd be of interest only to true crime authors and conspiracy buffs but for the macabre effort of our former President to grant him a posthumous pardon for unnamed crimes. Crimes I bet you could enumerate. Now this presents another sticky sitch where *your* name comes up, not just in connection with an ex-con's suicide in a squatter house. Your name was the *only* thing accessible in a case jacket on Bracht that's been sealed by a federal judge and redacted by Homeland Security—all consented to by the current U.S. Attorney and my predecessor, oddly."

Guess they were lying when they said they'd keep my name out of it, and now I got a Krakatoa of acid's in my gut. Pure will's the only thing keeping the mess down.

"Those snazzy business cards on your dresser—city program help you get those printed, right?" The stuff's climbing my throat. Yeah, she don't fuck around. "But are you licensed as a P.I.?"

"No."

"Then I'll be waiting downstairs," Figgis says with a grin. Another motherfucking grin.

. . . so I'm back in the bathroom, swapping peels. Wrinkled, faded Hawaiian-pattern shirt . . . equally crumpled baggy khaki trousers I got darned at the knees. At least they're clean and it's still hot as fuck outside and they'll batter-ram my apartment door if I dawdle too much longer. For all I know they've clocked the .380 Ruger in the dresser before I came home and know I got no paper for it.

Well, what they definitely don't know is my john's one big keester stash. The wall panel, behind the tank, comes right off. I stow the bear with the rest of my life's flotsam.

I text Ernesto over a piss and flush. He's a good boy, I swear.

Stripe watch my spot. Cops all up in it. Got you a better phone, Keesh will network.

And now, I'm in the mirror . . . and yeah, I know what you'd say, Daddy. That this white woman's gonna handle me. Oh how'd you do it? You, the liver lipped motherfucker who allowed the redneck DI's to call black boys in bootcamp "specks" and then you'd *yowsza* to any white officer who'd pat your bald pate like dog. You, who had the nerve to say my brain's "too big and addled." I can handle this Chief of Police. Watch.

And yeah, it's just me and her and the Le Labo in back of the Suburban. Figgis reminds me like I'm a child to buckle-in; the plainclothes female behind the wheel hits the running lights, no siren. The other Chevys follow.

My affliction delivers again. Can't stop it. "You went from patrol to Chief in ten years. Mayor was your college friend at U of Maryland. Lady Terrapin . . . hoops?"

"*Wowzers*—when did you have a chance to Google me?"

"Um . . . memory," I whisper. "Remember?"

"I see. I'm asking as parent, I mean no harm here . . . but were you ever tested as child for—"

"No! I mean. I've been on my own, a long time . . . " I recall Daddy tossing an Easter ham out the window when

Mom got a letter from a shrink over my tests. "Soooo . . . Chief, you were point guard and the Mayor was power forward . . . two ACC championships back when the ACC meant something, huh?"

Figgis nods. Guess she's okay with that little diversion. "Imagine me at nineteen and *many* fewer pounds. Interesting, though."

"What?"

"Your memory and due diligence yet can't tell me more about Al-Mayadeen. Makes me feel bad you can't trust me. I trust you. You are in my command vehicle, I extend the hand of friendship . . . "

We're blowing through more intersections, zoom onto North Capitol Street, southbound toward the gleam of the Dome and spot-lit Union Station. Long silence and finally I break bad.

"I have a jacket, Chief. I'm no saint. What do you want to ask?"

"This isn't what you think. File says your mother's deceased. You have no other family?"

"Alma, my older sister. About two years ahead of me."

"Has she been around to check on you? Seen how far you've come since being sober, cleaning-up?"

Yeah. Someone's been studying. But a few details are missing. "She committed suicide when we were in high school."

Figgis gives me a tepid pat on the shoulder.

"Who's the other brass?" I ask—diverting once more.

"Oh . . . uh . . . Patrol Chief Patterson, Commander Gates."

"What about the scary mug in the suit . . . looks like a James Bond villain?"

"*Ha*! That James Bond villain is Deputy Chief Dante Antonelli. He runs our SOD . . . Special Ops Division."

"Shit."

"Their rep is something we're working on. Dante made his

bones in the counter-terrorism intel and organized crime sectors so he's a smidge . . . heavy-handed? Been so since I was a patrol officer." She switches up, "Listen, did Al-Mayadeen go into detail about his wife . . . K'ymira Thomas mother, CiCi?"

"Never said she was neglectful, abusive if that's what you mean."

"Any mammal can push young from a womb. Yet we pray to the Madonna, sacrifice to the mommy cult."

Cult? "You're being hard on ladies. 'Suffer the little children . . . '"

"My-my . . . a theologian too?"

"No . . . look . . . it doesn't mean what you think it means. Jesus said you gotta act *like* kids to get into Heaven, not *be* them. No special admission ticket for kids."

She's staring me up and down. "I disagree, but I'm curious."

"The Coptic Gospel of Thomas, ever hear of it?" Hell no, she hasn't. Just me and my afflicted brain. "Source for the 'suffer the little children' line. See, when Jesus touched nursing babies on the head and their mamas smiled, the Disciples were disgusted—sexist mugs that they were, huh? But Our Lord schooled them: 'Heaven is like this—a nursing child and a mother's love.' Means mothers're *good.* Like mine was . . . "

"You had good mother?" Figgis quips, accompanied by an odd shrug. "You were lucky."

Her words are reaction's truly fucking with me, and I don't say a thing the rest of way to the Daly Building. Funny, she doesn't either.

CHAPTER 6

"Shut Up and Play Ball"

FIGGIS IN HER OFFICE SUITE'S BATHROOM, changing out of her golf or tennis vibe into her uniform. Weird, because it's late as fuck . . . sometime after eleven p.m. . . . and she did the press conference in her civvies. "All about approachability," she'd said to me with a wink.

See, I'm peeping this fancy paper box of what the jake who brought it in tells me are "Kobe beef sliders." The Police Chief's late dinner is on her desk. Thai shrimp salad. I shift in my buttery leather chair so I can check if my nutsack's still there. Nope. It's in the container with the salad. The pain of losing my balls and the smell of all that stuff's about to get me to blow . . . I chug almost the entire can of diet Pepsi—only thing Figgis serves—and blast a belch of relief into my sleeve.

Okay, that's not the only reason why I'm nellie'd and nauseous. I stole something off Figgis's desk while she was in the bathroom. Cameras in there? We'll find out. Yet here she comes, all cheery . . .

"You okay, hon'?" she chirps. She's all brass and official but for flipflops, and her feet are even fatter and paler when bare.

I jerk a nod. Not feeling great but if Al-Mayadeen's the benchmark, I'm glittering like the Silver Surfer.

Little over a year past, I was playing with key chains, slips of paper, the caps off pens . . . all glued together from mucilage and rubber bands and toothpaste I'd scrounge from behind the Staples down on Fourteenth and K. Drank broth I mixed from tins of sardines. Tins I stole from the curb piles—the scavenged bones of families who couldn't make rent. Saw Stripe carry off a fifty-inch flatscreen all by himself. Me, I was content with sardines and the loose change the landlords paid us. Now here I am, lounging with the Chief of Police and Kobe beef sliders.

She's propping those fat little dogs on her desk. I clock an ankle bracelet. She notices I notice. I'm fantasizing all right. Not the way she probably thinks. I'm figuring how the ankle thing would look glued with mucilage to a found pair of reading glasses, a discarded old watchband. Dr. Kapoor *loves* rocking my "collection fetish" but swear to God there's no allegory. It's all anesthesia. Can't help myself . . . even now.

"So," says after a sigh you give after you've fucked someone over and they got no way to fight back. "Let's see what the tooth fairy's left for you." She hits a button on her phone console. "Bonnie, the folder."

Bonnie's this sullen, plain-Jane skinny white chick; a civilian who you can tell's got nothing going on a summer night so she's probably glad to be checking the Chief's Twitter feed and typing bullshit at eleven at night. She hands Figgis a opaque blue plastic file folder, excuses herself with a meek whisper.

"'Bonnie' was Commissioner Gordon's secretary . . . in *Batman*," I mumble because that's the kind of shit my brain still does. No meds for that . . .

"Hmmm, you say something?" She's signing a document in the file, then bestows the folder on me like some priestess or queen'd do some amulet or weapon on a Greek hero before cutting him lose in Hades. It's a letter, and pdf of a web image.

"You now own me."

Yeah, she hears that one. "*Stoooooop.* It's not that sort thing."

Oh yeah, Daddy, it's that sort of thing. I read the title of the pdf and get queasy.

District of Columbia Provisional Temporary Private Investigator License.

The letter says I have twenty-four months to pay the bond. *Uh-huh,* she owns me, all right.

"Thank . . . thank you," is all I muster. Because the other shoe's damn sure got to drop . . .

Yet Linda, *wow* . . . she's so damn fucking gleeful she squeaks as if we'd been in there boning. She's the Queen of the Pig Poke and life is good now that Trump's Reich is done, though its second wave, like the 'rona's fourth or fifth, is rearing up on the beaches. Fuck it. She's spearing a prawn as if yeah—one of my nuts. And that's all that matters to her, right?

"You know, hon'," Figgis says, chewing as she speaks, "I didn't mean to scare you, bringing up Bracht. Just to motivate you . . . needed you on my team."

I nod, sigh to camouflage the gurgle in my gut signaling the surrealness of this shit. Pray I don't puke right there on my gourmet sliders . . .

"I need reliable people," the Chief continues, "not these 'violence interrupters' the 'defund the police' crowd's got me administering. So you can rest easy about Bracht, okay? There're a lot of gaps in an already sketchy file. The Feebees and DHS knew he and a lawyer named Aleksander Nimchuk had you on the payroll for something. That something's redacted, that's good enough for me."

"Bracht got me off the street, outta the shelter. That's all."

"Relax! Not that kind of party. On the other hand, you may think whatever you did for him preps you for your current 'vocation.' It didn't. It doesn't. But at least now, you are official. Congratulations."

Can't hold out any longer. "I gotta use the bathroom, is that okay? Man of my age and all . . . gotta stay near the head . . . "

"Women of a certain age, too, hon'."

I close the door and turn on the faucet to mask a heave into the bowl. That does nothing to quell my shakes, my fright. Did she really just hand a piece of paper, a gift of a real life? Me, who she doesn't know from Adam. Me, a nobody, a street dog?

I swallow some water, and then over a solid stream of legit piss I hear her say, "You are savvy enough to know this isn't Humphrey Bogart in a trench coat, right? It's paperwork, it's boring, it's full of assholes: overweight retired cops, pinheads who do nothing but monitor skip-tracing apps, tatted-up rednecks, gold-chain Guidos. And hackers . . . ex-identity thieves. Those are worst." I flush and I'm wiping down everything as I hear her shout, "Had to refer one to the U.S. Attorney because we discovered he was casing the Capitol in advance of the January Sixth riot, catch my drift?"

When I settle back in the chair, my chickenshit self is relieved to see she hasn't noticed anything missing from her desk during our soiree.

"Is me being an amateur any better, ma'am?"

"Jeez-louise, enough with the 'ma'am.' *Linda*, all right?"

"Sorry."

Her eyes narrow. "You aren't as amateur as you look. And I'm not talking about whatever you did for Jaime Bracht."

"Pardon?"

"Ever hear of an evil little bastard named Jian Kann . . . half Chinese, half black . . . sorta looked like the fella in 2 Live Crew. Bet you didn't take me for a Luke fan, huh?"

"I-I dunno." I cross and recross my legs as I'm dreading what's coming.

"Well, he bedeviled Deputy Chief Antonelli for sure. Plugging rock, loveboat PCP . . . and the 'killa K-two,' the 'Kush.' Had the Benning Road Boyz and One-Six Crew as vassals . . . city councilmen in his back pocket, girlfriend was his mole in MPD . . . basically ran Northeast so he crowned himself 'Ghenghis' Kann. Still doesn't a ring a bell?" I'm mute so she adds, "You apparently knew his little sister . . . and in return for your high, you offered goon services—collections, finger breaking and such."

"Um . . . Linda . . . you got my jacket. You know how . . . fucked up I was."

She's mute, studying me yet again, then springs, "Ghenghis was killing your people and a fair number of suburban white kids, all with Scooby Snax adulterated with herbicide. The dead and convulsed were downtown for the hick tourists to see. Word was he was trying to wipe out his competitors by blaming them. *Somebody* figured it out. Next thing we hear, that nasty piece of work and his sister got green-lit. Their homicides are remain a cold case. *Good work.*"

We're exchanging deadpan stares. "Looks like . . . they got what was coming to them."

"*Yeah,*" she whispers, with frost. But with a chuckle she's changing up on me. "By the way, how'd you like the presser? Lead story for the eleven o'clock news!"

I exhale as slowly. "From the nosebleed seats?"

"For your own good."

"Ain't gotta flex with me, Linda. I'm a nobody to those bigshots."

"I'll be the judge of that. Hey . . . you aren't touching your dinner!"

"Um . . . chops and gums hurt. First things to go, after the feet, on the street."

She guzzles what's maybe the third can of diet Pepsi, gasps as if she wasn't fucking with me. "Toothache or not, you can't be such a Glum Gus! Tonight, you've turned a corner."

Tonight, she's shanghai'd me more than Al-Mayadeen did. She's going to lay her jont on my ass soon enough. Just praying she doesn't ask me to kill nobody, spy on folk.

I deflect with, "Linda, think it's smart to lay on like this girl K'ymira might still be alive?"

She rocks in her chair like one of the pinktoe nuns back in the day, debating whether to hit me or let me finish what might be a decent train of thought once I get through the blasphemy.

"The Feebees can cite you data," she replies, low and slow, "showing how many children and young women were recovered alive or we turned a lead that resulted in us finding a body—because we affirmed we weren't going to stop. Perps get sloppy because they're *scared*, not because they're complacent. Teaching you gems, Mr. Cornish."

"Uh-huh." Jesus, Mary and Joseph make her let me go home . . .

Now she's scribbling on one of those Post-it things, reaches it over to me stuck to her finger tip. "Toy Thomas, at that last known address. Talk to her about claiming

Al-Mayadeen's body or having us cremate him. If the latter, the urn goes into—"

"Potter's Field. Know like I owe it. But . . . what if word gets out you got an ex-fiend, ex-drunk . . . homeless slob . . . doing your dirty-work on a closed case?"

There it is!

"Dirty-work?"

"Linda, please . . . an hour ago I was a grown-ass man making hobo pizza in a hundred square foot shitbox apartment. *Henchmen,* however," I point to the Kobe beef, "eat better."

"Did your father ever accuse you of over-thinking?"

"All the time. Then he'd hit me. Then he'd flip the script and call me 'retarded.' Hit me again. If I cried I was a 'slack-jaw lil' pussy.' If I didn't I was 'artistic,' because the motherfucker couldn't pronounce the *real* word."

Now I grab one of her little burgers and stuff it in my mouth.

"You poor dear." Sounds sincere. "Did he hurt your sister, your mom?"

I don't answer that. "*So* . . . you want me to share Al-Mayadeen's tox report with his mother? Seeing that I'm on your payroll and shit . . . "

"Ah yes. Benzodiazepines, competing with meth and cocaine."

I nod. "Called 'Tina.' She's your girl when you wanna run wild but come down easy." Or to cancel pain. "Why didn't the meat locker do full autopsy?"

"Cause of death was obvious, you'd agree?"

"I'm . . . talking about . . . he didn't look well. Hinted he had cancer."

"Six-in for armed robbery and assault with a deadly weapon. Hard time ages you."

"So does being on the street. How old do you think I am?"

"I know how old you are."

She's off her chair, moves right in front of me, arms folded and yeah, it's like the nun about to slap me silly and make me recite the math problem again even though I got the right answer, just won't show my work. Only relief is there can't be a camera in that inner office for sure because this looks jenky with her standing there, maskless, tits-high and almost in my grill . . .

"See the man in the picture with President George H.W. Bush? That's my dad. When things got real bad . . . that was before we moved here from Detroit . . . I'd ask him if he was okay and he'd swear yes, we're fine. Then he'd take off for the UP of Michigan in his gear and rifle and yet all he'd hunt was the whiskey bottles he'd drain. Served me well. Because I'll always know when you're lying."

I grow as dumb of a *Sling Blade* face as possible. "Can I go now?"

"We aren't done."

"Yeah. Top secret an' shit."

"Don't be facetious. You have to promise, no nosing around the Colonial View stuff."

"Pardon?"

"Dickie, we are barely a foot apart so no need to read my lips. The Colonial View's demise is a mess—endemic and emblematic. I won't have you distracted by it, okay? I won't have it affect our friendship."

Friendship? Yeah, it's gotten extra. Now I see the lines in her face, cutting right through the Maybelline paint and powder that gave her what I thought was a suntan.

"There's . . . some stuff . . . about the Colonial View and cops you should know." And I'm peeping jarhead jake's florid face in my mind's eye, with his pencil dick inside a minor.

"Go on."

I'm a pussy. Nah. "Never . . . never mind."

"We have to be frank for our little arrangement to work. For you to be my eyes and ears, right hon'?"

"It's just . . . " I pivot, ". . . those people. They were . . . begging me. Al-Mayadeen's last wish . . . was to help him. Their children . . . "

She's peering right through me with those sapphire marbles. "You think they care about their children?" she offers, a little rim of fire in the ice blue. "Aliyah Hannigan. Her mother owed a debt to a Benning Road Boy scumbag . . . scumbag calls in the collateral. We seized phone video from mooks in the Colonial View of him collecting little Aliyah, nine years old, from mom . . . carrying her down a hall to . . . to strangle her . . . while he . . . penetrated her. His first trial ended in a hung jury. Can you believe it? Mom's too. We fixed that, fast."

Fixed? Again, not here, not now. "Seen horrible shit, bent people. But I've seen good people rise above that . . . "

"Oh really? Graciela Gomez, age three . . . *boiled alive* in a Colonial View bathtub ten months ago by her aunt and uncle. When they weren't torturing her, starving her, yet collecting EBT and TANF benefits, they kept her in a closet. Last check we still had five open child endangerment and abuse folders out of that place alone . . . and those are the one's referred from Child and Family Services. Unreported, who knows."

"So that means a bunch of kids, unaccounted for?"

"You're missing the point," she huffs . . . garlic from her salad still on her breath. "There's no 'Q-anon' perv party. It's all garden-variety inhumanity the average cop sees each day."

"So what happened to Graciela's parents? Why was *she* with perverts?"

"ICE detention," she says. I see something hard and mean form in her eyes. "Uncle and aunt had papers, mom and dad didn't. That's how it went, that's how it goes."

"You saying the world sucks. Yeah. You saying can't do shit about it, or won't?"

I get her heavy sigh again and then, "Dickie . . . let's review your 'dirty work' as you call it. Go to Toya Thomas, tell her son's dead, get permission to cremate and inter the little box, press her for anything Al-Mayadeen might have told her. Easy peezy. Then review a file I'm going to give you . . . "

"File?"

"Task force memo and exhibits on K'ymira's disappearance. I want your impressions."

The fuck? "Again, I'm an amateur, and . . . my concentration's still not good . . . my meds . . . "

"You see things differently. Maybe share anomalies with Mrs. Thomas, jar her memory."

"On a cold case?"

"On a cold case. Tell no one."

"*Guh* . . . you can count on that."

"But gimme your word, Dickie. Stay away from anything to do with Colonial View."

"One condition." No clue why I blurt this. Maybe it's my ailment . . .

"Seriously?" There's a knock on the door to the outer office. "*Hold on*!" she screeches.

"I want someone in Fed custody out . . . "

"W-Wait . . . "

"Female, prolly mixed-race female, a minor . . . street name

'Sweet Sunshine.' Five-five or six, freckles, ruddy hair. Don't know her government name. She's got a baby."

Now the grimaces end. "A baby, huh?"

"Yeah, maybe eighteen months, a walking toddler."

The Chief yells toward her door, "Bonnie, is she here? Send her in." Then, oddly, she looks back to me and repeats, "Toddler, eh?"

A female jake, all geared up in her black tac vest and those dark blue BDUs steps in. Figgis' height yet lean, not a meatball. Black hair in a ponytail . . . olive skin tone. Matching black 'rona mask. Wish they'd go back to their old "officer friendly" peels—before they looked like Navy SEALs in a shoot 'em-up video game.

"This is Officer Sanchez," Figgis announces. "Officer, Mr. Cornish here is . . . is one of our *new* contractors, handling some special work. Run him over to the safe room, get him set up and tucked in, then make sure those guys from the Second-Dee secure his apartment . . . "

What? "*Kill* . . . lemme box my Kobe sliders and you take me *home*."

"Look, it's late . . . best you stay out of sight till the morning . . . "

"Come on . . . "

"Christmas crackers—I'm talking a Hyatt Recency. Be siced! Get a head start on *homework* if you refuse to relax."

Her voice is like a fingernail in my eye—fake-ass Maryland slang with the Midwest twang? I'm *siced* to say eat shit but selling tickets in the Daly Building, hundreds of po-po around to kick my ass? *Nah.*

When we hit the corridor the thwap of Figgis' flipflops on the polished marble makes a sick echo and she's returning salutes and doing fist pounds with adorning piglets. I'm clocking this Sanchez girl's tatts and I'm getting a real exotic dyke vibe from her. Daddy'd say what a waste. We all stop at the elevator bank and there I get my prize, as the Chief prattles on about the Mayor's philosophy of alliances and "rising together" bullshit.

See, all this time Sanchez is toting a pretty sizeable envelope, taped up. "Be careful with this Mr. Cornish," Sanchez tells me as shoves it in my hands.

"I would have put it all on a flash drive," Figgis adds. "But hey, I'm old-school, like Deputy Chief Antonelli." She offers her little pale hand. I shake and her grip's moist and limp this time. "It was a pleasure, *Mr. Cornish . . .* " Uh-huh, false formality and cheese is opera for someone, and it's not Sanchez.

Before the elevator light pops and the tone sounds, she asks, "By the way . . . so you're going to the dedication of the children's dorm at SFME?"

"Huh?"

"The red envelope I saw at your apartment. It's an invitation to fundraiser. *Verna Leggett*?" *Uh-oh.* Feels a thousand needles're piercing my tongue. "I met her when she was fresh out of grad school, counseling there at the munie shelter. SFME was the gold standard these past two years. Vaccinated more people in an afternoon than my poor hoops teammate the Mayor could did in a week."

Sanchez ushers my ass into an open elevator but I press the button to keep the door open.

"I-I . . . know her."

"Shame what happened at SFME before the vaccine," the Chief offers as the "close door" warning beeps. "Far worse across the corridor at St. Jude's, where you used to sleep, right?

I knew the late Father Phil Ruffino and Sister Maria-Karl Busch very, very well . . . "

Is she fucking with me?

"New children's dorm at SFME will be named for K'ymira Thomas, by the way . . . "

The door shut.

Sanchez isn't even looking at me and I'm alone in my head, thinking of Verna, St. Jude's. God was cruel. What better place to drop a plague, than on an already plagued place . . . a shelter for families, kids . . . and a haven for lost old men. And so all Verna's heard from me since the shit began has been through bank drafts on drawn from Nimchuk's trust account. Evil money cleanses with decent purpose. That's what Mom said about your paychecks, Daddy . . .

. . . and we arrive three floors down . . . and I'm still in my feelings. I see a garage bustling with rows of Ford SUV Interceptor white-blue & red units, motorcycles, panel vans . . . all getting waxed and wiped frantically despite the late hour.

Sanchez speaks. "For Fourth of July parade . . . maybe gonna be a mini-make up for Inauguration them Trump *bobos* an' *patáns* messed up, belie' that? You ride in the back."

Not a thing, as this time the seat doesn't smell like vomit or ass. But there's a piece of paper on MPD stationery, red stamps of "Confidential" and "Warning" decorating the margins waiting for me.

As she starts the engine, Sanchez explains through the clear barrier separating her from the rear, "An NDA. Deputy Chief Antonelli wants your session with Chief Figgis cloaked. You don't say shit."

Sanchez busts the unit from the garage onto F Street. Hits the siren.

"You the hatchet lady?" I ask.

"Did I say sign it? Jus' tole you what it is. Hand it up here." I do, through the narrow slot and she lowers her window, tears up the document. Tosses the pieces like confetti. *Fuck . . .*

"Are you nuts?"

"Dude. Relax. The Chief, she likes you."

Then why're my hands shaking from all the love? "Yeah? And she's your hero, huh?"

"She's our Athena and Artemis. You know who they are, mope?"

"Yeah. Greek Goddesses on Mt. Olympus. Prolly two most important . . . stronger than the most powerful male gods."

"*Bueno* . . . and why?"

"Because the male gods had fragile egos and would think with their dicks?"

I see her smiling at me in the rearview mirror, then she declares, "We would fuckin' *die* for her, dude. So shut up and play ball . . . "

CHAPTER 7

Desparecida

WE DRIVE BARELY THREE BLOCKS TO a Hyatt on New Jersey Avenue. Sanchez dumps me out . . .

"I haven't stayed in a hotel . . . a real one . . . in, shit, twenny years."

The *chica* huffs, hits the lights and siren, peels out.

My Man Friday answers when I swipe him. Stripe swears the cops haven't been around my place in hours.

"Take the spare key and go in. First, make sure the gat and clip's still in my dresser. Second, pop the panel by the toilet. Old paper bag in there kinda messy. Toss the old bag, put that shit in another clean bag. And get my *meds.* Popped the tops but they are in the CVS prescription white bags, near the sink. Little white bags. *Don't forget.* I'll wait . . . "

Silence for a couple of minutes as I survey the empty boulevard . . . should be lousy with tourists this time of year . . . cars and shuttlebuses clogging the by-ways. Tonight, the only thing in common with summer nights past is the pungency of the air . . . heavy as Da Nang, Daddy'd probably grouse.

"*Coño . . . wha' the fock . . . en serio?*" I'm soon hearing on my phone. Guess he found it the bloody teddy.

"Hustle come down to the Hyatt on D and New Jersey Avenue, fast . . . "

"Así . . . an' bring this shit . . . oso sangriento?"

"Yeah and try not to lunch. Don't need you profiled and picked up."

Checking into a hotel, rather than skulking in to take a dump, cool off in summer or thaw out in winter is a bit alien to me. Good thing they were waiting for me to arrive upon MPD's call. I use my height to look over the counter and sure enough the Becky's fingering a hard copy of my mugshot. Prolly the first time ever a black man's pic turns frowns into Chicklet-white smiles. The girl indeed whispers, as if I'm a rapper *in cognito,* how MPD, the Marshals, the Bureau hold some rooms for "government guests." Witnesses and snitches, I suppose.

The spot's on the seventh floor, fresh with that clean hotel smell I recall way, way back, maybe as a teen travelling for football? I try the bathroom first, clocking the nickel-plated fixtures as I piss, wash.

And suddenly I'm weeping.

Gotta nut-up. Not think about nice stuff, clean places I once didn't rate.

I rummage my trouser pockets, pull out my trophy . . . my fetish, housed from Chief Linda Figgis' desk. A mini-magnifying glass, tchotchke from some cop convention. Dumbass riff on Sherlock Holmes and now it's mine. How do I explain that to Kapoor? I hide it under a room service menu and return to the lobby.

Out on New Jersey Avenue I hear the rev and putt-putting. A fire-orange Vespa slows and stops. Double-take . . . it's Stripe seated there, rocking a riding helmet, a delivery medallion, reflector safety vest. In the front basket there's a paper bag looking like it's full of carry-out. I run out to the curb and he tugs down the garish bandana he uses as a mask.

"*Vea,* Rain Man, I learn from you—use cover," he announces. *Jesus, Mary and Joseph* he's pimping the gold fronts in his grill. Told him stop wearing those. And yeah, I still let him call me *Rain Man.* Still fits, I suppose. "*Mi cipote* Carlos loan th' bike." He dismounts, chains his ride to a No Parking sign, says Carlos'll lift it later tonight.

Carlos. I'm up in my feelings, bad. So bad I'm thinking Sanchez'd be back when the white tourists call 911 on my ass. "The fuck, kid! Didn't I say stay away from Carlos? He's slinging more China White than the plugger who almost put me in Potter's Field!"

"Da *fock,* Jefe . . . " He pulls these clam-shell big as shit headphones from the reflector vest, encloses his ears like he doesn't expect me to kick his narrow ass. "You say bring this nasty thing here, covered in blood, huh, an' you give me shit 'bout Carlos? Carlos ain't puttin' no fennie in needles, bro' . . . is that new shit. *La Nita.* Think I stupid, bro'?"

Yeah. Because he's young. Nitazene's starting to take what the 'rona's left. "Don't clown me, *chivo* . . . this is real shit. Stay clear of his head shop, and don't fuck with me about the teddy bear. It's evidence."

I tolerate a lot. But he's gone from under my shoe to under my wing. And I'm not you, Daddy.

"You promise, no more *loco* shit. But you be Cap, I be Bucky, bro' . . . Winter Soldier by you side . . . *siempre.*"

See? Ride or die.

Okay, the front desk folks and bald-head toy cops in blazers are staring. I mean, Stripe still got that faux-hawk fade with the day-glo yellow up the crest, so yeah that's the vestige of the name I stuck him with. A little less reptilian in the smile, gold fronts notwithstanding. Acne's getting better. After all, he's got me using my VA bennies on his for skin meds, on the low. Delivery boy cover's a nice touch but he's mumbling some obscene shit aloud, spilling from his headphones.

I get him in the elevator and scold, "Told you about being a potted plant when undercover, that's what the video courses say . . . so why the loud music?"

"*Rake it Up* . . . Yo Gotti an' Nicki Minaj, bro'!" He pauses, noting the bright and shiny things decorating the glass box we're in. "Man . . . air conditch-in . . . smell good, too!"

"Stuff'll rot your brain. What's wrong with some Pitbull?"

The door opens on seven. "Why you say Pitbull? Pitbull *old* as you, bro'." He tosses that gremlin grin then asks. "Linda Figgis? *Coño . . . ella tenía buenas tetas* . . . from I see on the TV . . . "

This reminds me again he's still a teenager. Indeed, the concept of a card key and a made, king-size bed is splaying is already dishplate-wide eyes. He takes a superhero flight onto the mattress.

Those Nike kicks—real ones I bought him—are soiling the good covers. I glower and he tugs them off, dutifully. "Bring bitches here, man!"

"Women," I correct him.

"Yeah sorry, *women.* So . . . *la policia* . . . they do this en El Salvador, huh. Treat you like prince when they wan' you do dirt . . . then cut you heart like the Maya . . . "

I tear open the package Sanchez toted, place the contents on the nightstand. "See?"

Not sure how much he understands. A lot, it seems . . .

"*Madre* . . . wh' this ops, Rain Man? Pics of CCTV . . . K'ymira Thomas . . . memo-randum, FBI an' MPD Join' 'vestigation . . . tran-script Cecelia Thomas. This real?"

"Yeah." I sigh and ask him, "Look, kitchen closes in like five minutes so if you want room service—means they bring food here to the room—here's the menu . . . " Quickly I snatch up the little magnifying glass before he clocks it.

"Hungry as fock, Rain Man!" Abruptly his exuberance down-throttles when he looks to the bag. "*El oso.* Cops know?"

I'm blown and bone-weary so rather than explain I just nod. So yeah, there are times I wish he'd grow up, act less the greasy kid. Right now, I'd treasure the squeaky snickers, a ribald moronic joke when he presses, "*Jefe* . . . they ask you . . . 'bout Jaime Bracht?" He pronounced the "J" as an "H:" the proper way that Bracht, ashamed of his own Lartino peeps, eschewed. "*Las niñas* tha' Bracht make hoes—you avenged them, bro'."

"Yeah but I lost Black Santa. Piedade, Fred and Eva. No, *m'hijo.* I didn't fix shit. And I can't help think she knew about . . . Esmeralda."

"*La bruja*?"

"I dunno," I say with a deep sigh. "FBI and Homeland Security put Esme on a plane to Mexico City, told her if she ever came back they'd jam her into a supermax cell."

"*Bueno*," the kid replies. He pats my shoulder, gives that imp' grin again. "Crab cake an' fries. Mos' 'spensive."

"I'll call it in. Now . . . go on my phone's Google because your old phone is shit. Search 'Colonial View Motel' with 'D.C. Youth and Family Agency. Child Protective Services' Anything about kids there."

Defying the Chief? Fuck yeah.

So now I'm fishing out two CCTV stills off the nightstand while Stripe's fiddling with my phone, waiting on his food. In one pic, a beautiful little black girl wearing a pink turtleneck and denim overalls . . . two puffs of hair atop her head like Mikey Mouse ears . . . and stands unaccompanied on a sidewalk.

Yet she's beaming at someone through plump dimples, clutching bear that is identical to the one in the bag and covered in her daddy's blood. Almost eye-level to her. Toward the street.

"Yo, kid . . . " I jostle Stripe. "What's this look like to you?"

"Lil' gurl . . . she get in a car?"

"Good job."

"Or . . . she jus' see peeps she likes, in a car."

Even better. But in the other, time stamped five minutes and seventeen seconds before, there's no bear . . . the child's face is twisted in the terror of abandonment. I've seen that on these babies out here in tents, or when Verna first takes them in.

Unh-unh. This is different. She saw a monster before she found a rescuer.

So what didn't you and your team see, Linda, all those years ago?

The house phone rings, startling both of us. I hit "speaker."

"*Chief Figgis wants thank you again for assisting her,*" a shrill female voice intones, "*and hopes you find the accommodations comfortable.*"

"It's cool. Um . . . I ordered room service. I apologize . . . regained my appetite."

"*That's fine. We just ask that you do not order alcohol or entertain visitors, Mr. Cornish. And as reminder, please return the materials the Chief loaned in the folio provided, within forty-eight hours. We were told you have an excellent memory.*"

"Yeah. Anything else?"

"*Some additional information you requested . . . a Federal detainee?*"

"Oh . . . yes . . . " I whisper furtively, "Stripe write this down," then "G'head ma'am . . . "

"*. . . Raynata Nehemiah . . . number bee-zero-nine-zero-twenty-twenty-one, being transferred to YSC Mount Olivet Road . . .* "

"Juvie?" Stripe mouths. I defer to him on shit like this.

"So she is a minor?" I press.

"*Seventeen. That's why the Marshals did the summary transfer.*"

"She has a child. I told the Chief."

"*No record of a child. Good night, Mr. Cornish.*"

The flunky hangs up while I'm in mid-fucking-stupefaction.

Jesus.

Well, at least Stripe's crab cake, fries, whatever else comes . . . Christ, a chocolate shake? He's got on his headphones but teases, "Is Drake . . . tha' sof' enough?"

I move to a plush chair by the window with the file and a cheese sandwich, cola. Yeah, why sit by a window but if there's surveillance, they'll tell Figgis I'm midnight cramming like a schoolboy, as ordered . . .

. . . and so I don't know how long I'm there in the chair, but the room's now dark but for the glow of whatever Stripe last clocked on that TikTok shit and streetlights below the window.

Nothing really in this file on the skinny motherfucker—skinny in his mug shot at least—named "Little," government name Hakim Alexander. Only tie to this bullshit who's still alive, if you call being as gorked as Daddy alive. Laurel "Medicaid Hospice" whatever that is . . . so I rewind the years . . . and poof the COVID and brain damage and deflated lungs. CiCi's jump while Al-Mayadeen was up in Rivers, that's it? He was only Stripe's age back then, full-up of piss and vinegar and boning horny older chick? CiCi lets him take the child K'ymira from the ole munie shelter because CiCi had her "mandatory welfare job" at a laundromat making shit an hour . . . when in fact she's with her cousin at the nail spot on Pennsylvania . . .

. . . okay so I'm seeing this in my dome like I'm bird overhead, and K'ymira's surly after Little, not her mother, takes her to the clinic for her school booster shots, he walks her to the CVS so he can pick up smokes, a snack to mollify for her, some mascara for CiCi . . . tells the child her to stand outside of store because she's cuttin' up, big tantrum like the teenager idiot he is. He goes in alone, buys the stuff . . . comes out. She gone and no one saw a damn thing.

Magic jellyroll bewitching a young, dumb nigga? Old story. But see, the previous stills show Ky hugging Little . . . he's kissing her, playing when got to the clinic . . . and after, when he's searching for her, I can see it in his face . . . terror. Same time another camera had the CiCi on Minnesota Avenue and Naylor . . . walking heading south . . . *toward Little* . . . she's on her phone.

No cell tower ping for that? Nothing. That shit wasn't new tech back then. Memo has a witness, a fellow shelter mom working at the laundromat say, "*CiCi caught a mind that something's up with Ky and left in a panic.*"

Four interrogations sessions with CiCi. Being a fiend, I know all about lying. That's how you pass a poly, why you don't lawyer-up. Keep to your words. But Figgis did the last interview got her on a lie about visiting a play auntie, a Miss Jocasta E. McQueen out in P.G. County. My affliction's triggered. Because my affliction loves maps. This addy is really Seat Pleasant, a little town carved into the county.

And I like the name, too. Jocasta. Reminds me of school, back when I read *Oedipus* while my classmates berated me for studying "dead whitefolks."

Anyways, the cadaver dog didn't hit . . . but they used ground radar in the cellar. Hard clay reflected-back in all but a little corner . . . the size of a six-year-old child. Disturbed soil.

Nope. Says here *two* dead cats wrapped in Walmart bags with air freshener. Like Oedipus' mommy, Miss Jocasta had gone a little crazy. Neglected her cats, asked CiCi to bury them but not too deep, because she "*wanted to hear them talk.*"

After Esmeralda turned me out, got me fiendin' . . . lost my football scholarship and ROTC so had to enlist or be a jail-bird. The Air Force locked me in room with satellite and aerial shit to look for *one* thing—whether the motherfucker *du jour* in Afghanistan, Yemen, Iran, Syria whatever was pulling a red-herring.

Like burying cats.

"Al-Mayadeen, you told me, didn't you," I say aloud. "High IQ. *Nolle prosquis* and getting' over on judges, Child Protective Services . . . just on brains not pussy?"

"*Oye, viejo,*" I hear and it startles me. "You take the bed for you elder bones. *Solo por favor no confíes en esta policía* . . . okay?"

"I'm fine. Just . . . how did the cops mess up this timeline. CCTV footage, cell tower shit . . . I mean, that's science, right?"

"Come on *Jefe* . . . cop do two thing good: lie, and fock-up. *Mira,* t'ree if you say blame us for lie, fock-up."

I nod. The kid's grown up with his eyes open. Real meaning of the word "woke."

Indeed, Stripe hands me a sheet of Hyatt stationery scribbled to edge with words. "I work, too, see? Tha hotel, bro' it *evil. Ocho niños* . . . eight . . . from that place. More from all those hotels on New York, on Bladensburg Road . . . city put families when munie shelter close down." I can feel the hair on my neck when he follows with, "Parents get jail . . . or deported . . . or they die in a beef anyway."

"I was told not to mess with the Colonial View," I reply with a yawn.

"Then why you ask, Rain Man? I know you, eh!"

"Listen, *chero*, maybe there's no connection between K'ymira Thomas and the motel but a headless Al-Mayadeen Thomas. One way or another we'll close that up in the morning."

"*Mira*," Stripe huffs, "*Mamas y papas* . . . they got no 'day care.' But each day, they find person come get kid, walk them home. Send aunties, uncles . . . even me, Stripe, for ten dolla, by apartment to check on becau' *La Peste—el corona*—close school but they still had to work. They no do becau' they scare of ICE. They do becau' lil' kid get *taken*, never see them again, an' no one care 'bout they screams. *Desaparecida*."

My mouth is dry again. "You grab my meds like I asked?"

CHAPTER 8
Anacostia Flats

Nope, he didn't.

And this morning, after a thirty-minute Green Line ride, I'm feeling cotton-headed and cotton-mouthed, and Stripe's trailing me up the slope along Good Hope Road, Southeast. Couple of shops peddling incense and African-looking stuff are fronted by clusters of folk throwing us shade and not the kind that saves us the heat and horrid sun, stamp . . .

"Don't like bein' stared down, Rain Man," the kid whispers through his mask.

"Hush the fuss," I say, pulling mine off to catch extra oxygen, salving my throbbing crown. The come-down from the pills is fucking with me but I got to play fearless leader. "We're here."

We halt at a cluster of low-rise red brick apartments—bland, bunker-like and frozen in time, from the laundry lines festooned with linens and clothing that flutter in the oven broiler wind, to the Eighties-vintage Chevy Caprice taking up three spaces in the project's small lot.

Indeed, through the window I see the hoopdy's full up of middle-agers like me, hot-boxing and sipping cold cans, grooving to Cameo, *Single Life.* Not a single fucking mask among them.

"S'up men," I lead, unabashedly loud to get through the glass and music. "Where's Toya Thomas, 'Miz Toy' . . . Al-Mayadeen's mama, live at?"

The front passenger window lowers. This dude missing teeth peeks me up and down.

"You loafin' on ya'self, Big Man. Don't come 'round here like that."

"Real live, I'm here 'cause her boy came to me for help about his lil' girl."

There're muffled voices inside the car; someone douses the volume.

I add, "Yeah . . . shot himself. Stamp, just here to help Miz Toy tie-up his stuff."

"Wha . . . y'all like her caseworker or sumffin?"

I shrug, hand this cat one of my business cards . . . on which the Chief joaned.

"Big Man here's a private dick," the tooth fairy chuckles to his crew in the backseat.

"*Ha*! Like 'Shaft?'" one scoffs. "He a champ Shaft, moe!" He's wrecking the movie theme with his singing voice.

If it couldn't get any worse, here comes a pride of local young lions—fit versions of theses niggas in the Chevy. They flank Stripe and saturate me with stank looks. At least these boys're masked.

I raise up from the car window, pull mine down to warn them, "Al-Mayadeen's mama . . . finna see her, is all."

"Folks is blown, Big Man," this cat in the Caprice muses when he also sees the teens gather. "Befo' the 'rona it was sugar or heart, cancer, bullets taking mugs . . . then this thing come to take the rest of us, and we now jus' able ta live when this Al-May come outta supervision, come to he mama's and start on 'bout he lil' gurl when folk put that chile long out they minds. Plucked some nerves. Let her rest in peace! He can go be homeless somewhere else!"

Before I can ask another question, one of the teens yanks down his mask to holler at the men in the car, "Gonna get kirked if you if keep spillin' ops ta this big nigga, hear me?"

Stripe moves to my exposed three o'clock, bluffing and puffing; the dude in the car whispers to me. "She in Number two-dee, North. Hell wiff these youngstas."

"Say less, man. Thanks."

We peel off until the junior varsity gets in our way.

"*Baboso* . . . wha'?" Stripe loud-talks the putative honcho. He's swelling-up his sinewy form so I better stop it before they pop it . . .

"Listen, Young," I call to that kid, getting between he and Stripe, "I told your elders we're not here to mess with anyone."

"Lan'lord come in here with lotta mugs look like *you*, Old, when folk sick, folk dyin' at home 'cause they can't get no hospital. Say they ain't gotta listen to new laws and they evictin' anyway. Pile my mama's an' my shit on the curb, while she dyin', nigga!"

Uh-huh . . . tarry spots, burnt patches, charred sofa cushions, melted rubber off toys, shoes . . . and up the block in a stand of ghetto palms lay the tangled wreckage of a couple of ATVs, dirt bikes. The trusty steeds of these annoying squires.

"*Dead*, Old," the teen snarls. "Twelve be a beast here, long wiff niggas say they wiff Health Department . . . "

Stick to the plan.

"Know a mug named Little?"

"*Guh* . . . fuck you, Old. Fuck Big, fuck Little and this bitch-ass Spanish you brung . . . "

"*Puto*!" Stripe fires back, "You gonna get glassed, bitch!"

I grab Stripe by his scruff and drag him with me . . . and the kids gasp . . . then melt away, cursing. Because they're kids. Kid don't shit when they clock a man being a man. Hope that sinks in with Stripe . . .

. . . and so the sweltering foyer is black as oil despite high noon outdoors, and it smells like greasy cooking and cat piss; the buzzers don't work but it's easy to jerk the door open. I roll up and knock on 2D North.

Toy Thomas welcomes us as if she knows we're coming. She's tall like her late son . . . bone-thin, with veiny brown legs poking from yellow shorts, yellow bedroom slippers shod on long, narrow feet. A wavecap tops her coarse gray hair. Look around at the spot: flat screen that sputters infomercials, a few sticks of furniture. A range and oven with the guts ripped out.

She shows us her vax certificate but we're keeping the masks up. "Suit ya'self" she mutters. But then with a sigh she eases up and points to one unmarred, painted wall, and there hangs a framed photo of she and Princess. Must be from the Seventies . . . cheery schoolgirls on brightly-painted bikes, tassels on the handlebars.

I smile. She sees it and answers it with her own, and it seems to buoy her enough to offer sweet tea from the old rattling fridge. Maybe the only decent thing about that place besides the picture on the wall is a full view of the Capitol, downtown, the monuments, spires of domes of cathedrals and basilicas in the background. Money shot for white gentrifiers making their first probing recons into Southeast . . .

"Miz Toy, pretty clear it was suicide, no police follow-up . . . no autopsy . . . "

"My boy was sick in the body, soul . . . an' head. Whatchew think I dunno?"

"His remains . . . "

"City can see him home, jus' like it saw ta Princess. Least it can do. Thas it? Thas why y'all come all this way?"

"Wanted to ask you . . . about CiCi Talbot-Thomas. You know she died a brick back, COVID?"

Miz Toy aims a squinted eye at me and Stripe. She grabs her pack of menthols and slides out a jack, lights it.

"Miz Toy . . . I-I didn't mean nothing. Just wanted some background. Hell . . . Ernesto, let's leave this lady in peace." Yeah, because I got my license. I technically did what Missy Anne commanded.

She blows a puff of smoke straight up into her nostrils and quips, "CiCi trap my boy into a wedding, she runaway and gits them drugs git her and my granbaby an' her in the shelter for years . . . *years.* But my granbaby so smart . . . she do her letters like a little white girl do. An' so pretty. When the pestilence come, God smote her an' put the scar on Little jus' like he mark Cain, sent him out to Nod." She takes another draw, taps the ash on the damn floor. "That it? Y'all have good day, Mr. Cornish. Princess'd be proud . . . "

Stripe's eyeing the marred apartment door. I say, "No." And now it's on . . .

"I want to show some evidence in the kidnapping no one's looked at in six, goin' on seven years."

She's picking at the cigarette filter with her thumbnail . . . she nods, stoneface yet hitting me in the softest of whispers. "Not the reporters, not the social services . . . not the po-lice . . .

been by since . . . or since that white woman in her uniform wiff all them gold braids who say back then 'we goin' find her bring her home, brung kidnapper ta the law.' Wh' faw *you*, Mr. Cornish?"

I set Stripe's "new" phone on the table after she clears off multiple unused carryout utensil packets and crusty microwave food containers.

"These are pics, shot from copies of CCTV video. That's Ky . . . pacing . . . Minnesota Avenue, broad daylight. Where's her teddy?"

"Lord . . . " she drops the jack on the floor, crushes it with her slipper foot and lights another. "Ain't . . . ain't never seent these."

"Chief, I mean, Commander Figgis . . . never went over the CCTV with you?"

"Whaffaw they would? Jus' look fo' Hakim, mess wiff me 'bout why I never could git custody of my gran-baby. Then axe if CiCi run her mouff 'bout any mo' men than Hakim . . . I mean . . . Little."

I exchange glances with Stripe and already I'm telling he's ready to book with that. "Um . . . check these out . . . is that her teddy in this pic?"

"*Ugh* . . . she call that bear Poob, like she sayin' 'Winnie the *Pooh*.'"

I thumb a few over. "Okay . . . in this pic, no Poob . . . but in this one, she's talking, eye level for a six-year-old, so it can't be a standing adult . . . it's an adult in a car . . . you see is a shadow for sec at the curb, see? Must be a car. Yet she's got the bear Poob. Now *third pic* . . . she's pacing again, crying . . . "

"Somebody . . . be helpin' her. Somebody she know? But it all be—"

"Out of order. Yes. If it's not you in the middle helping here, not not Little and not her mama, then who? Al-Mayadeen was locked up. Look. Here's CiCi, five blocks from the shelter yet still across the river, *not* some damn nail salon like she said, on the phone . . . this one, this dude Little, at another intersection, on the phone. . . . time stamp barely six minutes later."

"Di'n't they boff say they be callin', looking fo' my Ky?"

"Again, timeline's all messed up."

"Little be crazy 'cause he los' her?"

"That first shot of Ky . . . video from a pole above the CVS, was the time CiCi claims Little called her and says Ky's vanished. Yet it's identical to the time Little was in the store. So, he's calling frantically in CVS without going outside . . . *where he left her*?"

Miss Toy shrugs. "Thas' . . . thas' why po-lice make Little and CiCi suspects, fo' killing my gran-baby . . . "

"Nah, Miz Toy. Official case report says Ky'd been abducted and had on a red jacket and was holding a teddy bear. BOLO that went out to MPD, P.G. County PD, U.S. Park Police, Maryland state troopers also said red jacket . . . teddy bear. Well there's the red jacket in the footage? Why's the bear . . . in some pics and not others? Doesn't show they were killers and sure as hell doesn't show they kidnapped a child who was in their own care anyway. Proves either CiCi and Little were fucking around with their stories tryna throw off somebody when girl's lost on the street. Or somebody manipulated the footage."

That second jack's tumbling off her lips as she mumbles, "Why di'n't the p-po-lice . . . why . . . "

I take her hand and I don't care how any of this shit goes over with Figgis. I want Stripe to see how you get at what's right, how you help folks. "I'm saying I went over this a couple times before sun-up and each time it came up more champ and shady."

And now Miz Toy's giving low, slight moans as I explain . . .

"Little's, not CiCi's, Sprint mobile records are referenced in this memo, as is CVS store video. Little was buying his cigarettes, stuff for Ky . . . plus a pack of jimmies . . . confirmed by store video . . . the same time a call comes into CiCi from *his* phone . . . *the same time CCTC video shows Ky still out front.* Now, how'd he make a call, pay for this stuff, discover Ky's not out front when she is in fact still out front, in the space of maybe ten seconds? Linda Figgis thought he lied the first time about going outside, discovering 'oh shit Ky's gone,' then calling CiCi in a panic. Figgis hauled his ass back in when the subpoena results came in . . . he doesn't remember making two calls just one—the long one where he's frantic about losing Ky and he's trying to meet up CiCi to look for her."

"Wha' y'all tryna say Mr. Cornish. Somebody messed wiff they phones, too?"

"CiCi's mobile subpoena shows two incoming calls from Little. But seconds before the first—which we know was *impossible* for him to make given the store video—she got an unknown call . . . one ring, cut off, then this one supposedly from Little, twenny seconds, then the long crazy call from Little: hey I lost your daughter, left her on the street like a dumbass . . . I'm walkin' here, come meet me . . . "

Stripe finishes, "Make it look like he was plannin' som-in wid *chica* . . . "

Miz Toy's quivering, shaking her head. "I tole po-lice tha' Little . . . he too stupid ta plot wiff that bitch . . . nor he got the sand to hurt a chile. But I never tole them 'bout Big. Big hurt that chile."

I nod to Stripe. Gingerly he removes the bear from the bag.

Miz Toy makes a shrill cry, moves to the picture window overlooking the distant condo towers and monuments. If Figgis saw this, Lord . . .

"Your son had this . . . before he put a gun to my head. Said your granddaughter's alive and I was help him prove it . . . "

Takes her a good minute to calm down. Looking at the frame photo of she and Princess helps a bit and indeed Ernesto, who Daddy swore up and down favored a evil reptile, says to her, softly, "*Su nieta* . . . K'ymira, she be in here, *señora.*" He motions with his thumb to his sternum.

"He . . . he say someone mailed it ta him. I say it a devil-prank. I say I throw it away. Got so mad at me he leff out. Next I hear he wiff them trap hoes ova one them motels. I say, Big, he gone. Little, he gone. Stay wiff me, son. Lord I di'n' wanna loose alla them . . . "

All—the fuck? Nothing about a "Big" in the mess of shit Figgis gave me. And Little was just CiCi's dick-boy. "Little . . . Big?"

She's throwing us both a horror movie smile now. "Had Al-Mayadeen wiff my late husband Abul. Then Big . . . an' Little . . . come from men I knew."

Stripe's eyes are clawing at me. *Jesus Mary and Joseph.* "Little—Hakim Alexander—is your son, *too*? Suspect in kid-napping or killing own . . . damn . . . *niece*? *Kill,* you never told the heat, Child Services, *anyone* . . . that you had two other fuckin' sons?"

Yeah I'm almost yelling this and she's nodding like it ain't no thing, swear to God. "Whaffaw I tell th' po-lice? Little, he love my granbaby!" She sighs, calms. "See . . . alla them . . . alla them cursed, in the Land of Nod like in Genesis say, each in they own way."

And this is Eden? I motion for Stripe to pack the pics and file. My vision's getting a little blurry now . . . I'm lightheaded but Hell that must be debris and stank air of this apartment. Mouth's gone from dry to saucy, like when you know at some point you might puke, but a good belch and you'll be right as the U.S. Mail . . .

"Miz Toy . . . you know Hakim's in a hospice up in Laurel, right . . . in a coma?"

She nods but says, "Folk wiff gov-verment say he move ta other spot when money run out . . . good thang 'cause Al-Mayadeen wanna kill he brother for messin' wiff CiCi . . . but not as bad as he wanna kill Big."

She saunters to her rusted fridge and pulls a scrap of paper from under a magnet. "He be in two spots before. Now but here but like I say, next time they moves him, it gonna be one them dead houses. Coughin', smells—shit they di'n't show on the news."

So thereabouts my dome's really starting to ache, like a migraine . . . and I'm clocking Miz Toy dig into her sleeveless T-shirt as if to adjust her bra . . . out comes green money and she grabs my hand, smashes the moist, warm cash into my palm. Through my blurrier eyesight I can tell it's two fifties and a bunch of fives.

"You take a hunnad fo' yo' trouble, for helpin' my Al-Maya an' clear he soul, find truth. Gives rest to Big, so he don't lie t'y'all." She points to the window. "He won't lie if he gets this, tell him it f'om Mama." She turns away from the window and us, peering Lord knows where in the universe. "Al-Maya, he wanna kill Big worser than Little. Worser than Cain an' Abel. Long as Big around, I cou'n't git no custody a Ky. But Big, he my baby still, ain't he?"

Stripe asks, all mature and officious, "He in th' park?"

"Them the Flats," she corrects.

"Anacostia Flats," I chime in. "Old-heads call it that. Used to be a marsh. Look . . . I can't take your money."

Before Stripe can say *Yes you can* she shoots back, "You doin' mo'good wiff it than any. So g'won ta Big. He live in the picnic place. Flats is his Land of Nod. Tha's all I can say 'bout mah troubled sons. Lord help you, Mr. Cornish."

The cold grape Nehi I slurp down as we descend to the Flats doesn't do a damn thing but make me all bubbly, make me forget her warning.

The baked, dismal air isn't helping . . .

. . . Stripe's clocking me and his expression is funky as if I'm farting on him, joanin' him . . . and we stop . . . so I can rest a second against this tagged-up traffic light pole . . . catch my breath.

Stripe's talking but I can't make out what he's saying, as if I'm trippin' . . . and he's moving in slow motion . . . and I think I'm falling to one knee as everything gets like a watercolor pic you paint and you spill . . . spill your mixing cup . . .

"Rain Man!" I think Stripe's shouting as he helps me to my feet. "You good?"

Little spick.

About as useful on this trek as tits on a bull, and here you are, choking on heated car fumes there under the I-295 overpass in view of the river park. Ole Gunney's back, Junior. Do let's do this shit right.

"*Vea*, les' go home . . . *hace calor* . . . the mama she don't care . . . "

"Nah . . . nah," you mutter. Yeah, unfuck yourself and stay on that skirt's good side. Complete the mission, even with this detour . . .

. . . and yet when you eye the National Park Service sign and blue-green Anacostia River beyond God love you, you are full speed ahead. "Keep your eyes sharp. Bad shit happens here."

Your sidekick has had enough, but even he's pressing you on that cryptic warning about the Flats.

"*Oye . . . porqué la gente tiene tanto miedo de este lugar*? Just a park. Picnics . . . "

"No. Jont went back to its mean roots," you say in that deadpan and monotone of yours, and now you already got this kid scared. "Nineteen-thirty-two . . . Depression's fuckin' everything. World War One vets . . . poor, jobless, came to D.C. to ask the President and Congress to help them. Wanted their bonus for fighting, bleeding . . . catching a killer flu as bad as 'rona. Motherfuckers in charge then were just the ancestors of the shit we got now. Called 'em names like 'bums' and 'communists'. With a few brothers marching with them, hell, the southerners who ran this city back then added 'nigger-lovers.' Hoover, he called out the Army. Not Five-oh, not his own *federale* goons. The Army. Chased them across the river to here, where they'd set up camp with their women, children. Dudes they served with in France . . . they tear-gassed them, beat them, ran them down with *cavalry* . . . yeah, horses and sabres, back in the day before lots of tanks. Eisenhower and MacArthur and Patton . . . motherfuckers you've never heard of except when whitefolk geek about *heroes*. Not on the motherfucking Flats, they weren't . . . "

Nice history lesson, *Rain Man*. Now tell the kid the truth. Bigshots wanted the park reopened for the sunbathers. Had to be sterilized . . . like back in '32.

At the riverbank you clock the gazebo-like picnic pavilion, yet surrounding it are large paper bags you usually see filled with leaves in Fall, yet this are overflowing with clothing—some stained with grim and oil, some with blood—and shoes, blankets, ripped up tarps, the poles of makeshift hammocks and chairs though not up to your level of workmanship.

Stenciled on the bags: REFUSE: INCINERATE ONLY—U.S. DEPT OF INTERIOR.

So sorry the little weasel forgot your murder pills, Junior—but why'd you be fixing to kick ole Gunney to the rear with the pogues when it's time for battle? Especially there . . . on the Anacostia Flats.

CHAPTER 9

Rough Penance

BEHOLD THE FULL GLORY OF "BIG." Mud-stained sweatpants riddled with tears, faded, smelly Redskins T-shirt, hiked up to his man-titties. Ashy, clawlike toes curling as he slumbers, twitches. Reminds you of someone . . . come on, just a little bit?

You tell Stripe, "Grab some cold bottles of water from food truck back there, under the freeway."

You hear a snort from the grass. "Nah, *Mickey's*, muvfuckin' green grenade . . . "

Ah, a cuvée from your past, son!

"And banana if they got it. Here're few more bucks."

"Ain't no monkey, nigga!" the giant complains as he wakes, sits up.

"Bananas're good, moe. Easy on the stomach, choppers. Trust."

"Jefe . . . come on." Guess Robin's not feeling this, eh Batman?

Your eyes and sigh motivate the delinquent to tromp off, whining in Spanish. Alone at last. You pull pieces of what seems to be a deck umbrella from the nearest refuse bag.

"Steel . . . acacia. Good . . . heavy black duct tape not the craft store shit. This is what I would have scavenged . . . why didn't y'all build a blind? Tarp, old T-shirts on twigs, get some trash, bottles . . . that misdirects them away from you. Stuff they expect: picnic tables, trash bins, put'em by shrubbery, trees. That's your blind. Who fucked with you?"

"F-Feds an' shit. Full-up a rednecks . . . they ain't leave when Trump left." He barks a dry cough, then uses his swollen black hand as a visor against the sun. "I-I know you, gee?"

"Dickie Cornish. Al-Mayadeen come by my jont yesterday. He's dead."

Nice rapport, son. Rather than talking you got this sumbitch swaying like a huge smelly kindergartener tossing a fit there in the turf . . . squeaking all high-pitched like a hog.

As he composes himself now you're treated to stories of his lil' niece. So pretty. Giggling when she'd loose a tooth, blowing ole "Unca Biggie" kisses as he watched over her like a surrogate dad. And there you are standing over him like a bear clocking a dropsy hippo . . . what's on your mind? Those pills . . . making you all murky?

Stripe's returning with a bagful of water bottles. The kid's busy biting up a Strawberry Shortcake ice cream bar from the look of it.

Big grabs a water and chugs the bottle so hard the thing collapses inward. With a belch he thanks you for being there for his bro'. "Al-Maya . . . how could I help him when I *jih*-broke, on the street m'self, moe."

"Not disloyal, like Little, huh?"

"*Guh* . . . Little a punk," Big elucidates after a gulp from a new bottle.

Stripe's got the ice cream down to the stick, elbows you. Yeah. What's your play?

"Mama . . . she maybe give y'all some cash f'me?"

Stripe stink eyes you when you shake your head in a lie. And your sleepy monotone you tell Big, "Did you molest K'ymira, your niece, while Little was fucking the child's mother, or was it after?"

"The *fock*, Rain Man!" Better hush that pup, Big Dog . . .

You loom closer. "You heard me, nigga. Something your dead brother said . . . confirmed by your mama . . . "

"Nigga ya best better jump back . . . "

"She couldn't get custody . . . not because of that dump she lives in. It was *you*."

"Imo get in ya chest!"

Almost cartoonish how Big abruptly corkscrews off the hot, wet grass like a reverse wobbly top, hissing and snarling, knuckled and flailing.

You square up and fire a right fist straight into his left cheek. He drops back to where he sat. Haven't beaten down a motherfucker in an age, boy! Feels good!

You search your sidekick's frightened face. "It's okay . . . okay . . . just keep an eye out!"

He nods, chest heaving. He's not important now anyway, huh? Onaccount you reach down and pull this dazed fat fuck up to his feet by his stinky T-shirt.

"I know how y'all are. I know y'all put in the work for each other. You pass her to another pervert?"

Something must be funny here, on the flats, onaccount this walrus motherfucker's giggling. Better watch that spittle and blood, Junior, pull up your mask!

"Jesus say brung the churlin ta me. An' they come, oh yeah . . ." He licks his lips and they're slick now with his blood and snot.

"Don't fuck with me."

"Ain't . . . ain't a thing," he pants. "See . . . lil' princess, she special. *Ain't nobody ta mess wiff her.* Off limits even ta ole . . . Unca Biggie . . . "

"*Vea* . . . " Stripe entreats.

"Ernesto . . . *cállate y aprende algo*!" Then you turn to Big, "Twelve says she was abused from birth. A horror show."

"I-I *know* you, nigga . . . yeah . . . I know yo' name from Princess Goins! An' the Queen, all these fools on the street, too—hear she say 'Dickie . . . he watch us all, protect us all.' But they all dead. An' you don' know nothin' . . . big faggot . . . "

You slap him. All it does is push out more bloody laughs.

"Stripe show him wants in the bag!"

Hands shaking, Stripe pulls the bear, Poob, halfway from the bag.

"Al-Maya give y'all that? Like that prove *shit*? Big Man you into the levels of Hell, you brung that mess 'round? You brung it 'round my mama?"

"Show me how much I don't know and we can keep Miz Toy out of this."

He nods, spills in glee, "CiCi trickin' alla time at the munie shelter. Alla time me, ole Big, was watchin' her lil' gurl while she given out ass."

You know the rumors, boy. Rollas up in there giving up cooch for cash and Pampers.

"Hell you say."

Oh, now the laugh gets voluptuous as fuck, son. "Y'all don't got a damn clue, moe. Weren't no janitors and shit fuckin' in closets. CiCi be top shelf, *untouchable.* Al-Maya be dumb like you, gee—never think no pimpin' down there befo' Mayor shut it down? Women. An' lil' boys." He licks his lips. "An' lil' *gurls.* An' makin' mad pimp bank." He pauses. "Cops. An' social workers . . . an' they peoples. Mad. Pimp. Bank."

"Bullshit."

"Oh yeah nigga. Twelve"

Figgis left that part out, huh? You're tilting your head like a dog struggling to follow a hyena's tale. Well, your *incredulity,* if ole Gunney may use a college word, gives Big his office to take off. He lumbers—barefoot and meat rippling—toward the shimmer of the river. You do a 1973 Chris Hanburger and Jack Pardee onto his back, slam him to the turf.

Forearm under his fat chin and lookie how all that evil mirth's disappeared.

"C-Come on . . . B-Big Man . . . ain't no beef. Don' kill me . . . "

"You mess with this kid? Answer me, nigga!"

"Real live . . . r-real, gee . . . they tole me ta watch out for the gurl when CiCi trickin' thas all. CiCi, she start-up wiff Little . . . fuckin' Little. Some some a her reg'lars, they we'n't down wiff that. Al-Maya's beef—tha' the *least* a Little's probs." He swallows some spit them seems to grow a conscience. "But Little, he all 'bout that chile even if he was smashin' he brotha's wife . . . "

"Who's 'they?'"

"They wha' run the shit. Wha run e'rythin' gee."

Yeah. Feel that? Your stomach, dropping to where your nut-sack used to be?

Breathless, Big crawls like a wounded creature as far away from your newfound menace as you allow, and don't think you haven't freaked out the kid by all this monstering. He's mumbling in Spanish and won't even look you in the eye.

"Who . . . who'd you put in the work for?" you press Big, now squatting in the grass. "You both know you never kept your hand from that lil' girl. Means there was others."

"Lotta them Chile Services mugs be bent, di'n'tchew know?"

"*Kill* . . . you mean . . . a caseworker?"

You jerk around when Stripe taps your shoulder, points you in the direction of where the park meets Howard Road, just under the Douglass Bridge. Youngster's eyes're better than yours, and at first you're shooing him away . . . but then . . . yeah. Your little session's been noted by the olive drab and brown Twelve. Parkies. See them? Two ofays in helmets . . . mounted on two lovely sorrels, and the horses are headed right for you sumbitches . . .

"I-I ain't a devil like Mama say," Big suddenly confesses. "I-I jus' get sick is all . . . *sick*, Big Man . . . "

"Who you puttin' in work for, man. Get it offa your chest?"

"Rain Man, *coño*," Stripe intones, onaccount those horses are at a trot now . . .

"I-I find the good meat. The good meat they say. The rollas . . . mos' fucked up . . . can't get into the decent places, like Section-Eight . . . like that SFME spot, right. Miss Verna's spot."

That puts you off balance. "What the fuck you know about Verna?"

"She . . . she was young . . . worked at the munie, gee." He gets real quiet, then, "She weren't evil. *They* evil. They make ole Big mo' evil, right?"

"*Jefe . . . mira*!"

One horseman, who turns out to be a horse-lady, cuts right. The other flanks to the left and now you can hear the hooves pounding on grass in a canter . . .

Big's blubbering and it doesn't even sound like English he's spitting. "Got m'own lil' gurl . . . thas wha' they hold ova me, moe! Axe her mama, Dretta!"

"No, you answer me . . . who you puttin' in work for, man."

"G'won—*n'more, n'more, n'more.* Ain't no Lucifer . . . *n'more*!" Guess he hears the rumble of hooves too onaccount he goes all frozen and mumbles, "W-White dude . . . a Jew . . . counselor . . . at the munie, all ova the jont."

No time to sink into a fog of disbelief at what this fat fuck just spilled. Yeah, this white lady up on her mount's swinging her iron between you and Big.

"Hand's up, asshole," she yells. "Palms out!"

The other's on his shoulder radio and his piece is aimed right at Stripe's face.

"I-I'm . . . a private investigator!"

"And I'm Ivanka," the female screeches from the saddle. As the male jake dismounts she adds, "Now on the ground, bellies first. Arms spread!"

"We no bums, officer," Stripe protests, ". . . we come talk to this one."

She notes his accent before you can tell him to clam up.

"You a citizen, Pee-dro?" the female menaces, flatly.

"He's my . . . associate, officer," you pant. "Pl-Please . . . check my ID . . . "

"Your *what*?" the male one scoffs. He's astride your back, cuffing you as the lady jake dismounts, re-aims her piece. The other grabs her set of manacles, cuffs a moaning Stripe.

"Easy *chero*," you soothe him. Good advice onaccount you know one thing Big's said on the Flats today is proven, like at the Colonial View: too many peckerwoods and Nazis still burrowed deep among the Feds, even the Army dogs at Ft. Myer, the Marine devil-dogs at the Eighth and E Barracks.

The boy equestrian's rifling your pockets now. The female pokes at Big's distended belly with her boot, inspects the blood trickling from his flared nostrils and lips.

"Fatso owe you money, Big Boy?" she sneers at you. "Thought you types settled these differences with a round to the chest, not an old-fashioned butt-whipping?"

"Aw check this out!" her partner crows, showing what Figgis gave you. "P.I. license . . . *damn* . . . and a business card . . . " You look up from the moist, peat-funky grass to see the male jake pass the lady your stuff. Another pocket jiggle and the sumbitch chuckles, "And what on earth . . . ?" He yanks out the little brass magnifying glass.

"Sherlock Holmes!" the female gushes. "Pee-dro must be Watson!"

"Hey Big Boy, you the ghetto Sherlock Holmes?" the male teases. "You have that dumbass hat and the pipe back at the crib? What'd you smoke in it?"

You plead, "I-I did penance and I'm sober . . . pl-please let him do *his* penance, spill some info to me . . . and we be gone and . . . and never be down here again . . . "

The male Parkie snickers, "Now he sounds like a preacher not a private dick." He twiddles with your stolen trinket and adds, "Says 'National Association of Police Chiefs & Sheriffs Convention, New Orleans.' You shittin' me, Sherlock?"

"It's mine."

Suddenly, Big lets out a scream and the Parkies flinch, re-reaching for their irons. You must've rearranged his plumbing, boy and just now the pain's registered.

"Mo-Moses Roffe . . . *R-O-two f's . . . e.*" Big confesses.

The female officer shrieks, "Cut the goddamn chatter!"

"Moses Roffe . . . *good, get it offa your chest,*" you praise.

"*Shut your hole*!" the lady jake's hollering as the male's now blown and demanding the status of their back-up. "Look . . . Jeez . . . let's just cut these two loose to MPD. Help me with this one!"

They stand-up poor Big and struggle to keep his teetering bulk upright.

"Big, listen to me . . . they gonna throw you down a deep hole . . . *Moses Roffe* . . . where's he at?"

Oh, now this fat fuck's had it, bloody snot bubbling in his broad nostrils punctuate your failure . . .

"Now get going, Sherlock," the female cop yelps.

Stripe scoops up the bag containing the teddy bear. Lord knows why they didn't grab it.

You nod, take a step . . . then, *oh, come on, boy* . . .

"Big . . . you don't gotta go to Hell like your brothers. Al-Maya sinned by suicide. Little's an adulterer, prolly killed his own niece?"

Father God you indeed have descended upon the cursed Flats, onaccount Big's got this serene Holy Ghost's coming look. "Moses he . . . he clockin' moms an' kids in them trap hotels . . . "

Just as they're about to run Big out the Park—runaway slave-style between two horses—he adds, "He leff tha' jont . . . now he at Miss Verna new spot."

What's the matter son? This shit get too real, real fast? Pick your your jaw up off the turf!

Guess the male jake's sensing some sudden ennui, too. He reins-in his horse, looks back at you over the rump.

"Yo, Sherlock!" He tosses you the magnifying glass you stole . . . sorry, *scavenged* . . . from Figgis. The magnifying glass. "Learn your Bible. No such thing as 'penance' unless you got a gun stuck in your face. Now get outta here . . . "

CHAPTER 10

Sitch-awareness

NO IDEA HOW LONG I WAS asleep before Stripe let himself in. It's dark so it's got to be at least past eight. I downed the meds soon as I broke into my spot and Daddy's been gagged ever since. Got Advil for my sore fists . . . from beating on Big. God help me.

"*Madre* . . . come on wake th' fock up, man." Stripe's prodding me, even karate-chopping my damn pillow.

"Thought . . . thought I told you we had to fort-up . . . get up to St. Stephen's grab your stuff . . . tell the dude I'll still be paying the seventy a month for your bed . . . "

"You say a lot, bro' . . . an' it sound cray as fuck."

"Stripe, lemme explain . . . it's meds . . . it's . . . "

"We in trouble, Rain Man. Them Park Police take tha' fat man to Hain's Point lockup, sweat him, he gonna say why we was there. You girl the Chief of Police—she no say go down in park and beat the fock outta a fat man."

I swing my bare legs off the cot . . . I'm coughing . . . "Gimme some ice tea from the minifridge. And they don't give a damn why we were there. To them it's just usual Third World spook and spick drama they complain about to their friends in West Virginia on the weekends."

He fetches me a cold peach tea. I drain the bottle as he schools me.

"Nah, Jefe, Big—him say po-po, him say social workers . . . all abusin' *los ninos, los mujers* in the munie shelter, in that Colonial spot. He go tell Park Police, Park Police tell all the cops. Piggies come f'us, bro'. But by then they grow tusk like boar, tear our asses up, man."

Point taken. I finally see his footlocker by my dresser. *Good,* he made the trip from up Sixteenth and Newton where he sleeps in the church undercroft. "I'm gonna bunk on the floor, you, take the bed."

"Wha' 'bout Figgis?"

"What about her, kid?" I'm up, stretching, scratching. Because what else is there to do? See, a smart man would've hotfooted it to Missy Linda straightaway. Spilled every damn thing Big said, his Mama hinted. Handed over that damn bear, Poob, the CCTV stills and dared her to do her yank my license. I was hustling before. Can hustle again. "Didn't mean to kirk Big," I add, partially to myself. "I-I know . . . it's bad, I was bad . . . losing my shit, lunchin' with those Parkies. I know it's déjà vu, back to the shit with Bracht, Mr. Sugars . . . Esme. You listening, *chero*?"

"*Sí . . . coño . . .* " He whispers. "You di'n't 'mean it.' You not 'cray' like before . . . "

"No . . . no it's not like that."

"So wha' it like—you tell me? Is it them pills, Rain Man? Spose ta make you right in the head. Who you be when pills don't work?"

"I'm *me.* Just . . . me, hear me? But . . . " I swallow hard. He's seen me in the jump crew vans, on street, talking to Daddy in the air. But this is different.

Swear to God he's gaping at me as if I told him I dreamed about molesting him. "Then you focked in you head more than you say."

Lord I want to hug this kid, I want to smack him down. His world was shades of gray, slithering by, surviving. Then with Bracht comes the reckoning and I take him in, and now he's about rules, black and white, yes or no. I shouldn't complain. He'd be dead on the street if he didn't change, grow up. "I'm not hearing voices, and it's *not* time to get Figgis involved. I feel it in my gut so trust me. We need to protect ourselves, gather more facts . . . because this pinktoe in blue has got more angles than Pythagoras, can put a dozen cops and detectives right on my ass . . . and make a call to the Feds and the whole Bracht thing stinks up the air once again and I know you don't want that. Just because they're different people in charge, doesn't mean they won't scoop you up, throw me under the prison . . . "

Ave Maria . . . he's nodding . . . then I get a smile. Crap, with those bamma gold fronts.

He says, "Is hot in here, bro' An' you took the las' ice tea. Nothin' cold."

"There's some green on the desk. Get me a black coffee to go, and one of those Philly-style water ices, large cherry, up on the corner before they close . . . and you get that guava shit you like. Stay alert though . . . "

"Can't carry all that."

"You'll eat the water ice, first, I'm sure," I laugh.

He's out the apartment door, still grinning, and hey all's right in the world again, huh?

My phone lights up. *So Families May Eat* is on the screen. Only one person calls from there and it sure as shit's not Verna . . .

"M'lord, Duke of Edinburgh, York, Cornwall and Chocolate City," I hear in a very poor limey accent.

"Oh . . . oh wow . . . did I call you this afternoon, Keesh? My head's a mess."

"Not even a bumpy ride to another dimension in the TARDIS would I, sir, as a lady-in-waiting for a champion, be so scandalized at this effrontery . . . I do not recall giving you office to address me so brazenly . . . "

Jesus Christ. At least LeKeisha's punted that damn "Mother of Dragons" tip long ago, but this Jane Austen shit's extra. And it's a wonder Verna hasn't fired her for streaming *Doctor Who* and *Star Trek: Discovery* on her work computer. Still better than how I came to meet her: camping in the Shaw Public Library ladies room . . . toting that shopping cart and three busted laptops. Once upon a time the bug-eyed lil' fat girl was a lean, mean imp, name of Specialist LaKeisha Murray, tech-nav spotter, Battery C, First Battalion artillery, Tenth Mountain Division . . . Battle of the Mazark Valley, Afghanistan. Married. Kids. Where does the unraveling begin? Maybe before all that, with evil things remembered, and so liquor and dust and pills and needles help you forget?

"Listen, Keesh—you know I don't do need Google when I got you. Ha!"

Her champ accent dissolves into her normal frenetic typewriter voice. "*You called me, all crazy about this K'ymira Thomas thing, old Municipal Shelter, naming names I can't talk to about . . . you know I get nervous when I can't keep track of these things . . . you know I can't talk to to these bitches at the group house every night when I'm nervous . . . when I miss my girls . . . "*

"LaKeisha . . . "

"I'm a real person with a real job now, a bus pass, clothes. Ain't nobody's 'Google,' good only for looking up stuff for you, hooking up

Stripe's phone, shit like that! Why won't you respect me? Why won't you come by and see me? Why'd you forsake all of us, Dickie?"

I hear the sniffles, imagine the tears. She was farther down the rabbit hole than me, so she's come a longer way into the light. "*M'lady,*" I offer, playing to her fantasy du jour. "My heart as the only currency that will pay what's owed for offending you."

There's silence and a whispered, "*Thank you, Dickie.*" And quickly she's back in character. "*My Duke, the child K'ymira Thomas, an ill matter of some infamy. Abducted, assumed dead, from the waif and wench shelter. We honor her with the new construction.*"

"So I heard." I look around for the red envelope with the RBG stamp. "Yes, the invitation . . . "

"*So you'll come. You need to come, M'lord. May I announce you?*"

Come to SFME. Come to Verna, after a year of ghosting? Shit. "Look . . . y-yes . . . I'll come see you. *All* of you. But . . . tell me . . . is a dude named Moses Roffe . . . a staffer? Don't see him on the website and I know you can access the human resources stuff." Now I roll over to my desk, open Instagram and Facebook—Stripe's accounts as I have no need for my own. "If he is, can you give me his CV, background, if he worked at the munie . . . or has anything to do with kids and the Colonial View Motel?"

There's some heavy mouth-breathing, as LaKeisha's prone, then, "*I your most loyal courtesan in need of a legitimate man, cannot break Moses's trust. The donors and clients love him.*"

There's my answer. Big's bugbear, hobgoblin, is working for Verna. Lord . . .

"Okay, I won't put you on the spot longer. So let's move to K'ymira Thomas. I don't want to know all that mess that was on TV, in the papers, what niggas were tweeting and posting—fuck

that. What was her background . . . her mother named Cecelia . . . D.C., P.G. Co, MoCo, Medicaid, EBT, SNAP, TANF background. All that."

She's run these reports before and knows damn well Verna's broken into the system for me in the past, a dangerous, well-avoided past, about one other girl, named Piedade . . .

"I'll . . . Dropbox you a file when I'm done. And I see you."

"I'll bring a *posey*."

"And you won't mess with Moses Roffe? He could be anywhere, making money doing private therapy and consulting, teaching. But he's here, with us. I don't know who's lying on him but you better fist check whoever is."

"I'll . . . take it on advisement."

"Bye."

Something champ from across the river suddenly tickles my memory. "Wait! Keesh, from your Uncle Sam days . . . any way to muck up CCTV footage—digital—or scramble up cell tower pings?"

She laughs. "*That's old black bag stuff, John Le Carré novels . . . I can reco some dusty tomes for you, my Duke."*

"Love you."

"*No, you don't."*

Poor LaKeisha . . . and I'm an asshole. I put the red envelope back on my cot. I'm an important PI now, after all.

It's time to figure out Facebook's intricacies. See, I'm now clocking eleven Moses Roffe's on planet Earth. Most of this shit isn't public and what few faces I have are doughy pipsqueaks and old rabbis, to swarthy, cage fighter types.

This has got me got me lunchin' on my own life. What would I have worth posting? No pics around of me and Esme getting high, cold-turkeying, throwing up, rinse, repeat. Or

Black Santa, Princess, Katie . . . Mr. Fred, Miz Eva, Boston, Benedetto, the Queen, Esteban . . . all hugged up on the curb in the sooty snow, cheesing for group selfie. Trading cigarettes for mouthwash. Nah, what glues my eyes in a permanent squint is always the same. What might have been.

And I'm crying like a bitch now and good thing Stripe's gone . . .

. . . yet through the tears, something on the screen synchs-up.

Meghan Roffe . . . smiley and blond . . . early forties. Converted to Judaism, backpacked across the Negev Desert . . . kayaked Potomac rapids . . . climbed El Capitan, "to make my husband proud of me." Birthed a daughter—she's K'ymira's age were K'ymira alive. "Petal." *Petal?* And, she's "content" that he's a *social worker* in the District . . . who graduated from Yale, and Yale Law School . . . yet his "passion is saving the children, not money or acclaim."

Motherfucker . . .

Only a few public pics posted. Here's something from the Obama times, before the Dark Ages . . . everyone smarted-up in tuxes and black cocktail dresses. Her Honor the Mayor, looking all young and fresh . . . in office barely a month. White dude in a chef's outfit.

And what did I say—*swarthy, hirsute . . . swole gym rat cage fighter.* That's him. Jesus, Mary and Joseph . . . that's *him.* Whatever image I get from Keesh'll confirm it.

This "geo-tag" thing on where the picture was taken—I guess this is how it works, because I tap and it leaps to more info . . . *Mercado Asiático* Washington, D.C . . . there's a page for the flagship restaurant of a chain. And there it is . . . a link in *Capital Life* magazine. Nothing I'd ever heard of, but I'd been eating other people's table leavings so what the fuck do

I know? I click and the article headline says, "*Deputy Chief of Police Dante Antonelli receives $15,000 donation to the Police & Children's Recreation Club from celebrity chef Peter Adonis and Meghan Roffe, Greater D.C. Planning Commission.*"

"Boris Karloff . . . Bond villain," I mumble. Fifteen large and he can't smile?

Daddy called it my "jigsaw puzzle" brain. Well, the pieces are moving now.

I rock back in my creaky chair. I'm not supposed to care about the Planning Commission. Or Antonelli. Or even Linda Figgis' front court teammate, the Mayor. Only supposed to care about Al-Mayadeen's mother claiming his body. I clasp my hands and ask the Mother Mary why she puts me in shit like this. "*Sitch-awareness,* dummy," Daddy would say in Marine babble.

Stripe busts in. His mouth and tongue almost as day-glo as his damn hair. Hands me a cup of coffee and yeah, he's demolished the cherry water ice and is assaulting the guava thing with alacrity. This time he's got in some decent ear buds what came with the unbricked phone, yet the usual mess is playing.

"Projexx . . . goo' song call *Sidepiece,*" he mumbles, plastic spoon still in his mouth,

"Hey kid . . . *lo sciento.*"

"I gotcha back, Rain Man."

"I don't want to clown you . . . but . . . you'd be lunchin' if you we really could make a living staking out cheating husbands, finding lost *gatos,* bouncing horny drunk uncles from *quinceañeras.* I guess I fed a fantasy on my side, too. When you that, the Gods have a way of throwing shit at you."

"I una-stand, bro'." He clocks the Facebook pages open. "So know we look for this dude, Moses?"

"Until Figgis calls me in or what happened on the Flats blows up in our faces, yeah. Got LaKeisha working on more stuff. But kid . . . more and more there's all kinds of stuff popping in my dome . . . can't sever this little girl's case from Colonial View. Hard to explain . . . "

"You drink that coffee you be up all night."

"Am anyway. Listen . . . those apartments and shit you'd talk about when we were on the jump crews—out in Maryland . . . "

"Mm-mph . . . Langley Park, Silver Spring . . . down Bladensburg."

"All of them got bulldozed for redevelopment, right? Poor folk got deported?"

"Not you *myates,* eh?" He empties the orange slush and guava pulp directly from the Styrofoam cup then remarks, "You blacks—they move you to next projects. *Mi familia*? *Foooooock*! Gone to ICE tents, then Mexico, then back to same village th' volcano, rains bury. The gangs kill. An' the rich fockers who get Uncle Sam money—"

"From HUD. It's called HUD."

"*Sí* . . . fro' HUD, they get dolla an' fiddy f'every dolla they put in. Ask them around *El Don Trump* who own lotta them apartments, *en serio.*" He's shedding his shorts and T-shirt, ready to commandeer my bed.

"How's it work—Section Eight inspectors come in?"

"Section Eight, if you lucky. No, firs' they come say it all you live dirty, or you squatters, or you traphouse—like they di'n't plan you live that way, eh? Then other come, say *niños* got bad school, abused . . . say they take them away . . . then e'r'one homeless. Like *mi mami,* me."

"Then the Planning Commission arrives?"

"Dunno wha' they call it, bro'. Official, yeah." He suddenly blurts, pointing to my laptop screen, "Shit . . . *Mira*! You on the news . . . "

LaKeisha got my laptop hooked up so that instead of screensaver the thing pops when to streaming shit channels for news, weather, sports. Ten o'clock news is usually Grim Reaper updates on the 'rona or shootings, robberies. But here's a D.C. new anchors, live and all sexy in a wrap dress and big earrings, seated across from yeah . . . Linda Figgis who looks like a squat generalissimo in her uniform. No wonder she hadn't called.

Stripe and I sit in our underwear, mesmerized . . .

"*My dad was Assistant Special Agent in Charge of the FBI's Detroit Field Office. I was actually born in Bloomfield Hills. We moved to Maryland when I was thirteen . . . but I still consider myself a PG County gal and I'm siced for my Eleanor Roosevelt High School Raiders*!"

This news chick's on a serious Oprah tip: soft-balling the politically scary Black Lives Matter or the Trump January 6 shit, and yet playing hardball with the rough, tear-jerk family stuff.

"*My mother left when I was five. She was an alcoholic, abused pills. Cheated on my dad. He was the custodial parent . . .* "

"No shit," Stripe quips. "She messed up as anyone."

Yeah . . .

"*See, when I was a girl my dad oversaw investigations of mayor of Detroit and the entire command staff of the Detroit Police Department: corruption, connections to murderous drug gangs*," and then the gleam leaves her eyes, "*but defense lawyers, activist demagogues branded him a 'racist cowboy.' Unfounded, unproven, scandalous . . . but the Bureau wanted a change. I recall seeing my dad cry, my dad who stared-down gangsters and bullets.*

My mother was the only other thing that could make him break down that way . . . "

Even Stripe, now monkeying with his new phone as LaKeisha's sending it signals from her own "cloud" in the sky, notes something troubling. "D.C. like Detroit a lil'. You *myates* still run shit no matter ho' many me peoples and whitebreads move in. No offense . . . "

"None taken."

"*Couldn't go to Europe to play, as my dad was getting sick, there was no WNBA, so at twenty-one years old I got married right after graduation, to a true motorhead . . . but rather than the NASCAR circuit he treated me to a double-wide in Beltsville . . .* "

"God-damn . . . "

"My Lady Terrapin teammates were going to grad school and such and here I was, surrounded by Budweiser cans. I got the marriage annulled, became a probation officer then later enrolled in the police academy . . . "

The anchorwoman chirps about the Mayor, then says something about Figgis' "life partner" and gay couples adopting kids.

"*Kill* . . . what?" Didn't see that coming. Stripe's mouthing the word "dyke" and I don't even correct him this time.

"*. . . yes, our daughter Tessa came from a foster home in Southern Virginia . . . family history of abuse, alcoholism, prescription drug trafficking. She's now a sixth-grade scholar and proclaims herself the feminist in our family!*" Strawberry-blond little girl with a science trophy's on-screen . . . then there's a tall, string-bean skinny brown teenager posing in high school ROTC gear. "*Our older daughter Tamara will be looking at colleges soon. Fingers crossed she'll be a Terp but she's got the grades for the Ivies . . .* " The Chief draws a sigh after the follow-up question and replies, "*. . . the family kidnapped her and tried to flee the country to perform* *a clitoridectomy. Tammi was eleven. I petitioned the Superior Court for a guardianship when the father decided to forfeit parental rights. Well look at my Tammi now!"*

And the anchor tosses to sports. My brain's churning even more.

I leave the desk, scoop up the red envelope before Stripe crushes it on the mattress.

Yeah, it's the invite. With a little more . . .

> *Dear Dickie, I understand why you stay away. Many of the men from St. Jude's who tested negative were transferred to Central Union Mission, or Mitch Snyder's at 2nd and D Street NW over six months ago. I don't know if the place will ever be the same, and often I feel guilty that we have re-opened while the church is in turmoil. I am relieved in a way that you don't come. I don't want your healing, your therapy and progress to end. I could have called but doing it old-school with pen and paper and a hero's stamp emphasizes* <u>my need to heal</u> *as well from a one-two trauma punch: Bracht, then the virus. But if you do come, smile for me. Verna.*

"Better look for good clothes for tomorrow," I say aloud. "You stay here, figure out where Little got moved to. Might be worth sniffing around."

"Ricardo . . . " Shit, he hasn't called me that name in brick! "Moses be at party wid Verna party. So will Figgis . . . you know that, righ'?"

"Gonna get his ass alone, soften or scare him, get info. Means I might have to ghost him after the party at SFME, yes. If you'd watched the damn YouTube you'd understand the methodology."

"*Pinche madre . . .* " he laughs.

I put a coarse blanket on the braided rug next to the cot; he's chumped me because he's going to be awake anyway, playing fucking games on his phone . . . and yet when my eyes acclimate to the dark I catch him staring down at me, like who's this crazy old man I hitched my life to . . .

. . . and the damn birds are the best alarm clock! Didn't need the AC last night so the upper window sash's open. Still, I'm slick with sweat down to my skivvies, as Daddy calls undershirts, draws.

Bad dream. Esmeralda . . . my Esme . . . stands above me, that college-age voluptuous body all bare, Stygian black hair on her shoulders. She hands me a gat and I eat it, Al-Mayadeen style. Then it's now, those epic tits and ass, hips are stretched and sagging and stuffed in a red dress, gold high heels . . . and she's smearing her older form with the blood smoking from the hole in my head . . .

Pop! Pop! Pop! Pop!

My apartment's window glass atomizes, the sash explodes into a barrage of splinters. Nah, this isn't the tail of the dream.

My eyes search for Stripe but he's already diving to the floor next to me, arms outstretched, mouth screaming something loud and terrible . . . spit streaming.

Now it's over.

I'm overwhelmed by the smell: that acrid gunpowder timbre that bores into your nostrils . . . ozone from the window AC, tore-up, sparking . . . I scramble to the kid and peel him off the rug, push him against the cot. His head in his hands and he's trembling, mumbling but I don't clock red on him. Yeah, I check myself, too. *We're okay*!

Not my walls. Rounds, or fragments of them, tore lots of little burnt holes in the plaster, now flakes of that and the paint are falling like snow. Somehow Black Santa's hanging image escaped the barrage; I spot a few gouges in my front doorway casing and the transom's frame.

"*Es un sicario,* bro' . . . shit!" Stripe suddenly cries from the floor, still quaking. "Is how they do. Is a beef . . . or . . . them peoples like Sugars!"

No . . . *no.* I know he's seen these boys out here spraying houses, blasting motherfuckers in broad daylight . . . but hitting my window . . . from the alley? Can't be a hit. Can't . . .

. . . so I ease up to my feet and edge along the wall to dresser, yank out the .380 and pop in a clip.

Been shot at couple times and yeah you do get twisted by having to suck it up and play it off. Worse part, real talk, is how bad it is if you can't shoot back. I can't because my fucking hand's shaking like I got Parkinson's or palsy.

I hear shouting outdoors and quickly the alarm in the cantina's ringing so a stray round must've busted something there. If MPD's got the gunfire sound detector on—the sensor's over by the old Banneker High—then a unit's on the way. Still, enough yuppies live here now so someone must've called 911.

"Stripe . . . *Ernesto,*" I holler. "Stay frosty, kid." With more voices in the alley I'm confident whoever was blasting out there's booked but they could be inside now, right on the landing. I hand Stripe the pistol as I'm not in position . . . like the YouTube videos instruct. "The door," I whisper, then gesture like I'm aiming. That's no toy. That's Crock's tiny terror, the Ruger LCP. As the kid keeps the .380 trained on the door, I hug the wall, turn the deadbolt . . . Stripe's not wavering and if these motherfuckers are out there, they know what's going next . . . I trip the latch . . . yank open the door.

Duck.

Nothing, so yeah I'm slimming that sucker shut. He's still aiming the iron and I'm in the bathroom with my phone, doing 911 something better . . .

"If you didn't want me to call you, *Linda* . . . then why'd you drop this number on me?"

"*Okay . . . darn it I'm still in bed . . . I'm messaging the Three-dee on my command mobile, and if this anything more than random street nonsense I'll have to call in SOD.*"

"No way!"

"*Why not?*"

"We . . . we have to talk."

"*Heck yeah, but . . . listen—are you coming to the dedication at SFME?*"

As if that sitch has anything to do with this fucking sitch. "Someone tried to murk us, Linda!"

"And that's why we need to talk. Be there tomorrow, on time."

CHAPTER 11

RIP

WE WERE ON THE NEWS, AMONG the five other shootings. Like, "*early-morning gunplay in Northwest near Howard University*." Made the right-wing press, of course: "*Wanton violence in the Nation's Capital on the rise while liberals demand revenge on over-zealous protestors who entered the Capitol Building to be just to be heard*." Wish I could choke out the crackers pushing these irons and lead in here with one hand, strangle the bammas pulling the trigger with the other.

Alas, I'm not ambidextrous . . .

. . . and I'm gazing out of what's left of my window, down at the jakes canvassing the alley, Euclid and Fairmount Streets. Okay, maybe not at the uniforms, but at the head dick. That Uncle Tom, from the Colonial View. Bald asshole, and now I know a name: Woodman.

He's clowning with other dicks. White dudes in Dockers and blazers. The brothers are wearing these warm-weather pimp linens and Panama hats and all of them are chewing on stogies . . . chuckling while the gentrifier neighborhood watch types are pacing, throwing fits.

Figgis sent him. How do I know? Because her text message is on my phone. Says it's only a coinky-dink that he was there are the motel, watching it burn. He's being considered for Commander, per the MPD website, with Linda all smiles. Funny, wonder what she'd say if I told her he was cursing her out when she revealed she was over at my spot, and he was to cut me loose? All's not well in the Blue Boy Band, and the Queen of the Pig Poke might be too busy doing TV guest spots to smell it.

Now, I see one female dick acting like she's on the job. A pleasant-looking and petite girl who might be like a light-skinned sister, though Stripe insists she's Filipina.

She calls me away from the window with, "These slugs are 'RIP' rounds. 'Rest in Peace' on the street, but tech name is 'Radically Invasive Projectile.' Been around for years down south, Detroit, Chicago . . . but still a newby here in the D-M-V. Spent round through soft issue looks like a claw." She holds her little fingers out like talons and damn if her nail art isn't boss. "This causes them to splinter into darts, basically. Thus . . . the pattern on your wall . . . "

"So you gonna dip someone, it better be into flesh. But they shot through a third-floor window—partially filled with an old Sears air conditioner . . . "

She nods and says, "An amateur or sending message. Either way it's a beef. Detective Woodman down there says you were at the Colonial View before the Feds burned it down. Anyone there got a problem with you?"

I shake my head, look to Stripe. He definitely *ain't* buying something, and on this kind of madness I defer to his more *contemporary* street sense.

Oh, and in comes Woodman. Masked up, suddenly, though not when the cigars were shared.

"Trouble Man!" he greets me again.

My affliction that embarrassed Daddy so damn much, answers back. "Nineteen Seventy-Two . . . starring Robert Hooks, dad of actor-director Kevin Hooks . . . Paul Winfield . . . directed by Ivan Dixon, who was more known to whitefolks for his role as 'Kinch' on *Hogan's Heroes.* Soundtrack by Marvin Gaye."

"Wow. A genre fan? That's why you a P.I. wannabee?"

I shrug. "No. If I was doing what I thought I'd be doing when I was a kid, I'd either be a retired NFL player, or an active priest or teacher. Either way I wouldn't be clocking a shot-up window and taking your shade . . . *Detective.*"

"*Grrrr-rumpy* aren't we? But you're alive, so count your blessings. In fact, I hear the Chief didn't SOD coming by? Well, I appreciate the vote of confidence on my police work, but Antonelli's cats are the Justice League and Avengers when it comes to this gang shit, *cuz.* Somebody definitely green-lit you. And we *and* SOD got a theory as to who."

"Already?"

"Monica you and the officers wanna give us the room," he calls to the female dick. "We finna clear out in a sec once the report's filed and canvass done."

She forces a smile. Woodman is indeed a wood-headed Tom because this chick goes and palms what's got to be a business card . . . slaps it square in mine as she shakes hands good-bye then gives him a look. Figgis isn't going to like one of her girls ghosted like that yet his smirk shows he could give a fuck . . .

"RIP," I tell the smug nigga as the lady dick head and CSI toadies file out my door. "But kinda bait—outdoors, pre-dawn? That's what long guns with night vision scopes are for . . . "

"You been brushing up on homework, huh, Trouble Man?" He motions me close but I'd rather be socially-distant.

Stripe moves in, though. Chest-first as usual. "RIPs . . . *es stupido,* dude."

"You wanna tell the kid to let grownfolk talk, Cornish? You remember Blinky Guzman . . . his MS-Thirteen . . . Mara Salvatrucha bastards up Mt. Pleasant and Fourteenth Street . . . you got into it with him and the Otis Street *Brigada,* apparently? File's very, um . . . *limited.* Well, Montgomery County PD confirmed that Blinky's successors are into the RIPs. Puts down the target in one shot."

"*Eso no es possible . . .* " Stripe mutters again, sucking his gold grill.

"Again, I wasn't addressing you, youngster."

"Kill . . . come on," I challenge. "*Salvatrucha* would've bum-rushed my flimsy-ass door, sprayed me in my bed."

"That's our intel, Cornish. Take it or leave it. An officer'll be up for you to sign your statement." Woodman's glancing at my desk now. Shit. There's the magnifying glass . . . my scavenged fetish . . . laying in plain fucking view! "Oh, and, there were two agitated yuppies in Jeep out there looking for you. Guess they own the block now? One of your neighbors prolly dimed you and said you brought the heat."

I'm done. "This is an Adult Assistance Services unit. They can't evict me."

He shrugs, moves to the door just as Stripe palms the magnifying glass. "We'll leave a foot patrol in the alley for the next forty-eight hours," Woodman then says, exposing his true feelings by a yawn. "Try to stay in. Good *empanadas* and brew downstairs I hear . . . "

"That bu'shit, *Jefe,*" Stripe intones, handing me the tchotchke. There're still jakes out on the landing and in the stairwell so I hold my finger to my lips. Less louder he tells me, "*Salvatrucha* . . . they *hate* Blinky for bein' in widde white-breads, an' paid by Bracht. No way, bro' this them."

"Go ask Pilar for newspaper, tape . . . couple pieces of plywood. Let's clean this up . . . "

And as Stripe leaves, I finger the magnifying glass as I thumb-swipe a number on my phone with my right. Figure it's time to panic . . .

"*S'up fam'ly? Or should I say, old nigga. Graydick muv-fukkah. You good, baby?*"

Can hear the beat in the background . . . Junkyard Band . . . oh shit. *Sardines.* Me and him, just tenderfoots, just kids.

"Who you calling graydick, Croc? Your geriatric diabetic ass all up in the nostalgia again?"

"*That a live cut from a concert a couple monffs before the 'rona, fam'ly. Buggs an' the fellas still puttin' in the work.*" He pauses then hits back, "*Wait . . . my shut-in ass heard on the news somffin popped on Georgia Avenue. You?*"

"Yeah. That was me. And I'm good, ok? Be an encyclopedia and tell me about RIP rounds. Asking because Twelve, well . . . one person . . . is saying it's our Latino brothers . . . "

"*Fuck that ops, moe.*" So Stripe's right. "*Them rounds big in the Dirty. Lotta niggas come up from Carolinas, ATL, the Tidewater, hang in Mur'lin . . . PG an' up Northeast.*"

"Kill . . . be specific."

"*One-Six Crew.*"

Damn. Lil' Sweet Sunshine's boyfriends.

"*Them bammas only ones I know using the shit 'cause they too weak to hold down they groun' wiffout 'exotic' shit. Toy niggas think they hardcore; delusion is comfort, fam'ly. H Street's too white now for them to claim as home turf no more so they keep most of the cray shit out in the frontier. An' Dickie—po-po should* know *that. Somebody in MPD loafin' on you so you need ta come see me.*"

Stripe's watching me wince at the thought of cops putting us at harm by design, not just indifference. "Hold on, Croc." I put him on speaker and hates that, but I want Stripe to hear, write it down. "What's these's toy niggas' jont . . . tags and such?"

"*Tag is white spray paint . . . looks a Zippo cigarette lighter open . . . word 'lit' in it but it's really spose ta be a '1' plus a 'six.'*"

"Thanks."

"Kill, cuz . . . whatever you into, y'all should fold up and come work wiff me, man."

"Yo . . . bruh I ain't got time for this." I'm already rattled and he's hitting with this out-of-left-field shit. "So . . . what you want me to come help you plug your dirt weed, goon at that dive?"

"Nah, cuz. I mean you do you, that detective shit, movin' outchyo' voucher hovel, in with me at the crib here, under my *aegis* as they say . . . not no Twelve. Shit . . . keep you from usin' that crazy lil' bitch LaKeisha and duckin' Verna Leggett—"

Stripe's yanking on me. "Oye . . . wha' he say, Rain Man?"

I shoo him away. "Watch your mouth man."

"Apologies, fam'ly. But wiff me, y'all got the street as yo' network, not no computers. And when shit gets hot, like it did wiff Bracht, I gots the hardware to close the book. Thank about . . . "

"Peace."

Be damned if I take up with him again. Dead ass.

Stripe's circling back like a puppy. "Croc, he ay One-Six . . . they do they shit at the motel, eh? Feds burn motel. One-Six, they blame you . . . "

I move to the bathroom before he voices more bewilderment. "Yeah. They blame me." I swallow hard, lock eyes with the kid. "Just like my benefactor Chief Figgis said they would."

I liberate Poob from the wall stash. The bear's stinking bad now. And I push up into the stash even further, for the larder . . . for the box. Not even Stripe's seen this. For clear reasons.

I empty the shit onto the cot as he watches, agape, from my chair . . .

. . . key chains and combs and uncollected coins and other baubles fall out. My fetishes. My treasures from another life. An old 35-millimeter Leica camera and unused roll of film found in men's room at Union Station. Couple of .380 and .45 rounds. Tube of lip gloss and paperback novel from a pretty black girl forgot on the bus. Gucci shades. Black Santa's old bus pass.

Now the kid truly bugs when he sees the big mama gwap. The true lard in the larder. A barrel-roll of Franklins. Compliments of Jaime Bracht. Set-up money, hush money. *My* money now. I peel off a couple for my pocket, hand one to Stripe. Some loose twenties in there so I give him two as a bonus. "The c-note and change's for you. Just you. No bullshit, Ernesto."

He nods intently at getting paid but says, "So, you say to Figgis this One-Six, not *Salvatrucha*?"

"I-I dunno, kid. Something's not right here. Disconnected, comprende? Not once has she mentioned Blinky's people out there with a beef, yet she knows all about the One-Six. Even straight up accused me of diming ole Ghenghis Kann."

"Shit so whas the move, bro'? No way I sittin' still here . . . "

"Juvie, Stripe. Got to hit juvie. Talk a certain girlie off the green-light . . . and then find out what really was going on at that place because the One-Six was doing sinister shit. But stealing kids, turning out their mothers? I don't care what Linda says. That's not them . . . "

I leave the rest of the stuff on the cot as I shower, shave; I see Stripe clocking the personal items and I don't care. There's Alma's face on that old Polaroid . . . the beach on Okinawa, just before the return to Quantico . . . she's wearing a one-piece bathing suit because bikinis are for pinktoe harlots. Ah, but she was only eleven, you say? Start young. And the one-piece hides the bruise she earned for sassing like our siddity, redbone mother. Breach the rules and you get the what-for.

Used to be I'd deal with this bit of adversity by scoring me a few g's, smoke 'em up with a Xanny, washed down with a non-premium adult beverage. Now, as Stripe shoots me quizzical looks I'm out of the head inspecting my one clean white button-up shirt in the closet. And summer peels: blue seersucker, three-button jacket with matching trousers like they wore in the Sixties . . . six bucks from Goodwill . . . and I wriggle into the boxy thing. Previous owner must've been a grizzly bear—it's loose in the waist despite my eating real food, not cast-offs from Mickey Dees trays at 13th and F. My craziness is talking again when I admire myself in the mirror . . . I'm Rock Hudson, Tony Randall in that suit, *Lover Come Back*, 1961 . . . nominated for an Oscar, best screenplay . . .

"*Porque estas vestida asi?*" my confused sidekick asks. "You look like a nerd . . . "

"What I'm goin' for, thanks. *Oye chico,* mind the YouTube classes: look the part . . . or blend in. Camouflage. Up at Youth Services if I look official they might let me talk to this chick Raynata. Might catch her loafin' on her homeboys, tease out a break. And what we need is a break. Hold down the fort. Gonna be crazy before it gets better."

"If you good, I good."

"I ain't good, *chico.* I'm scared. But at least I'm making moves."

"The Chief, bet she don' wan' you makin' this one, Rain Man."

CHAPTER 12
Green-Lit

No matter how much reclaimed ancient bricks and timber the architects joined with stainless steel and planted gardens, this Youth Services jont's every bit a jail as the CDF. I'm in my feelings and prickly because I'm barely a mile from the pile of smoldering wreckage that was the Colonial View Motel.

The "receptionist," a C.O. in plainclothes reminds me that the spot closes to visitors in half an hour, and I got no appointment, and we are still on stage red for the 'rona with the staff and "residents" when it comes to vaccines. He holds a digital thermometer to my forehead anyway.

"Your Intake Counselor can clear this with Chief Figgis' office at the Daly Building," I say with as much phony white man bass I can stir. I show my new gumshoe ID and my vax card from the VA. "This resident was a Federal transfer, so the answer to how I know this person is here that's the answer. Also, y'all have a voluntary pass authorization—if the resident consents to a visit and you clear me?"

He looks me up and down. Big nigga in a white man's summer suit from a different damn epoch. Rock a costume, not a "look," the YouTube video on undercover taught me. See, I clocked this suit on the street, seeing all the lawyers like Sandy Nimchuk pimping them on the hot K Street pavement, but yeah all the whitefolk went casual. But real live, the peels hooked me when I saw the movie they made from one of Alma's favorite books, *To Kill A Mockingbird.* Gregory Peck. 1962. The lawyer, defending the innocent brother they found guilty of raping a white rolla anyway because that was what they did for real.

Well . . . it's working. They are letting me in on the consent pass after they call up to the dorms. They take my pic, print an ID sticker . . . buzz me through.

I sign some forms and loll in a stark white waiting room, AC blasting more to keep the 'rona vented than to cool . . . distanced from blank-stare parents or grandma's, squirming siblings . . . a single TV playing PBS cartoon of all things—reruns of Sesame Street—and the scent reminds of the shower room at St. Jude's. Lestoil and Clorox. Kind of hoped someone would ask me if I was a lawyer despite my height, my look.

A "counselor" arrives. Butch-looking sister topped with intricately-laced corn rows, big hips straining some jeans, Washington Mystics T-shirt. Masked and gloved. Best believe she's got the mace and some zipties hid; for every cheery poster of a kid with schoolbooks or planting a tree, I know there's a flesh and blood child laying up in their bunk: plotting or being plotted on.

This chick sits me down at a table in another room with ever more cheery posters. Reminds me that the resident may rescind permission to speak to me at any time, and the conversation is not confidential as I'm not an attorney or the child's shrink.

I stand when another counselor brings her in. No longer Sweet Sunshine. Back to a girl named Raynata. Nappy brick-colored hair all tame and pulled back behind a headband . . . denim capris shorts, simple leather sandals, flowery and frilly top. It's like she's going to cookout or the mall.

She sits down across from me at a round table with a potted plant decorating it. Can't let the occasional cries and curses beyond door fuck with us so I tug down down my mask, but she speaks first . . . in a scary dead earnest, almost like the stick-up boys in the CVS . . .

"I know why you here," she whispers.

"Yeah. Playing a hunch."

"You wasn't no *hero.* He was 'spose ta bring a *hero* . . . you a big snitch faggot." Guess she doesn't seem to care that the counselor sucks at pretending not to eavesdrop.

"You think I'm undercover Twelve or a Fed . . . Raynata?"

I'm praying this swole lady with cornrows is fiending for a coffee break and is just watching to see I don't try any grab-ass or passing her something. Tough because Raynata's balling her fists, scowling. The counselor cautions us both, then retreats to her snoop position.

"Sweet Sunshine" puffs her cheeks, trying not tear up as she reveals, "Feds took my son. Chile Services say foster care but caseworker say he not placed."

"That why you green-lit me? If so that's a damn good reason but I say it ain't so."

"I been alone, on the street and shit since I was fo'teen, handlin' my shit. See . . . I pretty, right? Mixed, light-skin, right? Niggas and white men boff want tha' ass, so thas what I do. So I don' give a fuck you mad I sent my boys on yo' big ass."

"I could give a shit whatever stash or product your boys lost when the Feds cooked the place—that's on y'all, not me. I'm mad at what happened to you, your baby . . . yeah and your brother. I remember what you said. And I ain't judgin' you . . . "

Her face softens. "Whaffaw y'all makin' me . . . act soft, like a baby . . . "

As she dips her head, I tell her, "Because I'm no villain. Neither are you. There's difference between a criminal . . . and a villain. Sometimes you gotta what you do you to eat, to shelter you and yours. But then you cross a line, and *bam* you a villain."

She lifts her head. "Then I guess I be a villain."

"No, you aren't. But villains can be *anyone.* Like social workers . . . *cops?*"

"Kill . . . "

"I ate the sidewalks same as you did, babygirl. You say your caseworker was next on that girl . . . girl cops was on top of."

"You want me to snitch. You the caseworker's name? You ain't gettin' it."

"I just wanna know what the ops is, why they're messin' with you."

She studies the ceiling for a few seconds, I pull back, silently routing for what's good in her to claw its way through the spoil.

"S-Sometime . . . caseworker . . . "

"G'won, babygirl."

"Sometime . . . he or he people, up Chile Services, say, we be neglectin' wiff a baby but we not writin' y'all up, we getting' y'all EBT cards, so you gotta do a date . . . fuck or suck a cop, or one they boys." Luckily, the keeper's two-way beeps and she's preoccupied with whoever called. "Sometime, it Feds, an' cop in plainsclothes in they cars. That keep 'em off

One-Six shit—guns, bullets, weed, pills, rock and shit—they got put in the walls. Thas why One-Six say, if cops and Chile Services wanna fuck y'all, the fuck."

"Was it worse in the shelter?" I swallow hard. "Verna Leggett's SFME, Central Mission, House of Ruth, Covenant?"

"Nah, man! One they turnin' into condos, by RFK. Municipal jont. Closed it when I was jus' getting mah titties and hips, bleedin' . . . not that no one care if I was a girl or not."

"Caseworkers set that up to, at the munie?"

"I ain't givin' up no name, man."

"Not asking." The guard isn't even watching now, still on her radio call. "Just listening."

"Rich white men mostly git the pussy there, not th' nasty muvfukkahs come to th' motel. Mens wiff wife, big house. Girls wha' don' get that Norplant shit . . . sometime they get pregnant. Baby's get taken, like my brotha . . . " She leans in close, unblinking. "If tha' happen ta me, I cut my baby out m'self first, then we *boff* die jus' ta fuck wiff 'em . . . "

That chills me to my nuts. From . . . a child. "Your daddy, he's white, right?"

"My daddy jus' some peckerwood who like that 'federate flag on he clothes, like ones come crawlin' up on the Capitol. But these muvfukkahs in the munie you got to be cleared more, feel me. Like a club."

I'm the one squirming now; she's cool as a fan. "Were they pedophiles too? I mean, people who mess with children?"

"Ain't I a child?" she whispers to the ceiling.

"Yeah, honey. And I'm sorry these motherfuckers stole that. But now that I got all that, now I'm comin' no cap. I didn't want a name because I already got one: 'Mo' or 'Moses Roffe?' Big dude, like a TV wrestler . . . "

Raynata's face goes slack, if a shot-through with Novocain. "N-No. Not een to take our babies 'cause we 'unfit.'"

"You a bad liar, babygirl. Okay—think Al-Mayadeen might've know this man Roffe?"

"Man, all Al-Mayadeen say all day an' night was 'bout CiCi. CiCi done this, CiCi done that. CiCi smarter than Chinese an' Jew gurls in school."

"Keep hearing that." I decide to string her along. "What was the spill?"

"Like . . . tests, ya know. IQ tests. Like the bitch a genius. Genius, in the shelter? *Ha*!"

"That's it?"

"Whachew wan', man?" she shrugs. "See you ain't no hero? Brung nuthin'"

"Al-Maya, he had brothers. Younger one smashin' with CiCi, other one always finna molest K'ymira. He talk about them?"

She folds her arms, stares beyond me. "See, CiCi in the shelter trickin', like all them bitches be, like we the street dogs and they the bottom bitches. But it like her coochie *golden* 'cause she say she always fucked wiff the rich ones. Stupid trick. Not like they took her ass out the shelter, gave her diamonds. Thought she was smart? Leff her in there . . . wiff her kid . . . who don' look a damn thing like that Al-Mayadeen. Feel me?"

Yeah. "Who's your baby daddy if it ain't a cop or such, then?"

With sickening pride she boasts, "Uh-huh, tha be mah Shawn! He be 'Thanos' now—name hisself like the god in them movies he took me to . . . 'cause he snap he finger and you be gone like Black Panther and Spider Man and all them 'heroes.' Trinidad, Holbrooke Street, Ivy City . . . whitefolk on

H Street . . . ain't nobody fuck wiff my Thanos. Or the One-Six has yo' ass."

"That's how you got the beef on me so quick, right?"

She smiles, leans in. "Y'all got the Insta? They took mah phone."

Matter of fact . . . yeah, with Stripe's account. Just for this kind of mess. The turnkey doesn't even clock me pushing her my phone, volume killed. She swipes.

"See?" she giggles. "Livestream . . . "

It's two youngsters, flashing pistols in the waistbands of their jeans. They are counting greenbacks then giddily, and inexplicably, pass the guns to somebody else off camera who admonishes them. The view cuts up to Rose's Liquors, a spot I know well—Ghenghis' old turf. One kid whispers, "*Tax collection, all 'bout the bidness, not the bullets.*"

So I press, "Then why didn't he protect you. Y'all's baby?"

Puffery drains to a weak goddamn little pout. "Befo' you brung . . . them Feds."

I look to the guard. Haven't got much time left and this chick's antics aren't helping. "Real live, Raynata. You just spilled pretty much everything, thinking you ain't told me nothing. So let's stop, and talk about Moses Roffe, okay. No more bullshit."

I outsmarted a child. Bully for fucking me . . .

"Um . . . dates—*dick*—feed the baby. Dates make Twelve leave the motel be. That's wha' that . . . man you say name is, tell my Shawny . . . Thanos."

"And . . . y'all ever heard of the Planning Commission—clockin' the motel for development?"

"I know ain't nothin' happs till Al-Mayadeen brung *yo' big ass* wiff the Feds . . . they burn it an' take ole Mister Manny away ta *die*!" She hushes when that shrill rebuke draws a stare from the keeper. "You look here, *hero.* Thanos . . . h-he know . . . wha' it mean . . . ta *hurt.* Hurt like a lil' boy, like my brotha hurt."

"I don't follow."

"His mama los' custody. She on the spice, pills . . . trickin'." Yeah, I know that tip. "She never seent him again. Then they come for him, give him to men. Like they do my brotha. But Thanos, he not goin' let that fuck wiff him. One-Six an' *me* . . . we be his fam'ly."

Swear to God I'm thinking aloud because of what she's dump-trucked into my dome. "Pimpin' . . . who was pimpin' her? Who gave the lil' boys to grown men?"

Raynata just folds her arms, rocks in her chair. "That white man. Man you say."

"Roffe"

"Wha'ever. Ain't nobody gotta slap a bitch when bitch jus' tyna make do, get food, clothes and shit."

"Were the pedophiles just messing with the kids in jonts like the motel, the shelter . . . or were they, like *kidnapping* the kids, never returning them?"

"Like Al-Mayadeen say happen ta his baby, long time ago?"

"Uh-huh."

Finally, I see a smile. More . . . a smirk. "I clock you when I firs' heard yo' big ass. A fool, no hero."

"Hero . . . no. But I got you away from the Feds and I'm gonna find your son, your brother."

"Good. Too many people wha own alla goin' stop ya, dip ya. 'Cause Mister Manny he right. We all already dead, an' nobody care. Ask my Shawn." She calls over to the counselor then turns away from me in her chair.

"I just might."

"I was messin' wiffchew! Thanos'll fuck you up, you talk 'bout him bein' less than a man when he was a boy!"

She doesn't word it right but I know what she means. And Lord because the jont I planned to go next, I got no choice now but to go now, based on what this child . . . I got no reason not to call her such . . . is spilling. Thanos' realm, where H meets Benning Road . . .

. . . and so the counselor stands Raynata up, takes her toward the elevators. I turn and tell the girl, "Thanks for clearing that up. About our little misunderstanding. Don't be a villain."

I think she's smiling as the doors close . . .

. . . and I'm loitering out on Mt. Olivet Road in the heat and exhaust fumes, knowing I got to be as clear about my next move as Linda Figgis' crystalline eyes. Before tapping a Lyft I swipe for some wisdom.

"Croc," I say when the big man answers. "tell me more about this One-Six Crew. I remember Lenny Mitchell down the Central Mission couple years back, talking about them fucking him up on Maryland Avenue . . . maybe Bladensburg Road . . . "

"*Kill, fam'ly . . . done told your ADHD whatever ass: if Benning Road was like the Tenderfoots, then One-Six was like the Cub Scouts to ole Jian Kann's crew—Ghenghis.*"

"Right."

"*Benning Road still venerates that nigga but One-Six got no love for Ghenghis' legacy, cool?*" He pauses. "*Still, my advice is come get a new gat, new ammo first. Them boys ain't got nothin' on moms n' pop or Rayful back in the day, but they so off the chain you safer wid them niggas across the river.*"

"Why they wildin'?"

"Because that's the Alamo . . . Dien Bien Phu, like we learnt as good Catholic school nerds. Whitefolk be the Mexicans, the Vietnamese, marching. Trump di'n't slow that. The 'rona di'n't slow that. The river sure as fuck ain't gonna slow that. City got plans, baby . . . "

"Planning Commission . . . " Just noodling aloud . . .

"*Stamp!"* he confirms, and I glue down another piece in my "jigsaw puzzle" brain, like Daddy used to say. *"Real talk, don't roll up on those toy gangsters without a plan. Hell, this fool who runs it now . . . yeah, Shawn Brown . . . calls hisself some comic book name, kiddie superhero shit but he think he Michael Coreleone."*

Making it up as I go. "Someplace safe in his turf . . . got CCTV all up and down there around ol' Hechinger Mall . . . up to that Dollar Store if it's still there. Used to score my g's a Scooby up there from Latoya Kann."

"*Nah, fam'ly—this boy's smart. He know where the cameras be and that's why his chain snatchers do so well on them yuppies on H Street."*

"His little goons are headed over to Rose's Liquors, do some collecting."

"Hmmm. Might work. Still lotta foot traffic. If Shawn Brown taxin' folk like Ghenghis back in the day, that's his cash cow . . . "

"Need back-up. My old-heads, cuz."

"*Put yo'faith in them ACP rounds, not human beings.*"

"You know me, baby."

"*Yeah. I do. Thas why I'm worried.*"

My ride pulls up, bald-head old Asian dude, looks like that actor Mako, from *The Sand Pebbles,* 1966 . . . Steve McQueen, Candace Bergen . . . directed by Robert Wise . . . the hero dies. Dude doesn't seem gassed by my hue and size. He even asks me if I want AC turned up. I'm a human being now. I get shit like AC, or being called "sir." Mako's still clocking me in the rearview, though. We types might try to rob him, if not stiff him for the tip.

We aren't going back to Northwest. Nope. Another ant hill, where the gentrifiers' H Street and Maryland Avenue meets ole Chocolate City's twin B roads: Benning and Bladensburg. I swipe up Stripe.

"New phone working ok? Good. Look, I need something in the dresser . . . third drawer, hear me? Special package, wrapped. Now you gotta pack it good, get it over to me on H . . . busy street . . . maybe at 14th Northeast. Can't get stopped, *chico.*"

"*I get the scooter back, no prob.*'"

"I told you to stay away from that dude! And listen, give Boston a couple bucks. Tell him Dickie says watch who comes and goes, who's clockin' the spot, got it?"

"*They ain't fix window too good yet.*"

"Don't care. Hurry up."

"*Oye, jefe . . . I look on computer an' check for you. Tha' 'Little'—he no in Laurel like* la mujer *say . . . but he not in hospital in Largo, neither. Some new place Keesh gonna help me find.*"

"Good job, kid."

As Mako slows up in the afternoon traffic, in comes a Dropbox file to my phone, from LaKeisha. Images of Moses Roffe's CV, his employment references . . . and "PTSD case studies" of children from "squatter residences and transient rentals."

"Gotcha!" I blurt and startles Mako.

The data on K'ymira's not as viscerally creepy, but confirms the fact that she basically did not exist digitally or on paper in this city until she was three. Keesh flags a report that this shit is rare . . . endemic perhaps to illegals fiending for food, vouchers and other shit for their kids and now clackity-clack, more puzzle pieces snap together inside my skull . . .

. . . so the driver lets me off where the old Hechinger's use to be.

I'm feeling big and bad. Making moves. A real gumshoe, a bad motherfucker . . . like dudes in the Chevy over in Anacostia mused: I need my own theme-song. No one's fucking with me ever again!

CHAPTER 13

Burning the Puzzle

I DO A QUICK RECONNOITER AROUND Rose's but the sun's blazing beyond the roofline and I can't fucking see a thing but slats of skinny shadows . . . Uncle Bob, Keef, Little Mary . . . counting on the old crew to be hanging around. Can't tell if it's them. Pray they'll be at the Dollar Store or milling around Maryland Avenue or it's my ass.

Over on H Street at least something's going right. Stripe's jumping off the red trolley, paper bag in his hand. I move toward him; he's bopping down the sidewalk. We make the switch and the loaded LCP and holster heavy in my palm.

I cross to the north side of the street to the old check cashing spot to get geared up in the shade and damn it as I hit the crumbly formstone wall here comes an MPD unit. Not that Twelve isn't thick here. Atlas—what the Chads and Beckies call H street, Northeast—is their spot with all the clubs and bistros. Still, did clock some "Potomac Ventures" signs up so the 'rona's done its damage here, too, and someone's making money off it.

But that's not the hairy pickle I'm in now. Normally I'd have side-eyed the cop behind the wheel, and they'd have gone on their merry way. Nope. This jake, I recognize.

And she clocks me.

"Well, you clean up nice, Mr. Cornish . . . " Officer Sanchez calls to me, lowering her shades.

Damn, I was *cabron* last time to this chick, and told to play ball. Maybe it's the suit and hard shoes? "Checkin' up on me?"

"Whachoo doin' down here? Need a ride?"

"Noneya and no, with all due respect. Shouldn't y'all be getting ready for the parade for Biden and my girl?"

Fuck . . . there's Stripe. He's got to re-cross the street to catch the trolley westbound and here we are in our little cabal. Can't draw attention to him but hey, *chica* might have been clocking him from jump, not me.

"Put up your mask, 'kay?" she says, "And come over here." I can't get too close or she'll see I'm carrying. I take two wide steps trying to keep the gun hid and I'm looking like I'm inviting her to polka with me. "Detective Woodman put a BOLO out on two dumbass freelancers thinking the beef Guzman put on you was still live. Chief wanted to know your thoughts on that."

"And what did Detective Monica Abalos say?"

"Detective Abalos is . . . not really part of the team."

"Then whose team is she on."

"Not yours and mine. But, for the sake of peace let's say it was MS-Thirteen who shot up your apartment. Sure you don't need a ride?"

"I'm cool." I'm not. "Tell The Chief MPD's rounding up the usual suspects." That's from a famous old movie by the way.

"Uh-uh, *The French Connection*, right?"

"No." I stifle my affliction, just this once. "*Casablanca.* You tell the Chief she jih-played herself when y'all put me up in the hotel that night—for my own safety. She mentioned One-Six and another crew. Not Salvatrucha. So you want to tell what the fuck's going on with you cops?"

She frowns, flustered as all fucking robots get when the sitch gets all tangled from the programming, right? "From now on, all communications are through me. If you got some info, text the word 'Artemis.' If urgent, 'Athena.' *Entender . . . Ricardo*?"

There are those names again. Two Greek goddesses who could give a fuck about what a man says. "*Sí.*"

"Be safe. Wear you mask and social distance . . . "

The unit's running lights flash—no siren—and she guns the Ford across the trolley tracks.

Not feeling big and bad anymore: skull-cleaving pain and there's gunk bubbling up in my throat.

"*Regina Maria . . . placere auxilium mihi servus tuus sum ego et puer.* Mother . . . please."

Can hear him now, inside my dome.

So I twist into a boarded-up doorway that's plastered with torn posters from concerts and dances, years past back when blackfolk ruled this street . . . marring that history are tags from straight white to dayglo green. One's staring at me straightaway. Looks like a cigarette lighter.

I heave my breakfast onto it. The street, my heartbeat . . . sound like I'm underwater.

Not now. *God, not now . . .*

. . . then don't be a pussy. Spit the rest of that gunk out and get squared the fuck away, onaccount there goes all your *ancora* and *veritas*, dripping from the wall . . .

"I-I gotta go . . . " you mumble to the air. "Make sure of my . . . backup."

Yeah, not a bad plan. Now you're in the Dollar Tree, clocking the tire lot next to Rose's. Triggers a vignette huh? Ghenghis' lil' sis'd buy shitloads of cellophane bags at that very Dollar Tree, then stamp them with a pic of your favorite Great Dane, Scooby Doo, or better yet, Agent Orange's daughter . . . with her simpering mug decorating the two-gram "Ivanka Crunk." *Ahhh,* the salad days!

No sign of the local thugs so best better bring the Mountain to Mohammed, son. Give a furtive tug on the .380's slide to chamber a round, pocket that lil' monster, step across the street.

Lots of local talent pissing, zooted. Few hipsters rolling in and out for exotic booze. Yet where's your hobo cavalry, loitering, panhandling half-naked in the muggy air?

Inside the store's a little queer—jont don't sell single cigarettes since the ofays started patronizing it. They also took down the Plexiglass maze of barriers so the Chads and Beckies could find their small-batch bourbon. But the area around the registers and lotto tickets is still walled-off behind the fingerprint-smudged transparent plates, and old Mama-san behind the defenses, masked-up, just shrugs as you pass. Bet the CCTV camera aimed at you doesn't even work . . .

. . . and then you hear the voices, in the back by the beer coolers, stacked liquor boxes. If anyone's got you scoped on CCTV they aren't making their move—you looking all cop-like.

There. Two rangy youngsters in baggy shorts, what look like vintage NBA jerseys from rosters back when you were their age—both looming over a seated, slick-haired old

Asian dude dressed oddly in white socks and shiny black tie-up Oxfords.

"You *late wiff tha cash,* nigga," one boy with a haircut like a broccoli floret screeches at the man. "Thanos say two hunnad a week, due Mondays . . . "

Two-hundred bucks a week? *That's it*? Lil' pussy pocket gangstas—that's this motherfucker's monthly lawn care bill over in Falls Church or Clarendon or Hanoi or the Thirty-Eighth Parallel . . . wherever these people roll in from to sell Hindu hair to you ignorant natives.

Out you spring from the shadows, the .380 pointed dead-on.

"*Oh shit!*" is all you hear from both these knuckleheads simultaneously. Feels *good*, huh?

You order Papa-san to beat it. Sumbitch's scowling at you like *you're* the criminal. "I got good deal from boys," he complains. "You take 'way outside, 'way from my store!"

The fuck? You doing this cat a favor, correct?

"Leave!" you growl in that low, sleepy Frankenstein bearing and yeah, he books to the front of the store. Given his 'tude he's probably *not* calling MPD but pray your balls are hanging strong, Junior, "You two . . . out the back!" You're pushing them like POWs, arms high, out to the loading dock. Lots of folk milling on the alleyway, son. Watch it. "Okay stop. Thanos—one of you bring him. Say Dickie Cornish wants to parley. Say I'm the motherfucker who's jont y'all lil' pussies aired out up Georgia Avenue . . . because Sweet Sunshine fucked up and greent lighted my ass and now we make things right . . . "

"F-Fuck you," the broccoli-head spits. The other's a bit shakier. He's the one.

"You . . . *go.*"

Don't got to tell him twice . . . he's off into the heat shimmer like a gazelle on the savannah.

Can't be but a minute when Broccoli's phone blows up. Yeah, put the spout on his neck. "Answer it."

"H-He be wantin' you . . . outside."

Now you a *monster*!

"Who are you?" you press Broccoli.

"Rodney. Shawn . . . *Thanos* . . . he be . . . m-my cuz-zin."

Even better. You yank his skinny ass off a stack of Miller Lite twelve-packs . . . choke-hold . . . keep the LCP's bad end at his shrubbery-heavy dome. "Comin' out . . . with your cuz!"

Okay . . . your amateurish recon's showing itself onaccount there's no way out unless you dodge rows of tires stacked along a chain link fence.

Too late.

Percolating through the stacks come pissants and toy-thugs who looked like they just came off a playground court, three-on-three, cowled like Arabs in sweat-sopped towels. Some don't look like they've been through puberty; they are the ones who scare you the most. No one to shepherd them, all with little piranha-toothed grins. Gats're somewhere under these billowy oversize white T-shirts. Not one of them's wearing mask; two of the older boys are dry-coughing.

"I don't wanna hurt nobody," you call, keeping your captive close.

The junior varsity parts a path.

Through it strides this ugly sumbitch . . . head looking like a grape lollypop someone picked up off a carpet laden with dog hair. *This* clown is the One-Six honcho? The troll's got on grownfolks' peels at least. Indeed odd, like he works at Best Buy. A dark polo, khakis, Nikes . . .

He curls his lips in almost an exaggerated snarl, like he's been practicing in front of a mirror. "Only reason you ain't dead is 'cause these folk in this shop is under my protection."

"That's what you call this kindergarten?"

Thanos puffs out his chest, ignoring the squirms of his captured hooligan cousin. "I got a tight ass-whuppin' schedule, nigga . . . an' you lucky I could pencil you in."

"Your girl Sweet Sunshine—*Raynata*—she says fucked up when she green-lit me. I just come from seeing her . . . I was the one who got her out of Fed custody, hear me?"

Your hostage shrieks, "Shawn tell this old nigga lemme go!"

Oh no, Shawn's changed facial expression shows he's intrigued.

"Kite for a word," you say, channeling Al-Mayadeen. "Because you know of me, moe. Kill . . . " Junior, his troops could be circling behind you already! "Ghenghis Kann . . . remember him?"

Hoo-rah. Thanos' minions are murmuring, confused until the boss calls out, "Somebody dipped him out brick ago, Old."

"How many folk . . . kids . . . got deaded on that bad K Two . . . the shit he and his sis' pledged was pure dynamite? I was the dude who stopped them. Street got its revenge. The street let you to rise, take his place."

"Meaning you done me a favor. Yeah . . . but you still walk up in here . . . like a bait Twelve dick . . . in that dumbass suit . . . barking and waving a gat . . . "

"Real live, moe. I'm a private detective."

"You? Come on, gee." He smooths down his sparse yet wild flyway hair so he doesn't look like he stuck his stubby black finger in an electric socket.

"Yeah, me . . . and you and your girlfriend need to get your stories straight if you gonna greenlight somebody.

Kite y'self to Mount Olivet . . . it'll show I was there, talking to her . . . "

Feel the sweat on your neck, boy . . . the tingling on your tongue? One rush by his niglets and you're done. But hey, you swing the hostage forward, release him. In response you hear Mama-san screeching in whatever language that is, onaccount someone's moving up on your six, cutting you off from escape.

Maybe you recognize the shaky footsteps from pained gaits, the odor, who the fuck knows . . . but Lord you're cheesing onaccount here's your grimy, sweaty, itchy rear guard to the rescue.

Lil' Mary leads them sheepishly from the store room's bay. She's sporting an upside-down visor on her shaved pate, looking more like a man than half those urchins menacing you.

"Real live . . . this Dickie Cornish. He come f'om the streets an' help us all. He stop Kann. He no Fed snitch . . . " Uncle Bob postures like he's going to box with all of them. Keef's smiling, showing rotted gums and the sight's backing the One-Six boys off faster than your little .380. Guess he lost that bridgework you rigged up for him years-past: his old falsies plus that plastic shit you scavenged and melted, fashioned with paperclips . . .

Your *bona fides* shown, you motion your back-up to scatter. Now for the hard part.

"Anything you don't want your boys to hear, you better pull them." Go ahead, son, holster the .380. You already showed your dick. "Boys and lil' girls being hurt by perverts . . . and their mamas made to trick."

Now you're clocking this sumbitch's rubbery face complete a wave of contortions. He waves his hand, and, with a lot of bitching, his troops disperse while dozens of hipsters dine or imbibe *al fresco*, oblivious.

The hobgoblin's face lifts, catching your full height as you walk closer, schooling, "Al-Mayadeen Thomas . . . the stick-up king . . . he brought me in to find his daughter . . . and to find Raynata's brother, and all those in the motel. Your girl, she told me part of the story. Cops, social workers . . . they were using people at the Colonial View like they turnt out women, children at the old munie shelter for themselves, rich perverts."

"Who you work fo'?" That's a good question, son. Who indeed? "Cause you *jhi*-stupid, coming up in here wiff tha' shit, Old!"

"Don't burn the puzzle, Young."

He grunts, "Oh you was spesh-ed, too? White bitches wiff clipboards pattin' yo' head like a monkey, too?"

Why you nodding? You were brought up right! "Had bad issues, moe. Got tested with puzzles and shit. Yeah, heard from other kids if you had enough of them thinking you crazy or slow, just set the puzzle on fire and they leave you be. All this to say, *Shawn,* is that Raynata says you was turnt, *too*."

"Kill . . . you callin' me weak, a faggot, Old? Clock this . . . I read books, watch big movies not dumb shit that Sunshine like . . . 'cause I be a mighty river to my niggas, but I stay poor."

God bless your affliction, boy. "*Lawrence of Arabia,* directed by David Lean . . . 'Auda' played by Anthony Quinn." This sumbitch's jaw hangs. He's impressed. "You ain't about your boys jacking these whitefolks' cars, murkin' them when they come outta Trader Joe. You *real,* right, Shawn? So help me, moe . . . "

"Past . . . is past."

"Come on, Young. I don't care about y'all's 'business' in the Colonial View . . . stashin' irons and product, buryin' cats you dipped out. Just tell me you aren't the ones who hurt kids like Aliyah Hannigan, Graciela Gomez. Know them?"

"Tha'was Benning Road Boyz, nigga. Not us. So gimme real talk. If I don't cop to where it's headin, you die."

"Moses Roffe."

Abruptly you're seeing this asshole's chest bellow like he's powering a blacksmith forge with his own breath. You've fished out his bogeyman congratulations . . . as if he's got to convince himself a bogeyman's long gone!

"His wife Meghan works for the Planning Commission," you add, " . . . knockin' down old shit . . . like fleabag trap motels . . . "

This sumbitch's trying to compose himself. "Yeah . . . yeah . . . his wife." He rubs his nose. "All she do is put niggas on the street when they bulldoze th' ole Federal Gardens, right? Then Chil' Protective mugs come an' rescue alla us wiff the 'dislocation an' anxiety.' Moses put me an' my mama in the munie . . . then Moses go and pimp her out . . . to horny muvfukkahs on lunch break, random dudes." He sighs. Turns from you for an instant.

"He had the power to do that?"

"Yeah."

Don't say you're sorry. These types'll think you're soft.

"I be in foster care three months, man . . . that foster family not happy wiff its cut so Moses, he come back an' say I gotta get passed 'round t'any rich faggot . . . white, black, foreign . . . who want my ass."

"Makes you feel evil. B'lieve . . . "

"B'lieve. But I ain't as evil as Moses. One time he want Mister Manny—you know Mister Manny? He want me to dip out the ole man. Never tole Sunshine 'cause she love Mister Manny. You keep that between us, hear me. Tole Moses got fuck himself. Tha' was las' year. Moses leff e'ryone be 'cause 'rona an' never came back."

"Al-Mayadeen Thomas—you knew him?"

"My firs' mind say that big stringbean nigga be thirsty fo' my Sunshine when he come after they emptied all them halfway houses. Look, he was all about his baby."

"His mama knew my friend who died on the streets. I got one more question."

"We done, moe."

"Ever hear of—"

"We *done.*"

Pushing your luck, Junior . . .

"You ever hear of a nigga name 'Big,' prolly in the men's annex of the munie when your mama was there? Big sloppy mug."

He's lolling that troll head. "No."

"Well he's Al-Mayadeen's half-brother and I got a tip he was Moses Roffe's . . . helper."

You're scanning the fence line, the stacked oily tires, just in case this sumbitch's troops decide to return but it's just you and him out there in the hazy sunlight.

"Motel was small time, right, Shawn?" you press. "Munie was the monster, right?"

Admit it son, for a second you thought them RIPs were going to separate your dick from your body. Instead, you get a whisper, a wide-eyed look.

"That fat nigga an' Moses use ta laugh . . . how the munie got the 'top shelf pussy' . . . an' the cutest lil' *sweetypies.*"

Hard to breath, like the 'rona just got in you. He pauses, finally locks eyes with you and then there's nothing but honking and traffic, whiteboy rock and roll blasting from the bistros on H.

"How'd it work?"

"Wasn't like these Spanishes here or up Gaithersburg, Russians in Bali-mo', Ko-rean in Virginia all runnin' squirrel pussy outta some basement, man. Cop protection, give each female lil' piggy bank wha' they keep, rest the females kick-up. Some go to Moses, some to Big 'cause I hear jus' got one job: keep nasty muvfukkahs off *one* lil' girl, while Moses keep 'em off her mama. Moses, he had plenny lil' girls, even boys ta play wid, so keepin' mileage down on one ho, no problem. But Big—"

"Big dig didn't the rules. He touched K'ymira. That was his niece."

The boss shrugs as if it's nothing. "So? E'rybody catch hell an' nobody come help. Look gee, Moses he swole like a jail-bird nigga so word is he beat Big's ass till it look like chewed grape Now and Later."

"Munie gets shut down when Ky's kidnapped, everyone runs for cover. But Twelve couldn't make a case on Al-Mayadeen's wife, CiCi. Sunshine says that bopper was a *most* favored lady, agree?"

He nods. "Mama say tha' bitch touched. *Liked* them white men wiff money, wiff uniforms. Man, the Mafia di'n't have they spots on lock like them bent whitefolk did in the munie." He palms his face, moans. Yet in an instant he's shaking off his woe like a giddy prizefighter in the ring. "Di'n't burn th' puzzle, amiright?"

"Stamp, Young."

"So wha' now? You th' dick. You find Moses an' 'bring him ta justice?' Bring down the whole a th' police force . . . get it all on *Dateline NBC* and *Sixty Minutes* and niggas all be dancin' to you on TikTok an' tweetin' who should play you in Netflix version a real life?"

"Why so bait, moe?"

"Cause wha' ya doin' is a death march for fools, don't matter who you client be. My solution: I gots whole boxes a RIP rounds, Old. Y'all come work fo' me. Put that shit up Roffe's ass. In some cop asses. I makes you my *con-sigli-eri* like old-school."

"Why'd I want to work for you, killing folk?"

This walnut-headed hoodlum's laughing at you, son. "Cause I ain't so bad compared to the police an' folk spose ta help kids. 'Cause you so ain't so good as you think."

Lord, he knows you better than any of those shrill pinktoe child shrinks, drippy therapists back when you wore short pants.

"I gots a for-real accountant what gives ten-ninney-nine forms fo' taxes. I needs mo' OG scury niggas like you. By the by . . . all tha' hit I say was 'off the record.' I hear it or see it anywhere you be smoked, hear me?"

"I'm out . . . got what I need," you surrender.

You can still hear him laughing as you stride up to H Street, turn the corner into the searing sun. And if you never peep me inside you again: kiss my ass and stay haunted by what that piece of shit said, son . . .

CHAPTER 14

Dead Ass . . .

I PASS THE ER ENTRANCE WHERE I came in, seems like a lifetime ago, about to dip out on fennie and heroin. I pass the lobby where I traipsed out, couple weeks later, naked under a hospital gown, yanking a shunt out my arm, dragging IV tubes.

Walk right into the guard booth and intake at the VA flashing my card and all they can say is "Put on this mask, bub . . . "

That this seersucker's comically soaked dark with sweat as if I walked through a carwash, spattered with road mud, shirt a grand mess, my face brick red from the sun—nothing to them.

And I don't fuck with the metal detector, and they don't stop me. Must be the magic suit? .380's still tucked on me, and I pass on through.

Indeed, passed a lot on the way. All the way, up from H. An entire city, from Union Station and the Capitol to the Basilica where my mother prayed. At least the heat baked him out of my head. Melted my brain, yeah. Small price to pay.

I want to rip the TV off the wall in the second floor waiting room so Steve Harvey and the Asshole Family from Asshole,

Alabama, with shut the fuck up about what the "survey said" on *Family Feud*; room's ancient Linoleum floor is starting to melt into the dull white cinderblock walls so saliva's foaming in my cheeks as I approach the brother in civies tapping on his keyboard; got on an American flag mask like most of the staff and he's talking to himself under it.

Hoarse, I say, "Excuse me, sir . . . "

He doesn't look up.

"No appointment but I gotta see Doctor Kapoor about my meds . . . the dosage, I'm losing it . . . this is an emergency . . . "

He still doesn't budge.

"I'm *not* a killer. I'm *not* scary. I'm helping . . . making moves. But I'm scared where this shit is leading . . . *dead ass,* bruh . . . "

"You say something, my man? Look y'all know the drill . . ." He calls for a nursing assistant.

She arrives, gives me a cheery how-de-do and cup to pee in. Take my temp and I'm at 99 but she says it's hot outside.

"I'm . . . nauseous . . . I think I have heat . . . heatstroke."

I'm told to go in the head, squirt. I do after dousing my face. Calling Stripe. He's happy I am where I am and not bleeding on the curb, ripped apart by RIPs.

When I come out, the nursing assistant says sit down and someone'll come by to take my blood pressure blah, blah.

"After the piss test," dude at the desk tells me, "you gotta wait on that . . . plus the doc, he got another therapy session just ending. Give it another hour."

"I-I can't. Dr. Kapoor told me—"

"I'm a Christian so all's I say now is calm down." He finally looks me up and down. "Do I gotta get security, playboy, huh?"

My phone buzzes and it's Figgis' private number.

"Ain't no calls allowed here."

"It's the Chief of Police."

"Yeah playboy listen . . . that's workin' my nerves and—"

He pauses when two women come in . . . both in those flip-down welder's visor-looking med-shields and masks. One's in VA scrubs and smock billowing like a tent, toting hypodermics: big, orange-tipped ones.

"S'up Nurse Lopez!" and he's sweet as pie.

The other is a sister in some skintight leggings and silky tank top, high heels and I don't understand how she comes dressed like that . . . yet she's carrying one of those tablet computers and sheets of bright stickers . . . got some weird peach hue to her skin and I say weird because the undertone's a deep bronze, more so than me. That stuff's all contrasted with this short cropped, almost bald cut on her head, but for some baby hair and wispy curls toward the front. Frosted white . . . like she's from the X-men.

She clocks me, looks to the gatekeeper. "Is that him . . . from las' week?"

"*Uh-huh* . . . Miz Agave. Everyone else knows the rules, but this one, looking all like the playboy on the Amalfi Coast, right? Comin' up on me like he's a VIP patient and everyone else in here ain't got no problems."

"*Agave?*" I mutter. I note under all that face gear her pinched whitegirl nose, what's got to be blue contacts in her big eyes. Blue like Figgis'. "That's Greek, right?"

The nurse with the needles says, "No that's cactus."

Agave giggles. She's hovering in her cloud of what my affliction says is old-school Issey Miyake she must've housed from an auntie. Lots of older women who were counselors and teachers wore that when I was going to Central Mission, second time Esmeralda left.

"Didn't mean to be like that. I don't know you."

"It's okay. Now . . . can you sit down wiff me?" We do, right under Steve Harvey, and she takes my hand. "I feel I know you, Mr. Cornish even though I never talked to you. You gotta stop all this foolishness whenever you here. You be doin' so well, meetin' all you markers . . . Dr. Kapoor tole me."

I forget myself and peer between her ample breasts and there's the badge dangling from the lanyard around her neck. "Epps, Agave, Patient Care Admin."

"Now, who you gettin' calls from? President Biden?"

"N-No . . . Chief of Police. For real." I shouldn't've said it.

Yet rather than air me out she purses those red lips, nods, "People trained to think you crazy . . . will think you crazy, right? So what I'm goin' do is expedite an appointment with Dr. Kapoor to go over your meds . . . and for group meetings . . . keep you busy. Outta trouble. But there's nothing today and you goin' be compliant partner in your own treatment, any questions?"

"I'm busy. I got work. Check my file. I'm hired to . . . *shit* . . . "

Can't tell her. She's smiling but . . . those fake lashes batting over those fake blue eyes are swatting away what I'm saying. It's what Daddy says they do here at VA. Nothing!

I don't know why I blurt this. "Pentheus' mother. Your name."

"Mmmm?" She then gestures to Nurse Lopez.

"That's what it means," I say. "Not cactus. King Pentheus . . . he was pissed off his mother, aunties, all the women were—"

"All freaky and nekkid around the woods with Dionysus, the God of Freaky. Mr. Cornish take off this jacket, take down your sleeve, okay?"

I just up and do it because I'm entranced by this chick. She's not even turned off by my sopping clothing, the funk.

"Yeah . . . h-he made Agave think Pentheus was a stag. She tore him limb from limb. Um . . . what're y'all doing?"

"You're on the vaccination cohort list. So sorry it's taken this long. Should have been two months ago. Nurse . . . there's his ID."

It's the super one-shot tip for we Third-Worlders in the room that day. Nurse tells me to keep my mask on, though. Keep washing hands. Agave, she thumbs a sticker on my shirt, then adds, "Agave felt real bad when she stopped trippin' on Dionysus's liquor," she quips as if it's a little kid's fairy tale. "Bad bitches can still get blind. But Pentheus shoulda let mama play and not get in the way. Nah, he wanted to show e'ryone he was baller. Thas the lesson."

I'm thinking, I could marry you. But I rewire, come back to why I was there. "My meds . . . real talk . . . y'all can't do nothing today?"

"You be a good boy, Tree-top," Agave purrs.

"I'm . . . I'm not schizophrenic."

"Who say that?" she shoots back with a laugh.

See, the heat-fever and Thanos and everything else is fucking me up and I wish they'd just sedate me and give me a bed . . . just to lay down on away from K'ymira and the Colonial View. Maybe call Figgis back for real and do what a rational man would do, like Stripe wants me to do . . . yet I still can't stop myself, can't stop babbling . . .

"I'm . . . going to a party tonight. Was thinking of questioning a witness . . . bringing a Ruger LCP three-eighty . . . holding it to his head. Same Ruger I got on me now. Wanna see it in my jacket?"

"Man get outta here wid that," Agave jokes with the nurse. "Oh snap I remember now, Mr. Cornish. You'd say just about anything for some milligrams of Valium. Nah-unh. You gotta cut yo' demons loose . . . or else you sacrifice. Alla us got to do it. '*Never will I have joy in you or see your bright young prospects.*'"

Holy shit.

She whispers to Nurse Lopez, who whispers to the nursing assistant who took my piss.

But . . . *holy shit.*

The nursing assistant hands me a plastic cup of water and like a half-deck of Valley.

"Re-ups are in yo' treatment profile, so call it a gift," Agave cautions. "Cause it won't happen again. No more a this foolishness. Go home and wait for you appointment text and the call. Peace."

Yeah . . . I'm out to the bus circle at Medstar, craning my neck for the Number Fifty-Six and I know Daddy'd tut and curse at the odds that someone he'd call a chippie . . . would be quoting *Medea.*

My phone buzzes on the bus. This time I take it.

"*Want to tell me where you've been, why you haven't checked in. Why one of my captains in the Seventh got an email from the Park Police saying a PI with a provisional license was 'obstructing justice' in Anacostia Park . . . a crime scene they were cleaning up?*"

"Linda . . . that's old news."

"*Ma'am or Chief now.*"

"I wasn't doing a thing in Anacostia Park but following leads Toya Thomas gave up."

"*Hmmm, okay. Now, you're leaving the shooting investigation to the Major Crimes dicks correct? They are working the MS-Thirteen angle.*"

"They are indeed. And you and I both know that's bullshit . . . "

There's silence. A very telling, scary silence, then, "*Okay.*"

"Okay?"

"*Why were you on H Street today . . . almost a hundred degrees out there! Sanchez said you looked like you were sick.*"

"Linda . . . Chief . . . about the One-Six Crew, I think we need to talk about—"

"*You coming tonight . . . to SFME?*"

Jesus, Mary and Joseph. Yeah, now I'm scared again. Fools like Thanos, nah, he's paper, he's all air, once you take the soldiers away. But this deflection, avoidance—this has got my dome clinking and whirring and calculating again.

"Yes. I'll be there," is what I give her. My friend. My ally. My sponsor.

"*Good. I'm speaking at the event then likely will cut out so I doubt we'll have a proper sit-down directly tonight, but hon' – you will spill mama a whole bowl of beans very soon, you follow me?*" When I don't answer, just loll in my seat, she presses, "*Um . . . where exactly are you now, if I may ask?*"

"On a bus. Smooth . . . as spider spit . . . on diazepam." Before she trips I say, "From the VA Hospital. Not my pluggers."

"*VA . . . hold on. Who's your care team at the VA? Dickie?*"

I swipe off. Then I turn the phone off . . .

. . . and I'm dreaming about this fucking teddy bear, and Figgis is laughing at me. See, I'm naked, and she's laughing like a real Missy Ann while she's sizing me up on the slave block . . . squeezing my ass, flopping at my privates. As she does so she cradles the Poob and the teddy's dripping with fresh, bright blood. Black folk cower from the pen. They are covered in soot for the smell, yet I'm slick with oil, for the sheen . . .

"Yo *jefe . . . mira . . .* " I hear, all tinny yet real close. "*Es tarde . . .* "

I shudder and flail and now the busted, mildewed tile on the floor's wet with puddles. Yeah, I'm naked all right. In a tub of now tepid water that's soot-gray. And I don't recall getting in.

I jump out of the tub, grab a towel.

"Dead ass you walk all the way f'om H to Medstar?"

"Dead ass." That's why I'm filthy.

"You phone . . . you were outta breath talking on the bus . . . *como*?"

"Dictating?" I say as I check the smudged mirror.

"*Sí* . . . an' you email to me, LaKeisha. I delete . . . it so long, make no sense. You talk to girl in Juvie but you talk to *boboso* wha' run One-Six? An' he no shoot you?"

I point to my naked body. "No holes but the one I was born with."

"*Oye* . . . Pilar, she got your clothes an' socks hangin' in window downstairs. *Mojados* an' nasty, bro'. You sweat like *mi tio* . . . "

"What time is it. Got to roll to the . . . "

He does this movie-like double-take. "Party? Party start like half hour ago but why you wan' show up like white people, Rain Man?"

"Oh no . . . " I'm slipping all over the wet bathroom floor like a drunk skater and fall square on my bare ass. "*Vea, chero* . . . " I play it off like a brotha should. "Give Pilar like ten bucks from my roll for my clothes."

I jump up, wrap the towel.

"Regional ho'pital . . . then hos-pice . . . "

"Huh?"

"Tha' Little muvfukkah, regional ho'pital, the hos-pice . . . he ain't there."

I'm looking for the only other shirt I got that looks civilized. "He's a vegetable and they're moving him? My father's been in the same spot thirteen years."

Stripe pops an imaginary collar. "'Patuxent Care', thas the spot . . . th' fock far out pas' Andrews Airforce Base. But it get better." He smiles that evil shit Daddy called reptilian like back in the day. "I call there . . . my new phone . . . I say 'Felix Villanueva' at Largo hospice lookin' for nurse to Hakim Alexander 'cause I clean his stuff an' he got personal stuff we forget to send."

I pull on clean draws. Always have clean draws and socks. I revere clean draws and socks.

"The fuck's 'Felix Villanueva?'" I then ask my impish sidekick.

He grins and says, "Somebody in them places *always* got a somebody workin' there wid that name, Rain Man! No woke gringo gonna say 'who?' Get them all confused an' they say 'Alexander, Hakim . . . Medicaid public transfer. Not allowed visitors . . . "

"Stamp?"

"And they ask him an' he say he got no shit at old place." Stripe nods. "He *say* . . . "

Okay he tries to squirm away maybe owing to my half-nakedness not being good for a mentor-protégé tip, right? But I catch him, bear-hug him. "Kid you are a better detective than me. Better everything."

Of course then my gloom returns. The fuck kind of jont'd lie about a coma?

"LaKeisha say this fockin' place sound like shit leftover, like tent jails for ICE, many sick . . . put squatters in so no one know they sick. A dead house."

Yeah, I heard about those places from rosy-cheek campers and fiends come in from the hinterland where they still think the world's flat or the 'rona vax comes from Mars, sprinkling among the blackfolk in the tent-towns. Guess Mister Charlie needed a couple more for the coughing poorfolk herded off premium real estate.

The AC's been replaced by a panel of plywood but lucky for us the temp outside's something bearable so all I do is powder up like a bone-in porkchop and for someone who ducked out of hug of pride Stripe's now got narrow-lidded eyeballs on me.

"You let me go, the street . . . hunt down shit like before." He hands me the ancient seersucker on a wooden hangar. "The *ropas*, you look like a pussy, bro'. But you fit in at white-bread party, maybe." He pauses, cocks his head. "See, *Señora* Verna, she be there . . . lotta memory, and then Figgis be there . . . Roffe. You gonna be okay?"

"I'm good."

"*En serio?*"

"What's on your mind, kid?" I button my shirt, glowering.

"If you not let me go in the street, then you promise you go to VA, get doc to keep them pills f'om fockin' in the head."

"*Soon* . . . and no. I need you here, like an HQ, *comprende?* Don't want you out there, marked." When he does a long-minted teeth suck and spin I get even more bass and chop, "This ain't about your people, and them taco gangsters, man! These is about the *niggas,* on high and very low . . . this is about bad cops! Uh-huh . . . some turnin' these places in brothels, smorgasbords for pedophiles, maybe even kidnapping little kids like K'ymira. And some . . . " I calm, squeeze out the bass, when I see him scared, ". . . ain't got that figured yet. It's dangerous."

He sees me grabbing for the Ruger and the holster. "This all crazy, Rain Man," he whispers. "Now you goin' to a party . . . wid *el machina?*"

"It's case I got to scare Roffe. He's big dude. And I'll take the Metro down. I can get on with a bazooka these days an' they won't know . . . "

"An' when you see old places, bad memory . . . Verna, you still gonna be good, dead ass?"

"Dead ass."

CHAPTER 15
Mea Culpa

AND SO I'M COMING UP ABOVE ground at Navy Yard Station and the humidity and river funk are glassing me bigtime . . . I swear the clean shirt is no longer clean after a block of hoofing, and I'm envying these stripped-down whitefolk who smell of split beer even at six feet away, not a soul wearing a mask because hey, why not? They're the suburban drunks who mob the bars surrounding Nats Stadium yet never seem to make it inside the gates, and the jont's all lit up like Star Wars and shit against the sky. As I cross K Street to the remnants of the darker, scarier region, I hear a roar and I guess our fellas have scored some runs. Like I give a fuck because those happy folk don't give a fuck about the ops on the other side of South Capitol Street.

See, St. Jude's hasn't changed at first view, even at night, bell tower with no bell lost in the glare and gleam of the stadium, the traffic. Carved gray stone and two-hundred-year-old red bricks, thick with climbing hydrangea, connected by that glass walkway with the cheap 1980's boxy functionality of So Families May Eat. The steel spine and ribs of the new SFME "K'ymira Thomas Children's Dormitory" prompts a stare, though—along with the white party tent thereunder and sound of glasses clinking, a jazz combo playing, a songstress crooning. Still, I note the one thing binding the two spots. Bent and withered men congregating on one side. Beaten and forlorn women and kids, entering the other, even as the champagne flows there in between.

Verna wished I'd taken more of Jaime Bracht's blood money. Wonder what she'd holler if she ever peeped what's in the larder, huh? I finger the Ben Franklins as I enter the St. Jude's Chapel, always open, guarded only by a lone CCTV camera I clock in the rafters. Something new. "New" was never Father Phil Rufino's thing.

Good to see the AC sitch's the same, eh? The nave is stifling, like a crucible with the burner under it set to melt bronze. The smell of candlewax and incense philters and cuts the dankness. I dab holy water and oil on my forehead despite a frayed notecard taped to the wall, warning about COVID.

Welcome home. Stripe's right. I'm shaking like day three of a third rehab.

Not a soul in there so I shove two of the five c-notes into a brass box to the left of the ornate alter. Once the rustling of skrilla ends, however, a few sandal-shod friars appear out of nowhere.

None are familiar. And I miss the cute little bronze-skinned Brazilian novice nuns. Wonder how many of them died from the virus back in Sao Paulo.

"*Cantatur hodie in cor meum,*" I hear, ". . . despite being broken, so long . . . "

A weathered, stooping Brother Karl-Maria limps close, and I grin for a second, recalling how his opposite number was a nun named Maria-Karl. The grin drops when I recall hearing 'rona took her in the second wave. LaKeisha told me some dickhead from the Diocese offered them tests, offered reassignment to some place safe, like where? They declined, demanding instead that the residents—bums, boozers, fiends . . . losers and sinners—get swabbed first, and then get them vaxxed first. Father Phil gave up a shot at a ventilator and life in the ICU, LaKeisha says. Told the nurses to hook up somebody who "hasn't lived a full life." Say what you will, Daddy, about the Holy Mother Church . . . because you're probably right. But I'd hold *these* individuals higher than the pulpit pimps and gilded first ladies of the tambourine palaces you dragged us to.

So yeah, I rush into Karl-Maria's arms and he feels so small now, fragile.

"Prodigal Son," I joke through the tears. "*Mea culpa . . .* "

He's shaking his now white-haired, pale head. "*Never*, Richard. I hear you walk around with a sawed-off pool cue stuffed down your pant leg. Come on son, what'd I teach you about using calm words . . . "

Okay, he gets more jonin' in and we both laugh. He wants me to join him for juice and bread fresh from the basement oven, and a tour of the garden the winos and dopefiends planted in honor of Phil Rufino and Maria-Karl.

"Can't." Yet I hug on him again. Got to go before I get netted-up and forget my mission.

"Ahhh . . . all right. Crab dip and erudite conversation next door, huh?"

I nod.

"Be gentle," he advises. He then points to his own back . . . in the spot where I've holstered the .380 and I knew I should've put on my ankle. Cagey old bastard. "You stop in here first because you have a metal detector issue?"

I nod again.

"I miss our talks . . . rather, your rants."

"Rants? Nah, dropping knowledge, Brother. Oral histories of the Continent, Hellenistic myths . . . "

God, listen to my pompous bullshit! And just a brick ago I was stuttering like Gomer Pyle, getting dropsy like I was having a stroke, drooling like a sick dog. See, I could just never abide by being called a *jock* in school. Trying too hard *not to* made me silly, vulnerable. That was Esmeralda Rubio's way into my soul back then, like a germ invades an open sore. And soon here came the stuttering, fainting, drooling. Till these folk took me in.

Well, the old white man's not peeping my inner soul this time. He's shooting me mock gasp and teasing again, "You claimed to have memorized Plato's *Phaedo* in one weekend, remember?"

"I was high. Prolly not."

"Fair enough," he says with laugh. "But whenever you'd dry out, and the shakes and nightmares came, I'd calm you with the tale of Bellerophon. That was one of Plato's favorites, too."

"Brother, I'm . . . still fuzzy."

"We all are these days. Okay, Dickie—close your mouth and think. Bellerophon, he was unique among all the heroes. Many indeed were drawn from his exploits: Perseus, Hercules, Jason. He was born high, yet lost it all . . . suffered scorn, pain, loneliness . . . the rebuke of the bigshots, ignored by all the of Gods but Athena, who saw the good in him, and it was through *her* he received the gift of Pegasus, the winged horse not even Perseus could fully tame."

He motions me toward the nave's side exit that leads to the connecting tunnel. I see him pull a two-way unit from the folds of his hassock. He calls into it. "Let my friend Mr. Cornish over to the other side. He's attending the SFME event." Then he stashes the radio. "Bye, Richard. It was a heart-song to see you again. Now go face what you must."

The man could throw shade and buck you up with the same words. Either way I'm swallowing hard and as I'm heading out of the chapel here comes his voice again, but this time it's amplified by the War of 1812-vintage stonework, so I halt.

"You really *don't* remember, the tale, do you?"

"N-No." I really don't. That's why it's no heart-song for me.

"Bellerophon vanquished the most terrifying monster of all. It was called the 'Chimera.' A huge fire-breathing beast whose body was an amalgam of all the predatory creatures of the earth. Invincible, irresistible. The bigshots and gilded heroes who shunned or reviled Bellerophon were too scared or corrupt to fight it. So this one brave man stood alone . . . "

"What . . . what happened to him?"

"He died."

"How very Catholic," I tease.

"Actually, his head go too big . . . Pegasus bucked him, and he fell from the sky." I hear him chuckle, then he tells me, "Or . . . he wandered the earth, obscure once more, having tasted heroism. I like that ending better."

"Why?"

"Fits the other meaning of the monster's name. *Chimera*: something contrived to fool and scare people."

Daddy would say it's a bitch move, coming in this way rather than going straight to the party tent but I'm no Bellerophon so bitch moves is all I got. Still, we embrace, and I whisper thanks for saving my life many times.

As he drops his frail grip he says to me, "You know . . . when I first met you, you were carrying around a paper you'd written as a student . . . it was so yellowed and torn I thought it belonged in the darn Reliquary. Ha!"

"I-I don't recall." And I'm pissed I can't.

"It was the usual politically correct history, my friend—that the Greeks stole their myths from older traditions . . . the ironworkers of the Volta River, West Africa, who supplied Ramses the Great with fine lanceheads for his charioteers. They also created a weapon to fight a monster very much like the Chimera. The creature killed people, livestock until a hero dispatched it similarly."

My brain's all locked up but this reply's a good bet: "Betcha I was using it to insulate my trousers against the cold."

He shakes his head. "No, it's because you were so big, so frightening to people, even police, when they saw you. You told the social worker you'd finished the essay the day your dad came to visit you in the athletes' dorm, found Esmeralda Rubio in your bed, and she was high, incoherent. He yanked you out of the shower, threw you naked into the cold, outdoors . . . beat you with a tree branch that had fallen from in an ice storm. Campus security ejected him. You never pressed charges."

Guess I left that nugget out for Dr. Kapoor. "I'll see you later, Brother."

"Richard, last time you said 'later' was like two years ago. When you note gray hair beginning to sprout on your chin, your head, it's tempting to think the failure and pain we endured from our sins, or sins put upon us, were the test. But for a select few, my fine fella, they're merely the *quickening*, readying you for the true trial. Anyways, tread lightly and lovingly next door, okay? They haven't seen you in a while either."

Motherfucker strips the bullshit away, doesn't he? And now I'm clocking the new paint and flooring at SFME yet drawing in my nostrils that old smell of Lestoil and Clorox mingling with the aroma of actual meals rather than the spartan soup and buttered bread of St. Jude's. It's conjuring visions of Verna, not a mythical monster.

And here's the noise! Tots mewling. Teen moms cursing, middle-aged moms groaning. Even a few white chicks in there: thin and hillbilly or portly and sloppy; their flip-flops slap the floor as they tote the squirming seed of black or brown fathers around on their hips.

Squeaks of delight yank me from that hard mind when I pass the huge steel door to a for-real larder they used to call "Fort Knox," full-up of Tide detergent, diapers, Cheetos, pain meds . . . and thus guarded like the gold depository. Of course, I were light-fingered numerous times onaccount Verna gave me run of the jont when I bop over from St Jude's. None of the staff realized my "addled brain" could memorize lock code tones whenever I watch them punched in.

But back to the squeaks. Kate . . . Lord, she looks twenty years younger as she rushes me, kisses me all over my face. I look down and she's still into Birkenstocks. Nice silver ones. Though she's missing some toes from the winters with me and Princess, hunkered on a Smithsonian steam grate . . . in tattered Birkenstocks, no socks.

"Skeleton crew here, working late 'cause everyone's at the party! How'd you get in?" She guffaws. The mirth switches to sobs as she digs her face into my shoulder. "I-I miss Princess so much. I miss you. Working here just made me miss botha you more . . . and there was rumor COVID took you and—"

"Shush now." I'm crying again like a punk, and now any swinging dick would see why I avoided this spot. Tears will kill you; look what they did to Al-Mayadeen.

"Say . . . where's LaKeisha?"

Kate blows her ruddy pug nose with a tissue and points down the hall. "I fixed her a plate from the party but she says he hates rich people 'little food,' not something ta eat! Let's surprise her."

LaKeisha's gaming avatar when she lived in the libraries was a pale porcelain-skin blond rather than her true self. Black as pitch-tar like my ole man, round face, thick lips. It's so good to see her in the flesh again. And trying so hard: stylish glasses, iridescent green frames! I recall the busted specs I re-engineered with wire, my miracle glue scavenged from mucilage, Manischewitz wine and denture cream. Look at Keesh: pair of shapely jeans, a pretty orange top, clean white sandals . . .

"*John Snow*, returned from the North," she huffs, in a faint monotone that's more cloying than mine, I guess. Barely even looking up from the big desktop computer screen the two laptops arrayed in front of that. "Or John Henry, rising from dust and rock of the railroad tunnel cave-in . . . "

Therapy's working, a bit, because she reminds herself to rise, hug me, sit back down to refocus on the screen. Baby steps, girl. That's why Verna hires damaged folk. They take life in small bites and give back their all.

"Verna's not going to like this John Snow," LaKeisha continues. "Sneaking in. Tactically advantageous, yes. Strategically sound, no."

I lean to whisper in her ear.

"I got you some money for your research help. I got Ernesto looking for Hakim Alexander."

"Stripe needs to pay attention."

"He's good kid, Keesh. Ain't how he used to be."

This girl will never hit me eye to eye. "None of us are, eh. By the way . . . was churning some stuff for you, oh roaming Paladin, on this CiCi Talbot. Maybe cops missed this years ago but to get TANF and stuff she had to do a quitclaim deed of interest in a house in Seat Pleasant, Maryland to the estate of the deceased, the majority interest owner."

Shit. "Stamp . . . what? Cops thought Ky was buried there. Cici owned the damn house?"

"She was on the deed, *M'Lord.* Put the copy of the quitclaim in your digital goodie bag, okay?"

Before I can chew on that more, I catch a deep audible deep sigh from the doorway. LaKeisha pushes her nose into her monitor and I'm standing there, too scared to turn around. Me, shot at, dumped in a traphouse? Smell that? The perfume. Better than Figgis'. So much better . . .

"This is *bait,* Dickie," the voice calls me out, though softly. "Even for you. Plain . . . damn . . . bait."

Verna's perfect when I turn around and catch her whole. Bobbed black hair falling in place and bone-straight, brown skin glowing. Sweet red summer shift flows off her body . . . I must've gained the pudge she's lost. She's got on these sandals and I've clocked the style before in pictures of my mother. Mom clocked them on Jacqueline Bouvier Kennedy and Coretta Scott King, when I was little . . . back when Daddy said the shoes made her look like a "redbone trick" in front of me and Alma . . .

"Jack Rogers sandals . . . " I mumble, my affliction bubbling up.

She looks down at her painted toes for an instant but huffs, "Why didn't you RSVP, why didn't you just come straight to the tent, why lurk in here? The event's almost over . . . "

"I-I know."

LaKeisha huffs in her own monotone, "Y'all gonna do this here, now, in front of me?"

Nah, Verna's not having it. "LaKeisha call the caterer and get an ETA because they are short clean-up crew and the residents aren't going to do it. Katie, will you tell the kitchen we need more ice. Hot as my auntie's armpit in Alabama out there so the punch's running low." She hasn't seen me over a year yet she's not losing a chance to get in a shot! "Dickie, the dedication speeches ended. Why are you late?"

"Who spoke?"

"The Mayor . . . and she just left. The City's new Director of Child and Family Services, poached from Johns Hopkins and Howard U. And Chief Figgis, Deputy Chief Antonelli."

Damn. One time you couldn't pay these bigshots to set foot in here or St. Jude's—and these were "nice" jonts. Unlike the munie . . .

"Come with me."

I miss being tugged around by her. Katie and LaKeisha know it. Staff and residents who've never seen me, well, they stare as their boss storms by, all five-feet tall of her, followed by yours truly, a galumphing bear in a hastily-cleaned seersucker suit.

I almost got her killed. All because of Esmeralda. And now Esme's face is invading my dome again and I got to stay sharp, remember why I'm here. Even if I see Linda.

"Why aren't you wearing a mask, Dickie," Verna stings me. "Vulnerable people here. The mutation can live in your nose for weeks." I note she's not wearing a mask; bet all the luminaries got their boosters a brick past. "I got spares in my office. Also—visitors must register on the website for contact tracing. Didn't catch that either, huh?"

Me coming strapped, ready to kidnap one of her prize employees, might be on that no-no list, too. "Brother Karl-Maria, um . . . he let me in."

"Yeah. *Shortcuts.*" She motions to her office door.

My hangdog look, the stammer and low tone . . . probably all reminds her of the simple big and bugged-out nigga she wanted to save. She forces a little smile, though, when she notices me clocking the refurbished jont. Updated with gray glass, brushed nickel. No artwork though, no tchotchke and family pics. Like it was sterilized. And no tea roses, sent anonymously.

"You good, Dickie?" she says, suddenly a bit more friendly than firecracker. She pulls of her Jack Rogers, straps her party heels back on.

"It's hard. Day-by-day, even before this."

"I know. And I'm not angry. Okay a little."

"Again, *mea culpa.* Sorry for . . . " I pause, shifting in the chair. "Lot of people I love or knew. Gone."

"Dickie I want this to be a restart, not about apologies," she suddenly gushes while I'm squirming like I got to piss fire.

"I'm not loafin' on you, Verna . . . "

"Of course not. Did you . . . did you find a family for . . . you know, the baby?"

I dare say his name. "Maximiliano. Uh-huh. Two nice folks. She's a lawyer for the Labor Department, he's a software designer just out of the Navy. Kid's gonna be fine."

"Because of you." I dip my head and she comes around from the desk and smells so good and my affliction wants to demand the name of the new scent. She lifts my stubbly chin with her finger and no she never has to ask permission to touch me. "Hear me? Because of you. You are a hero. And I am overjoyed to see you again, no matter your lil' eccentricities, huh?"

"Th-Thanks," I whisper, knowing she will hate me when I see Moses out there. Or maybe even before . . .

"Oh *shit*—heard about a shooting . . . at Howard's campus. Was that near you?"

"Um . . . no."

"Thank goodness."

I lied. So why not deflect, too. "You look more beautiful than the Mercedes e-class renovations, the dorm. Must have some big donors."

Thankfully her weight loss didn't deflate her dimples. "Got a nice check from Bezos through the Washington Post . . . Bill Gates . . . some local rich folk of color, yes. Pity and guilt maybe. I mean, look how all the dog shelters got cleaned out—folk needing stuff to hug. City's broke from the virus, from Trump. All of the shelters and food banks got lotta staff on permanent disability. But the grim truth is we got more dollars per head now . . . because a lot of heads . . . old, young, just born . . . have moved on from this Earth."

Fuck, think I went and got her depressed and down.

"*So* . . . the Mayor was here? Linda Figgis and other bigshots—how about that!" Could my ass be any more ham-fisted?

Yet she gives a weird snort and says, "Well, I am *thirsty* . . . no peanut gallery commentary, hear me? So let's get back to the party, get some punch and food in you. And speaking of Linda Figgis . . . " Now Verna's whispering playfully as we head for the exit to the courtyard bordering St. Jude's. " . . . keep this on the low, 'kay, but the Chief's going to resign in a few months and run for mayor." I try to close my mouth, but the trapdoor keeps hanging as her heels tap the shiny new floor. "The Mayor's gonna work for Biden and Harris. Linda's her girl, to carry the torch."

"What do you mean?"

"Wake up, okay! Running . . . for mayor!"

"Oh yeah. And . . . wait, she's still here?"

"Of course, silly."

"And your senior staff?"

"Yeah, them too, Mr. Private Eye. One I'm *dying* for you to meet. Moses Roffe."

CHAPTER 16

Ten Commandments

THE FIRST PEOPLE I CLOCK ARE the shelter teens dressed in blazers and skirts, all safely masked unlike these vaxxed bigwigs, all serving punch or champagne, fancy canopies. They got a music combo out there under the tent: four instruments, lead singer who looks mixed, like Sweet Sunshine under a wig of tight blond curls hair, body undulating in the sultry evening breeze. The song's something from a memory . . .

. . . sixties psychedelic rock ballad or the first neo-soul, who can tell . . . but my affliction knows it P. P. Arnold. "The First Cut is the Deepest," and my lips are muttering the lines my mother crooned when Daddy was on duty station . . . she was barefoot, wearing those capri pants and one of Daddy's civie shirts, sleeves all rolled up and so baggy I could see her bra cupping her small breasts, not big, veiny, hanging udders like those hillbilly moms on post . . . and she pirouetted on our chipped linoleum kitchen floor . . . swirled around the cheap sofa, the old-school console TV. And Alma joined her in the dance as the song's chorus played. My sister, bubblebee clip in her own rust-colored hair . . . and they looked like two feathered dandelion seeds floating together on an easy puff of wind . . .

"I still want you by my side . . . just to help me dry the tears I've cried . . . "

Guess I know why Mom liked it now. Why its words are a porcupine inside in me, still. Second chances, penance—they ain't rare. They just cost, right Esme?

"Dickie?" Verna nudges. I realize she's linked arms with me like we're prom dates.

"Huh?"

"You okay?"

"Sorry . . . " I'm checking myself. Next door just over a year past, I'd have to be hosed down at intake, dried out or put on suicide watch. My belly'd be howling for food, yet I'd vomit from a single spoon of porridge.

Not tonight. Tonight I'm a VIP, you motherfuckers!

"*Chief*! Wanted to catch you before you leave!" Verna suddenly gushes. "Sorry I missed Deputy Chief Antonelli."

The Boris Karloff-Bond Villain's bounced, it seems.

"Yes, Dante's old-school po-lice," Linda Figgis chuckles with half-twirl to face me. "Warrior code. Hits the hay early, rises with the sun, no vacations."

"Hard for his family?" Verna muses.

"Oh, his wife died. She was old school, too, from the stories. Their home was his castle, she cooked. Went to Mass. No children. Interestingly."

Verna speaks up. "Well Chief—*Linda*—again I'm glad you stuck around because this is the person I'd told you about awhile back . . . " I'm wrecking my neck between Verna's giddy smile and Figgis' champ grin. *Told her about*? " . . . my dear friend, a success story despite enduring many . . . many horrors—Richard E. Cornish, Jr. 'Dickie.'"

Damn. I'm dreading her play . . .

"Mr. Cornish." Okay. So far. She extends her pudgy hand. She releases her grip before she frees me from that look, that grin.

"Dickie was homeless," Verna explains, "and often a resident next door at St. Jude's." She leans in and now whispers, "Helped the FBI, as you may know in that . . . *stuff* . . . with that finance guy, was in Trump's Cabinet . . . *Jaime Bracht* . . . " Pulls back up and says in a non-CIA-ish voice, "Was accepted in the Mayor's Fresh Start Housing Program . . . is learning to be a private investigator. Tell the Chief, Dickie."

And like a golem—a clueless, silly one—in my monotone and deadpan I clown, "Um, yes, ma'am, um . . . before the virus we'd, this kid Ernesto and I, do stuff like security for safe parties . . . uh, finding runaways and of course truancy, and . . . "

She cuts me off, like a cat bored with a ball of string. "You're on contract, correct?"

"Pardon?" Verna huffs, clasping her hands "You know each other?"

"Verna, I'm surprised Mr. Cornish here didn't share his news . . . a provisional private investigator license through MPD. He's already had a task to perform for us." She looks me up and down. "And from all reports, he's gone *way* above and beyond the rather pedestrian limits set for him . . . "

Maybe she's not that bored. "Chief, I . . . "

"*Linda.*"

"Linda . . . I want to explain some things."

"Never apologize for being a self-starter. But hopefully you *will* share your time with Officer Sanchez . . . if she were to come calling again."

I'm frozen in place, jaw'd be quivering but for shear will. She's fucking with me. And it's scary.

"*Nice,*" Verna quips with a little spice. "See, this is what happens when you don't keep in touch, Dickie." She grabs a full flute of bubbly from a masked server whose name tag lists a name and an "aspiration"—this one's is "Simone" and "ballet dance teacher." "Is it good work?"

Figgis is playing shit tight to those Zeppelin breasts straining her uniform. "It's confidential, sorry Verna. And I ought to be running as well. It's been a wonderful evening, sweetie." They embrace, and it's weird looking down on them doing so, as neither clear my chest in height. "Ky could have been saved had you the room, the resources. The child shouldn't suffer the mother's sins."

"Amen," Verna whispers. Never seen his sister show such reverence to a white woman before, especially a fucking cop.

"By the way, Verna, I'm doing a big event at the 'Gingerbread House.' See you there?"

Verna does something else I never saw. Shrink away. "Aw . . . you know . . . not my scene. It's your party and I don't need myself . . . in any group's Instagram feed."

Figgis laughs. "My peeps'll be snatching mobiles. Official pics only. Think about it coming."

When she turns to me I extend my mitt and her fat little fingers disappear into it. I pull her close and I don't care who's watching.

"*You know MS-thirteen didn't shoot-up my place*?" I whisper in her ear, crouched and smiling like any good deep-pocket asshole at fundraiser.

"*Let go,*" she growls into my ear, smiling as if on a movie star red carpet.

"*None of this about Ky, is it?*"

"*You should have stayed away from 'Big.'*" She gives a playful shove, giggles, aloud, "You are inspiration, Mr. Cornish. Proof that programs like St. Jude's and So Families May Eat work. Good night!"

She steps away with an Amazon in blue, saying nothing else.

"Okay spill, Dickie," Verna presses, head wriggling. "How did you get hooked up with her?"

I shrug head. "Confidential." She'd kick my big ass if I told her it was about K'ymira Thomas, and Mother Mary I'm thinking about fessing anyway. A kid named tagged "Jasper" and "attorney" bops over with some cold shrimp and sauce. Grab a couple and I'm chewing greedily, wondering if I'd made a big mistake tonight. But at least I got to touch Verna.

Then, from the band's little plywood riser, I see him. Little under my height, but all meat—body shaped like a letter V with arms as thick as lightpoles. Swarthier in person—looks like a fucking werewolf in a lavender polo shirt stretched over his muscles and thick body hair. Pair of white slacks . . . those Teva sandal things, like he's at a luau! But swear to God I'm thinking some 1960's sword and sandal epic, *Hercules* . . . Steve Reeves. Lou Ferrigno.

No Missus in tow, however.

"Who's that, Verna?"

"Oh . . . dang it Dickie . . . he is someone you *definitely* must meet! My right hand, responsible for much of this growth, fundraising, remodeling. And to think I had to apprentice under him when I was back with Child and Family Services, now I am the boss."

She breaks, calling out "Mo, come over here," as I nervously finger a certain mini magnifying glass that's in my trouser pocket. Funny, it didn't tingle when Figgis was near.

He pops over, and says hello with that sing-songy whiteboy familiarity and I'm reminding myself I have a pistol and holster at the small of my back. Did I think this through—ask him to take a piss with me like women do to the "powder their noses," then house him in the mens room? Clearly, no . . .

"Dickie Cornish, Mo Roffe," Verna offers.

He extends an elbow instinctively but then draws it back. We don't shake. "Our boosters at the VA's been . . . held up," I mutter. Got to remember I'm a guest, not serving these people.

"The VA, huh?"

"Air Force . . . by default."

"*Awww* . . . no degree? I was ROTC in New Haven. Drove my proto-woke parents nuts. See what you avoided."

I shake my head. He's digging on digging at me. Predators love softening-up meat.

Verna's probably clocking the testosterone, so she chirps, "Mo, you might have heard in the news, year before the virus—awful sex trafficking ring up in Columbia Heights . . . girl and her baby kidnapped by a woman named Esmeralda Rubio . . . the late Jaime Bracht, guy who ran Homeland Security . . . was implicated after his death?"

"Oh snap!" Roffe intones. "This is him?"

Fuck this cat and his *oh snap*.

"He helped break that case, singlehandedly kept dozens of people from being deported by ICE. Even protected me." She exchanges a sweet look then swoons back to him, looking like he's Spartacus or some bullshit. "Sorry your better half couldn't be here. Oh my God, you heard the banter about Chief Figgis and the Mayor . . . somebody's going to need fundraising soon . . . "

"Aw, I don't like politics, Vee. Besides Em's packing up . . . tomorrow after morning therapy we're off . . . kayaking at Great Falls. Gotta get you out on the water, Vee . . . "

She's giggling and I just want to punch him.

"Hasn't rained in a while," I toss. "Guess less white water. Still, watch the mosquitos."

"You sound like you hit the Potomac a lot, dude."

"I've *camped* on the shore a few times."

"Ah, boys, I'm glad you met," Verna intercedes. "Sorry the party's winding down."

"Vee you need a ride home, gurl, say the word."

"Car service has got me tonight, from one of the sponsors."

"Cool. So, Dickie . . . count on you to see our gurl doesn't stay up too late tryna clean up every crumb, escort every guest back and tuck them in? You know how she *be* . . . "

"Got to get up early too. VA appointment. Meds. Paying for an old life."

"Hey, I got an idea," Roffe suddenly offers. "You come by after your appointment—see how we're doing new programming?"

"Um . . . Mo, Dickie probably wouldn't . . . "

"Love to."

"Cool, cool . . . see, my thing is early child trauma and post-trauma milieus."

"Figures."

"Pardon me?"

"Figures, given the peewees who come here."

"Yeah, well this is self-actualization, meditation therapy," he explains. "Better to conduct these without a parent, more often the mother. Children are protective of their mothers but that's concomitant with fear of loss, fear of the unknown associated with their mothers' homelessness, addiction, dysfunctional relationships and domestic abuse. That's one of the therapeutic tenets of Dr. Wilhelm Steif, ever hear of him . . . no? Yes, *ten* commandments in all, and I follow them to the letter."

"Because you're Moses."

He and Verna crack up. I pretend to laugh. This motherfucker . . .

"Dickie . . . it's a *date,* eh?"

Yes, pervert. Tomorrow. Thank you for making this easier. Though I wish I could part his Red Sea with an ACP round in his smug mug right now.

"Boys," Verna says, "I've got to glad-hand a bit. Don't go anywhere."

When she leaves I turn to this tanned Mixed Martial Arts block of concrete in front of me. "So, you fix little black and Latin kids?"

See those nostrils flare? "Um . . . no . . . again. Therapy."

"All homeless, poor. Mamas're pretty low?"

"I don't use value terms like 'low.' Or 'homeless, poor.'"

"But see, I was one, still am the other. I have a right to use the words because they actually mean shit to me."

"I heard you are studying to be a private investigator?"

"You do something wrong I should know of?"

"*Awwww* . . . no. I read you perfectly Dickie. You see another male . . . married but male nonetheless, for example, me—stuck close to Verna Leggett. A woman who you pretty much abandoned before the virus. Am I close?"

A bit. "Mr. Roffe . . . "

"For real Dickie it's just 'Mo.' 'Mr. Roffe' was my father and grandfather. More accurately, *Judge* Roffe and *Rabbi* Roffe."

"How'd you get *here,* Mo? Word is . . . you were at the old munie shelter, that fucked-up place."

"I'd been a resource teacher in DCPS, then counselor, yes. I'm also a LCSW . . . "

"No. I meant, rabbi . . . judge . . . and you went to Yale? Yet you're *here.* In the *real live.*" He frowns so I elaborate. "I was a Catholic Diocese and McDonald's-Giant Food award recipient—for D.C.'s top high school scholar-athletes. Full ride to Howard. Literature major, football, a badass fraternity. And yet I've been bum and dopefiend much of my adult life. That shit put me *here.* So what about you?"

"We don't know each other well enough for that. By the way, I also direct security staff when there's an incident with an at risk or special needs child . . . doing home visits. I work them like a drill sergeant."

Verna jumps back. "So . . . you gonna play nice tomorrow?"

"Cool, Vee," Moses signals. "Gonna bounce, walk the dogs, pack up Em correctly, then snooze. Dealbreaker if I cut out tomorrow after I give Dickie the tour?"

"Do your thing, Mo, honey," Verna almost gushes.

And the pervert's gone.

"Um . . . Verna . . . I know I just got here but, this—"

"Ain't your thing. I know. Good night, Dickie."

I'm chuckling now and have no clue what to say next.

She says it for me. "Don't be a stranger. Oh, I forgot to say, Dickie, I really like your . . . suit. You look like you need a pair of suspenders to go with it . . . a corn cob pipe . . . " She's teasing and I'm trying not to laugh. "Straw boater . . . piece of fried chicken . . . "

She doesn't touch me, just scrunches that nose, waves, mouths, "*Thank you,*" fades back into the dwindling crowd and the singer channels P.P. Arnold again with another Sixties psychedelic ballad, "Different Drum." It's like Mom's putting quarters in a jukebox up in Heaven. Or that middle place, where she's working off some shit . . . and she's giving me a strategy . . .

I take out my phone. "Stripe, yeah, coming home."

"Jefe, you sure you okay? Please leave Moses alone."

"Got an idea. Old is new."

"*Rain Man . . .* ?"

"I'm going to stash the piece now. The Ruger. Place here no one will find it but me, tomorrow . . . "

"*Qué*? Aw . . . Ricardo . . . "

He's never called me that before. Undeterred, maddened, I tell this poor kid, "We aren't done visiting the iniquities of the parent on children, like Commandment number two announces. His name's Moses. He should know . . . "

CHAPTER 17

Real Live

Another Green Line ride . . . and two transfers later, I'm walking the halls with a masked Moses Roffe, a jittery tourist in a jont that was once a sanctuary.

"Whoa, big guy . . . " Roffe teases. "Too much champagne last night? Or . . . sorry, I apologize . . . I'm betting you're *recovering*, right?"

"Whole time," I huff, catching my bearings and breath, "just been through . . . a lot . . . in the last day or so. I'm not a young anymore, you see. By the way that wasn't champagne because the labels said 'Oregon' so it was just . . . sparkling wine. Only a few brands are technically 'champagne.'"

"Of course."

See, this cat's giving me the eye as we tour the repainted and rewired digs . . . not with shade but like he's figured me out. He waves to mothers on their way to a parenting class then tells me, "Vee talked you up, Dickie. You've overcome quite a lot. But, um . . . ever been diagnosed, back in the day . . . for Asperger's? It's a whole different ballgame in the DSM now but—"

"No," cut him off. "I'm good."

"Well, you really weren't, per Vee. History of alcoholism, addiction . . . check it . . . sorry for the out of left field tip, man. It's how I'm wired—*to diagnose, to help*—and sometimes it rubs people the wrong way."

"Wired to rub people the wrong way? So have *you* ever been diagnosed autistic?"

"Touché. Apologies." Of course while he's yapping he's winking at more residents and staff like he's a rock star. "My granddad, Rabbi Roffe, taught us to do God's work. God's work is service, says my dad, Judge Roffe. Teaching, healing is service, says plain ole Mo."

"So where're your peoples, huh? Accent says local but not the District."

"Neighborhood of Baltimore . . . *Bawlermer,* just up the Parkway, *hon* . . . "

"Ah. Always around black folk? Don't mean any offense but you are pretty chill."

"Let's say the high-born WASPs, lowbrow rednecks at my high school used to say that Park Heights Avenue, where our house was, was the longest road in the world, because it went from Africa to Israel."

He's still all smiles, yet I discern the lingering hurt in his face. Almost made him human. Almost . . .

"Stamp," I reply, hoping to get his guard down, "look at any atlas and you see Israel's smack up against the African continent at Sinai. Those kids are grownfolk now, prolly show up for anti-mask rallies. Privilege of ignorance and arrogance, right?"

"*Preach,* Dickie. Preach. You have a very scholarly mind."

Uh-huh.

"Well, this is me, here," Roffe chirps, almost like girl despite his sinew and bulk. "Post-trauma program. This place has come a long away from just food, a bed, and a roof."

I peek in the small classroom, I recall it used to be ceiling-high with bunkbeds, stale smells. Several ten black and brown children are sitting cross-legged on colorful foam pads. Most are little girls, two boys. Stone fucking quiet and still. Yet they all snap-to like Daddy's leathernecks on deck when they clock Roffe.

"Trauma," I bait, "from sexual abuse?"

He chuckles. Yeah. Chuckles. "By custodial mothers or caregivers?" Roffe asks.

"By men preying on the mothers who are homeless, addicted, plain terrorized, so they look the other way."

"Dickie, I shoot video of the sessions—if that's where you're going."

I point into the room. "Is that what that is, on the desk?"

"No, I use my phone. That's the GoPro I use when I'm kayaking, climbing."

"You were at the old municipal shelter before it was closed, right? That's where you met Verna before she got the gig here."

He's squinting hard on those brown eyes. "Mr. Cornish, this is very strange . . . "

"I'm not 'Dickie' now?"

"I have work to do. And if I may take a shot in the dark here, I am *married* and Verna Leggett is my boss—in case this is some Byzantine torch you are carrying for her."

I want to drop this cat, veiny biceps be damned. I stick to my outline . . .

"On the street I knew this brother who geeked about a white dude, a counselor, at the munie . . . and, interestingly, investigated child endangerment cases at traps like the ole

Colonial View Motel. Said everyone loved this cat cause he helped children. Just wondering . . . "

"Who this person?"

"Kevin Washington."

"Never heard of him."

"Folks called him 'Big.'" I get nary a twitch. Oh he's a frosty bastard. "Haven't heard about Big in a brick, though. Hope he ain't been murked or died of the 'rona."

"I'll pray for Kevin," Roffe says. "Now if you'll let me get to my kids . . . "

"Speaking of prayer, I got a question about the Moses in the Bible . . . " That gives him pause . . . oddly. "Seeing that you come from rabbi and judge stock. First of the Ten Commandments, it always confused me. More poetic in Latin and Hebrew than King James English, but why is it 'You shall have no other gods before me,' rather than, 'There are no other gods out there in the cosmos but me.' Catch my drift? Almost sci-fi, huh?"

"Rabbi Roffe would ask if your confusion is genuine, or do you just get off on being profane . . . from your years as a *bum*."

"My years as a *bum* brought me to this horrific understanding of that Commandment, Mr. Roffe. One way to God, is to *be* a god, huh? Every pervert or killer, plugger . . . and pimp, they knew that. Holding absolute power over a helpless child who has no choices, defenses, is godlike. Pimps say the same thing about turning a woman out. That sound familiar . . . in your trauma studies?"

He's laughing. "Verna's moved on, Mr. Cornish. I hope you do, too." Then he finally leverages all that gym time, when he comes right under me and with deep snorts and unblinking eyes growls, "Now *fuck off* . . . before you get hurt, real bad."

I nod, I don't wolf or smirk. When he's in doing what he does with the kids, I duck into the old supply room where Fitz—Black Santa—would change into costume and literally be a black Kris Kringle for the *po'* kids on the SFME side. Gives a clear sightline to Roffe's playroom.

He's not even in there five minutes before he's calling it quits, hitting his phone, whispering something coarse, rapid. His eyes, face—I can tell he's scared. Not worried. Scared.

Indeed the kids are all filing out, bewildered, willy-nilly and he's brushing by all them with not another adult in sight. I text LaKeisha, tell her to get Katie into the hallway, as something's wrong with Moses Roffe. Verna's in a meeting and said stop by before I leave. Can't, Verna. Because I buried a gun . . .

. . . yeah, right there in the detritus and moss and ivy where the ancient basement steps to the kitchen at St. Jude's meets the delivery bay at SFME. Camera's always faced the bay, not the steps, so the steps are where we'd party. Me, Big Stevie—Esteban. And Black Santa. Sure enough, Roffe's breaking from that rear bay in his bullshit outdoorsmen peels. Unless he's portaging a fucking kayak on the subway he's not going to nobody's river!

"Real live," I whisper inwardly, feeling like a genuine gumshoe despite the pains in my head. Got to hold it together . . .

I watching him cut over from Half Street to South Capitol. Yeah, moving up toward the ole Capitol Skyline Hotel.

Lord, he's storming right into hotel's lobby and I got to roll, *fast*, into the poolside fence to keep out of sight. Until very recently the jont serviced a lot of hayseed tourists in their red

Trump hats. Then again, how am I welcome with unlicensed .380 hidden in my damn trousers?

Hotel security's thick with dudes in green windbreakers—Africans, judging from the mic checks just over the pool fence in accents or whatever Bantu stuff is.

Gotta get eyes on the smoked-glass lobby!

Stripe's suddenly blowing up my phone, killing that effort for now. Probably safe enough to answer. He says he's leaving Navy Yard Metro Station and will close in from that side.

"*Bueno, chico,*" I reply. "*Sígueme con la aplicación en tu teléfono* . . . like Mr. Sugars had on me. My phone'll be the blue icon on your screen, okay?"

Okay, I see him now . . . bellying up to a window table in the lobby coffee shop . . . tapping his phone now. With fury. Texting for a meet. I know it. I will stake my life on it. Can't be with Big; got to be with someone respectable-looking among his pervert group . . . otherwise, why this jont? His wife Meghan, maybe? Just got to wait, see what falls from the tree . . .

. . . and it's going on ten minutes now . . . I've had to relocate twice to stay out of the guards' eyeballs and I'm really getting nauseous, achy like I got the flu and I know it isn't from that shot. Vax can put down for awhile out's said, but it ain't that quick.

Then I see it. Black Chevy Suburban is pulling up on I Street, Southwest, yet stops well out of sight from the coffee shop windows. Dashboard cop lights. Big cop whip antenna. Cop plates. Just like Figgis'.

A plainclothes piggy, earpiece in, idles the Suburban and I'm biting my lip till I taste salty blood, praying it isn't the Figgis . . .

. . . and I swear to God I should've called this off. Head's killing me again. I twist away and fucking dry heave into a big potted shrub belonging to the hotel and Lord I know what's going to happen next. Agave . . . I told you I needed to see Kapoor . . .

You don't need the Mumbai medics. You got Gunney!

So . . . keep your fucking eyes on the Suburban onaccount look who's getting out. Onaccount your dumbfuck problems have evolved into wet-ass trouble.

Tall sumbitch, slick gray hair. Bond villain bearing, Boris Karloff face. This ofay should scare you more than Figgis, Junior. And he's communing with Moses Roffe.

Antonelli's in the lobby now, at the table.

You call Stripe. "Hold your position a sec." Wise move. "We got cops."

"*Dios . . . okay.*"

Whoops. Antonelli's pointing a finger at Roffe. Roffe smacks the table. Roffe's leaving . . .

"Stripe. F-Forget the hold. Just . . . just shadow me. I'm the blue dot or your screen, okay? Easy to follow. You are the red dot on mine."

The son of the judge, grandson the rabbi, the pious yogurt-eating hipster . . . he's not headed back to SFME and then challenge the whitewater. He's charging down I Street; gives a middle finger to the idling Suburban.

You slip behind a pile of construction sand where I meet the exit ramp to South Capitol. The big Chevy literally creeps after this Jew at single-digit speed. Forget Roffe's swagger—this is *gangster.* This the FBI in the Sixties, NYPD in the Seventies and Nineties. Shit your commie Black Panther profs at Howard used to babble about, right?

Abruptly, the Suburban does a three-pointer back toward the hotel. You see it scoop up Antonelli and gun the engine. The vehicle disappears just as Roffe's moving across Lansburgh Park.

"No . . . this is right. He's crazy."

Possibly son, onaccount the dude's charging like a bull into one of those last islands of Negrodom, the ghetto Atlantis in Southwest: the Carrollsberg Dwellings.

Jont's all pitched-roof, one-story townhouses with doors fronting the street, unlike the ramshackle cinderblock boxes with tore-up foyers across the river where Al-Mayadeen's mother lives. And they're tidy: no garbage or car tires and bicycle parts strewn about. Back in the day this housing project was a wellspring of customers, live-in hostages and recruits for the crack rock empire Croc's parents built. Now, other than an occasional nine-millimeter beat down over bootleg or Tina, or random fisticuffs over intra-family drama, the spot's quiet.

Roffe's entering a ring of houses where parking lot forms the inner ring.

Couple of cars there, one getting waxed by some white-haired old dude . . . peewees horse around on their bikes or jump double-dutch, and boy, you best better tip-toe onaccount you are almost as out of place as he is. To Housing cops, you're a stranger—there to score. To those peewees on recon for the pluggers, you look like an undercover Housing cop.

Wonderful. This ofay's pounding on a townhouse door, hollering. The peewees and old man wiping down his whip are staring. Whatever's going to pop will do so most ricky-tick so get ready.

Roffe desists only when the door flies open and raggedy sista, looks to be her forties but who knows . . . pink flannel bathrobe, leather sandals with busted straps edges out. She got something on her face and you see it's a plastic mask connected to a small thermos bottle-looking thing. Oxygen? Okay . . . remember when DC Medicaid gave out a lot of those cheap-ass things when whitefolks got the ventilators and high-tech hospital suites? Nevermind . . . Roffe's going in, shutting the door behind him.

Why you got heavy feet? This is the life you wanted, son: tough sumbitch, P.I., gumshoe! Get your ass moving!

There ya go. You're flush to the wall right under a window occluded by dingy, water-stained blinds.

Muffled voices, yeah . . . then a thump . . . a squeal. Then clear as day, Roffe yells, "*You fucking ugly black bitch I'm gonna crush her turkey neck. Now you tell Big to be a man and come out of that room, understand?*"

Big . . . ?

And the reply, "*Y'all fetch him from Hain's Point an' he gone, Mistah Roffe!*"

Do you really need to hear more? You lift the .380, thumb the safety.

Your big foot hits the door in the sweet spot. All project doors got sweet spots. Cheaper to replace rather than get something safe . . .

. . . and it splinters off the hinges and you're inside, aiming the .380 between at a spot between Roffe's wide-as-dinner-plate eyes.

You glance down at his hairy-knuckled hand . . . it's around the throat of a bawling little girl, her braids flapping as she squirms.

"*Who da fuck's dis?*" the sista with oxygen tank screeches through her mask.

Roffe flexes like he's getting froggy despite the gat pointed at him. He gets wise when he senses that meanness in your eyes. Yeah, you can thank me later. He shrinks backward, releases the child.

The girl scampers to the woman but this heifer promptly snarls and back-arms her, hard, onto a sofa. The girl rolls into a ball.

Damage done, this nasty bitch yanks off her mask and wheezes in anger—at Roffe, not you, "You promise po-lice leave my man alone . . . now they back?"

"Shut up!" you shout. "Ain't no police, no Fed." Then to Roffe, "On your knees, pervert, hands on your head!"

"On my knees . . . on this nasty carpet?" he sneers. "I got *friends* asshole. You're just a speck."

Ruger's barrel isn't but a thumb's length long, yet when pressed against his cheek this muscled-up asshole sure enough quiets. Yet as he leers at up at you, the little girl abruptly starts screaming, "*Daddy*!"

And behold, the plea summons Big like some tore-up black genie . . . materializing through a bedroom door . . . congealing into a human cannonball that mows down you and Roffe in a blur and there goes here goes your lil' Ruger, out the door, bouncing on the pavement. Far the hell out of reach.

Now it's skin on skin. You're the old fart. You're going to catch the damage.

Maybe not, onaccount you're the cat who's seen the foulest shit, the days on the street, nights at the CDF when the C.O.'s turned off the lights in the dorm, snickering.

So when Big rears up to hammer down two fists down on your crouching form, you pull back then pump your legs to power an upcut to his jaw. Swear you must have made him bite his damn tongue off onaccount he's slobbering ruby snot.

With you in a melee, Roffe's either going to kirk you or run. He makes his choice. You feel a sharp pain across your back. You see the glint of a spindly floor lamp's sections. The pieces fall harmlessly to the carpet yet he's taunting you to square-off.

Sumbitch's younger, swole and yeah, those pecs're rippling under the Ivy League T-shirt.

Thoughts of little Ky flood and the Colonial View flood you with rage and raise your paws and go hard at him. He lands a bad kiss on your forehead but damn you might as well have a steel plate up there, eh son? Your revenge is a hip-driven right hook to his lower ribs. A pivot left and twist is all you need to for an opposite hook into Roffe's cheek . . . and the sumbitch's running now . . . rather, stumbling like a wino . . . out the front door.

He falls on the oily pavement . . . and lucky him . . . he is in easy reach of that fucking little .380.

Now you are standing there, thinking you are going to get shot in this miserable place when all you had to do was stay in Dr. Kapoor's waiting room. Wish you had your mama's rosary, now?

With a satisfied roar, Roffe stretches for the pistol.

Pray, son.

CHAPTER 18

The Gingerbread House

*P*HEW . . . HEAR HIM? THAT'S GOD, whispering, "*Not yet.*" Onaccount you're clocking a Nike stomping Roffe's big were-wolfish hand.

"R-Rain Man!" Stripe stammers.

This kid. Who'd a thunk it! Stripe scoops up the .380 and aims it, shakily, at Roffe as you call, out of breath, "*Guay*, kid. Come 'round here, pass me the iron."

He does. Too late to stop someone you forgot about from charging past you, out the door, taking even Roffe by surprise.

All you see is an oxygen tank trailing behind this crazy snipe as if weightless. She halts only to scream the names of random dudes into the lot and courtyard. Sure, the Carrollsburg's tamer than back in the day, but damn if the ghetto cavalry's not going to come blasting when one their own's in peril.

She'll start the massacre with the kitchen knife you see in her hand before Roffe does. She's on him, yet in the second it takes for you to debate whether to fire a round to separate them or jump in, the hairy ofay easily gets the blade from her.

His first thrust glances off the oxygen tank. The second tears into her abdomen and she makes a burping noise, drops to the ground.

Neither wrath nor horror's on his bearded face when he whips around to you and Stripe . . . blade high and drooling red. Just a weird, robotic calm.

Dinosaur brain and muscle memory, right son? You go and put two ACPs into the sumbitch. *Ba-bam*!

Easy-peezy. You've done it before. In a weird, robotic calm . . .

"S-Stripe . . . *Stripe*!" you sputter. "*Coño* . . . go inside!"

Wouldn't move if he could. See, you forgot about Big. He's crawling out of the apartment as if a pathetic creature in a silly horror movie's death scene. A bloody froth covers his jaw like a pink beard and the big nigga's nudges his writhing woman like a wounded dog to a dying master. She's leaking hepatic blood from the smell of it.

And then you hear the sirens.

Like, *a lot of units*, shrieking-in from I and K Streets.

You know goddamn well nobody in the projects calls Twelve that fast. And even if they did, the whole force doesn't show up as if space aliens dropped them from the sky. And here you are, LCP barrel still smoking . . .

"Antonelli," you mutter. You bark now at Stripe: "*La niña*! *Muevete*!"

Impressive! You even got enough mind—given how *fucked* you now are—to hit your knees for the two ACP casings.

Now you and Stripe look like leathernecks evac-ing the fallen. He's got the girl, limp from shock. You're half-dragging, half-carrying Big's stinking bulk.

Panting, frantic, loaded down . . . but stay aware, son . . . think of Esteban . . . *Big Stevie* . . . remember back in your hobo days, how he'd shown you a garage on Delaware Avenue . . . shaded nooks to hide, sleep, piss . . . an unlocked spigot for cold water . . .

"Down this way!" you direct.

Your party serpentines through this warren of po'folk hovels and yuppie condos, and you better believe, Junior, that all of them are gawking so you better pray the niggas won't snitch and the ofays don't want to get involved. You end up in sight of a huge concrete garage serving the playhouse and waterfront businesses. Just in time, too, as the sirens are almost up your asses . . .

. . . and so you're into the garage, about to bum-rushing the elevator. Suddenly Stripes stops dead, gasping. You're about to scream at the little bastard, and then you feel something pressed hard to your temple, and it ain't Big, kissing you. It's a gunsight.

"Put this fucker on his ass . . . drop the three-eighty on the ground. Raise your hands."

It's woman's voice, calmly commanding you despite the encroaching sirens. And it's one that knows you're carrying an LCP. Dinosaur brain's telling you to fight, then flee. But pain like your scalp's being ripped off your crown is assaulting, yanking you down to the blacktop with Big. Got to work fast, son, onaccount your monkey brain's coming back, and that's curtains for ole gunney. You catch a glimpse of dark blue BDUs, cop kicks.

"Officer . . . *Sanchez*?" you mumble.

Yep. She's keeping her Sig level as you drop your Ruger. "H street, then up at the VA," she recounts. "Hard to keep up with, Big Papi."

Monkey brain's such a pussy brain, but hey, you did indeed put two slugs into a white Yale man. "I-I want to report an assault on a minor . . . attempted murder . . . with a knife . . . self defense . . . I'll talk to a lawyer before I talk . . . to Chief Figgis."

Funny that. Chica's stuffing your pistol in her thigh pocket. "You have about thirty seconds to hide yourselves." She then looks to Stripe. "*Oigame, bicho! Mantenga a la niña quieta.*" Back to you she huffs, "All right . . . they want the one called 'Big.' He was sprung from Park Police holding at Hain's Point this morning . . . "

You're mind-fucked. "This a set-up?"

"They're coming, Cornish . . . "

"I didn't start this shit!"

"No, you swooped into this like Batman and then wild-carded like the Joker, *cabrón*. They know who you are but don't know you're here . . . but they will in about ten fucking seconds."

"Why are *you* here?"

"Because they will kill you."

Audible radio mic calls from cops on the ground obviate the urgency. You and Stripe are now tumbling over a low concrete wall, huddling . . . struggling to keep Big and the child from making noise.

There's a drainage opening where the wall meets the pavement; now you catch the action at ankle-level. You spy the piggies converging on the projects. None of these motherfuckers are patrol jakes. Crazy mixed bag of plainclothes: undercover jump-out squad spooks trailing dreadlocks, crew cut rednecks wearing tac vests over T-shirts and jeans, detectives in business suits and blazers!

Two male voices soon push up on Sanchez. Legit question: she's out of her district. She tells them her brother's a Housing cop. She was on her way down to hang with him on his break.

"I heard the ten-thirty-three and Code-One for SOD. Came to see if I could help."

One of them's doing a radio check with D.C. Housing on her brother. The second asshole presses, "The other patrol units heard the follow-up ten-twenty-two and backed off—so why didn't you? This is top security SOD business, not patrol."

"Then where are the tac officers?"

They don't answer about SWAT. A honcho shows up, wolfing at them, then her.

"Officer, someone's put a *critical* confidential informant in the grave unless we can get an ambulance in here . . . "

Yeah, you heard him. And Stripe's groan almost gave you all away. Should have stayed at the VA? *Nah* . . . should never have been at that fucking CVS, letting Al-Mayadeen Thomas stick to you like your sweaty soaked towel. The boots, kicks and penny loafers are getting closer to the wall . . .

. . . then one cop's voice confirms, "Tell HQ and that she checks out. Her brother's a uniform at Housing. Give the media mopes the usual shit when they come snooping around, make it consistent with One-Six-Threes if the Chief demands a review."

Your ears're almost flaming-up like back in the day when the Scooby smoke and boat fumes would congeal in your Eustachian tubes. 163s are incident reports—as you learned in your little YouTube class. Oh yeah . . . "*if the Chief wants a review* . . . "

Sanchez peeks over the wall when these sumbitches depart. Cooing at the shaken little girl. Scowling at you.

"Get up, we're leaving," she orders.

Black Santa'd be so proud of your figuring, boy. "Who's the rogue. Figgis . . . or them?"

"*Mierda,* Cornish . . . "

Stripe's eyeing you for the move and it's clear from his shallow breaths and whispered curses that staying there isn't the tip warming him. So what's going to be, Killer. Remember when Mr. Sugars stung with that nickname? No matter which side of Twelve's jocking you, boy—Dr. Jeckyll or Mr. Hyde in blue—you're lunching on attempted murder with an unlicensed .380!

But Sanchez is cool as that green dip those people eat, eh? She smirks, pulls your LCP from her pocket. Even the little girl you've rescued is staring as Sanchez pops out the clip, ejects a round . . . and then dumps the gat in a storm sewer intake fronting the wall. Hasn't rained in a week but damned if your eyes down follow the fucker down, and yours catch a splash. She's re-pocketing the clip and round, though.

Your jaw's down there in the sewer as Stripe whispers in awe, "De fock?"

"Happy?" Sanchez barks. "Now get in my unit . . . them in the back, you up front with me."

"*A dónde?*" Stripe mumbles before you can ask, onaccount you're still paralyzed from what this cop just did.

"We call it the Gingerbread House."

Don't know how long you all are criss-crossing bridges in and out of Virginia to give SOD a wide berth before pain's spearing you from behind your left eye socket. Ooops, then your right. Like somebody blinded you; your nose's clogged and swollen now and your only reliable sense is through your ears.

You hear yammering in Spanish: Stripe and Sanchez. Then Sanchez, only . . .

"Is it diabetes . . . *el sucre* ?"

Your Tonto replies, “No . . . he get *pills.* Make he head right. B-But . . . they mess him up more. *Oye* . . . fock . . . *por favor, Ricardo* . . . don’ leave like this, bro’ . . . ”

I know. I fucked up.

And the unit’s running lights are off, siren stifled . . . a long way from Southwest . . . a long way from the projects. Leafy lanes, cobblestone . . . elm, ginko, dogwoods and tall forsythias hiding old homes, nice as shit old homes . . .

“I know. I fucked up.” But this time I hear the words outside my ears, not in a dream.

“*Awake*?” Sanchez quips.

Yes. I am.

I clock the street signs. “This . . . this is *Georgetown.* We . . . in custody?”

Rather than answer, Sanchez motions to the back, through the cage separating the rear seats from us. I see Big’s slumped over, handcuffed. “I think he shit himself?” Sanchez complains. “Check him out, *bicho.*”

Stripe, still holding and stroking the little girl, scoffs, “Is jus’ *chivo*!”

“*Oye bicho* . . . mind how you talk to adults,” Sanchez snaps back, turning the unit onto Avon Place Northwest.

“You don’t get to talk to him like that. Sanchez—*look at me*!”

She ignores me, pulls her mic. “HQ-Artemis-HQ . . . copy? This is Sanchez, two-dee-four-seven-one. Open the gate. Got some visitors. Ten-four.”

A set of iron gates open and you are out of the cloak of trees and barrier shrubs and onto a drive bisecting a broad lawn . . .

. . . and damn if there isn’t a gingerbread house . . . materializing at the crest of the drive!

A custardy tan with white trim. Old as fuck, identical wings and cupola over the entrance. Sanchez parks the unit and another female jake—this one a sister looking all tough with corn rows and shades—trundles over to the driver's side window, hands on her piece.

"This unavoidable?" she barks at Sanchez, lifting her lunettes to us.

When Sanchez nods the sister yanks open the back door and snatches the little girl from Stripe's unexpectedly tender hold.

The child'd been sleeping. Now she's thrashing, mewling. Big remains cuffed in the unit, in a trance, babbling Lord-knows.

I climb out with Stripe, and he's dazed and I'm too fucked in the head to savvy whether we're guests or prisoners. As to "we" I don't mean Big. Oh, he's now wide awake, and screaming for me to help him as Sanchez motors away . . .

CHAPTER 19

Lay Down with Lambs

"Welcome to Tudor Place," this little white chick calls out to me. She's pale, freckled—all summer cheer in a diaphanous white shift, short denim jacket, flip-flops exposing her toes painted in intervals of yellow and white. "They're in the Gardens. I'd ask that you leave your mobile phones and any dangerous implements with one of the officers to the right. Now I'm going to take your temperature with this device . . . and ask if either of you have been fully vaccinated for COVID."

I grunt yes. Now Stripe's clocking me as if I'd been beatified.

"They do you, bro'?"

A gloved cop comes over to hand Stripe one of those super masks, slather his hands in antiseptic goop. She gives him a flyer for a free vax. Me, they just hand a mask.

We're escorted through a rotunda. Ornate, compelling. Never been to the jont before, not even for a school field trip.

Stripe's wandering toward a bank of huge windows fronting a rear slate patio.

"*Escuchar* Rain Man," he abruptly signals. "Like school recess . . . *dios* . . . "

Indeed, I hear laughter, shrill calls, play growls and grunts. Music . . .

. . . and out there I clock maybe thirty kids, from tots to teens, most black and brown but a few white, some Asian-looking little ones, too. Running barefoot in the manse's garden, prancing to pop tunes crackling in from massive speakers, blowing bubbles, painting their faces, studying a Ronald McDonald-looking clown manipulating creatures from balloons. Masked adults are in identical blue-and-red aprons with logos, tending stations all up and down the garden's paths and on grassy spots . . . grilling D.C. half-smokes because no other hot dog hisses and smells like that . . . spinning cotton candy . . . dripping batter in hot grease for funnel cakes. At the grounds' far-end is a massive air-inflated bounce castle next to a trampoline fitted with safety nets.

And while there are a few other men out there, *all* of the jakes securing this spot are women.

"Dickie," I hear. "Please . . . come with me."

Linda Figgis looks like a mom from the 1980s: frilly yellow peasant top, white culottes, big clear-rimmed shades resting on her head, flat clog-looking sandals . . . and one of blue-and-red aprons. She's got a marionette's apple-cheeked blush from the sun, and I smell the Le Labo rose under the timber of sweat, burnt sugar, grill smoke. Her face is juicy with chirpy-cheeriness. Those blue eyes, nah . . . cold, almost purplish in hue.

Without breaking my glance I order Stripe to go get a lemonade and a half-smoke, chill.

He yanks down his mask. "Nah, bro' I stay. You need back-up."

"*Esta bien*, kid . . . " I tap his boney shoulder, smile. "Keep your mask up, keep me in your line of sight." I address our "host" I'm figuring. "Is that okay if the kid eats?"

"That's the theme of the day. He's welcome here."

As Stripe moves off, reticent and reluctant, I press, voice breaking at times, "What is this place . . . who are these people . . . who are these kids?"

Figgis is leading me to a bunch of Adirondack chairs, "Stripe's come a long way from Mt. Pleasant chain-snatcher. You've done well with him."

"Cut the bullshit. You've lost control of your own fuckin' department. Who is Roffe to them . . . who was Big to them?"

"Hey," she tuts, "watch the language, look around. Smile but speak in a low tone." She sits; my knees are shaking but I stand. "Ah . . . more like it," she continues, wriggling her toes. "Been on my feet all day. And . . . you're sweating heavily . . . you look peaked. Nice and shady here, pretty . . . "

"I want the truth. Everything. Because everything you said in your office, was a lie."

She smiles. Iggs me. "This was the Peter family's house. Designed by William Thornton, first head of the Patent Office, helped design the Capitol. Mrs. Peter was a Custis, related to Martha Washington. Here they indeed hosted Martha . . . the Tayloes, who lived in Thornton's famous 'Octagon House,' the Brents, who build the Brentwood neighborhood, the Smiths, who built the Eckington neighborhood, the Barlows, who built Kalorama . . . "

What choice to I have but to play? I sit my body relaxes, my head still feels like someone doused with kerosene and lit a match. "Their slaves did that, not them."

"Fair point."

"Now that we got that out' th' way . . . I have Antonelli's entire division after me. I was in a shoot-out. Your officer tanked my pistol."

"Shoot-out? Reports filed already say it was a *one-way* shoot-out, so you may want to thank Raffi Sanchez."

"Don't clown me, Chief." I'm whispering, for the little happy lambs' sake.

She purses those Betty Boop lips pensively, tells me, "Moses Roffe was DOA at GW Hospital."

Yeah, I'm sliding around the wooden chair and the thing squeaks and shudders as if I busted it.

"You went by the VA—pretty much begged for inpatient status. That true?"

"*N-No* . . . how'd you know that?"

"Don't unravel on me now. I need you." Yeah, and those blue eyes are still dark, chilly.

"You . . . need me?"

"Everything will be apparent soon."

For an instant my first mind is to grab Stripe and walk on out, daring her Amazons to stop me. But this spindly white dude appears, toting an old-school clipboard and his phone. He's clocking the bloodstains on my shirt, my mask down to expose my swollen lip, bloodcaked lip . . . my mean, distant look.

"Uh . . . Chief . . . Emmie wants to serve just fruit for dessert, but the volunteers already made funnel cakes and cotton candy."

"Tell Emmie to serve all of it. You hear, David? We have some potential campaign donors here and I want them to see I mean business for our children. *Abundance*!"

"Um . . . okay," he replies, doubtless looking for his balls. "And, well . . . "

"Oh . . . Mr. Cornish here is . . . my guest. He's a *famous* private detective. A sleuth, like on TV shows. Mr. Cornish, did you see my piece in Vanity Fair, on the *Law and Order* character 'Olivia Benson?'"

"No."

"Um . . . hey, hello Mr. Cornish. Uh, Sergeant Brooks also was wondering if you wanted the . . . *new* . . . girl . . . driven over the volunteer house, or can she be released here so she can attend the party with precautions."

I'm leaning-in now. "New girl?" The one I killed Roffe to save?

"Do a rapid-test on her, if okay, then get her cleaned up, let her join the party."

"Of course, Chief. But this . . . atmosphere . . . might be overwhelming."

Figgis twists in her Adirondack, seemingly more annoyed with him than empathizing with my afternoon of flying lead and rogue cops. "*Take care of it, David.*"

He skitters off.

"Campaign donors . . . yeah," I quip.

"Walk with me," the Chief commands, flipping down her mask.

So here we are, among the rollicking flock . . . Daddy'd call them porch monkeys and yard apes . . . and every single one stops and stares at me, almost enthralled. Can't be the wrinkled, bloodied camp shirt or dingy trousers. I still exude "bum" no matter what I do.

"It's your *size*," Figgis asserts, however. "Many would be frightened of big males, but . . . there's something about *you*. Kids know menace. However, they also can sniff out when menace can be a *protector*. My experts tell me that a lot of these children who go on to manifest dissociative disorders when they become adolescents . . . and even *adults* have imaginary friends who can be downright ugly, cruel."

She's jabbing close to my dick. "You're talking out your neck. You have no idea."

"Oh, I disagree," she comes back. "Dickie, who'd you rather have on your side when the real world's abusing you? A tittering sprite princess . . . or a fucking ogre? It's no accident, for example, that *teddy bears* . . . are bears, right? Who's your bear?"

Not siced for her choice of words.

More kids start to gather as we approach the cotton-candy apparatus so she's maintaining the cheesy smiles and waves as she says, "Things got out of hand today."

"I started a war," I whisper.

"No, hon'. You shattered the attrition, the stalemate of the trenches. Had no choice but to bring you here . . . "

She's clocking the beads of sweat blooming on my brow. A lanky, brassy-toned girl whose mouth is sticky with that pink cotton candy goo rushes up, hugs her. As Figgis embraces the child I push, "So you and the Mayor are queens of civil rights when the TV cameras are on and little kids are around. When they're not, I guess folks're beat down, shot down . . . suffering, ignored . . . when there's bigger picture involved?"

Still squeezing the child Figgis mocks, "There's a bigger picture involved, hon'."

The girl peels herself off the Chief and runs away. "Today SOD bumrushed the Carrollsburgh," I press, "like it's Iwo Jima—over a little girl? Over Big?"

"Will anyone miss Big?"

"You're serious?"

"Tamika Kemeh Washington's mother is Dretta Kemeh, age thirty-eight . . . from Ghana originally, green card marriage to Kevin Washington a.k.a. Big."

"You didn't know he and Al-Mayadeen Thomas were half-brothers, did you?"

"Glad I sent you fishing. And you caught a 'big' one."

"Shit . . . yeah, you are an Oscar-winner, Chief. You wanted him all along . . . and Roffe?"

"Before we go on, you realize this relationship makes Tamika and K'ymira cousins. I had to find Big before Dante could bring him in. I didn't count on the Park Police. Dante has more friends embedded there than I do . . . "

"And I'm your friend?"

"*Christ-on-a-cracker* . . . " she complains as we approach an iron gate to a smaller topiary, a bit farther away from the kids. "Listen. Dretta Kemeh is an abusive mother. Allowed Big to molest Tamika, just like we're sure he molested Ky, years ago. Now, we'd lost track of Tamika when Fairfax County Virginia Foster Care returned custody of her to Dretta based on a false report from a D.C. social worker who also's staff at SFME, then Dretta moved back to D.C. in her own subsidized townhouse miraculously available at the Carrollsbugh, with the blessings of this official and even MPD. Not *my* MPD."

"Roffe? And—"

"And someone in SOD, countermanding what our new liaison with Child and Family Services recommended. I'd heard rumors since Ky's kidnapping that Al-Mayadeen's mother was stonewalling something. You broke that up in less than an hour and managed to link him to Big, to Roffe. Good work. Anything else you want to tell me?"

"Nah, anything else you wanna tell my big gullible ass? Like why is the Chief of Police tracking one kid. *One*?" *Unless* . . . oh yes . . . my chest's heavy, I feel cold despite the summer sun.

"I'm tracking dozens and dozens." There it is. And this woman just shrugs. "Let's get back. Everyone's looking at us by ourselves. People will talk."

I hit her straight. "You couldn't put a case on your top suspects for K'ymira . . . because someone fucked with your evidence. You gonna tell me now it was SOD, mutinied against you. You gonna tell me know that everyone out there among the blackfolks was right, and the true crime documentaries and all that other shit was dead wrong, magpie-ing your lies. You gonna tell who among your Blue Boy Band kidnapped, even killed, that little girl . . . "

"Oh it's worse than that, Dickie. Those sots who broke into the Capitol to steal electoral college ballots, ziptie 'enemies,' whatever. There's subset of them who say the government's filled with pedophiles, rapists—in the basement of a pizza spot, remember that? It's a page from a recipe book written long ago."

"Cut the parables, Linda, I'm not a child."

"Invent a scarecrow for the rubes and hillbillies, distracting them *from what you yourself you are doing.* Can you guess who thought-up that cover story, years ago? Dante Antonelli. I mean, something so ridiculous yet plausible to an audience of lunatics and their enablers."

Jesus, Mary and Joseph. "And you knew he was a pimp. Covering for Roffe, who's a child molester. Yet here you stroll in this garden, allowing it to happen, having me to do . . . yeah, *dirty work.*"

"Have some lemonade."

Her retainers in blue are clocking us, like workers eyeballing the queen bee.

"Dickie, I'm going to hurt you with what I'm about to say. So think about what I said to you in your apartment, in my office. And why indeed I found you, at all. Do you really think I haven't seen the full file on you, what happened to you?"

"You . . . you said . . . it was redacted."

"I'm Chief of Police of the capital of the civilized world. And fib when I must."

I swear it feels like I'm pissing my pants. I lean on a bench, praying it's not actually happening.

"Two years ago former DHS Secretary Jaime Bracht's murdered in his hunting cabin, along with an ex-Ranger and private Iraq contractor named Burton Sugars—Bracht's fixer. Feds say a slick K Street lawyer of Bracht's and a Mexican national named Esmeralda Rubio survived the carnage . . . and the attorney is now a solo practitioner . . . with a mysterious client who pays with old school money orders . . . for *adoption* services? Sound about right?"

"No . . . no that's right."

"The cover story was manufactured days after a Bracht's death *and* a gun battle in Mount Pleasant. We're told the Otis Street Brigada and MS-Thirteen were involved trafficking of teenagers from Central America. Only when the smoke clears, we're arresting innocent Otis Street folks and civilians, not MS-Thirteen. But someone says you and your sidekick Stripe were there . . . "

"Why are you doing this to me?"

"Because what you did to rich scum like Bracht . . . " she gets real close, right under me because I'm so tall and I don't know why suddenly she's not nervous about the kids looking. " . . . made an *impression* on me."

"W-What?"

"How did Woodman's officers corroborate your Princess Goins connection so fast through Al-Mayadeen's mother? How'd you think I mobilized the command staff and made a big show about invading your miserable little hovel on Georgia Avenue. I've been a fangirl for a *long* time. And indeed, *your* fans are my friends."

"Verna? Nah . . ."

She nods. "All this time, I'd been looking for a monster to battle the *real* monsters. Then I realized I didn't need a monster, a weapon."

I'm staring at blue eyes now . . . with tears in my own. "So what am I?"

"Oh hon'. You're my *pig*."

"I'm done, I'm out . . . *fuck you* . . . "

"*Whoa . . . whoa big boy*. My officers get tense when they see you making big gestures. See, my daughters love this classic movie . . . well, classic to me at least. *Babe*."

My malady takes over. "George Miller . . . wanted a change from the Aussie *Mad Max* films . . . made tale about a little pig . . . who thought it was a sheep dog . . . "

"Yep! A brave, honorable little pig," she repeats. "But the farmer, the animals knew Babe wasn't what it seemed. Hiding there, in plain sight. But wolves, villians . . . *monsters* who hurt without consequence, all they saw was a pig." Her eyes narrow. "Ghenghis Kann, Bracht . . . Roffe: how many others *never* fucking knew what hit them, huh Dickie?"

"That's . . . that's not me. That's not me . . . " The children are all shooting admiring glances at me from the great lawn and I'm ashamed . . .

"Hey . . . it's all right," she coos. "We need to get you back in the poke, hunker down a bit, before I unleash you, little curly tail and all, on Dante . . . *again*."

"You're . . . you're the clever one, Linda, not Antonelli. Jesus. Lot had to fall in place . . . for what—so you could prove to him that you didn't fuck up K'ymira's case? That you're the better cop, the queen bee? They didn't just pimp out Ky's mother. Nah, she was something *special,* some asset to be guarded."

"So?"

"So your pig wants to know—you answered the 'why me,' so . . . why *now*?"

"All right. The virus. CiCi Thomas dies. Al-Mayadeen Thomas, who'd been writing me, Dateline NBC, Discovery ID, any true crime nut or 'no one cares about our missing children of color' activist is released early. Then Biden and Harris close the private prisons like Rivers so he can't go back anyway, and now this highly-motivated yet stupid man is loose. He's dying."

"He was your lightning rod. And . . . the teddy bear?"

"Yes. I arranged to have it delivered to him. I saved it from being 'misplaced' in our evidence storage . . . so parked it with a friend at the Bureau."

"Misplaced. So a cop was involved in this kidnapping, after all?"

Before she can dodge or lie I hear this earsplitting noise: a toddler's scream, the kind emitted when they demand attention for a simple task they mastered. A kid's pushing a stroller, likely its own, across grass . . .

. . . I'm remembering an imp with nappy, brick colored hair.

And now I see more of them. Faces on those cracked screens. Proffered in that Hell Motel. Some a bit older, some just as their images in frozen my skull. They are laughing as they chase each other, chewing on half-smokes or dusted in a funnel cake's powdered sugar . . .

I'm dizzy and nauseous, like after my first ever hit of the K2.

"*Raynata . . .* " I swing back into the Chief's face. "*You bitch.*"

"We use the same tools as our enemies," she tells me. Matter-of-fact, no biggie.

"Kidnappers . . . from *mothers* . . . same ones being abused themselves? That's why you wanted me away from the Colonial View?"

She pulls me in close, and the lambs think we're all huggy. "*Mind yourself . . .* "

"I tracked Roffe to the Colonial View, too. All my leads go through there but you had me snake-bit from rip, goddamn you! You're no better than Antonelli . . . "

She's trying so damn hard to make it look like we are in a playful clutch she's almost muffled into my chest. "Is that how you think of Verna Leggett?"

I clinch my eyelids and release her, fidget away to a stand of red roses when she mentions Verna. Like it's the *coup de grace.*

I raise my head when I hear thuds in the warm, moist turf. A couple of older kids are suddenly in front of me, asking if I'm okay, offering to get me fruit punch or a slushie. One girl with afro-puffs almost as big as her head, huge almond shaped eyes, is squeezing my hand . . . my calloused, scary, giant of a hand. And its she's so tiny but her grip, so damn tight . . .

"My name is Jazz and you look like a football player," she whispers. "Is your wife here?"

I shake my head, try to will my eyes clear. "I'm alone."

"Nah you got the Chief and the good lady po-lices. You wan' some popcorn?"

"No . . . no. Um . . . where's your mommy, daddy?"

She shrugs. Figgis doesn't intervene.

"Don't you . . . miss them?"

Another shrug. "*Why?*" And she scampers off.

"H-How long as Verna been helping you?" I pose.

"Since she was at the munie. Straight out of grad school."

"And you do this to . . . rescue them . . . from people like Roffe?"

"Hon', I've been doing this since I was on patrol, a dozen years ago. We are Artemis and Athena . . . because we have to play the long game, do distasteful things like hire or hobnob with the likes of Moses Roffe, Dante. So . . . now, you are all-in, all caught up."

"Let me and Stripe go. Now."

"Okay, just correct these misassumptions first. When we started years ago, it was to return children who were trafficked here. But then we realized some were put in the meat grinder by their own parents . . . "

"Who're prolly sick, desperate. Get to the point, Linda."

She taps my shoulder. "So smart, so focused photographic memory but yeah, you miss things, and forget things . . . on purpose. I'm thinking of a baby, taken from a dead teenager, trafficked by Jaime Bracht . . . ."

I shrink away. She knows. "Jesus . . . "

"Then that baby, through the lawyer, or crony, more accurately, of the baby's father, gets a new life, *new parents.* Aw, but that's a *noble* undertaking because you're Dickie Cornish, and we're scum?"

Now I would be dissolving into the grass like the kids' melted ice cream but for one thing: three figures approaching from across the lawn. Figgis becomes maladroit even bumbling as she tries to coach me into what to say.

"Uh . . . yes . . . this is . . . my partner Alecia." Then she sighs and says, "And my daughters."

Alecia's got a beach tan, streaks of sun in her flaxen hair. Retired supermodel thin. She and Figgis resemble a number

"18" together. The tall older daughter—the black one—she's got this insouciant air and mobile phone fused to her hands. The little white one's staring at me like I'm a carny freak.

"Hey, you're big . . . you look like you've been fighting!" the brat exclaims. Neither mom pulls her up. "Is that your son with the zits? I can tell he smokes marijuana!"

"He's not my son. But . . . he does smoke marijuana."

The older one giggles.

"Are you on SFME staff, getting the K'ymira Thomas Dorm ready, Mr. Cornish?" Alecia asks.

Figgis mutters, "Allie, no, he's—"

"A troubleshooter," I jump in. "Ma'am . . . young ladies, wish I could stay . . . I gotta tend to some business. Been a *bear* of a day." I face the younger kid, "Fireflies'll be out at sundown." Then I look to Figgis. "Guess we're done. Good-bye."

I watch her jaw bulge through her jowls as she says, still keeping the pretense pasted-on, "Oh, we'll talk more, Mr. Cornish . . . "

Yeah, the Amazons follow me as I hunt for Stripe but they don't stop me, even when we bolt for the street.

I remember Bracht and Nimchuk joanin' me in a . . . calling me a buzzard, a hyena, a maggot. A scavenger. Now . . . I'm her pig. *Mother Mary*, I'd pray for you to take me to your breast, tell me that's not me. But it is. Where else can I go? I'm trapped, penned . . . like these screeching, *happy* little lambs . . .

CHAPTER 20
In the Blind

"Here." I'm handing over the Mickey Dees' bag to Stripe after eating my fill of fries. We lay in our own blind—a low brick wall and shrubs surrounding the university's oldest building—and further obscured by the late afternoon shadows. Boston earned his own burger when they confirmed the hoopdy—big old greasy-gray Crown Vic Ford—parked farther up near Fairmount Street, and a hybrid Fusion stopped right in front of the cantina I swear had been tailing us since Figgis' lady jakes dropped us at Columbia Heights. Back there we tried to blend in with both shoppers and loiterers. So much for that. Antonelli's got SOD's monstering all for lil' ole me.

"*Lo sciento, chero,*" I tell Stripe. "For dragging you into a war."

"As long as we on the good side."

"I'm not sure what that is."

He bites into a cheeseburger, says, mouth full, "Then the winning side?"

The hybrid pulls out. Then here comes the Crown Vic, pulling a U and heading up Georgia. They're bugging out, coming back for us another day . . . else they risk going toe to toe with Figgis' Amazons. Yeah it's a dance. Can't fight the war in plain view.

"Okay let's go," I grunt.

Stripe follows me off the hill and we rush across Georgia above the Banneker Pool, slip through a spot in the fence. As we amble over the alley behind my apartment, Stripe huffs, "How she know you at the VA trippin' yessirday, bro'? Bitch got eyes all places?"

"Seems so."

We come in through an old coal hatch in the basement, go up metal steps into the cantina's kitchen. Pilar says yeah, there was heat, all right, selling tickets, threaten deportation . . .

. . . and see, my door's almost hanging off its hinges, my thin mattress is on the floor, my chest of drawer gaping . . . my laptop's buzzing on and off like some digital Dracula sucked its neck.

"*Coño* . . . " Stripe gasps as he rights my little fridge.

I'm beelining for the bathroom, and relief soaks me when I see the wall panel fronting the larger still intact.

"G'won back and chill at the church on Sixteenth. We goin' to the mattresses like in the movies. Do not fuckin' come out till I call you . . . keep the track app *on*, hear me?"

"Wha'?" he gasps. "Ain't no monk like them white faggots wha' run *Santa Jude*!"

"*Hey*! Check yourself damn it!"

But he's kid, he's shaken up. I repeat my order. I get a snippy, mumbled acknowledgement. I slip him more bills, send him back out through the cantina and the coal hatch. I don't even think we shook hands, certainly didn't hug.

I'm tracking his phone on mine though. He's zig-zagging, good. Looking for an indirect bus route. He's learning more from YouTube than my old ass is.

And so I prop the chair against the door. I wash myself, just with a rag and soap, no shower. Can't take that chance. Clean T-shirt, some gray trousers, my comfortable slippers and there I am trying to reboot this laptop on my cot. These motherfuckers are no cleverer than LaKeisha but they managed to strip everything I've saved.

There's a knock on the door and I spring up, this time with the sawed off Balabuska. It's Pilar, with a shitload of ice in a big plastic bin, some ginger ale, my good ole Rock Creek Cola. Paper cups. Suddenly so nice, eh?

My phone's buzzing and I know it's Figgis' private number. No way I'm talking to her now. I look up Stripe's moving dot and he's almost up Sixteenth Street to Newton, thank God.

Another knock.

"*Gracias* Pilar . . . bologna and crackers is all I need."

"Open the door," I hear in a hushed voice.

I'm trying to slow my breathes and I'm digging at my thigh with the cue stick. Yeah, I know who it is. She wouldn't bring the heat, at least not on purpose.

Verna stands on the landing, behind my wreck of a door. Her face is raw and sopping from tears and the sweltering heat there at the top of the stairs. All kinds of bad must be coming.

She's wearing one of those long tank dresses and sandals . . . nothing like she wears to work so I'm wondering was she really even there at SFME when I arrived at Moses Roffe's invitation, to view his miracle cure for those poor, poor Third World-ish children.

She slaps me.

Despite her size the momentum's enough to backpeddle my big ass in the apartment. Now she's a flurry of fists, tears, phlegm. "*You killed Mo*'!"

It's starting to hurt and so I grab her, shove the door shut with my butt while she's flaying. "He was a pervert . . . he abused women, kids!" I yell. "A pimp!"

"Shut up!"

I let her go. "Figgis knows it. So take it up with her next time you scheme to kidnap a child."

"Wh-What?"

"The Gingerbread House."

"Aw God, Dickie." But Verna calms herself with a tissue.

"Linda says you shot Mo and . . . she's not sure how to protect you . . . he was going to do a welfare check on a girl and—"

"Verna listen! Yes, I did it. Self defense. I followed him from SFME to the projects, down I Street . . . he attacked me."

"Stop."

"No . . . listen damn it. If Linda's such a friend . . . how'd she allow you to hire that piece of shit, put him around more vulnerable kids, more women huh? What—she coming to put a case on me? Fuck that!"

"Stop saying that about him!"

"Take out your phone and ask her about this guy. Because Big . . . Kevin Washington . . . gave him up. Now Big's gone. Ask her where he is. Because I talked to the One-Six Crew's leader Shawn Brown and you how these niggas are in the their macho . . . yet he admitted what Roffe did to him, forced his mother to do."

Oddly, she calms, looks around. "I-I hadn't been here since Adult Social Services found it for you . . . what . . . what happened?"

"One-Six fucked up and thought I'd snitched, so they aired me out. Then someone . . . Linda will say it's SOD officers,

SOD will say it's the Chief . . . tossed the place, looking for something or just to send me a warning. They emptied everything off my hard drive, near as I can see."

Verna's been a samurai of sorts for the poor folk of this town. And certainly for me, believing in me, believing me. Two different things that got tested as this shit with Bracht exploded. But I wonder if she still thinks everyone is good down deep, and the few evil mugs out there all got some angle merely because they got played and had no recourse.

I fill a cup with Pilar's ice, pour her a ginger ale. Now she's on my cot and smalling herself up, like she's making room for me. Forces a smile through the tears. Doesn't mean I got to talk less. Just that I got to listen more.

"I-I don't know what's going on, Dickie—she won't talk about Mo beyond what she said, and what she said was between us . . . because what's being said on the news, internally."

"I don't understand."

"It's down as a homicide . . . but that he was killed by a known pedophile and part time plugger who hung there." She turns away when she says the name. "Kevin Washington."

"Jesus." I roll to the cot, slide in beside her. I say what's on my mind, not trying to be cagey or an asshole . . . "Your friend and Antonelli . . . for mortal enemies, they sure do know how to dance with each other."

"I don't pretend to understand. Look, Linda even called it a dance once."

"So you know."

"No . . . *yes* . . . "

I kiss her forehead before she can react. It's a sibling peck, a guardian's show of affection. "Two years ago I got you in danger, being around me. You coming here, it's happening all over again. Like with Stripe. Don't think he can take it again."

Okay, now she's leaning in. Kisses me. No peck. Unh-unh. *Mouth . . .*

I jump off the cot. I've yearned for that even when there was no way anyone would come near my nasty grill.

Well, this little chick's crazy now . . . she's kicked off her sandals and is up on her toes . . . elbows on my shoulders, fingers gripping my throbbing temples and tongue seeking mine. Now what?

"Cops might come back," I tell her after each bite on her lips.

"Don't care," she almost growls, now tasting the gray beard stubble on my chin. "Just don't want to think about today. Just want to think about . . . *nothing*. Is that okay? Nothing, damn it!"

She's reaching at my trousers. Moaning a bit and I don't know whether it's disappointment or sated curiosity.

"Verna . . . the street's made things . . . y'know, bad for me, *down there*. It ain't the meds—I mean, my mind's ready. The body's . . . I dunno."

She's got the fly open and thrusts her fingers in anyway, because Verna's a trooper.

Women are funny that way, I guess. I mean, who'd I have in twenty-odd years to compare making love? Esmeralda . . . *la bruja*. Do I really think Verna wants to give up that jelly, rawdog, on this narrow bed, in this tore-up spot? *Nah*, she just wants to know that I *want* her, and if I want her, that means the universe isn't the cruel and bloody place it is.

"I understand," she trills.

She never, ever looked better. She's pulling her dress off her shoulders.

"Dickie. Still want me to stop?"

"Kiss me, and I'll tell you."

She swallows my breath. And this time, she feels me responding. I'm more embarrassed than cised or proud.

Is this a bad idea? Hell yes. But I'm not going to turn her away. I mean, her skin's so soft, those breasts only slightly deflated from her weight-loss . . . sliding over top of my bearish bulk . . . it's not fucking, right? And it *ain't* making love because I can't say we are in love but it just feels so good . . . and she seems to like it . . . even when I pull out and I'm dripping everywhere just as her thighs tense and spasm . . . and in a quaking voice she tells me she's *very* happy and I sort of believe her, because I want to forget how I looked back then, my smell, my stammer . . . why would any woman want me . . .

. . . and so I'm watching the alley streetlight pop on beyond the ghetto-palms swaying under my half-assed fixed window. I follow the trickle of light right to Verna's head on my chest. She's snoring right into the salt and pepper curlicues of my hair. Me? I'm just digging on her scent. Pungent moisture . . . orange blossom . . . argan oil . . .

. . . and she's now barefoot and wearing one of my T-shirts. Doesn't complain about having to tip-toe around broken glass piled up from my airing-out, or the hissing toilet.

I'm popping my meds. I'll show her all of me as I get better.

Nothing so lofty from her, however. Like with all women, it's pretty simple: she tells me to head down to the CVS on Florida and Seventh, where I first met Al-Mayadeen, to grab hair products for her, a toothbrush. Says if anyone can do that and avoid Twelve, it's me.

"Want something sweet? Can make you a cake . . . "

"Uh . . . a cake?"

"Yeah . . . mash up Little Debbie's Oatmeal Creams, find some mixed nuts watch the peanuts because folks can be allergic, some packets of cream cheese and—"

"How 'bout you stop on the way back at Mickey Dees for proper coffee and apple pies?"

Yep. Just a normal, easy vibe. Something I could get used to, as I pass the mess on the floor from cop hands, the bullet holes in the plaster from the One-Six. Fuck all of them. Sorry, K'ymira . . .

. . . and Verna's brushing her teeth after polishing off an apple pie and joe, and I'm recounting, "This girl at the Colonial View . . . y'all have her kid at the Gingerbread House . . . she's in Juvie on Mt. Olivet Road . . . "

Verna spits in the sink and begs, "About Tudor House . . . the Gingerbread spot . . . let me explain . . . "

"It's okay. Listen . . . gonna call Figgis and tell her I'm done, she can yank my license, I won't snitch her out about these kids to Feds if she leaves me be, keeps Antonelli off me."

Verna wriggles her dress over her head, grabs the brush, oil and such I bought along with a coffee. "Mirror in the bathroom's cracked. Can I use the one over your dresser?"

Verna doesn't seem to be paying me any mind, and indeed she pauses at Black Santa's picture on my wall. Not even askew, despite the gunfire. "A complicated old fella. Guess you miss him, even though . . . "

"Though what?"

She's tending her hair and she'd look boss with just a bandana and a little wisp hanging across her face. "Though he . . . betrayed . . . *endangered* you. Us, eventually."

"He never lived foul. He did bad because he was in a spot. He paid the price. In the end he was still . . . *my friend*." Before

I stop myself, I mutter, "You . . . you did bad. Whether you knew and did nothing, or conspired . . . I mean Vee, it's *stealing* kids no matter how you shine it. But like Fitz, I still . . . " *Love her?* " . . . care about you."

She's not missing a beat slipping on her bangles, her pendant, but damn—that look she's stapling on me. "Really Dickie? You wanna pick a fight . . . now?"

Don't know where this is coming from. "Come on, Vee . . . who's your clientele?"

"I beg your pardon?"

"Ratfuck rich people don't gotta fly to Africa, buy themselves a baby—you got them here? You were at the munie all that time when your star boy, Roffe, was turning women out, abusing their kids."

"Dickie? Walk that shit back . . . "

"Then a year at Child and Family Services and you didn't suspect a thing? Why, 'cause he's white . . . Yale? He tell you that kidnapping kids is okay, long as you don't have sex with 'em, pick 'em yuppie parents?"

"How . . . dare . . . *you*!"

Yes, Verna. Linda would say who does Maximiliano Soloronzano live with now and I'd be a hypocrite. I've been alone my adult life. Clear to see why. "I was invisible, degraded, like these kids, like these women. You know that, you saw it!"

"You think you're the only one who was invisible, degraded? Gonna tell you a lil' fable then I'm out . . . *out*, okay? *A Christmas Carol* . . . Ebenezer's schooled by the Santa Claus-looking ghost, and under the ghost's robes are two ghoulish children. He schools that boy's Ignorance, the girl is Want, but be more afraid of the boy."

"Vee, I-I got your back, always . . . but stamp, nona us get to decide who's worthy and—"

"*Pay attention*! See, the boy's all grown-up as a smirking man . . . in a banker's Italian suit or casual Friday Dockers or hunter's camouflage, and under *his* clothes he hides two new waifs. The boy is Nihilism, the girl is Fatalism . . . "

"Vee . . . "

"I'm not finished, *dammit*!" Her eyes are both wet and burning; I'm breathless, as if drowning. "*He* is homicide, suicide . . . agony, anguish. *But beware the girl,* 'cause she destroys with slow, meticulous, deliberate ease, and I will battle that little bitch with every weapon, *legal or not.* You feelin' me, Dickie?"

"Was this the real you, back then . . . or did you change?"

She hiccups her tears, grabs for her purse, phone. "I didn't make love for your approval or clemency."

"Then why?"

"So you'd meet me where I am, like I've been doing with you for *years.* At your worst, you made me smile. Stay safe, Dickie . . . call Linda when you can, but do *not* call me. Or LaKeisha—she is *my* employee, not yours, and I will not put her in harms way."

Like I've done to you.

She's down the stairs.

I catch up to her on Georgia Avenue. Under a streetlamp's buzz I hook her by the arm . . . just as what looks like a summer session class is disgorging students.

The dudes are slouching types with earbuds affixed, or swole and back in football camp. I can do my mad dog and back them off, run. But they aren't the problem.

It's young women who are shouting, aiming cameras-phones or hitting 911 when I bet up on campus they were running their mouths about defunding the po-po. They exhort the dudes to kick my ass, and after the boys dither for a split second, I'm treated to a full-on charge in the dark.

Whether it's the night's cover or they didn't want to mess with me, they peter out, scatter, and thus allow me to scramble down the steps leading to a basement apartment counting on the shadows as cover, pulling a recycling can with me to position at the top. Perfect blind against them, but no match for any MPD German Shepherd tearing at me like I'm a pork chop. And yeah, here come the running lights of a unit, flashing blue. They pass me by in two seconds that seem like two hours.

Eventually I find Boston, shirtless, sucking on a Nutty Buddy cone.

"Guess y'all run inta th' rapist, huh?" he muses. "Twelve roust me jus' as I wuz getting my ice cream an' churry bomb-pops. Dang college gurls!"

"They gone? Any plainclothes?"

"You mean like them fools wha' come by today? Nah. Jus' jakes."

"Bang the drainpipe out back if you see anybody don't belong—anybody!"

He gives a military salute. "By the way, yo' rolla be waitin' on you."

"Huh?"

"Inside."

I'm bounding up three steps at a time, heart about to bust my ribs . . . just to see those small feet, the big eyes and oval face. She's crosslegged on the grimy landing, swaying.

"I-I'm so sorry," I puff. "Dunno how to act . . . dunno about being . . . with anyone."

Verna nods, sniffles. "I'm not saying I came back for you. Just that . . . those students called the police . . . police could have . . . hurt you."

"They'll do a different hurt on you. And to Hell with this delicate 'dance.'"

She starts giggling through abrupt tears. "Yes, careful choreography . . . and then along you come with them big-ass feets." She tells me someone's been blowing up my phone, based on the sounds through my wrecked door. "Maybe it's Linda's people?"

I push the door aside, right off the jamb. Me and Verna have a blind . . . if only in our minds.

And it's at that moment I realize that Stripe's out there among his pals . . . smoking bud, talking shit, slurping his lime Jarritos in the muggy, frenetic night-time, tossing rude comments at *chicas.* Being young.

Young people don't think they need a blind. "*Oh my God . . .* "

Stripe's sent three voicemails but strangely no texts. I call him.

He doesn't answer. Instead . . .

"*S'up Trouble Man, Big Homie?*" Detective Woodman greets. "*Sorry . . . I mean* 'moe.'"

I turn to Verna, whisper, "Maybe . . . maybe you better go home." When she shrugs why I get back on with this motherfucker. "What did you do to him?"

"*Nothing. Why would we? Well, seeing that there was a disturbance on Park Road, at the All-Smoke Tobacco and Pipe Shop . . . bodega that switched over when the weed got legal. Your friend happened to be in altercation with another Hispanic male named Carlos Ramos . . . we had our eye on for selling nitazenes. Worse than fentanyl, that stuff . . .* "

See, I'm shrinking into the seat upholstery, throat tighter, drier. If I'm lucky I'll suffocate long before I disappear, less than a germ. "G-Go on . . . "

"*You're aware of our BOLO on two of Carlos' hommies for shooting up that hovel you live in . . . figured it was best to take young Ernesto in on a material witness warrant, for his own good. 'Specially if he was contemplating sampling Carlos' wares, and there was a disagreement on price or payment.*"

"He doesn't do . . . do needles. Where is he?"

"*Oh yeah. Needles. That's your thang, forgot. Well, he's at the Second-D, Idaho Avenue Northwest. His civil rights are fine and he's getting his three hots and a cot.*"

"Listen, Woodman. It was the One-Six Crew, not MS, who got the greenlight on me. And I cleared it up."

"*Oh you didn't hear, you the shamus of the shelter? Shawn Brown, aka 'Thanos' got himself three GSWs to the chest last night in front of the Addis Ababa Grocery up on Benning Road.*"

I'm grimacing and Verna's standing in front of me. I wave her off, mouth to her: *Dangerous. Please go.*

She's not going.

"Y'all did it."

"*That'd make us a street gang in blue and that's so very Serpico-old-shit.*"

"Al Pacino." Can't help it.

"*Whatever. Thing is I got a witness, a Mr. Park Cheung of Annandale, Virginia who owns Roses Liquors and he was about to work out a protection tax deal with two of Thanos' toy gangstas when you rolled up on them and treated them harshly, let's say. Someone else spotted Shawn arriving there. You're on store tape. Now my brotha, if you had pointed words with Mr. Brown, then he's found dead . . . you better come down and speak with us.*"

"You got a gun? Slugs?" I've got him on speaker now, and I'm gathering clothing, armfuls of shit, gesturing to Verna to grab this army surplus duffle bag that can hold my whole life . . . and my laptop. I spot a sheet of paper they must have missed, filled with Stripe's chickenscratch . . . in Spanish. I piece together an address . . . and the words *El Poco* circled. "*Little*."

"*Where are you at, Cornish*?" He's either blowing smoke or he doesn't know. I thumb to my tracker screen. Yeah, Stripe's phone is indeed at the Second District, way over by the Cathedral, off Wisconsin Avenue in Chez Whitey. I disable my own trace. "*You really need to clear this up for real. Clear up a lot of shit 'cause there's a lot of shit being spoken and your name is now in every other sentence.* So *come down here or let us pick you up. Call no other cops but me. Bring lawyer if you want. Legal Aid opens at eight in the morning. Of course, skeleton crew due to COVID . . . I hear there's a hell of a line . . .* "

"Or?"

"*You saw what happened to them folk at the Colonial View. Still a lotta Trump cowboys left among the Feds. An' this boy ain't registered as a Dreamer. Plus, well, other personnel might want to have a deep, deep talk with him about your caseload and whereabouts.*"

"You hurt him, I'mo beat you bald-ass head bloody with my shoe."

"*You listen here you big Lurch-looking retard motherfucker! Don't get twisted by these dykes out here who—*" Other voices cut him off until a new one breaks on, whispery and cold . . .

"*Cornish. This is Deputy Chief Antonelli. I apologize for Detective Woodman. Bottom line, I'm trying to rescue you from this grand mess.*"

I swipe and turn the fucking phone off. I look to Verna and yeah she's peeping my ashen face, like Dracula himself put a beef on me. "I-I gotta ask a favor. Just drop me anywhere, it's a warm night, I can find a spot. Just need to stash my laptop no matter what they did to it and—"

"Don't be crazy. You're coming home with me."

"Not again. Won't do that to you again . . . "

"I'll get the ladies downstairs; they can find someone to secure the door . . . "

When she leaves I'm back in the bathroom again but not basting in relief. Oh no, I give an ample heave into the toilet, stumble back to my rack, and it's then when I see it on the dusty floor by the baseboard . . . must've been displaced and missed by these assholes when the rolled my shit.

Detective Monica Abalos, imprinted on the little white card. I pocket the card as Verna comes back.

"Pack whatever you don't want anyone to steal," she whispers. "No shame in hiding."

CHAPTER 21

Chimera

YEAH . . . I LET HER SEE me pack Mom's rosary and Figgis' magnifying glass. Yeah . . . I let her see me bust open the bathroom wall panel and open the larder.

And yeah, she stood there, mute and clocking the grimy teddy bear, gwap of bills. See, all my people dead from 'rona, they taught me two things on the street. First, you don't share *nothing* hidden, even with a ride or die. Second, there's no running away from winter's cold, or summer's oven. You run to it. You tuck in. You survive. That's what blinds were for yet now I feel I've betrayed everything they taught me.

I'm rabbiting, with a chick.

So now it's taking the better part of an hour to get to Verna's spot with all the zigging and zagging to shake whatever tail these assholes may have put on Verna no matter them claiming not to know where I'm at. Worse, I'm netted up because we're only a few blocks from where I parleyed with Thanos. This Monica Abalos' card is burning a hole in my pocket but she's a chick, and odds are she's in Linda's tribe no matter what that Leather Tuscadero-looking jake Raffi Sanchez says. They all lie. Two evils are two evils, none the lesser . . .

. . . and so I sleep on Verna's sofa. Maybe not sleep. Lay lateral. I see no one in the dark but Stripe. I'll fix this, kid. No more promises broken by my stupidity, my mania.

We're up with the sun. She's calls in sick. I don't let a soul know I'm with her, even my living, human Google LaKeisha. They are all safer that way.

Except for Stripe. Daddy . . . what do I do? Murders me to ask, but what do I do . . .

. . . so the Mini's ragtop is down and Verna's hair's in a kerchief like she's in the 1960s and so sporty. We stop at this spot on Maryland Avenue for coffee, egg sandwiches and see that in the hours since Shawn "Thanos" Brown's death, the twins nihilism and fatalism have been damn busy in this little piece of the town. Three drive-bys. A car on fire with two dudes in it. Deputy Chief Antonelli calls upon the Chief and the Mayor to "take the gloves off . . . " And as we hit 295 at Benning Road, all we see are big black X's through every One-Six tag in sight.

"Linda told me she told you about K'ymira's toy, Dickie. It . . . it doesn't shock me. She was like Captain Ahab in *Moby Dick* with that case, back when law enforcement, the media, didn't care about abducted children who weren't rich or blond. Figured it was one of CiCi Talbot's tricks who kidnapped and killed her, not a child molester at the munie. We dedicated the new dorm to keep the child's name alive for the community, even though the community hated Linda for getting frustrated, giving up."

"You think you could have saved her if you'd gotten CiCi into SFME?"

"I could have kept a better eye on her . . . but CiCi, she was . . . "

"A most favored lady, I know."

"You'd've hated her. Bamma as fried dirt but book-smart . . . read real books you'd've recognized from college. But whatever she had between her ears, on the surface she'd O.D. on reality show vixens and their plastic surgeries, Jezebel make-up."

"Look at my dumbass . . . keeping the fucking teddy bear as a bargaining chip for a bargain that never was. Never was."

I rise and announce I got to hit the head after a nibble on the sandwich, a sip of coffee. The Jurassic payphone's still connected and I wipe it down with my breakfast napkin, like I'm fronting to the 'rona lounging in its innards.

Guess someone's on-duty, as one ring does the trick.

"*Monica Abalos, may I help you?*"

"You were right not to buy that RIP round bullshit."

"*Mr. Cornish? Mr. Cornish where are you?*"

"Did you hear about some ruckus at the Carrollsburgh in Southwest?"

There's a sigh and, "*Intel, Spec Ops lost a CI. Murdered.*"

"That's bullshit."

"*I-I know. Or I . . . suspected. Please, sir . . . where are you?*"

Sir? "And I've been to 'Gingerbread House.' Ever hear of that?"

Dead air, and maybe there's no trace setting up because then I hear, "*Come to Metro Center Station, get a farecard . . . then let's pick a meet-up on the train at—*"

I see Verna buzzing around the booth. "I'll find you, if I need you . . . or will Chief Figgis?"

"*I'm not with Chief Figgis, sir. I'm—*"

I hang up, brush by a bewildered Verna and grunt, "Let's go. The monsters are circling . . . "

. . . and the blue Potomac emerges before us; to our left is the shimmering casino and hotel. Verna guns the Mini onto the Beltway, then exits to what my mother, ever the North Portal Street debutante, distained as the "primitive Maryland suburbs" along the southern rim of the city rather than urbane Silver Spring, manicured Chevy Chase, sparking Bethesda. In minutes I'm seeing signs for Waldorf, La Plata . . . the bridge to Colonial Beach, Virginia. My affliction tells me this is the way that cracker Boothe rabbited after he shot Lincoln. This is country heat, country bugs, dust.

Verna nudges me. "This is a hell of way to work off the walk of shame, Dickie."

"A real date."

One side of my cracked brain's cherishing the humor as the other's chewing, digesting Abalos' words. These are likely the last smiles anyone's giving or getting for a long ass time, or nevermore. Yeah, because we are now in deep in the tide-marsh boonies on U.S. 301, all suffused with this country heat. Even in the daylight I bet you could clock the ghosts of the slaves rolling tobacco in barrels down to the water, or of John Wilkes Boothe, riding away after murking Abe. Not the best head for checking in on Hakim Alexander.

Indeed, we whiz past a weathered temporary sign like the one Stripe describes in his Mayan pictograph-like notes; I bark for Verna to bust a U-turn. When we get back on the road northbound I get a better look. Basically a U.S. Department of Health and Human Service decal on a painted slab of particleboard. And now we're kicking up red dust like it's Mars . . . as damn if the place resembles the hooches we had back on Okinawa when I was little. Not even a guard in the ramshackle booth . . . maybe they're taking a piss in portable johns down by the fence. Portable johns, yeah. At a hospital . . .

. . . and the front desk is populated by slow and ill-smelling hillbilly types in dingy, once white uniforms; the lone TV's playing the original *Batman* movie . . . Michael Keaton, Jack Nicholson, ole Billy Dee as Harvey Dent, and the staff seems transfixed by his smooth mane instead of helping us. A sign above the counter reads PLEASE PRESENT VACCINATION CARD OR NEGATIVE TEST BARCODE UPON DEMAND.

We mask-up with the free ones there in a stack, but I don't have any other credentials. I just tell Verna to slide them one of her business cards.

"Un-huh hon' whas' this mean?" says a young white woman, blond-frosted extensions sprouting off her brunette scalp. Name tag says "Bree."

"Means we're to see a patient. He's a witness in a child welfare case I'm working on . . . for the District of Columbia . . . through Miss Leggett's non-profit."

Damn if it doesn't work. What the fuck do they care? Not like many others—family, physicians, whatever, have visited per the sheet I've committed to memory . . . at least from the first page going back four days.

No one escorts us down the barrack-like corridor and I clock not one surveillance camera. Cleanser's hiding smells worse than St. Jude's or SFME at full capacity. And from each room comes beeps and ticking and pumping sounds.

A knock prompts a slight, boney woman to greet us ay the entrance to bigger sick bay area. She's swarthy, probably a Filipina like the ones who could have been my mother in another life at the Subic Bay base in Manila had Daddy forgotten his jimmies. She's wearing blue scrubs, purple gloves and a mask yet no name tag, and you swear she smells of menthol jacks and cabbage. Sure enough you spot a crush pack of the former peeking from her back pocket when she bends over.

One bed by tiny window covered with oversize drapes is stripped to the mattress. The other's surrounded by what looks to be Nineties hardware substituting for human lungs. Two IV bags also hang there, with tubes infusing the arm of a twenty-six-year-old black man who looks older than you. Eyes as jaundiced as banana skins, skin like wax papery.

"Family?" the attendant asks, not that she cares.

"Um . . . official . . . b-business," I say through the mask.

Yeah, I'm stuttering and as "mush-mouthed" as in my old life because swear to God I think this man's eyes are tracking mine. If this he's a vegetable than I'm an asparagus.

"*C-Cops*?" the poor bastard whispers, laboring with a betadine-swabbed, bandaged hole in his throat. He waves off the woman in scrubs and she gladly leaves.

"N-No. Um . . . private investigator, hired by your brother Al-Mayadeen, your mama, Miz Toy."

He's grinning—at Verna. "Wh-who this r-rolla?"

Verna huffs, pulls back.

"Listen, moe. Got some bad news about your brother. He's dead. He . . . committed suicide."

Nothing. Just rapid blinks, a squirm of his boney body under the sheets. "That it?"

Mother Mary, I'll play along. Came this far. "Kill, moe—ain't that enough?"

"Y'all be here jus' tell me that? He live foul."

"Unlike you."

"*Dickie*!" Verna disapproves.

"Sorry, gee, but it's like this. You won't be here unless your time's close. You need to come clean about your niece. About Big. About shit done at the *munie* . . . to women, kids."

"Yeah," he says, looking away. Yet he then mumbles, "The shelter . . . it all 'bout dick and pussy . . . "

"Little . . . that sounds like something Big'd say."

His sleepy eyes narrow even more. "B-Big . . . he got filthy h-habits."

"Big molest K'ymira? A white man on staff at the old shelter, Moses Roffe, he knew about it . . . and CiCi let it happen 'cause she was busy fucking everyone including *you*."

"Nah . . . *nah*," he wheezes, squirming.

Let's see if they can continue to scare folk. "Vee . . . could you get that . . . *bag* . . . out the car for me, please?"

"For real Dickie the fumes in this place are making me nauseous anyway."

"Whole tee, Little," I begin, no back-up. "First, cops think you're in a coma. Second, how long before Feds tell them you alive. Third, your mama lied to me about where you were. Fourth . . . check it out . . . you ain't a suspect in my mind. You're a what my study videos'd call a material witness."

"Y-You aint think I think I hurt Ky?"

I shake my head. "You consent to being interviewed on the record?"

Damn if he doesn't up and nod so I take some pics of him awake, his chart. Then I swipe the recorder app, and put the phone on this little wheeled table next to the bed. He repeats his consent then scoff, "Wha' tha' white bitch cop F-Figgis still be sayin'?"

"That you and CiCi killed lil' K'ymira over six years and got away with it."

"Al-May . . . he say it too? C-Cause he wou'n't." He's seizing up, coughing . . . points frantically to an O-2 mask. I give him a blast. As he calms he asks, "You the . . . Angel of Death, nigga?" He gestures to some sticks jutting from an ice tray. Tiny popsicles.

I place a popsicle on his cracked lips. "If I am the Angel," I declare, "wanna get it off your chest before you go?"

"I say I di'n't kill *no one*," he slurs as he licks at the popsicle.

"How 'bout CiCi or a pervert cop . . . "

"*CiCi*?" he says, slurping, "S-S-Smarter than them muvfukkahs."

"Smart enough to cover up a child homicide, implicate your girlfriend at the time? Dumb enough to have to sell pussy to survive?"

That got him. He spits melted popsicle juice. "*Smarter than you, if you here 'bout her . . .* " He breaks out into another coughing fit and I hit him O-2. "Can't die hard like this," Little mutters. "There go that pillow, moe—y'all do it for me?"

I nod. "Spill."

"Y-Y'all really see Al-May . . . Mama?" I stay mute, so he motions me close. "Nasty muv-muvfukkahs di'n't go to shelter for *kids*. They be goin' 'cause . . . jont was a big-ass brothel. Kiddie-lovers be out in the group homes . . . "

Corroboration. "*Go on . . .* "

"High-falutin niggas an' ballers, maybe a few yeah, but it was mostly . . . mostly, rich white mugs, *politicians* feel me? All coming through the Distric' . . . C-Congressmen . . . *boo-coup*, gee." He coughs, I hit him with the O-2. He names folk. Swear I could move to The Wharf the hush money I'd collect.

"Cops . . . they the pimps? Turning women out? Finding kids for perverts?"

"Sometime. Mostly . . . like, protection 'cause some Feds, some cops weren't down wiff that mess. CiCi say . . . they dick get *harder* when a rolla *scurred*, desperate, no hope. Th' real nasty ones like ta see *kids* scurred . . . "

I dangle another popsicle by his lips. "Ky, too? Pervs wanna see your niece scared?"

He shakes his head, licks the popsicle . . . yet's now giving me names of officers, division commanders he heard were all up in this shit. Nothing about Figgis or her command staff yet, and I'm about to put words in his dying mouth but the machines making him some sort of cyborg are whining and beeping faster and I don't need that little bait nurse fucking with my shit here.

"Repeat—Ky, too?"

"Big Man. You my Angel but you *don'* see. How y'all goin' lullaby me if you *don'* see?"

"See what?"

Abruptly I hear the thwap of Verna's sandals back in the hallway, "I really think we need to talk, Dickie," she calls from the doorway.

"*Not yet*!" I'm also distracted by the battery level on the phone. The recording app gobbles up juice. "No more riddles, man. I'll let you die here in agony, no pillow, real talk."

"Dickie?" I hear Verna gasp, "I got a call . . . *scary one* . . . from Linda. We need to wrap this up."

"*All right*, Vee." Then I turn to him. I'm not gentle. "If she didn't alibi one of her tricks who killed Ky, then—"

There's another spasm of coughs and I think he's going to die right in front of me . . . I grab for the mask and a cup for the sputum but he's motioning me close again . . .

"CiCi . . . she . . . she be *alive*."

Virus ate up his brain. He was my last card. And these motherfuckers got Stripe . . .

Verna's shouting. She's waving her phone. "Charles County sheriffs are coming . . . "

"Folk're waitin' on you down in the bad place!" I curse him.

"N-Nah . . . *Angel* . . . " he grabs my wrist. "CiCi, she switch-up on a f-female on them lung machines . . . h-hospitals all full-up a coughin' niggas . . . babies, old folk, people like me wiff the sugar. Apocalypse, moe. N-Nobody keepin' track . . . just us, dyin' . . . " And I'm just about to gently pull his hand away . . . when he offers, "Her play mama, Miz Jocasta, die of it, in a shitbox like this one 'cause white docs they don' give a fuck . . . "

"*Stop* . . . who?"

"CiCi. Miz . . . Miz Jo-casta. Her ole teacher, Jo-casta Epps. E-P-P- . . . "

"There's no . . . " And it's then that I'm needing my own hit of oxygen as the revelations suck the breath from me. "Aw . . . *no.*" He's frowning as I monkey with the phone . . . here's a pdf from LaKeisha. I repeat aloud what see.

"Estate of . . . Jocasta Epps McQueen."

"You awite . . . Big Man?"

I'm staring down at this talking corpse, shaking more than he is. "Little . . . think. I-I believe you. So . . . who did she switch-up with. Think . . . hard . . . " I tap the record app again.

"CiCi . . . she go into the hospital sayin' she sick . . . but come out in nurse outfit. Like she house the clothes, an' then tell me bye."

"Miz Epps, she have any relatives at all that CiCi spoke about?"

"Niece. Down Florida. She real smart too but she ain't no project gurl like CiCi."

"She died from COVID too. I bet she looks a lot like CiCi."

He closes his eyes. "Naaaaaah man, she was zooted from all 'rona shit, couldn't handle it . . . drove her car offa bridge into a creek." Maybe animated corpses can read the thoughts of the living, because this one's snickering, blowing bubbles alternatively between his nostrils and that hole in his throat. "Wooo . . . Big Man . . . CiCi fuck widchew? Betcha Al-Maya say ta y'all CiCi, she ain't she wha' seem. Findin' tha' out jus' now?"

I'm falling back into the chair, tugging at the hair on my dome. "*Yeah.*"

"I-I get sicker . . . go off inside m'head for a year, bruh . . . I come-to and Th' Donald ain't the prez-dent . . . then they move me here, monff ago . . . "

He pauses, clocking me kneading my forehead because it hurts. No . . . it's the jigsaw puzzle pieces inside, *snapping.*

"Little . . . if you had to guess, what . . . what would she look like—*now*?"

He shakes his head and whispers, "CiCi kiss my hand t'rough her mask thinkin' I be out, but I clock her, smell her perfume. She say . . . say she goin' get a *better* face, lift her titties, new life. But she said for me, like in her old shit book she read, 'never get joy no more . . . by not seein' my bright young—'"

"*Prospects,*" I mutter, almost sickly, like him. "It's a story about a mother named *Medea* . . . "

"Wha' tha' be?"

"Greek name like *Jocasta* . . . *Agave.*" Now I'm back on my feet, hovering indeed like the Angel of Death. "Medea said it . . . before she kills her children."

He's nodding. "Only reason I be safe f'om her, moe, is 'cause I be dyin' or else she woulda smoked me befo' she run off jus' ta close tha' door. Tha' bitch play poker wid Jesus and Lucifer an' not blink."

"*What* did he say?" Verna scoffs from the doorway. Don't know how much she heard.

Little calls, "Baby . . . look at your man here. He be *seein'* now, like Gawd's Angel!"

He's right.

"K'ymira," I tell him, making sure my phone's sucking its last bit of juice. "*Chimera.* Greek also." Right under my fucking nose. "But . . . how's the girl . . . a monster?" I'm so netted, so drained . . . my forehead just dips into one of his dirty pillows.

"Y'all still don't get it." I'm raising my face right to his, almost like we're kissing. Yeah, he's geeking so hard that pinkish foam jets from his nostrils.

"Dickie . . . *let's go,*" Verna warns. "They know we're here . . . "

Already got a nuke on my phone, not just scary ordnance, so fuck him, time to go.

But he blurts, "Mah gurl . . . *special piece a ass fo' special muvfukkah.* She tell this mug she on guv'ment Norplant. But she lie." Not even the heaves and coughs reign in the giggles. "*Special muvfukkah* . . . an' he goin' kill me if he know where I be . . . awake or no. Thas where you comes in, big dawg . . . "

I hear sirens outside. Uh-huh. And it isn't Linda with funnel cakes and half-smokes.

"Verna . . . listen . . . go the car, pretend like I made you drive me here. They won't mess with you. They want me."

Maybe Little sees my eyes widening, discerns the approaching heat because now he's gripping my shirt with whatever strength he's got left. "Light me up a fatty . . . ya got herb? Then push the pillow . . . promise you do that."

The sirens morph into radio chatter and feedback, spraying gravel as the units roar to a stop.

"You coulda stopped this, all of it. You coulda helped . . . your brother."

"Do it matter, Big Man?" Little mumbles, his face drained of guilt, remorse, regret.

And my own lungs are deflating, likely just as achingly as his fill . . . because there's a racket coming at me from the parking lot . . . now the receptionist desk . . . and now Verna, shouting at me that there's a side door we can cut out of . . . yeah, those are jake shoes pattering on that cheap floor, getting closer.

"*Name*!" I shout. I got to get this on the record. "The father. Who bumrushed this whole thing! He's *cop*—is it Dante Antonelli?"

"He *untouchable*, gee . . . b-but y'all still ain't got the joke. Lil' girl. Who ain't what she seem, either . . . "

He had his chance to die clean. Got to give this worm his due . . . so he can give the worms their due.

" . . . *ego te absolvo a peccatis tuis* . . . " I say to him.

"Tell CiCi I still . . . love her," he begs.

Yeah, like your brother did. I answer by yanking the dust-caked window curtains aside, raise the sash, bust out the screen.

Little wails, "You s'poseta lullaby me! *Aw fuck me* . . . "

" . . . *in nomine Patris, et Filii, et Spiritus Sancti* . . . " I'm calling to him as I drop out of the window . . . through a cloud of biting gnats . . . landing with a thud onto the baked red country clay. "*Amen.*"

I lope around to a stand of spent oxygen tanks laying against the building like torpedoes, spy a Charles County deputy inspecting the Mini.

Verna's in the driver's seat . . . where yeah, she left that bear. Next to the Mini sits . . . oh Jesus, a gray Crown Vic. No plates. Doors wide open.

I freeze. Not because of that, oh no Daddy. It's the shrieking.

Sounds like Little doesn't want to die after all. Least not the way he's dying at that moment.

CHAPTER 22

Idle Vain Fancy

THE MINI'S BRAKE LIGHTS GLOW RED . . . so the car's running. Means I'd better be, too . . .

. . . and so clock this chunk of busted concrete in the weeds, pick it and heave it at the spent oxygen tubes stacked against a wire fence. No Daddy, not like Sonny at RFK. Like Doug Williams. The bang and pings startle this lanky Charles County deputy and he's scampering away from the Mini. I forget the years of abusing my knees, my dogs, and sprint as fast as big man can and dive into the tiny back bench seat.

"Verna go!"

Verna Leggett's no bourgie hothouse orchid. She's stomping the pedal. We slingshot out of the motherfucker . . . and Barney Fife must have been real scared of the whomever arrived in the Crown Vic because all I see out the back of this little clown car is his dumbass running through the dust we're kicking up—straight into the building to get fetch them rather than chase us!

"Where? *Shit*!" Verna screams at me.

"Get off this road next turn!" From the rear I point to her GPS display. "Up on the left, another road loops back and shadows three-oh-one." Then I grab Verna's mobile, yelling to her, "plug in mine, and raise the top up, hear me?"

"Dickie gimme my fuckin' phone!"

"They killed him, Vee. They killed Little and they will dip Stripe!"

My phone's dying gasp is Dropboxing the audio file and pics to LaKeisha. At I'm praying that's happening. No confirmation before the thing blinks out.

She says nothing. I help pull the ragtop closed and hit the last number she called.

"*Verna for christ-sakes what has he done?*" Linda Figgis answers.

"No, this your little pig, squealing. They prolly getting a ping on this phone but, I found Hakim Alexander."

"Where is he? He's conscious?"

"My YouTube classes they call it 'a dying declaration' . . . it got one from this motherfucker . . . all kinds of ill shit . . . uploading that cloud thing . . . "

"*Mother Mary . . .* "

"So you a good Catholic now, huh? Then listen up. I got you and your Goldilocks kidnapping ring. I got these bastards under Antonelli. Who I go to the U.S. Attorney to fuck first depends on *who* . . . does *what* . . . for *me.* Now I got a soft spot for you, Linda I guess so I'll give you the benefit of the doubt, hear me? I want protection, I want . . . *Stripe* . . . Ernesto Rivas . . . freed from custody before the Antonelli's Nazis tear him up!"

"You ham-fisted brute how dare you! It wasn't supposed to happen like this!"

Like *what*? Yeah, if I wasn't drowning in adrenaline right now I'd be suffering that hoe with no money on the dresser feeling!

"Dickie!" Verna tries to intercede as she swings a left turn into the bowels of the sticks and I'm expecting a chopper above the cypress treetops any second.

"Oh God . . . put Verna on. Do it please, if you want to get out alive."

I hand her the phone and my girl doesn't put it on the speaker like I ask. I hear, "Wicomico Landing Road was the last sign. Uh-huh . . . I *don't* know, dammit . . . two white males, plain-clothes or detective . . . maybe in their mid-thirties . . . one blond hair, one a ginger. God, Linda . . . you had to put on a show for your admirers, bigshot with big pocketbooks?" And then, "Figgsy *please* . . . I love you but this shit's gotten *beyond.* That man Little, he told Dickie some things that I . . . I just . . . "

She surrenders the phone back to me, jerks a right onto road so narrow we're dead if another car comes around a bend, head-on.

"Listen carefully, I have friendlies, from Calvert, PG and St. Mary's Counties so get to Route Five . . . Charlotte Hall . . . I can have units meet you. Dickie?"

No thanks. "Linda so you know your Greek shit, huh? Artemis and Athena. Rescuers of *worthy* woman and children? So who was Agave? Gave birth a king, named Pentheus. Mama and her girlfriends went off with the god Dionysus, and Pentheus ran after them to tell her to behave, stop embarrassing his uptight male pride . . . but she and her ladies were in such a frenzy they tore Pentheus's uptight ass . . . right off his body. Then his head. In blind passion. Or fury, like another Greek mom . . . Medea, who murders her kids to teach an arrogant asshole a lesson . . . "

"Christ . . . I don't know what you are insinuating but you don't know shit. And am your only hope right now because the FBI, the

U.S. Attorney would laugh you out and then flip a coin as to who'd they dump you with, me or Dante! Dickie? *Dickie*!"

I swipe off. I see Verna weeping, little brown hands on the wheel going all gray she's gripping it so tight. "I'm turning off your phone. Bust a right up here!"

No particular reason why. Just to get off that road. Now we are back on something better-paved . . . yet in the open. Chickenfeed trucks lumbering in front of us, watering towers spraying rows of leafy stalks to our left. Only advantage is they think we'll hide, not run for civilization.

"Dickie," Verna whispers. "Little . . . he said . . . CiCi Talbot-Thomas is alive, right?"

"Uh-huh."

"And those men'd kill over that."

"Uh-huh. So much for your 'dance.' Guess you gotta rename your dorm."

"And Mo'. Wh-What about Mo'?"

I see Roffe's eyes again when I pumped the ACP's into his pervert chest. And I bounce her question. "We can't . . . can't be certain either Linda's people or SOD's not headed to your jont now to toss it . . . or worse, plant evidence Gotta think . . . "

It's my jigsaw puzzle brain that tells me to make a call. "Yeah, my name Richard E. Cornish, Junior . . . ID seven-four-four-nine, dee-two . . . I'm on my way to talk to Patient Admin *Agave Epps* . . . and Dr. Kapoor. Got it? I'm fien'in' to hurt myself. Got it? Yeah . . . "

She seen too much of the real me, of the instincts my Daddy usually feeds me. "Whoever you called . . . we aren't going there. Then where are we *really* going?"

"Up to Route Four, into PG County. Only place we can go . . . "

I turn off the phone. Not so much to interrupt the pings but so I won't answer when they call, when they put Stripe on and he's bloody and broken . . . and so I won't have to tell him there's no shame in crying out, because jumping bad will only piss them off and they'll kill him. And so my puzzle-mind goes back to the file Linda gave me, seems like a lifetime past . . . and methane probes . . . an address in a pdf.

Jocasta Epps McQueen's house is a ranch-style home with a carport. Sits at one of D.C.'s sharp border angles on the Seat Pleasant side, on 69th Place. Unlike the adjacent yards, the grass here's been cut, de-weeded. Central air whirring rather than sputtering cheap window units, concrete padding re-poured. Old C-class Benz in the driveway. Someone's got income.

We park then circle around to a backyard un-penned by rusty chain link fences or shrubs.

She's swaying back and forth on one of those enamel-painted glider sofas everyone had on their porch back in the day, and the whitefolks pay out the ass for at these West Elm type jonts. I can smell both the menthol from the lit jack and drying nail varnish from fluorescent orange toenails. Short-cropped hair, all frosted silvery like some rapper's wife. She eyes me, blows out a cloud and smiles as it's only then a clock her gear: pair of black bike shorts bareing her belly. And something else bare, too: her plum-hued areolas proudly and unabashedly free on one of those demi-cup lingerie bras.

She points to sweaty, slender cans of adult beverages in a small ice pail, swings her feet into some flipflops as the nails are complete, I guess . . . all like the world can go fuck itself.

"That was some boss thinkin' Mr. Cornish," she coos, butting the jack in the grass. "Callin' into the VA." She wraps her blood-red lips around a can, swallows hard. "Now jakes an' Feds be bumrushing Irving Street." When I nod she calls to me, "Just, uh—how'd you know I'd be home?"

"I didn't." She raises up and I see she's clocking Verna through blue contact lenses more than me. "But like your ex-husband told me before he goes and blows his brains out, 'CiCi's smart.' A tactician. You'd lay in the cut soon as whoever's feeding you four-one-one hipped you to me. Prolly since I found Big couple days back."

"Why wouldn't I have jus' gone ta Jamaica or some shit?"

"Because you're curious how all this'd lay down. Curious about me, too."

She grins. "And if I'm so smart, whuffaw I need ta be fed info."

"Because you're smart enough to know you ain't all that smart."

"Smart enough ta stay here, y'all stupid, not know."

"Cause you had help. And you knew who I was."

"Not at firs'. But then . . . like when I made sure you get you dose, I think damn . . . God punkin' me . . . what're the odds, huh, in the damn shabby-ass VA Hospital."

"Uh-huh what're odds Al-Mayadeen goes and finds me. Because Linda Figgis upped those odds, right?"

"You trippin'." She cranes her neck at Verna again. "Yeah, whatta th' odds . . . that Miz Lady here'd be co-trespassin' wiff you . . . "

"Is that really you?" Verna whispers after clearing her throat, like she's at a séance talking to a real ghost. "Ima ask you before he does—what happened to your daughter?"

"Boff y'all borin' me. So say yo' proposition then get the fuck out."

"Could you put on T-shirt, maybe?" Verna presses her.

"Wha' y'all don't run the show. Ya got five seconds t'impress me."

"Okay . . . Dickie talked to Hakim Alexander," Verna fires back, smug.

"*Pssst* . . . Little in a trance. Double-dead."

I really want a six pack of that fruity booze-in-a-can she's got, then a hole to climb into. Too late for all that.

"Little's dead, yeah," I explain. "But not when we saw him. Out of the coma for a month. Ready to speak to me, now, Miz Talbot-Thomas-Epps or whatever the hell."

"No caps."

"Real talk. I got him on audio before some white men came in chased us through alla mosquito-ass Southern Maryland . . . " I'm clocking her lower lip start to quiver and those boobs rise hard, fall with each of my words. Tactician yeah. Poker bluffer, not so much. "We came to snatch you up, make you come clean, get to sanctuary with us. You're gonna help me get my boy Stripe from being hurt by the same motherfuckers who killed Little."

I hear a bullish groan from inside her sliding screen door.

"Ya know, Seat Pleasant got its own cops," CiCi announces, blithely reaching for her pack of Kools. "I got one in there, asleep after I rocked him wiff some afternoon delight. Can't stand the snoring so I came out here . . . "

"I can shut you up and break a bottle over his head before he gets his draws back on . . . "

"Dr. Kapoor really *does* need ta adjust yo' meds, Mr. Cornish."

So I clap back. "And Al-Mayadeen snatched me at gunpoint . . . pleaded with me to find out what really happened to his daughter. K'ymira . . . the *Chimera*. Gotta say, you curve-balled that right by my ass and I'm the expert, baby. This was my shit in school, when I knew shit."

She's shaking her head. "Not this shit. *The* Chimera? Child *ain't* a monster. Monster's all 'round you."

"Your world, sis . . . spill."

So she points a painted fingernail at Verna. "Y'all dispensin' cheese sammiches an' cream a'wheat and Pampers and false hope . . . then take 'donations' from the same rich white muv-fukkahs wha' be the monster, amarite Miz Lady? Folk need houses and real jobs but naaaah, Ima chickenhead wiff cases on me so me and mine, we gotta go *rot* in the munie . . . where the monster chew up mamas, babies."

"I'd be wellin' if I said I didn't feel for you, what you endured," I tell her, real talk.

Verna's not having it. "You got this story down pat, don't you?"

"Nah, Mr. Cornish an' me know what it be . . . ta be a animal. Not you, bitch. Twelve say it can shoot you . . . rape you while you handcuffed and it ain't no thing. *So I changed the game.* Ain't a mother no more, ain't CiCi no more. And that lil' gurl—*never was.* Now, I be *Agave Epps.* Now, a lil' gurl who never was . . . is growin' ta be someone who *is.* And her name ain't 'K'ymira.' *Never was . . .* "

"You're a sociopath," Verna scoffs.

CiCi's catching something and I interpose my body between her and Verna while listing for any more groans.

"'Vain, idle fancy,'" CiCi mutters. "Thas what Chimera also mean. 'Cause that's wha she was . . . to her daddy. So I had to erase her. Make her a dream. That piece of shit first made me name her some wop Catholic name ta remind him of ice queen-no-lovin-wife. Miscarried a lil' gurl long, long time ago."

That's why LaKeisha said the records were wonky. "What was your daughter's real name?"

"*Vittoria Sofia Antonelli* . . . an' Al-Maya thought that child wiff her baby hair still at age three was *his*? Almos' as stupid as simple-ass Hakim or that fat evil Big . . . "

But lil' Verna's not backing up. "That child was not a mirage . . . she was flesh and blood and you sacrificed her for an old white man?"

Oddly, she grins. "Oh no. Ta him, Vittoria was still part 'animal,' 'specially after he be fallin' more in love wiff these rich white Nazis and fool-ass Uncle Tom niggas who jus' want the crumbs . . . an' so he keeps my baby in that munie hole, in trash schools . . . no joy, no comfort. Jus' a teddy bear he gave when she turn five and money in some bank account for when she eighteen . . . warning that her ass leave town on that birfday . . . *or I go to prison.* So nah, he was the one who wanted her gone, not me, her mama."

The tactician just made a mistake. "But he did change his mind? Maybe do without you, yet still want a child, even a dark one. Give him no incentive to shield you. Who'd believe you anyway—Linda Figgis, maybe?"

She's giving me this weird open-mouthed stare and then I realize I'm the one who fucked up. I was being clever when I should have been watching, as something's now leveled at both of us. Looks a lot like a Sig Sauer, based on Croc' gunnut schooling.

"You always disarm your sleeping lovers?" I quip. "That's cop issue, right?"

"*Agave* . . . 'dis-armed' . . . her own son. So wha'm I gonna whidchew?"

"You gonna go with us. Antonelli's people got my Stripe and Figgis doesn't give a shit."

"Baby, if Dante got the boy then he already be dead, sorry. Now y'all get out."

Chill blains in the summer heat—they suddenly wrack back and thighs . . . my stomach's bubbling. *No . . . not now Daddy*!

She can smell it on me. Probably learned over coffee with Kapoor, flashing those fake blue eyes, for now she's whispering, "I should just do you, Mr. Cornish . . . put you outchere misery 'cause it not never goin' away—trauma's voices an' pain. *Ever*."

The screen door to the house suddenly slides open and a brother naked as the day he was born trundles out, dick swinging . . .

"*Da fuck*? Bitch you took my piece?"

Verna's either a quick study or she's so netted and pissed the adrenaline's juiced her into being Catwoman! I'm slack-jawed watching her little self leap onto this chick. And I'm right behind Verna, dead ass.

CiCi's got the wind knocked out of her and Verna gets the Sig. As her She-Hulk power wanes and reality oozes back, Verna starts aiming the damn thing at all of us in wild swings.

"Vee . . . take it easy," I cry.

"Y'all . . . with . . . this trick?" the nude Seat Pleasant cop jabbers.

Not the right word with CiCi, as she's cat-clawing at me to get at him. I get her in a wrestling hold—thank the D.C. Catholic prep schools for that move—and for now I'm safe from those nails as she screams, writhes . . .

"Where's your unit?" I yell to the cop. Can feel cool blood and a hot cut on my temple. He mumbles and I look to a quivering, armed Verna. "Get him inside, tell him to find his cuffs, keys to his unit . . . have him cuff himself to anything like a railing and shit . . . "

"I-I'm . . . not myself, Dickie," Verna whispers.

"I know, Vee." I roll onto CiCi and even with my full weight she's thrashing. As the jake steps into the house, Verna behind him, I yell at him, "My girl'll shoot you, officer, if jump bad, hear me?"

"Shit . . . whatever . . . just keep that crazy trick away . . . "

CiCi goes limp under me this time . . . chuckling. "You can't run. But I ride in a *chariot* . . . "

I pull her arm back behind her back, threaten to break it if she moves or speaks again . . . but that reference is digging at my dome. "What'd you say?"

"Fuck you."

I holler to Verna, "Bring her a shirt and . . . a belt. Hurry."

I watch neighbors peeking through blinds or curtains . . . praying they mind they're damn business till we can book. Still, I roll off her, stand her up.

She's unfazed. "You fuck with me, an' Twelve ain't at war wiff itself no more. *They be at war wiff you.*"

Thought has occurred to me, which is why my old man bladder's leaky.

Verna's out the screen door and shoves that Sig in my hand and Mother Mary thank you for it not blowing a hole in my palm because the damn safety was off; she helps me bind this divine spitter's wrists with a fashionista leather belt.

"That's Banana Republic, bitch," CiCi hisses at Verna, who just sighs in reply.

We jump in the Mini. I'm driving and it's no macho tip . . . because I'm passing the iron to Verna . . . in the back . . . safety *on* with the spout pointed at CiCi upfront in the passenger seat.

We're shooting onto Addison Road. I ask Verna to slowly

pass that paper bag up to CiCi's lap. With difficulty our passenger manages to get it open and screams when she beholds what's inside. No more venom, huh? Nope she's staring right at Poob.

"Linda Figgis admitted she sent that to Al-Mayadeen. She not tell you?"

Verna pops between us, whispering, "Don't shade Linda in front of her."

Sorry, Vee. Here's what's got the jigsaw pieces clacking. "The goddess Athena rescued Medea in a *chariot* before Jason could come after her for killing their kids. Likewise, the goddess Artemis guarded Agave from Pentheus's soldiers after she realized what she'd done. Ask CiCi, here."

CiCi's not saying a damn thing until, "Why I get wiff the same bitch who wanna put a case on me and Little for dippin' my own blood, my baby, huh?"

For once Verna's in accord with the queen of the boppers. "Wrong, Dickie . . . *wrong*," she scoffs from the back. "Linda'll rescue Stripe, protect us . . . you'll see."

Well, Verna senses pretty damn fast that her little ass car's going nowhere near the Daly Building, or the press, or the Justice Department.

It's headed, full bore, to the one place I prayed I'd never have to hide. Croc's ramshackle duplex and its basement full of guns is no more than a mile away.

I hit the radio, WTOP, to pick up any news that might help . . . and to drown surfacing echoes of Daddy voice up in my dome. Mayor's down at some "socially distant community carnival" at the Reeves Center—with Figgis. Says she holding a press conference tomorrow or Wednesday on whether she'll run for "an unprecedented third term," or retire and endorse a successor.

CiCi gets geeked up and quips, "She gonna pass the reins to the chariot to some *other* bitch . . . " I see her stare at Verna, then purr, " . . . *amarite?*"

And now I'm starting to wonder about a lot people who aren't what they seem.

CHAPTER 23

Vittoria Sofia

CiCi needs a couple of seconds to clock ol' Croc and his Aussie slouch hat beaded with crocodile skin . . . the mirror shades . . . the reptile cane. It's some extra shit, especially as he's breathless just from ushering us up the iron steps from the alley to his duplex's back door.

Hard to imagine he and I as teen anchors of the D.C. Catholic League's irresistible power sweep . . . me as tight end, coming around to knock the fuck out of any Gonzaga, DeMatha, or Carroll linebacker who got in the way, Croc as pulling guard, taking out the knees of whatever gorilla D-end gave chase. Now his gut's parting that ratty blue terrycloth bathrobe . . . Ace bandages wrap both knees . . . his dogs swell out of his slippers like loaves of bread. And he *ain't* the kind to seek a vax shot. Not that he goes anywhere since his grandniece and her baby moved out, and the house smells of that fact.

"Yo, fam'ly . . . " Croc grunts to me after directing Verna to a cleaner bathroom on the second floor, " . . . y'all better pray Twelve don't check last-known associates. If my name or my parents come up, them mugs be batter-ramming my bran-new door from Home Depot."

"Thought you had Cee-Four wired to your shit . . . " And I'm only half-joking. " . . . like when your pops blew up that garage near ole Club Fifty-Five so DEA couldn't get the product?"

"Kill, nigga that was Christmas, Nineteen Eighty-Nine. Cee-Four all spoilt now."

CiCi suddenly screeches, "This hermit nigga's got explosives up in here?"

Croc's eyes narrow. "Ain't my tip to be peevish, young lady . . . but my moms and pops and the Colombians were the only folk Rayful Edmunds be scared of back in the day."

"*Who?*"

"Lil' gurl you prolly think Rare Essence's a shampoo. We ain't museum exhibits . . . "

CiCi, wrists still bound, gives him a wink. My jaw goes loose when this rolla up and starts a wop . . . perfectly timed to a D.C. swing beat in her head, then busts the lyric, "*Put yo' Gucci watch on . . .* "

Damn. Croc goes from crusty to all melty . . . waddles over to his Nineties vintage stereo and cues up the Rare Essence. "Do You Know What Time It Is" pops from those column speakers, loosing puff of lint and dust with each bass vibration. CiCi's there shaking that ass and boobs like the girls at Club RSVP, once not too far from here . . . when I was callow and stupid, and Croc was worldly and stupid.

Now Verna's descending the stairs to the bizarre scene. "Look at her, dancing with this old goat," she tells me. "Sociopath, like I said . . . "

Indeed, same motherfucker fretting battering rams is utterly mesmerized by this chick so I pull him aside and school him. Swear to God he hears me but he's not *listening*.

"Didn't ol' Croc cover you in your last pickle . . . wid Bracht and that merc Mr. Sugars? I gotchew, moe."

"Turn off the music, gee."

"Fade-up." He's all sore-faced now, waddling back to the stereo to kill the volume.

"End times," CiCi huffs, all sweaty, smile as odd as her statement. "Wanna untie my hunnad-twenny dollah belt from 'round my hands so's I can pee?"

I point to the powder room by the kitchen . . . the one Croc blows up on the regular, so she's not pleased. "No good reason to trust you," I quip as I dig into the belt's knot.

"Wish y'all'd let me bring my bag. Monthly came down on me."

Bullshit. But now Verna's rummaging around in her own bag, produces something cylindrical and wrapped in pinkish paper.

"Spare . . . emergency one."

CiCi bats it away onto Croc's dusty rug. "Pooh-butt trick. I *manage* . . . "

The door shuts and I'm not moving till I hear a solid stream of pee under her cursing.

"Doesn't play well with others who have vaginas," Verna jokes with a mock-sigh. "And I know what you're thinking, Dickie, but that child is dead. Fits every profile, every metric so don't let her say this 'Vittoria' is in Wisconsin somewhere and passing for white, as a lure . . . "

I hear the toilet flush and then, "Pennsylvania, *bitch.*" The door opens. "Wiff a white family who think she all Sicily dark, not a nigga. An' by the way I took stuff from under the sink, maybe Mr. Croc's ole ladyfrien's mussa leff."

Verna's folding her arms, exchanging a nonplussed look with me for an instant but I just say, "CiCi, sit down on that sofa and don't move."

"Dickie I gotta call SFME," Verna adds.

"Make yo' call, trick," CiCi hisses.

"Fuck you say?" Verna retorts. Verna'll slap her, so I'm ready to intercede.

"Pure as the driven slush . . . makin' mamas cry," CiCi whispers upon deciding to retreat.

His girl-fight leer unrequited, Croc calls out to Verna, "There go my landline right there, suga-pie. I can make it look like it's a call from the Supreme Court or the White House widdat lil' box an' keyboard on the table."

Verna's not digging the paranoid gear or "sugar pie" but hey. I'm rolling into the kitchen to grab a bottle of cold water. Chug it as I pray the meds hold . . .

. . . and this girl must be clairvoyant because now I'm hearing, in a mocking, sing-songey pitch from the living room, "Need your meds, Mr. Cornish? I can call Dr. Kapoor . . . "

Croc's now watching me finish off a second bottle. He whispers, "Like I say, they'll figure out y'all're here sooner or later. Be a Bonnie an' Clyde bloodbath, real live . . . "

Turning to his triple-pierced ear I tell him, "I look like I want that? But Ima be needing a bad stick. Twelve gauge. And a forty or a nine millie, maybe a little twenny-five for Verna so we can dump that Seat Pleasant Sig Sauer."

"*Grasshopper.* My teachings on the ever-loving firearm have gotten purchase!"

"Real talk, man . . . I don't like gats, but we gotta stay breathing to get truth out."

Guess he clocks no bullshit in my pupils. "I got what you need downstairs, cool? Scrambler radio unit, too, so fuck the mobile phones. Lemme order some grub."

"No James Bond shit, moe. Just the iron and lead, okay? Which brings me back to *her.* What I recorded from this boy Little don't mean shit if SOD perishes my live witness. "

"And yo' gurl . . . the Chief of Police?"

"Shit, she and her ladies club prolly wouldn't mind if CiCi's dipped, trust. Nah man, with her I can play it twice—with SOD to get Stripe back, buy some safety, and Figgis, as a block on SOD."

"Jus' be careful. You did that with Bracht—his babymama—and it blew up in your face."

"The baby's fine. The baby's got a new life." Shit, I sound like Verna.

"And what about this kid—this *Chimera?* Kill, you say the rolla in there say the babydaddy didn't give a fuck 'cause the kid's part speck? You believe that briar rabbit shit?"

"Something's not tidy about this, Croc. I told her he changed his mind and loves the child, just to throw her off. Serve my hunch."

"What hunch, cuz?"

"Nevermind. It was just my bullshit . . . in reality there's no way this motherfucker wants that child."

"Ole Croc must retort. Maybe it was so when she was young. But six years away from the shelter, from the niggas in the District . . . out wid whitefolk? Maybe that's enough to bleach the mambo sauce outchere till she's a just another Becky wid curly 'air and a lil' knob nose. He might want her back now, regardless of who snatched her in the first place."

His logic's causing my bladder some issues again. "If she's alive."

Croc chuckles at my dilemma then achingly descends the basement stairs on his diabetic legs.

I find CiCi chillin' all sandals off, feet up on the sofa underneath framed, autographed photos of Marion Barry, Elvin Hayes, Redskins cheerleader squads going back forty years maybe?

The pep squad shots seem to intrigue her and here's my angle.

"I coulda did that in school," she says, longingly.

"Croc's mama was among the first blacks out there. Then . . . made her leave when they found out she was a single mom, Croc's daddy said hey lets get married . . . instead of a housewife she became a narco-queen. Crack rock. Spending paper at Tysons Corner or Mazza Gallerie with the ofays, as my own Daddy called them."

"Dayum," CiCi huffs, as if she could give a fuck about her current captivity.

"We got food coming. Waterfront Fish Market."

Her face lights up beyond her cosmetic illumination. "Crabs?"

"I could get by with a can of deviled ham and some Ritz Crackers, word. But this ain't no alley or stoop set, eatin' off newspapers, okay?"

"How would you know 'bout eating Fish Market crabs on the stoop, Mr. Bourgie?" she joans with a disconcerting grin. "Saw your intake file. Your grandfather was a dentist, high on the hog over there on Sixteenth an' Kalmia. Sister went to private school wiff white bitches in Bethesda . . . daddy's some baller in the Marines." She's leaning now, and her breasts are spilling from her shirt. "You down here in the dirt wiff *us* 'cause you got on the pipe in college. *Guh* . . . Mr. Croc's parents turn you out?"

My videos say: *Connect with the suspect on a personal level . . .*

"Clever girl. But it was a sherm stick, not the pipe. Embalming fluid my girlfriend Esme procured. Pipe came later. As for the rest, you *jhi*-lunchin'."

She bites the lure. "You been on the street twenny years or so. Most niggas don't last half that time. In the file it say folk call on ya to do goon, gorilla shit—is that the truth?"

"I'm just an old man."

"Wha' you like fifty? Tha' ain't old!"

Those blue contacts don't seem the least bit dry, the fake lashes are batting like Bette Davis' in *The Little Foxes* . . .

"Nineteen Forty-One . . . directed by William Wyler," I mumble.

"Huh?"

"Just more stuff I roll around in my dome that Dr. Kapoor needs to fix."

"Oh . . . yeah," she giggles.

I pivot. "Why the VA? And how'd you get past background checks even using what . . . Miz Jocasta's niece's creds?"

"You an' me . . . we peas in the same pod, watchin' the rest spoil slow or die fast. We *survive.* At school, Miz Epps asked my mama get me tested. See, I already knew I was special 'cause I had ta grow up fast, be the mama."

"I don't understand."

"Had ta pay bills, get shoppin', make dinner, put my goon half-brother in check 'cause he was always fuckin' up, worthless. An' go to school, do math problems an' shit when I was ten and rest of them niggas couldn't add. Let x equal fiddy percent alcohol an' y equal ten percent alcohol an' shit . . . " Now she's got this empty, distant look, not pensive. Pensive would be too warm for what I'm clocking. "Then at night . . . be the mama . . . for my *daddy*, too. See, he went to college, okay? Coulda been in law school but no money, my mama drain he money. So he *Twelve*—a motorcycle cop. But I couldn't be mama for him 'cause I be young, stupid . . . so he leff, married his side bitch . . . "

If she's telling the truth, my heart bleeds for her. If she's not, I should be more scared of her than I am.

"All that trauma . . . then going into the munie's madness . . . "

"Oh so now *you* be Dr. Kapoor and I be the patient?"

"Not tryna get into your head. Just tryna see—how we're alike?"

"I hunt. You clean up the mess. We alike 'cause we ain't prey."

"You sound like someone I used to know."

"A woman?"

"No. Someone who tried to murk me."

"He still beefin' on ya?"

"No. I killed him first. *Bad*." I stand, push my grill real close. "I ain't Al-Mayadeen or Little, or Moses Roffe, so don't fuck with me."

Suddenly Croc's hollering for assistance. I leave her teeth-sucking and neck-rolling to help him lug a nylon Redskins duffle bag from the basement stairs and wrestle it onto the kitchen table.

I hear Verna say, "Dickie, I dunno if LaKeisha got your upload . . . "

"The cloud . . . she talks about the damn cloud!"

"I told her to go home, don't talk to a soul, lock the doors to her room in the group house. Katie's gonna to check in on her." She eyes me fishing a Glock from the goody bag and doesn't muffle a gasp. "Lord . . . this has gotten outta hand . . . I *don't* want anyone else hurt . . . "

"I'm screwed if she can't back up my interviews, pics, notes. It's all I got."

"All you got to nail Linda, too. Implicate me?"

"Melvin be back, getcha grub, people!" Croc calls, quashing that conversation. Melvin, the skinny brother on the other end of Croc's little beeping two-way he keeps in his bathrobe pocket, is at Croc's newly-installed Home Depot door. Croc's snatches away a bag of white Styrofoam containers, then tells his gunsel to post-up across the street, signal if cops rolls up.

"Fried fish, mac an' cheese, greens, *and* fries?" Verna huffs after popping open a container.

"Oh thas' mine," Croc snorts, switching her out. "Y'alls is the shrimp . . . "

She takes her dinner and a water bottle upstairs without another word. CiCi's wants hot sauce and another towelette packet. I've lost my appetite.

Croc's hitting his stride with impressive belch as he feasts. I'm nursing a Rock Creek Ginger Ale.

"Think Verna's getting nervous . . . wants to hit her place, grab clothes and shit," I tell Croc. "I told her it's a bad idea. Undercovers and jakes might have the jont on lock."

"Kill, gee . . . not necessarily," Croc replies, grabbing for a toothpick. "You said you stashed shit there. Better get it. Leave the toy car here, I call you a Lyft. Maybe red cab back? Get in, get out. Long as it ain't like Bruce Willis in *Pulp Fiction*, cool?"

"Might work. Might clear her head a bit, too."

"Can't help you widdat moe."

Verna comes down, hair pinned up, to find us in the living room waiting on her.

Croc's all cranked back in his Lay Z Boy. "G'won now you lovebirds," he quips. "I'll watch Miz Gurl, here." He lays a pistol on his lap. "We good, Missy?"

CiCi, mute, jumps a painted-on brow.

When we blow out the back. Still hot as brick kiln out there; daylight's likewise melting into streams of yellows, blues and reds and the airs thick with that fermented summer sniff of weed, spent firecracker gunpowder, barbeque charcoal, alley garbage . . . and it's like a mini Ginza from Tokyo when we get out near Sixth and H, Northeast . . . with the rising moon outshone by the lit-up bistro fronts, posh shop windows, live music brew pubs. I smell the sweat and strawberry scent of gangs of Beckies in their summer dresses . . . craft bourbon odor of Chads, all in cottons and linens . . . ravenous for what the previous summer of 'rona denied them . . .

. . . and Verna's quiet, stonefaced until she tells me, "I'll go in through the garage we share with the Whole Foods . . . then run to the stairs to my floor. I'll pack as much as I can for you."

Not a jake in sight anyway but for the traffic cops ticketing along the trolley lane before the tow trucks swing-up. Undercovers? Not a problem because there's the perfect blind and even reinforcements out here: new meat's pitched tents in the patch of dirt under a big poplar across the street. Bunch of hourly cats are on break among them . . . bumming smokes off one another in their busboy aprons and dishwasher gloves and such. Not much into the conversations I figure out they use to live around here as children. Tonight they're either sleeping under a filthy vinyl dome or rushing to keep their battered cars from getting ticketed or towed . . .

. . . and so Verna's taking too damn long and I move to the big smelly construction Dumpster obscured by the poplar, doubling as a latrine for the campers, based on the familiar scent. Old habits die hard—and as I piss on the dumpster I note an old One-Six Crew tag. The lit lighter. *And again,* with another red "X" spray painted through it. *And again,* not a difficult task to noodle through: after they dipped Thanos, they probably framed Benning Road or others for it like they tried to pin my airing out on fucking MS-13.

Anyway, here comes Verna, manhandling my heavy duffle and her fashionista leather satchel bag like she's a midget stevedore. She drops the duffle hard on one of the poplar's gnarled roots and I cringe. The fucking .380 and clip are in there.

She runs back into the night bustle and gets a hack who's no doubt thinking here's a pretty black woman with cash needing to get to Reagan National or over the bridge to Union Station. But then my big ass edges into the backseat with her and he's huffing and hawing when I tell him the address.

Maybe it's a blessing because he minds his business just as Verna's reticence abruptly ends.

"What you said about the U.S. Attorney. Equating Linda with Dante. Good people will be punished, bad people will go free, even boast . . . even kill to silence the truth."

It's not on a high horse when I tell her, "Kidnapping these children . . . abusing the system?"

"Do you want me to go to jail?"

I fish for my meds. Swallow the pills without water. They don't need to dissolve for me to whisper, "I shot Moses. Before they took us to the Gingerbread House. He was coming at me and Stripe with a knife . . . "

"I-I . . . "

"Vee . . . I did him. He was dirty but it was self-defense." Not really. Just being a little killer pig.

Her expression's blank, unblinking and it doesn't change until this asshole dumps us off Potomac Avenue Southeast, and even if my long Frankenstein's monster gait I can't keep up with her scamper . . . and she won't even turn around to look at me with disgust. But she comes to a halt in the alley. Gestures.

Croc's house is usually a *Munsters* or *Addams Family* brand of keep-the-fuck-out.

Not this time.

The rear is lit up like H Street; the back door off the iron landing hangs open. I dig out the .380, pray it's not the po-po who did this.

A figure appears at the top of the terrace stairs and swear I almost pull the trigger. With my temples throbbing I call to Croc's gunsel, "The fuck, moe?"

"Man . . . you gotta see this!" the skinny narrow-headed dude pants, holstering his own iron.

Inside, Croc's writhing on the floor by the Lay Z Boy, face bloodied. His draws are down by his swollen ankles.

By the way, that red on his shrunk dick sure as hell isn't blood.

"Fucking loafed on me, moe," I whisper. Not to him, *nah*, inwardly. Hell-else am I going to do? He fucked up . . . *he's* fucked up . . . he's fucked me. But he's my friend.

Verna's panting behind me, dropping her satchel. "Where's CiCi?" she cries.

Yeah, she's more netted up than I am and I don't fathom why but I suspect the evil gods on Mt. Olympus will hip me very soon. And it'll hurt, bad. "Dickie . . . Lord . . . see this?" she adds, waking me from my dithering stupor.

The gunsel's passed her an old PEPCO bill envelope, something scrawled in red marker on it and now he adds the golden commentary. "This bu'shit was taped to his dick."

"I'll get some towels, ice," Verna tells me as I try to focus on the message.

Mr. Cornish, Agave was heart-broken when she wake up and saw she murdered her son. If Medea didnt lov Jason so much she wouldnt hav killed her kids. Vittoria Sofia is here: Michael and Randie DiSilvio 2000 W. 4th St. Harrisburg Pa. Susquehanna Middle School was her school. -C

CHAPTER 24

From a Great Height

"WHAT ARE YOU PLANNING?" YEAH, VERNA'S not playing. She's already pulled up Croc's shorts and elevated his head. "You aren't going anywhere with a damn bag full of guns."

We smell of a sweltering day and sultry night and I'm shy that I'll stink more, but she's the one grabbing at me, poking as if this is a game. "Kiss me, Dickie. Show me you're not going to throw your life *back* in the garbage . . . "

Nice Vee. The life I changed so you'd respect me as a man, right? And now I'm all up in my feelings and shouting at her, "Wanna call me stupid, wanna say you gotta stop making this shit up as I go along, huh? I didn't *ask* for this . . . it followed me into a fucking drug store, put a gat in my ribs . . . stood right over my mother's rosary and said nigga you're involved. Just like with Bracht . . . *and Esme* . . . here I am again!"

Verna puts her small hand in my big, gnarled mitt as I struggle to come down. "This address . . . I'm telling you, it's fake. Anyone and anything useless to a personality like CiCi's is jettisoned including her own daughter. Now you got but one card to play."

I hit back, "Linda's behind this. I can smell it."

"What, she made Croc pull his pants down for a blow job so CiCi could escape? Are you decompensating? I'm dead ass serious."

"She could be with 'Figgsy' right now."

Lil' girl drops my hand and her look is icy, stabbing. "Don't you dare mock me while you have a bag of guns and nona the damn sense God gave you . . . 'cause if you did you'd be calling EMS for your friend."

"GW . . . " we all hear Croc moan aloud.

"GW . . . Myron'll run him over to GW. Croc likes GW. When the Justice Department finally got his parents on a case that stuck, they beat his Croc's dad like a slave when served the warrant. Docs at GW who stitched up an set his bones wouldn't let the Marshals and FBI near him till he was out of surgery. Robbed George Bush the Elder of a drug war photo op."

"Forgive my lapse in DC lore—what happened?"

She should have stopped me there.

"He had a stroke during his trial. The Justice Department moved him to a secure Army infirmary Ft. Myer where they claim he died in his sleep. His mother was found guilty and went to prison. No club-fed like the whitefolks. She died up at Lewisburg in Twenny-fifteen." I sling the Croc's nylon duffle over my shoulder. "You know Croc never was pinched, never served a day? Wanted to be an engineer and work for some big German or Japanese company overseas, no lie . . . like I wanted to play pro ball then retire . . . then start my own school, teach . . . crazy shit like that."

"I know you've done ugly things . . . out on the street."

"White girl who was president of the Glee Club . . . dude who was prep school lacrosse phenom . . . she was on her way to Princeton, him to UVA . . . and likely both'd Beltway famous and plain rich today had they lived." I swallow hard. "They roofied my sister, assaulted her when all she wanted to do was fit in. Black girls on post, who went to public school—they called her a wannabe and teased her 'cause she was shy, a nerd. My dad pissed on her when he should have protected her. My mom abandoned her because that's what Daddy wanted and Daddy was boss. My sister killed herself and I had Croc kill them."

Before Verna can lean to kiss me I holler for Myron the gunsel, swing the duffle so she can't reach me. I'm down the rickety iron stairs and don't look back.

Myron hips me to where Croc's got his Cutlass stowed. Under a tarp, where he left it with instructions no one fuck with it. Last time I needed this thing Croc loaned it with great relish. Now neither he or the gunsel are in a position to deny me. You'd be proud, Daddy . . .

"Myron—the keys?"

"Dunno, gee," the gunsel grunts. "But the 'oh shit' key be in the wheel well, right rear."

"*Dickie*!" I finally hear Verna scream into the alley. Maybe she was too scared to add "If you love me you'll turn around." Or she didn't want to lie?

My last stop in my ole District of Columbia is a BP in Silver Spring. Gas the monster with my shirking gwap. Grab a map from the little Eritrean lady wearing her mask dutifully and who doesn't treat me like an armed robber despite my tint and size.

She shows me the men's room. It's bright green tile and clean, air conditioned to an Arctic level. Maybe a good omen? I wash up, read the map, change my draws . . . put on fresh

T-shirt and button up this short sleeve shirt that's sort of blue chambray I got at Goodwill. See, a car like a red Olds Cutlass is a rolling target and I am walking taser collector per the current wisdom, so what does one do? One just rolls. Plain sight. I turn on my phone . . .

. . . lots of messages, full voicemail. I call Stripe's phone. Pray they haven't busted up and buried it in a hole. Goes to voicemail. Unsure whether that's good or bad . . .

. . . until I get my ring, a voice.

"*Is this Cornish. Hold on . . .* " No clue who this late-shift goon is. It's not that Uncle Tom, Woodman. Then after about four or five weird clicks . . . speak of the devil. "*Is that you, Big Man? You lucky I'm a night owl.*"

"Don't bother with the hi tech. I'm in Silver Spring, Georgia Avenue and the Beltway."

"*You slicker than we thought, Slick. Steve McQueen yourself outta Charles County then disappear. Radio silence. But you put Verna Leggett in a lot of—*"

"Shut up. I will send a sample of my interview with Hakim Alexander along with a teddy bear, my notes . . . the whole wad . . . to the *Washington Post* with a 'cc' to Kamala Harris so don't lunch on me. Where's Stripe . . . Ernesto? I want to speak to him."

"Hold on."

More clicks . . . couple of seconds and dribbles of piss I'd rather have back. Then . . .

"*It's frickin' late.*" The hushed menace generates a few more dribbles. "*I understand you're a member of the Roman Church . . . there's a* novena *for those in peril . . . and I pray you're ready to come in on your own, rather than on a gurney or in a body bag.*"

"Deputy Chief Antonelli . . . "

"*I don't care if you're recording this, Cornish. Indeed I'm showing you the courtesy of zero trace, no tricks. This is you and me. All we need is you, or your phone, whatever we lifted from your laptop to shut you down . . .* "

"Is Stripe okay?"

"Didn't just hear what I said? We want you, not him. Hurting him does us no good. We aren't the Gestapo. But given a citizenship issue and lack of a fixed domicile . . . he was automatically remanded to the CDF, okay?"

"So you didn't kill Little in his bed, send Roffe to murk Big, give Thanos of the One-Six Crew the nine millie beat-down . . . then maybe game out setting me up for all of that? And I hear SOD can manipulate . . . *hmm* . . . CCTV video, cell tower data? Or is that old news."

"*You watched too much HBO in the men's shelter. But here's some juicy intrigue for you: Chief Figgis has gotten you and herself in a bind, and she's going to fall very hard, very fast, bringing many with her. Prosecutions, lawsuits, disgrace . . .* "

I hit mute, turn over the Cutlass's engine, pull out onto Georgia. "And?"

"And, I read files, too. Two years ago, you were on the street in a hospital gown, nuts-out, picking through garbage cans. Now look at you, Slick. You aren't part of her scene." There's silence and then, "*Again, it's late, I'm tired, I'm not into grandiloquence. That said, to 'rule,' one requires power, not legitimacy. Linda's 'throne' is papier-mâché . . . and it's about to rain. You want an umbrella or not, Slick?*"

"Funny I was gonna offer you the umbrella."

There's dead air. One Mississippi . . . two Mississippi, then, "*I've shown restraint. You've shown folly.*"

"Saw online you're member of Knights of Columbus? They're still around? What would they say if they knew about your babymama . . . and baby? Or did you hook them up with frightened women, underage treats, too?"

"*Young Ernesto's now in detention gen-pop. From my review of your rather storied past, you had a run-in with one 'Blinky' Guzman of Mara Salvatrucha. His surviving disciples might want a word with Ernesto . . . some of them have been in the CDF for over a year awaiting trial, thanks to COVID. Hopefully, the C.O.s will get him in productive custody . . .* "

He went and did it. So I swallow hard, spill, "CiCi Talbot-Thomas is *alive.* Your daughter is *alive.* Guess you could pop by the 'Gingerbread House' for cotton candy and ask Linda what the intel is, Mr. Intel Expert, but I'd rather you hear it from me."

Well, what I hear next is cursing in English and Italian . . . and then dead air, then, "*Linda is not what she seems, Cornish.*"

"No one seems to be."

"Yeah? *when that's manifest with your balls in the wringer, you'll whimper and whine for me to open the door and let you in you dirty black bastard . . .* "

"You just make sure the C.O.'s are extra watchful over Stripe. Matter of fact have him call to me in an hour to record a message. Then I'll be in touch. And we'll both take our chances with Chief Figgis."

I'm done, and just in time as I'm on 95, less than hour plus from Baltimore and a brick on top of that from I-83, which snakes in Pennsylvania.

Yeah, but it's not Figgis I'm worried about right now. Braving another cell ping, I call Verna.

"Vee . . . it's me. Maybe . . . you better just go home . . . go back to work. Do normal shit so Antonelli's cops and the Feds . . . they can't see what's up."

"*Where are you? Why did you do this?*"

"Vee, *stop*, okay? Look . . . how's Croc?"

She's saying something about some jackleg preacher who used to have a medical license giving him stitches and an ice pack but it's all melting into blah blah blah so I tell her, ask her, to have Croc send Melvin to put eyes on a group home on Riggs Road, Northeast. Yeah, it's a jont where LaKeisha sleeps, keeps a tidy room with cots made-up for the day when she can get custody of her kids. Small cots, Katie once said, because that's how she remembers her babies. Oldest got to be at least thirteen now. Like the girl called K'ymira.

"*Dickie please . . . don't tell me you have that bag of guns with you,*" Verna presses, voice getting wetter. She's hiccupping, all frantic.

I lie. My heads all balloony, like I'm not even there, just floating.

"*Linda'd believe you about CiCi, Dickie. She'll put five hundred officers on the street to find her and dress it up like it was someone else they were searching for.*"

"Vee. Peace." I cut her off before I get a second mind that abandons my course, my plan . . .

. . . and yeah, Croc's got no tech in this whip so I try to catch the DC stations fading the farther north I go, sideswiping Baltimore. Nats won, Orioles lost. Wizards out of playoffs. Whatever . . .

. . . ah, here. Multiple gunshot victims at a city BBQ, including three toddlers. No suspects. Mayor's press conference on whether she will run again, cancelled mysteriously.

"They're waiting for me," I say and it's Esme young and voluptuous, nodding along from the passenger seat. I'm not hallucinating, no. I just feel her, and she haunts me with whispers . . . into the inky dark, General Motors hemi gobbling the white lines on I-83. *Ave Maria* . . . most favored lady . . . I'm so tired . . .

. . . no decent music on the FM. So I'm laughing now, as one side of my brain's watching for deer and Twelve while the other's aghast and says to Esme, "Here I am again."

Uh-huh, in the Keystone state . . . with a shotgun . . . at night, alone. *Déjà vu*? Oh yes, that hunting lodge couple miles from Breezewood. And I put some faces on the evening news and Google that night.

Quickly those memories melt into a scene of dried-out, rehab clarity . . . of scholarly debate in the shelter kitchen, below the chapel . . . and Brother Karl-Maria quizzes me, with Father Phil Ruffino looking on, silently rooting for me.

"What brought Bellerophon low?" the celibate friar asks. Ruffino's cheating, whispering "Book of Job," but *fuck* the Bible here, huh.

"Hubris!" I answer to them in memory and that Cutlass, in the dark.

And Karl-Maria'd school me, to get me to dry out, "Doom, reckoning, came in the form of a gadfly. Pissant with wings."

Bellerophon, up in his feelings, caught another ride with Pegasus and flew too close to Olympus. Zeus sent the little bug buzzing close to the mighty winged horse's eye. Pegasus bucked. Threw Bellerophon from a great height . . . and a huge thorn bush "cushioned" his fall.

And I see myself whispering . . . timidly, afraid . . . my head hurts so much. I repeat, "Here I am again. Pennsylvania in the dark."

Here I am again. Esme, naked in my bed . . . Cook Dorm, full-up of my teammates, who hadn't seen me in weeks . . .

. . . you're pounding on the door, cursing your only son . . .

. . . I feel the tree branch snapping across my bare back . . . Yeah . . . *here I am again.*

Yeah. Here you are again, dummy . . .

CHAPTER 25

Contrapositive

ONACCOUNT IT AIN'T THE PILL, IT'S the will, Junior. Wish you'd've learnt that by now despite your murder attempt on Ole Gunney. But I forgive you . . .

. . . no need to stop for caffeine and a hard roll and to hear the little spick caterwaul from his jail bunk; they'll protect him as leverage while you flail about in Pennsyltuckey looking for the leverage on them. And time's running out on that . . . see? You're creeping up on this cowtown, Harrisburg.

The sun breaks the eastern rim of the planet . . . and that dawn fog shrouding your arrival now is going is either going to burn away most rikky-tik or be thin cover. Pray for the rain foretold on the radio, because there's only one way into this burg stretched out along the Susquehanna River like Stalingrad unfolded along the Volga. Hard to believe this broad sewer births the regal, mythic Chesapeake Bay.

You cross the bridge, circle off the cloverleaf, pull the Cutlass in a hard left onto empty streets rimmed by the red brick shells of ancient buildings. The stone, concrete and glass edifices housing the state government loom ahead, no doubt still vacant from the 'rona, and that's funny considering the

Trump iconography fluttering from same windowsills and light poles wrapped with July Fourth bunting!

Get over to Front Street . . . you'll have a cheek to the river . . . better idea if anyone's on your six, or flanking you on your three.

"No."

Thinking like a boot! Okay, announce yourself by driving straight through downtown's rabbit warren of intersections, most still flashing red? Shit, the architecture could be in D.C. or any eastern city from Richmond to Boston frankly: ancient rowhouses. None of your hobo tribe are lying about so you can't stop for a guide. Worse, that Motown muscle engine isn't for stealth. It growls and sputters, leaving folk rattled out of their beds in its wake . . .

"I-I can't read the neighborhood . . . no one's out . . . "

Listen boy, if this *is* a Bohunk enclave and they make you as a big spook in a red Oldsmobile you'll be scooped up faster than dog turds on a yuppie sidewalk. Then they find the shotgun in your trunk and black lives definitely won't matter, so what's your play?

"Dumping the car . . . map showed an alley off Peffer Street."

Now you're thinking! Slow up . . . that's the house. Stained and dented pale blue siding nailed over the old brick and timber to make it look like the more "modern" pitch-roofed townhomes across the street. Windows fronting the street are dark . . .

. . . you get off 4th, come around a couple blocks then recross Peffer and still no activity but a *Patriot-News* truck replenishing vending boxes.

The alley's perfect for you and you're breathing easier. Couple of abandoned brick buildings on one side, tall plank fence and stands of thick tree-ferns on the other. Perfect cover from the yokels long as you stay quiet and relocate. You stash your gwap in the trunk, pull a heavy pair of rubberized grip binoculars from the duffle, next to the almighty the shotgun.

Feeling like a gumshoe now?

Only sound is a big stray tabby groaning almost humanlike hissing when you scare it from the stack of plastic milk crates some yokel's been hoarding back of their hovel. Gives you a view of both the rear of the house on 4th and its little sunroom covered in blinds. The DeSilvios better not be at the shore with the rest of the ofays. Still, you've lucked out—the morning mist off the river's given way to roiling blue-ish clouds. You're going to get wet but at least you won't be—

"*Stop* . . . shut-up. Movement. *Lights* . . . "

Well, well. They blink-on upstairs, then the lower level. Sunroom's still dark. Check the street, dummy! Can you see 4th Street from this position?

"Swear to God . . . brake lights . . . saw a car stop . . . wasn't the traffic light . . . "

First drops of hot rain are hitting your head, spattering on the alley concrete and fern leaves. Garage or big utility shed ahead and all you must do is get over a chain link fence, undiscovered. You struggle over the fence like the old man you are.

But at least you're at the shed. Front row seat!

Of course, that bopper could have been lying. She's got that voodoo to make fools be fools, right? Ask Al-Mayadeen. Or Dante Antonelli. Now you, out here in the morning rain, jumping fences . . .

"Youze gotta move yer fuckin' truck fore Christsakes!"

Startled, you spin wildly and almost give yourself away. *Calm down.* It's some old bat hollering in the window, see? She's hollering at a pot-belly codger emerging from rear basement stairs in his skivvies, toting a garbage pail.

"Trash men'll b'here soon!"

"Shut yer hole, ow-kay? Wakin' the neighbors."

Yeah. A Bohunk hood. That stupid accent.

This old dude would be heading right for the Cutlass but for the squall line coming off the river driving him back inside—and soaking you to the marrow. You raise the field glasses one more time and yeah, now the sunroom's lit up, glow slicing through the shades. You thumb the focus toggle just a bit . . . yet . . . catch it, to the right of the room

"*Mother Mary*," you mumble.

Pray the Papist mumbo jumbo all you want. But that's a Ford . . . an Interceptor SUV . . . white, blue and red. Now you're really straining, leaning . . . rainwater's occluding the lenses and mouth's full up of pin pricks, acid . . . *yeah* . . .

"MPD unit. *Fuck me* . . . "

Getting toward breakfast and thus more lights are blooming in the steamy gloom; you lope across a lawn and are now moving parallel to 4th Street, away from the house but with a better of the street and *Lord have mercy* it is indeed an MPD unit. Parked snug to its bumper is a Nissan SUV—black, weird D.C. plates . . . four letter that must be code. Running lights on the dash far as you can discern.

Listen, you can make it back to the Cutlass before Pennsylvania state troopers and more of Antonelli's brown-shirts arrive. Your afflicted brain's imprinted with a line of retreat north along the river to I-81; they'd expect you to go south on 83.

Yet as to hustle to the shed, you're finally clocking figures in the sunroom. You freeze. There's some ofays, in bathrobes.

White woman, white hair. There's the male, older probably sixties. Odd, he's pacing the room, arms flailing while the gray broad's a statue, head down.

See this? *Third* person seated . . . maybe a female . . . finger pointing up at the frozen woman, *not* the pacing man. You can still run, boy . . . but this is getting extra!

Hope that phone works in the rain; you power it up, zoom in on the sunroom, then the MPD and Nissan. Email it to LaKeisha and you best better renew pray LaKeisha's on planet earth, Junior.

The rain mercifully slackens just enough for you to make out the arrival of fourth human being and still none who look like Antonelli's SOD officers. Before you thumb the wetness from your eyes you hear, "Hey you . . . *you*!"

Much is a milky blur but what looks to be a white woman in a lime green rain slicker's gesturing at you dead-on like that *Invasion of the Body Snatchers* flick with you being the sole speck left on the planet . . . and a peeping tom at that. Rather than exercise some Second Amendment on your black ass the pinktoe jumps in her car and wheels away, no doubt pecking 911 into her mobile.

No reason to lurk now. You roll up on a line of hydrangeas all pale blue like the house just as that fourth figure comes into some light. And that figure's not some old turd like you or the others. It's smaller, slight. A robe hangs off its delicate shoulders showing a red tank top and deep bronze skin . . . but her hair—it's almost auburn, like your mother's and sister's . . . and at this distance, bone-straight. *She's got to face you.* Get one final good view from those tired peepers of yours, before they pop-out your head. *Hoo-ah* . . . now focus the binoculars . . .

Father God, Father God! No idle vain fancy. No monster.

Onaccount the age progression pic Al-Mayadeen sickly tree clutched with that bear . . . it matches the eyes, nose, lips exactly!

Abruptly the girl rushes out of view and whomever was seated is up after her. The older whitefolks stay put as these other figures are framed by another backlit window . . . got to be the kitchen . . . judging from the cabinetry as backdrop.

Fifth figure there—a damn convention! It grabs at the girl.

"Aw fuck me . . . "

Yeah, these arms are attached to an MPD uniform, not SOD plainclothes.

And it's a lady jake. Tits and black hair.

Feels like a gallon of blood's surging through your neck's plumbing each second. See, Antonelli's isn't down with the female affirmative action. But you know who is. So play your hunch, son. Or drive that Cutlass to the Canadian border, sink it in a river, hike the rest of the way and hide.

You peck out a number on your phone. Clench your eyelids. Listen.

The rain returns in a gentler hiss . . . and you hear the ringtone in the house.

A woman's voice answers. Your lungs empty. And when your wind returns all you manage is that pagan gibberish. Yet somehow, Junior, it fits this shitshow when you say, "*Kyrie eleison. Et tam mihi quam imperfectus.* Look . . . outside . . . the window."

Faithful Officer Sanchez is bolting through the kitchen door, Glock drawn. Coming right at you.

"*Puto bastardo*!"

When you're escorted in, there's Chief Linda Figgis, certainly not as wide-eyed from betrayal as you are. All five feet of her in pair of khaki shorts, Terrapins hoody, Teva sandals on her stubby little feet. Like she'd been driving all night, right?

Like someone'd tipped her, right?

"Don't you say it's Vee . . . "

"*Christmas crackers, Dickie,*" she groans. "We could have closed this on Dante's head, had all of these perverts, traitors on a list. But thanks to you . . . *argh*!" She hollers at the lady in the bathrobe. "Where is she, Randie?"

"I-I sint'er upstairs."

"Go get her back down here. *Now.*" Figgis turns back to you. This bitch is finna quarterback a way out of this hot mess! "You're the 'black prowler' HPD got the call on just now? You realize I can't trust a soul up here, right? Someone in SOD is monitoring activity anything deviating from their algorithms and snitches, from Ohio to North Carolina to Manhattan . . . "

"*Fuck you,* Linda."

The older man also in a robe tips out of his threadbare easy chair, ranting, "Who is this mouli-nigger in my house?"

Figgis almost clotheslines him, barks for him to sit down, shut up. Sanchez is cuffing you and you're pretty much kneeling like a slave before Missy Anne.

"How did you find her?" Figgis yells at you. "Chief in Seat Pleasant said there was an assault on an officer, he was naked and gun stolen but I said, no, no way . . . "

"You didn't do all your homework, Linda. You let CiCi take a job at the VA of all places . . . but that's not what's fucking with me the most, oh not by a damn side."

Sanchez rifles your pockets, makes a face when she pulls out the magnifying glass, your fetish. "Chief . . . I seen this before," she says to Athena, Artemis, Goddesses of bared breasts and snakes and bull-riders.

"Oh, Richard. My 'Babe.' What happened to you?"

"Me? Me? You . . . you been on the other end of CiCi's leash from rip! You concocted the biggest child kidnapping story in the city's history, then you punt so it looks like a cold case. For a fucking *sociopath*?"

"To rescue a little girl I had to deal with her mama. Both got a way out. Vittoria first, then comes CiCi . . . Agave, with the virus as a gift . . . a terrible ironic gift."

"You sabotaged your own phoney case . . . "

"I let Dante sabotage an artifice, yeah. To complete the artifice, lull him, make him think he'd won, saved his whore."

"You are the monster, Linda . . . you are the vain fancy, too. And that chick's played both of you."

Sanchez is fingering the taser so here comes the pow if you don't zip it. Your ticker might not re-tick if you get a juicy enough blast.

There's some creaking on the second floor and Figgis looks toward the stairway.

Against a backdrop of gaudy, peeling wallpaper . . . descending one step, pausing, then hitting the next, a girl joins big chocolate eyes with yours, and you're thankful the rainwater's drenched your face. No child wants to see a goon weep.

"*V-Vittoria*?" you babble with a retard's addled earnestness . . . sort of like when you came to see Ole Gunney's shell at the Old Soldiers and Sailors Home in between diaper changes and new catheters, right?

"N-No. V-Vickie," she peeps, cocking her head, raising her hand slightly. "Are you . . . you my *dad*?"

"I wish I was. A man who also wished he was . . . he wanted me to find you. He loved you."

Boo-fuckin'-hoo, son . . .

Figgis snaps her finger and Sanchez pretzels you into an illegal choke. Chick's half your size and you're wheezing like a pussy.

The Chief's voice softens as she pockets her missing tchotchke magnifying glass. "Vickie, hon' this is the man who you will describe to the locals when they get here as someone who hurt you, stalked you. Look him over, then *quickly and quietly get packed.* I can't order a chopper in from ninety miles away . . . "

"Vickie," you cough, "I came up for the truth. For you. These people don't care . . . "

"*Callate cabrón*!" the lipstick lez jake shouts in your ear as she twists the cuffs' steel into your wristbones.

"Auntie Linda?" The girl's shaking like you told her Dracula's in the next room and Sanchez will light you up, for sure.

The old bastard in the bathrobe adds, "Randie, I ain't takin' this shit n'more!"

The graybroad cries back, "Stop it Mickey . . . stop! We could get kilt!"

"Cause we're on the wrong side! You part of that cabal, cult of homos and libs down there in Wershing-don, Linda! Control us with them vaccines and masks! We're coming to fix alla youze!"

"Mickey shut up!" Randie pleads.

Figgis nods to Sanchez, and this hot tamale, despite her stature, shoves you headfirst onto a rickety love seat then puts her Glock's spout right into one of Michael DiSilvio's gray hair-sprouted nostrils. Randie cowers, moans. The girl just stares, mouth open. No shrieks or gasps. Wonder which creature she inherited her cool from, huh?

Figgis scoffs, sickly nonchalant and in that fucking Detroit suburban accent, "Remember why you are in this arrangement, and where you and Randie'd be without me. So pack . . . you two are coming as well."

"Carpet-munching commie cunt!"

This ofay's a true believer so what Figgis has on him besides twenty pounds must be a motherfucker. He's not going to get you out of those cuffs except in a bodybag, so forget him. Indeed, Figgis huffs back to him, "You and Randie'll ride in the SUV with Officer Sanchez. Randie, hon', we'll drop you guys in Lancaster at cousin Willa's . . . "

"N-No, Auntie Linda," this living ghost named Vickie whines, wriggles in place. "I-I want to know . . . like . . . what this big black guy doing here, okay. He came looking for me?"

Residual memories of Al-Mayadeen . . . or Little? Doesn't matter because Figgis promptly pulls out her two-way, announcing calmly, "Seven-Fred-Niner, this is Athena. We clear outside? Might need you in here to control a prisoner while the subjects pack. No time to change clothes."

"*Uh, negative, Athena . . . HPD unit approaching. Might be the peeping tom thing?*"

"Acknowledged," Figgis growls, now aiming those blue marbles dead at you. "Stand-by. Vickie, listen to me, hon'. This 'big black guy' is a loser—a homeless drug addled scumbag . . . who could have been a hero had he stayed in his lane. Could have been your protector."

"*Figgsy.* Let's show her what's in the whip I drove up her from DC? What you stole from evidence to hold over Dante, then dropped on Al-Mayadeen." I look to the kid. "Antonelli was your real dad but this man Al-Mayadeen, he thought he was your real dad . . . "

"You shut up!" Figgis screeches at you.

" . . . and he killed himself 'cause he was sick, and couldn't find you . . . "

"Get him ready," Figgis hisses.

"*Poob*." I hit back. "Your bear."

"My bear?"

"You were alone on the street but someone found you, had Poob, right?" You face the Chief. "Was it you 'Figgsy?' Had to get the look of terror on her face, then relief because Dante's jump-out squads were getting close. They could've found her first, like they flush out the pluggers hidin' in the corner traphouses."

"Or killed her," Figgis mutters. She whips around to the DeSilvios . . . and a cowering Vickie. "Do all of you understand that?"

Figgis steps to you . . . you're still slumped, bound. *Damn* . . . that little fist hurts, and you're tasting your own blood's bitter warmth right inside your lower lip.

Vickie's cowed right into Randie's trembling arms.

"Damn you, Linda," Mickey sputters, "brung this shit in my home . . . tearin' the poor girl up . . . again!"

But *ahhh*, the Ice Queen don't melt a drop.

"Sanchez, stand Mr. Cornish up, take his phone." She grabs your mobile. "Take off his shirt." She's rips a of couple buttons and tears your cotton shirt at the sleeves, like you're field slave about to be whupped . . . and in that rain and sweat-dampened "wifebeater" *Lord have mercy* you make a convincing big, bad, black criminal . . .

But ole gal ain't done. "Follow my lead," she calls to Vickie. "Hon' . . . *look at me* . . . you nod when I nod, shake your head I purse my lips like this." The graybroad Randie's into a full whiny breakdown. "Randie . . . *Randie*! Keep crying. That's good. Mickey, I swear I'll put a round in your fake wound from your fake Gulf War service if you fuck this up!" She's back on the two-way. "Seven-Fred-Niner, this is Athena . . . show your ID . . . tell the officer we're coming to the front door with *our* suspect in custody . . . "

"*Repeat, Athena*?"

"You heard me."

"*Copy* . . . "

CHAPTER 26

Deus Ex Crazy

Working so far. A testament to deviousness or dumbfuckery . . .

. . . and so here's a black female jake escorting this Harrisburg yokel inside. First rule of po-po rules is to get the sumbitches outdoors and manageable, not walk into a cramped Bohunk rowhouse mudroom. Still, you're clocking the whiteboy's parked unit through the rain-spattered dining room window—the running lights are still flashing crimson and blue, and that's a beacon for nosey neighbors and a zillion more Twelve. And see this? Under his billowy yellow cop slicker? His pistol's grip is turned outward in the holster like he's some gunslinger in the old west so maybe he's not the dullard he looks to be.

Got on a star-spangled chin bra and tugs it down only to speak to Randie and Mickey as if the 'rona only pesters outlanders. They whimper or grunt their acknowledgements so finally this twerp deigns to speak to Figgis.

"So . . . mornin' . . . I'm Officer Tim Kudla."

She extends her little mitt. "Honored, Officer Kudla."

Lord have mercy . . . *he's the jake, she's a chief.* He should be honored to shake her hand. Instead, he looking you up and down, shaking his head. “A big so-and-so, huh? I mean, I wish it were just a perv or peeper or B & E ’cause we know how to handle his type here, no matter what these protesters and Ka-Bala Harris say . . . ”

“*Kama-la*,” Figgis’ black female jake corrects him with a sneer.

“Yeah, sorry.” After finally giving Figgis what looks like a limp shake, he loops his thumbs under his tac vest. “But . . . um . . . this being a fugitive come to harm Randie’s niece all the way from DC . . . we coulda gotten our Tac unit fellas in here as support . . . maybe even made the collar ourselves.” He looks to Vickie, who’s trembling, searching puckered and ruddy-stained ceiling plaster. “You okay, sweetie?”

The live ghost doesn’t even look for Figgis’s signal. She just nods, twitches a shy smile.

“Now . . . what’s his story?” Kudla re-centers on you. “For you to come up here yourself . . . ”

Figgis explains, “Mentally ill . . . homeless, was on dope a long time. Had to do with that sightseeing tour you guys did right, Randie?”

“Um, the Washington M-Monument . . . he stalked us all the way to our . . . hotel.”

“Officer Kudla, I again I know it’s odd . . . and we didn’t even have time to bring the lead detective along. They will Ten-Twenty us closer to Baltimore, as I’m taking Mr. and Mrs. DeSilvio with me and Vickie as material witnesses. I’m in touch with the U.S. Attorney in Philadelphia to obtain the proper order; there’s no need for your department to get into needless paperwork beyond calming the neighbors . . . ”

You sucking all this in, Junior? Figgis is starting to puff out her big tits like the cat who buttfucked, then ate, the canary.

Being the expert on deviant human nature you are, best bet is to watch Mickey. He's mumbling, his gray hairy chest's billowing under ratty pj's.

"Finally," Figgis wraps up, "we will arrange to have a car, secreted a few blocks thataways, Maryland plates, towed after we inventory it."

"Car?"

"The subject boosted it," Officer Sanchez adds.

"Uh-huh, well lemme take Big Homey here to our Cooler while youze-all guys wrap up."

"I'm mentally ill," you moan.

The cop cocks his head, snarls, "Anyone ask you, asshole?" He returns to the Chief, the snare still glued to a narrow, pale face. "I don't agree with these bleeding hearts who wanna send shrinks and social workers out on the street. My Captain won't even let us process these mooks for robbery, armed assault . . . "

Randie breaks character. "Timmy . . . it doesn't . . . matter . . . we just want Vickie left . . . in peace. *Oh God . . .* "

"Hmmm . . . maybe I gotta call it in. Just a notice to the Troopers HQ you're transporting a prisoner."

"Really Tim—" Figgis objects.

"*Officer Kudla,* ma'am. And maybe a statement from Big Homey, just for my report."

"We read him his rights," Sanchez growls. "He's not speaking."

"Yeah I bet he'd talk to me if motivated."

Vickie jumps in, blurting, "He's got my bear. My old bear, Poob."

"Pardon?" he says, wincing like his brain hurts. You doing a sitch assessment, boy? This whiteboy's in over his head yet still got to play the role and damn if you aren't watching ole Mickey there in the corner . . .

. . . but Figgis readjusts, takes over, "Officer Kudla I've instructed my people so we're going on respecting your standard ops and the fact that we are guests here. Indeed, I'd like to contact Major Isaac Washington of the Pennsylvania State Police. He's headquartered here . . . "

"Yeah, I know that—why wouldn' I know that, huh? Major Washington . . . heck . . . is always on frickin' TV . . . hangs out with the freakazoid running for governor . . . "

Uh-oh.

"Officer—"

"And my Captain . . . and us, we deal exclusively with Commander. Colonel Arnie Stanz."

"I've met Colonel Stanz, and—"

"Maybe he should talk to youze-all . . . "

Get ready, son. Never a dull moment with ofays . . . feel Sanchez's grip on you tensing?

"I'm calling Major Washington . . . " Figgis digs for her mobile and you'd think she was drawing down on this noodlehead as Kudla's now got his hand on his piece's grip.

And then the kid mewls again. "*H-He knows my mom . . . my dad . . . my real dad*!"

Don't know why you're twisting to look at Sanchez and Henderson. The next move ain't theirs. And yet before Figgis can slither out from under this bullshit, here comes the *deus ex* crazy to your hubris, Junior . . .

. . . with Mickey charging into Figgis, bashing her against the stair banister as he raves, free at last, "*Timmy . . . the nigger and her are liars*! A *cabal*! Put 'em down!"

Okay. You're looking at two seconds, max, before this sumbitch has a couple of synapses tell him what it means to pull a piece on the chief of police of a major city . . . *the* capital city . . .

Despite your shoulder joints yawning as if about to be torn out you shake off Sanchez and launch yourself into the mudroom . . . yeah, just like the linebackers did to you back in the day. Luckily, the money blow is with your back and not your head . . . still mighty enough to smash a small console table and topple a grandfather clock onto Kudla and *Lord*, the tones and gongs are all sounding off as you the cop hits the floor.

Randie's jumping over her the crumple of limbs that is her hubby and her cousin, scampering back up the stairs to likely cower in her bed.

The girl's just frozen, though, eyes wide as if she's seen the span of her true life. Every lie, every outrage.

"*Uncuff me dammit*!" you scream at Sanchez.

But she's pulling her Glock so it's Henderson who does the right thing but as she unlocks the cuffs Mickey's screaming, about to jump through the front door to Paul Revere the neighborhood.

You hear Figgis' muffled voice order Sanchez to stand down, but . . .

Pop-pop!

Mickey DeSilvio's catching two slugs in his back as he's running away. He falls face-first to a concrete sidewalk now steaming from the cooling drizzle.

"*Raffi why*?" you hear Figgis cry to Sanchez.

Time for your own magnificently futile *banzai* moment . . .

. . . as you knock the wind out of that child when hook her body . . . on a dead run through hallway, tear-assing to kitchen . . . then out the back, busting a screen door off its rusty hinges.

She doesn't squirm, flail or gnash-about until you're a couple of fences and chunks of ruined of alley pavement from the Cutlass . . . and the "oh shit" key's right where you left it.

God help you, what that must look like to any whitefolks who happen to clock you over their pours of half and half into their mugs of cheapass coffee. You toss the kid in the back of a whip, click her in her seatbelt. Look, she just witnessed one of Linda's Finest putting lead into that guinea sumbitch Mickey. No way she woke this morning thinking her summer vacay, all free of the 'rona for camp was going to morph into this shit, huh?

And so the freakout begins. She shrieks, bashes at the rear window with her sock-shod feet so hard you're afraid the glass with shatter.

You're tugging something out of the trunk . . .

Yeah! 12-gauge stick, the nine-milly iron. Brave, Junior . . . very Pork Chop Hill . . . but the yokels and State Trooper will fill you up with so much lead your dick will be pencil.

"*No.*"

You throw open the back door, shove a paper bag now tattered beyond usefulness, onto her squirming form.

Crazy. She's quieting herself as she strokes this nasty thing.

You hop in, start the car. The engine strains, purrs . . .

. . . and soon enough, there's the sign for I-81 along the river as the sun's burning off the rainclouds. All this time the girl's mute. Squeezing that damn bear as if she'd reverted to a tot. You know you can't stop for food, gas with her. Can't give her a what-for to the cheek to shut her up—it'll leave marks. Scare her into staying cool . . .

"You had a daddy who loved you," you meekly whisper instead.

Vickie's dropped her chin to her chest—see in the rearview mirror.

"You're shitting in a diaper, blowing saliva bubbles on you lower lip as the nurse mixes your oatmeal."

Ouch.

"Who . . . who are you talking to?" Vickie hollers. "*Stop*! I'm scared!"

"*Vickie*," I mutter . . . as I throttle back on the engine.

Yes, *I mutter. I'm* driving. Fuck you, you're the vain fancy.

I can hold it together.

I can keep my head.

I can save this girl . . . and Verna, and Sweet Sunshine, and Croc. And Stripe! *Stripe* . . .

"Wh-Why'd you do this? Auntie Linda said—"

"Auntie Linda's in trouble now, girl!"

Wonder if her black Trooper ally's got her back? Given Tim Kudla's disposition, and Mickey with two bullet holes, that's unlikely. But hey, I owe the reality check to Vittoria . . . *K'ymira* . . .

"Honey, I tryna be lucid, okay . . . listen."

"I'm not anybody's 'Honey.' I'm *Vickie*!"

"Vickie . . . this road . . . *my* road, it's gonna end soon, so your road can start."

"That's stupid . . . that's stupid . . . I wanna go home now . . . ."

"I'm taking you home." The truth is the only thing keeping me sane. "I thought I could trade secrets, bad stuff your dad . . . biological dad, did. Trade secrets so a friend of mine can go free and your dad leave me alone. But your Auntie Linda . . . she doesn't want that to happen."

I figure I went way deep or way over her head, but after some silence she breaks. "Is my dad . . . a bad man? My mom . . . Auntie Linda says she was bad, but did a good thing coming to Auntie Linda . . . when I was little . . . "

"I dunno. My dad's . . . bad. My mother . . . she was full of love but she let him smother it, chew it. Your Auntie Linda said good mothers are rare . . . and I got mad and said I was lucky. I-I dunno. Hard being a good mother . . . 'specially when a hunned folks tell you a hunned definitions of what being 'good' is. "

"Didn't ask about moms. I asked about dads . . . "

"Okay then yeah your dad's bad. And I'm a bad dad . . . 'cause I got sloppy. I let a boy who's like my son get caught. And your dad will hurt him!"

"I-I'm sorry," she whispers.

"It's cool . . . cool." Though it's not . . .

"I was bad a lot. They wouldn't let me on Insta . . . cock-locked my phone . . . *my phone*!"

"'Cock-Locked' it? Whoa . . . I you mean it was bricked at one time?"

"Huh? *Nooooooo.* I could only call them, nine-one-one, my school . . . and only they and Auntie Linda could call me. Dead . . . it was like being in jail with old people . . . and kids in school would drop shade at my clothes . . . tell me I was sus', say if I wasn't black I'd be Amish or a Mormon. I'm not black I'm *brown* . . . Puerto Rican, I'd try to tell people, or I'd try to sneak make-up from Rite Aid and then glow-up and say I looked like Doja Cat, right?"

"Who?"

Her big eyes are filling the rearview mirror . . . pleading for something and I don't know what. "Girls in my class, my church group . . . were the meanest. Especially when Randie'd do my hair. Take a hot comb to it to make straight. Dye it brunette. Then it'd fall out. The thots, they'd laugh . . . "

"I'm sorry about that."

"It's . . . okay. You . . . you said there was a man who loved me when I was little?"

"Uh-huh. A tall black man with that funny name: Al-Mayadeen Thomas. And he had a brother name of Hakim . . . 'Little' like when you were little, and he took care of you, too."

"They're gone?"

"Yeah. Gone."

"I was always having dreams . . . nightmares . . . about my mom . . . and places we'd been. Auntie Linda said that was good. Being scared would save me from mistakes. From evil people."

My dome's tilting back to Mister Manny's weathered face and weary eyes. That dude knew the world where you could barter to save your life, keep things from blowin' up, is long gone. To Hell with the rules. It's all about who rules.

Next thing I see, she's out cold. Snoring, even. Best for both of us. Still, it's nuts: no sign of state troopers or even much traffic—just bright sun shimmer on the interstate's pavement, signs telling me I'm past Chambersburg with the Mason-Dixon line and Hagerstown maybe fifteen miles away. I-70 and Chocolate City just beyond that.

I'm saying aloud, "I kept my promises. I found her. I found the other kids, some in the Gingerbread House. *I am worthy.* Don't need a flying horse or iron spear to be a hero . . . "

CHAPTER 27

Sanctuary

Midday mass, or Sext as the old fellows called it, was always pretty empty at St. Jude's. Ragged men, busted men—they'd rather argue over a checkers move, eat noodle soup and lunchmeat sandwiches than pray. Not that they aren't thankful. They are bashful about coming before the God they thought said didn't give a fuck about them, and learned different.

So the Brothers, and what's left of the Sister Maria-Karl's nuns after waves of 'rona and lovely mutations do the praying in their stead.

Guess they haven't found a replacement for Father Phil so there's Brother Karl-Maria in the vestments, and he's singing, because unlike Father Phil and his fucking Trini Lopez folk guitar, Brother Karl-Maria's old school . . .

"*Evangéli i secúndum Lucam . . .* "

"The Gospel according to Luke," I translate in a whisper to Vickie, who looks almost as messed up as me. Even more so because she's too old to be clutching both my big hand and that bear. Still, what few bodies are in there have turned to see us grab a pew.

"Dico vobis: descéndit hic justificátus in domum suam ab illo: quia omnis qui se exáltat, humiliábitur: et qui se humíliat, exaltábitur . . . "

"Two guys to the temple to pray, one a baller, rich, everyone says is cool, successful. One's just a low government worker. The rich smug guys prays, 'God, I thank you that I am not like other low, dirty people—even this jerk next to me. I fill the collection plate, say all the right things.' But the other dude, he just beats his own chest and whispers, 'God, have mercy on me, a sinner.'"

"God told the rich guy who believes in God he's a good person," Vickie explains. "Auntie Randie and Uncle's pastor says that."

I shake my head. "*Nah.* God favored the regular government jerk. 'For all those who exalt themselves will be humbled, and those who humble themselves will be exalted.' Jesus was the one who told these stories."

"Is that why you believe in him? You say 'Jesus' and 'Mary' a lot in the car."

"Not many people dig this kind of Jesus. Maybe he loves me, too. I just . . . dunno. 'Cause we're in . . . trouble, right?"

"Can we go to BK or Wendy's?"

She gets a "shush" as the incense starts to swing and philter sweats liquid. I smile when the enforcer turns and realizes who I am, wearing the awfulness of my mission to Pennsylvania all over my face and body.

"Dickie?" Katie gushes. She genuflects her way out of one pew back into ours, skittering along in her Birkenstocks and tent-like dress. She squeezes my arm. "Oh, we were so worried. LaKeisha's . . . disappeared . . . " *Shit.* "Verna's been downtown to Judiciary Square, the District Building . . . they say some of the cops are on a 'blue-flu' letting shootings, carjackings just happen . . . others are out rousting, oh Gawd, even beating up street folk like back in the day . . . "

Her only slightly muffled cackle's now bringing a look from Brother Karl-Maria, but it's not one of frosty reproach. He nods to me. I nod back, point to Vickie . . .

"Who's this?" Katie presses.

"Someone who has to kept safe. Is Verna in her office? Can you plead with her to part with some clothes, hair stuff, toiletries for my teenybopper, here?"

"What's a 'teenybopper, huh?' I'm Vickie DeSilvio. I'm just hungry, 'kay?"

"Her name was K'ymira Thomas at one time . . . "

"Oh?" Katie sighs. Then it fucking sinks in. "Wait . . . *ohhhhhhhh . . .* "

The recessional's just Brother Karl-Maria, and an old dude I recall from back in the day carrying he staff-cross, think his name's Nick. Couple of nuns who are new faces. Pretty *pro forma* because Karl-Maria simply busts a U-turn at the last pew and hooks my arm.

"When I said welcome back to the Prodigal Son, I didn't mean this malarkey, Richard . . . "

"Zeus sent a gadfly. But I'm done falling."

"And this young lady . . . ?"

"Not the Chimera. The Chimera's out there, looking for us." I turn to Katie. "Kathleen, stamp, girl . . . please . . . Verna?"

She skitters off toward the vestry and the connecting tunnel to SFME; Karl-Maria strips his gear. "You need a bath, Richard, a shave. Nothing new, eh?"

I follow him to the cramped, dingy office in the undercroft. I smell the cheap Pillsbury rolls, the mediocre coffee—ambrosia and ichor for folk sleeping in a piss-smelling tent or *al fresco* in the mosquito-filled muggy night air.

"Here." He tosses me a towel, a fresh shirt from a donation bin. More like a white dress shirt for some office moe, a size too small as I push through the sleeves and try to button the fucker. Vickie just scans us both.

"Anything in the news about the Chief of Police? That's she in some pickle, out of town."

"Not on any outlet that I follow. Religiously, so to speak. What're you getting at?"

"P-Policewoman . . . shot . . . my uncle, my play dad," Vickie mutters.

"One of her officers shot a dude Linda stashed this girl with for six years." That stings the kid and she immediately goes into hermit crab mode on a chair in the corner.

"Oh my. Okay . . . and it gets . . . *worse*?"

"Her mother is CiCi Talbot-Thomas, also alive . . . whole kidnapping, murder thing was big news back then. All bullshit."

He releases a long sigh like a leaky tire, turns to the girl. "And your dad? Do you know him?"

Before I can interrupt, Vickie moans and fires back, "My Uncle Mickey, kay? I-I don't know who my dad is!"

"Deputy Chief Antonelli, Brother. Donates to St. Judes, right? And SFME. Good Catholic, fights evil."

I would have said it was impossible for the old goat to get any paler, eyes grow any wider. *Nah.* "*Sanctorum, placere adiuva nos . . .* " he whispers with dread.

"Amen."

The old white dude Nick, I guess he's "hobo altar boy" for the day, as Daddy would label . . . he's rushing in without knocking. Tries to announce Verna, but Verna's through the door before he can stutter her name.

She's looking me up and down like I'm a corpse, freshly fished from the Potomac, now reanimated. Swear to God, baby . . . you don't need to be clocking me. Don't you see who I've brought?

"It was CiCi who told Figgis where I was," I tell her to calm her. "Thought you'd sold me out but I had this bug swimming in my gut ever since we left Little. I'm sorry."

"Dickie . . . I-I couldn't just stay underground with Croc. All I told Linda and her staff was you'd left me, ghosted me."

"So . . . so you did speak to her?" I say with a cough. Bitter phlegm oozes out. Not the 'rona. Just badness I'm siced to get rid of.

She nods. "Then Linda yesterday, no one could find her. Mayor's been going batshit looking for her . . . more shootings last night . . . Fourth of July parade coming . . . unvaccinated Trumpers wanting to come back dish out trouble . . . "

"And?"

"And? *And*? Yesterday was supposed to be the announcement . . . aw, dammit Dickie that she was not going to run again and that Linda had formed a campaign committee! Can you please just—"

Yeah. Now . . . finally, she stops getting high on her own supply long enough to notice the visitor sitting cross-legged on the brocaded Queen Anne chair. Rocking like I'd see the rock and smack orphans and runaways do when I was first at Mitch Snyder's shelter with Esmeralda . . .

"Verna Leggett, meet Vickie. *Vittoria Sofia . . . Thomas . . . Antonelli.*"

The girl gives a somnambulistic, limp wave.

"Father God . . . " She then looks at me. "Y-You . . . did it. You found her."

"Ain't no Gingerbread House for her, Verna. Now that my phone's kaput, all I got is her, unless CiCi miracles herself up in here. Speaking of miracles, why don't show Vickie here the new construction—posthumously named after her."

"Dickie . . . *stop.*" Verna whispers.

Uh-huh. Being mean's all I got now. "What's Croc saying?"

"He wants his car back. But not if every cop on the East Coast is looking for it. Mostly he just . . . wants his friend back. Like I do."

"Besides that," I snap, cold. "Melvin and his boys get and lead on CiCi?"

"No. Me, I called up to the VA first thing this morning, *to aid you* . . . and they said they got an email last night from a closed account that she's resigned, moved."

Suddenly we all turn in unison toward Vickie . . . she's tapping the chair like a little nutcase and saying, "Someone named a place after me? Can I see?"

She's old enough not to lunch like that, and maybe I've added to that invisible trauma.

I tell to wash up and change, maybe figure out where Auntie Linda is and the bad people out there. I turn to Verna. "Katie says LaKeisha's gone under. Think relapse . . . or cops got her?" I put my hand on Brother Karl-Maria's shoulder. "Don't wanna mess you up more than I have by being here, but . . . need a favor. Need you to call the Daly Building, MPD HQ. Need you to find Deputy Chief of Police, Special Operations Division, tell him I want to talk."

"Dickie no . . . " Verna pleads. "He's going to have you killed. Straight up. You can't be walking the streets knowing what you know." She dips her head. "And I begged Linda to leave you be. She was ready . . . ready to do that."

"Brother, tell whoever answers Dickie Cornish will speak to him. Face to face."

Just as my stomach's about to drop to my knees with those words, murky shape beyond the diffused colors in the stained-glass windows of Karl-Maria's little enclave. Now I can make them out. MPD units, a motorcycle cop . . . a black Chevy Suburban. No sirens just the lights.

Verna sees it now, too. "Oh no . . . "

"How would they know?" Brother Karl-Maria aptly posits. "Who told on you?"

"They can't be after Vittoria. Because to either the Chief or Antoinelli's goons—she doesn't exist."

"Then who are they?" Verna scoffs.

As she moves away I catch her arm. "The lawyer. Nimchuk. Maybe you should call him just in case."

She smiles. "I'm a big girl in a little package boo-boo. You watch her."

"*Sanctus sanctorum*," Karl-Maria mumbles. "They know better than to pull anything here."

My head sinks when Vickie asks, "So I don't get to see what they built . . . for me?" At this point realization rather than unfolding reality finally smacks her adolescent dome like a cinderblock. "Built . . . when they thought . . . I was *dead* . . . "

As the voices and those cop footsteps get closer all I can think of is a misshapen troll people thought was an animal, stupid . . . protecting . . . yes . . . *Esmeralda*, in a church. "Charles Laughton as the Hunchback . . . Maureen O'Hara," my affliction mumbles.

"What'd you say?" Vickie quizzes, scrunching up her nose.

"I had problems when I was a kid . . . memorizing stuff, blurting it. My father thought football would smash it outta me. It didn't, and the drugs, liquor . . . the street . . . made it worse."

She smiles at me. "I-I don't mind."

No one's ever said that to me. I smile, too. "Stay close. Follow my lead."

"Mr. Cornish . . . are these the good police, or the bad ones?"

"Good question." Bad distinction.

And then like a superhero's brother, Karl-Maria's out, slipping on his vestments like his cape and damn if he's probably grabbing the staff and Gospel and Holy Water, too, for battle.

I can't make out the voices, especially if it's that scumbag Uncle Tom, Woodman, but it's getting heated. Still, heated means they don't have anything near a warrant, and a warrant for a place of worship—yeah, it's a bed and clean shower for turds like me but still a church.

Vickie grabs for my hand. She doesn't scream, she doesn't weep. Yeah . . . my hand. She's either more fucked-up than I could ever know, or I'm less so, despite my bumbling crazy shit, and somebody sees it.

But then the ubiquitous radio feedback hushes; footsteps fade.

Karl-Maria returns, bathed in sweat, bent . . . and smiling as if he's exorcized all of Pandemonium. "They're on the SFME side, with Verna now. But they aren't coming here without a warrant to me and the Diocese, or they can kiss my old Polock ass . . . " He's gotten florid in his old age!

"Did they say they were Special Operations Division?" But would Antonelli flex like that?

"Honestly, I don't know. It was two detectives, two officers. Was pretty heated . . . one left his card and its says 'Major

Crimes Squad,' see? Mentioned coming back with the FBI next time. Did not mention this child. Just you."

"FBI . . . " Uh-huh—the kid's still got a Maryland blue crab grip on my fingers. "But no warrant?"

"Richard we're not lawyers."

No, yet my jigsaw puzzle brain's clackity-clacking again. "I grab this child across state lines—and they say Feds, yet don't mention your name. Something's up, Brother."

"It always is with you, son. Be that as it may, we can protect you here but so long. And her . . . a minor? God knows what the narrative is out there."

"Don't call the Daly Building, then . . . I'll figure out what to do about getting a hold of Stripe."

Karl-Maria has lunch brought in: the St. Jude's staples of lunchmeat on bread and a mug of soup. The latter's just what I don't need when the sun's cooking these stone walls and the humidity's about to collapse my chest. Indeed, I'm clocking Vickie's hair. Yeah, so carefully monitored by ol' graybroad Randie, yet in a day the D.C. weather's wrung out the auburn, and it's back to black, with a little frizz. When she bites into her sandwich, swear to God she favors fucking slick-back Boris Karloff . . .

"You haven't had a nip in the middle of this?" Karl-Maria presses. "Or a joint, a snort?"

"Nah. Not one pang, not fiend. Think I'm cured?"

"Hmmm. No. Look, there's a blanket, pillows in that cupboard. You know where the showers are. I'll have one of the sisters take Vickie to Verna when the police leave . . . "

"No!" Vickie shouts. "Staying with *him*!"

"This place is for stinky old men . . . like me, okay? I need to clean up."

"A . . . *shelter*?"

Suddenly her eyelids are fluttering, the tears come. Memories, sensations, flooding back?

I rush to her and hug her. "This *isn't* the munie," I declare with as much paternal bass in my voice as I dare. "Over there, at SFME, it's better. They're building a place for kids to be safe and they named it after *you*. Doesn't matter what your name is."

She nods, tearful . . . fretful.

I whisper to the cleric, "She ain't the only one with flashbacks. My meds. Don't know if I can hold on . . . even here. Any suggestions?"

"That's the fee for sanctuary, Richard—remember? You must *pray*. And join-in folks' spirits who you've trespassed against, with those of the people who let you down. Now take a knee. *Both of you*. Hold my hand."

CHAPTER 28

Jackals and Cuckolds

WHEN THE FRIARS GET THE ALL-CLEAR that po-po have vacated, I take Vickie over to SFME and of course no one but Verna has the slightest clue who she is. Real live, it'd be like Jesus wearing modern clothes, bopping into the Basilica of The Assumption up on Michigan and saying what-up and whoa, nice work on the crib. So yeah, she's plain Vickie, little white-acting "brown" teen. Not like she has horns growing out her head and tail, as Verna's got plenty of runaways of all races leaning up against the door each sunrise, dressed in their pj's.

The second we are over there, Katie's grabbing her away and it freaks the kid out. She doesn't come back to cling to my big scary ass and yet nor she doesn't let me out of her sight, either. Katie's not helping. She's jumpy, curt with the kid, huffing and puffing. I tell Vickie, look you don't want me in a bathroom with you, do you? No, so cooperate. Lord, it's like a female Stripe's come to me. Katie gives her over to staffer and they let her use the staff ladies room to wash up, so she can hear my voice.

I don't want her to hear this: "Katie what the fuck is up? Where's Keesh?"

"I-I dunno . . . I-I . . . Dickie, everything's been so wacky here. Morale is crazy, scuttlebutt flying, Jeez . . . and then . . . you heard about poor Moses, right? Oh my God."

Poor Moses. Whatever. Her cheeks are going apple red, like on the street in winter but we are in the AC working overtime so I sit her down.

"LaKeisha got your last message about uploading something and some trouble you and Verna were in the other day . . . and she, well, you know about her and stress."

"She's not at the group home?"

"I-I called, no, she's not."

"The library in Shaw? She says she goes back every now and again."

"N-No . . . they've limited people in there since quarantine ended the first time. Even kids."

Not good.

"Dickie, I am so sorry. Verna . . . she won't say a thing and she's been so . . . so mean to me since she got back from whatever you were doing." She finally looks me up and down. My sweat-stink trousers, torn shirt . . .

"It's okay. I'll find her." As if I don't have Hercules' Tasks ahead already. I just said to make myself, not Katie feel better. "Take me to Verna's office."

As I pass the restroom I hear Vickie call out "You'll be back, yeah?"

"Can't ever get away," I tell her, and it sure as fuck wasn't to be coy or sarcastic. My body and soul are weary. My brain's plain terrified and cruel with its own failures, that's why I said it. No telling how she'll take it.

Verna's in her office with a bunch of counselors, the kitchen manager. Only two of them are masked so I guess this is the sterile Fortress of Solitude. There are condolence cards on the bookshelf. For Roffe.

But it's the wall flatscreen—something I missed the first time I was back here and realized the grant skilla's flowing again—on which these mugs're all riveted.

Linda Figgis.

She's masked. Boom mics appear extended at maximum length, with a beefy nigga in Pennsylvania State Police gear and of brass attached to it at least a body's length from her, also masked. Don't see Sanchez. Caption is "WTOP Fox Five Live from York, Pennsylvania."

"Is this gonna be bad?" Verna turns and asks, as if these folk in the room need to know.

"You tell me."

"I mean—for *you*."

And of course a couple of pairs of eyes lock onto my ass. Oh, it's bad. If you consider Linda Figgis having more lives than a fucking tabby, more angles than damn Pythagoras, *bad* . . .

"*Yes I may have to quarantine for a week—in solitude, as will my officers . . . one also on admin leave now . . . we didn't have a clue the couple was in an anti-vax anti-mask group . . . but what is important is that a cold case has been solved, and while it does not excuse my impetuousness and jumping out of bed to drive a hundred miles north, and I face you all in the press and officially for that decision, I stand by the result . . .* "

A reporter fires, "*So Michael DeSilvio was in fact Michael 'Mickey' Tasco of Detroit, a money launderer for that city's major criminal drug crew there in the Eighties?*" a reporter's disembodied voice questions. "*Your father headed the Task Force that had federal warrants out for Tasco's arrest when he absconded . . . and this is during the 'Whiteboy Rick' Wirshe controversy as well . . .*

would you call it irresponsible for the chief of a major city's police force to act personally on tips and not consult the FBI? Ma'am . . . it could be said that you were out to save your father's reputation and endangered yourself and a local community."

Some camera flashes pop and the Chief calmly replies, "*Tasco, as law enforcement knew, had probably migrated to the metropolitan area and even the District itself, in Northeast, by Nineteen Ninety-one eight, then disappeared once again. I stand by my actions. I await the consequences . . .* "

The black man steps to the mics but I'm not paying attention to that hocus pocus. If you got away with it, Linda, then it was with Dante's grudging complicity. Too much heat'd burn the whole rotten house down. Say less, Verna. This is no dance, Jesus and Lucifer, Skins and Cowboys. Nah, its old high school biology symbiosis in the Pig Poke . . . and that's scarier.

An SFME staffer, one of the newer bright-faced ones corporately-sponsored hands me a business card. "This person said give this directly to you. She just smacked it in my hand, not Verna's and gave me this look and, well . . . here . . . "

Shit.

"I already have one." I crush it in my sweaty, quivering palm. Drop it in Verna's wire mesh trash bin.

Yeah, Verna takes notice. "No Dickie you don't throw away anything the police drop on you. Especially in *my* office." She hooks the can with her leg, pulls it closer, retrieves what a tossed. "Monica Abalos. What's this?"

"A way out, maybe." I say, "Or another bait alliance." I point at the TV screen. "Linda was hooked, about to be gutted but now she's this close to swimming free and she'll be back to close up loose ends like you and me, before she finally settles this shit with the rebels in her department."

"Rapists and pedophiles and their protectors," Verna whispers, eyelids shut.

My mouth's suddenly desiccated when I hear her say it all in one line. I hear Vickie hollering for me as I escape to through the security doors to St. Jude's.

I hear her still, now inside my head like you, Daddy, over the hot spray and groaning pipes in the shower room.

No more overwhelming Lestoil and Clorox smell . . . there's mold in the floor and wall tile grout as if the ceramics are outlined with mascara. Guess I'm like Katie now: gone soft and thus intolerant of the rot that was once comforting. At least on this visit to the shower I got no clothed staffer standing there as I shave, ready to collect my sharps. The geriatric altarboy even loaned me a bottle of Clubman—lime green, old-school and pungent—to splash on. Stings and I still have red dots from the razor nicks as douse my whiskerless face with that shit.

I reach for my towel but freeze when I hear footsteps out in the locker area. Always got to be aware in the showers. Yet the sound's followed by a familiar voice.

"Richard . . . please finish up," Brother Karl-Maria says, almost somber.

"Vickie—she tripping? Po-po back for me?"

"Well . . . you have a call holding."

"This isn't the Mystery of the Cross, man. From who?"

"He claims to be Deputy Chief of Police Dante Antonelli . . . "

"Uh-huh."

"We set out some clean underwear, T-shirt, summer shorts Collection Services on the folding chair out here . . . "

I'm back in his office with a towel around my neck rather than on top of head, where it usually is in the summer . . . and dressed in cast-off beach ware. The cleric points to a flashing button on the phone console.

I nod, feeling my nutsack in my throat. He presses the button. Leaves, to give me privacy.

"So your scouting party reported in," I say, testing him.

"*Don't know what you're talking about, Cornish. So let's cut the bull. You need to come to see me. A-S-A-effing-P. Something's happened, and I think you better see so we can talk.*"

"Is Stripe all right?"

"*We need to talk.*"

"Did you see Figgis' press conference? Aside from black magic an old flame of mine used to carry on about, how'd she wriggle out of it?"

"*I said . . . we need to talk. I'm going to send a car.*"

"Fuck that." There's dead air. Maybe I should have been easy but damn, I'm netted, tired. "You still there?"

Oh, he is. "*Okay tough guy . . . gumshoe . . . whatever you think you are beyond a piece of trash troublemaker, a homunculus assembled by jackals and cuckolds. Pedal your tricycle down to the CDF . . .* "

No I don't mind the epithets. I've heard worse, just not as creative.

"You're letting Stripe go?"

"*The CDF medical unit . . . between the CDF and the Correction Treatment Facility. Main entrance is shared with CTF . . .* "

Swear to God I felt an artery burst. "*Kill* . . . is he okay? Deputy Chief?"

"One of my people with be there at check-in instead of a C.O. Just one, so as not spark questions. You will come alone as well. I know you won't be so stupid as to come armed. But leave any recording technology in its toy box."

"I asked if Ernesto was okay."

"I'm offended that you'd think I need to game someone as low as you, Cornish. Get down here and you'll see you lil' butt buddy, we clear?"

Boris Karloff hangs up.

I ask Karl-Maria if there he's got anything *less* to wear. From the way the shower room looks, the budget's bare.

Lucky me. Says they've got a couple of men's suits, white dress shirts, all still in dry cleaner plastic . . . black and brown shoes, worn only a few times. Not too many takers. When the geriatric altarboy brings the gear in now I see why. Belonged to a funeral home that went out of business, used the suits for temporary "display" before the motherfuckers headed to the oven . . .

. . . and double lucky. One black suit fits; black shoes are tight but my dogs don't feel it—calluses or the sugar's come, right? At this point some bigger fish got to fry me so I'll worry about my feet later.

Verna knocks at the open door to the cleric's office. Been on the street twenty years . . . so yeah, even a Catholic School boy, an HU Bison, can forget how to tie a necktie. Some of the other brothers watch, maybe in celibate jealousy or utter curiosity, as Verna wraps and knots it for me.

I whisper as she's close-up on me, "Suppose Linda's coming for you when she gets back. Be careful."

She twitches a grin. Her eyes are wet. Nah, she doesn't kiss me.

"No *you* be careful."

"I gotta grab something from Croc's car. You aren't gonna like that."

"Do what you got to do. Just come back."

I turn to the assembled, robed white men. "Got to leave a duffle bag here. Please don't look inside it. Hide it. Or bury the damn thing. Whatever. Just don't let anyone who isn't me near it. Miss Vee here's got a number of someone who can pick up the red Oldsmobile in the lot off Half Street . . . get it outta here fast."

Finally, I look to Brother Karl-Maria. "Richard, did I ever tell you what I did before I was called to the order, Richard?" Karl-Maria announces.

"No."

"Good. Because I want you to see how much you've overcome, conquered by sheer constitution, while the rest of us remained the same."

My nostrils, eyes, throat are suddenly slick, wet. I hand him something I've been carrying so long that what was white and stuff is now yellowed, tattered. "You hear something bad, like if my 'constitution' didn't hold, I want you and Verna to call this Detective, Monica Abalos at MPD. Here's her card. Get the girl to her."

"Why?"

"Because I got no other play." I wink. Dry my eyes on my fists.

Now I'm walking with Verna to SFME. Longest walk ever, it seems. I'm so damn scared but I got to get Stripe.

We find Vickie's alone in Verna's office, watching gameshow, clad in sweatpants, flip flops, tank top. She's demolishing box of snickerdoodles.

"I wanna . . . wanna get a pedicure and paint my fingers, too," Vickie declares, wiping the cinnamon sugar crystals from her hands. Guess she gets a second glance of me, clean and suited. "You look like an old guy still . . . like the old black guy that *Men in Black* alien movie. Mickey and Randie love it. Real old special FX."

"Vickie . . . I want you to behave. I want you to do what this lady says." I swallow hard. "Even if it means you have to see Auntie Linda."

Vickie' scrunching her nose, shaking her head. "W-Why?"

Verna adds, "Dickie . . . I got her. It's okay."

"I'm realizing there was only one way to handle this when this started, when I got involved. Just like with Bracht . . . Esme. Head-on." I turn to the kid. "Vickie . . . I meant . . . I won't let Auntie Linda see you unless me and Miz Leggett here are with you."

"I see the new building from the window," the kid muses. "I see the kids outside, playing near the fence around it. They wouldn't believe it was for me." Suddenly we get a smile. "Maybe I can name it for another kid bad things happened to . . . "

"Gotta go."

"Thank you . . . Mr. Cornish," Vickie calls to me.

I nod. "Grab Poob . . . lemme take shot." Verna takes out her phone, takes some selfies of us, gives it to me and I double tap and take video of Vickie musing about her life in six years, and then singing to the bear.

"Happy now?" Vickie huffs. "I look like a dismal dog."

"No, you're perfect, baby." I look to Verna. "You too."

Once away from anyone's eyes I check Croc's gifted .25 in my sock. The Glock and stick are back in the chapel in the duffle. Can't afford to lose those; this I can sacrifice to make a point if and when I'm frisked.

Before I can cross down to M Street Katie appears at the entrance to SFME. She's swaying, making clapping motions with her hands, calls out finally, "Come back to us. Don't do bad."

"Keesh'll come out of hiding, I promise . . . and she'll find you. This is her, coping, like I said. You tell I love all of you and I did my best . . . and if all my stuff, everything I found, is up in that cloud place, keep it locked, safe 'cause they took my phone."

"Take mine," my plump pink girl offers. "I just get coupon updates and my family never calls anyway. Just my sponsor." She puts it in my hand and it's got glitter tinted violet and green glued to the cover. Katie whispers, "LaKeisha can trace it. I lose it all the time. Really."

"Listen carefully. When she surfaces you just say 'counterattack needs time on target, then zone and sweep.' That's her Army talk. No wizardry, dragons or sci-fi shit—tell her *exactly* what I said. Yell it at her if you must."

It makes her cry. "I-I will. Princess is watching over you."

"Whole time—she's the one got me into this shit, sweetie." I look up. "Hear me, Princess? You owe me, ole gal."

Katie wraps her meaty pale arms around me. Hope Princess isn't the only one siced on my head. Could use you, too, Daddy.

CHAPTER 29

Enemies

I STEP OFF THE NUMBER 51 at 18th and E Southeast. Mister Softee truck that's seen fewer dents and less rust in the Eighties plays its disjointed music-box tune; to slow my heart I recall me and Alma sneaking off the Barracks grounds to 8th and line up with the other kids for Good Humor Bomb Pops. Of course, ole Gunney . . . nah, now Sergeant-Major Cornish . . . well he'd bruise Mom's lip for allowing us to mingle with "them project pickaninnies."

Well, my memory's cut off by a couple of plump old ladies fanning themselves on a rowhouse stoop...who ask if I'm an undertaker, owing to my peels. Ask if I can service someone's niece, faded in a drive-by not far from here. People dying on the street, and all these cops can do is make war on one another, why? The simple answer's the scariest, and I'm just trying to grab Stripe and not get faded.

Immediately I clock an MPD Suburban idling near the bay doors to the medical wing, attached to the CTF, where male fiends and boozers dry out, and where all female jailbirds roost.

As I approach, two dudes in blazers pop out of the entrance and start talking into their sleeves like Feds but fuck, they ain't. I can see their MPD lapel pins from here, sun glinting, the size of old silver dollars. And not a single jail administrator or C.O. in sight. Yeah, Antonelli's got that kind of dap I guess.

The Suburban cuts off. This time someone familiar pops out.

"S'up bruv," Detective Woodman greets with a fake-ass grin. "Lookit you, all fresh and clean and walkin' like a for-real dee! How dick! You found Hakim Alexander . . . and then pulling that Pennsylvania shit . . . you continue to impress. S'pose it's all contingent on stayin' off the liquor and controlled dangerous substances. Sometimes you can hear the screams of these sorry-ass bastards in here goin' cold turkey clear 'cross the street. Don't seem to deter our folk, though, huh?"

I'd like to beat him with my shoe, as promised, but . . .

"Where's the Deputy Chief?"

"Inside. But someone wants to holla first . . . "

He gestures some flunky pinktoe in plainclothes seated in the Chevy—beyond the tinted glass so I can't get a full look if anyone else's in there. They frisk me and of course find the .25. Then Katie's phone. "It's a loner. Ain't got no crazy apps on it, just check."

"Kathleen?"

"Yeah."

Moron doesn't turn it off and tosses it to me. It's then that scent of Menthol jacks and perfume wafts from inside the Chevy to my nose.

"CiCi . . . Agave." I whisper.

"He . . . he don't like it when I smoke . . . " She leans into the light. "He waitin' on you, Mr. Cornish."

All I can do is tilt my head like an attentive dog when she speaks . . . to keep my dome from imploding. "It figures . . . you snitched me out to Linda, you go running to him. Playing both ends. I knew two females like that—one with a baby—and it didn't end well."

"I be smart, like you an' him, right?" Now she's swing her legs out of the seat so I can see her whole. Crop-top—silver lame. Tight denim capris, heels. Like she's on the way to the MGM Casino over at National Harbor for some foolishness. Kept and owned, foolishness. Her eyelashes bat, her moist red lips twitch, awaiting my affirmation.

Fuck that.

"Someone broken like you is like a mouse to cheese with the motherfucker who broke her. That one female with the baby? She was girl who name meant 'Piety' in Spanish. Choose her rich babydaddy three times her age over freedom, a fresh start. Stripe and I found her with two bullets to the head, on a traphouse floor. All dude wanted was the baby . . . "

No effect whatsoever seems to register under all that Maybelline, MAC and shit. "He don't want my baby. He want me. *He always want me.* Tryna tell that white bitch cop that shit years ago . . . till today. Nah but she say she 'save' boffa us. *Ha*! I makes stone choices, Mr. Cornish, then an' now." She flicks the spent butt out the doorway. The female plainclothes picks it up and that's a smart or a scary thing. "Why you look so sad," she continues. "Now you got something on him. My baby safe but ain't living in bullshit, no mo'; Figgis . . . fuck that bitch. You get your boy Stripe in there, and Dante—he be gentle wiff me now, not hard, now that I come back . . . "

"Angry fuckin' is the best kind, I hear."

"That's enough!" the female plainclothes spits. "Go inside. He's waiting!"

Woodman jams the spout of a nine millie in my shoulder. I igg him . . . *he finna to shoot nobody!*

"I feel for you, Agave. I really do." No clue why I'm catching this shit for her, now...

She frowns, still vaguely beautiful. "Why you still me call that?"

"Cause the Greek one who killed Pentheus, her own son—she didn't know what she was doing. All part of this fucked up game, and we little humans get played, bleed." And as her frown softens I tell her, "Thanks for the vax shot by the way. Prolly saved my ass."

Now she's grinning, and coos, "Somebody got to tell the tale. You come look me up, Mr. Cornish."

The female plainsclothes shuts the door, and I don't see Agave . . . no more.

I turn to spy the CCTV cameras in the bay and over the sallyport. Their indicator lights are dark.

Woodman hands me off to more goons in blazers and suits who shove me through the sallyport's steel door; the C.O. at the main desk, the other at the metal detector . . . a white chick, young intake nurse . . . none of them even look at me or say a thing through their masked mouths. My ass's tough to miss, right, so the whole jont's on lockdown as if Uncle Joe Biden' visiting.

Still . . . I hear the squawking from elevator bank going up to where the lady jailbirds roost, and the wails from the drug rehab cots. It's not like those folks're roaming free. Thing is, we aren't going to that bank. They're pushing me to single elevator open on the opposite wall.

Sign says "Lower Level: Physical Therapy-Lab-Pathology."

When the doors open it's like an arctic wave hits me, but I'm already shivering. If I'm going to get murked at least I won't have to go far. Then it hits me.

"Why . . . down here?"

"Shut up."

We pass the labs, weight room and stuff for when you're missing a leg or have a head wound . . .

"In there!" the goons bark.

They open the door. And it's even colder.

Dark, but for a spot-lit metal table.

And on that table, a sheet pulled up to narrow, hairless chest, is my Ernesto, my Stripe, my boy. And everything I've ever promised, taught, lied, joked, scolded plays in my dome for an instant . . . until I'm howling . . . or I'm kissing his swollen, black and blue cheek, struggling to wake him up. Or I'm doing both I don't know.

And I hear, from the shadows, "Yeah, I feel terrible. I mean, I told these *scimmie,* these *testa dura,* look—keep the kid in solitary, safe. But they're 'short staffed' from the frickin' virus." I guess they're showing me his arm . . . I don't know . . . I'm floating, I'm sinking, and I hear this devil, this white piece of bloody stool say, "Lotta holes. Who's to say they are recent or old . . . but I'm thinking one of them was the Nita . . . protonitzene . . . this piece of shit Carlos Ramos was selling through his homies locked in here, and the homies gave your boy a final taste. Carlos died, by the way. Some of my friends have friends still in this shithole from January Six. Can't have them near any spick drugs, eh?"

My wet eyes dart to the Deputy Chief. "You . . . " *You* what? What can I do?

"Look, if he has legal family here, we can get them a settlement. Off the books, of course . . . "

Like it's no big deal to him. He's the monster, not Linda. Death's just part of the job; this is a piece of meat.

I have no further need for grief.

I'm at him like a were-bear . . . I'm my own snarling, phlegm trailing Chimera . . .

. . . and yet before I can separate his ghoulish head from his turkey neck . . . I hear a click, a pop. The probes pierce my hip, my ass.

And with a buzz comes the what-for . . . and the electricity puts me down like Mike Tyson's hammered my head and only smoking roast beef would meet your eyes if you clocked my brain now.

I come to, seated in a small office swivel chair, and the room's more lit up much to my horror. My Stripe's still on that table, bruised and quiet forever. My courage . . . I dunno . . . it's a mere puddle on the concrete floor.

The Deputy Chief's pacing. Holding the .25 Woodman took from my sock. A goon fingers Katie's phone, still on.

"Nasty little gun. My cousin . . . yes, blood cousin . . . was a cleaner for the Philly mob. Nicky Testa's crew. Used these rather than larger caliber for reasons only criminals understand."

I think that's what he's saying, as my ears have gone all tinny. "I'm . . . gonna kill you."

"No you aren't, Cornish. You're going to sit and not interrupt, okay? Because every minute I get to know, means you aren't dead and there's a possibility we can work out a system where you stay not dead. Now, where was I? Ah yes, I was a street cop in Wilmington, Delaware after college because I wanted to belong, to kick ass and take names but Wilmington was a joke. Yeah, corporate headquarters in shiny buildings, but beyond that it's a ghetto . . . in a marsh . . . like the District. Yet in Delaware. *Frickin'* Sleepy Joe's Delaware!"

Even that quick pop of electricity could re-scramble me, undo me, kick me back if it hasn't already wrecked my ticker. Still, like an idiot, groggily hiss and curse to keep myself from sobbing like a child.

"Stay with me Big Boy. You need to know this *truth* because a lot's gonna come to light very soon and I must know who'll be in my corner."

Even in my fog I note his underlings almost roll their rolls when he says "truth," like it's some cultish mantra he forces them to memorize.

"I sure as Hell wasn't going back to Philly so I joined the Army as an MP and did the counter-terrorism training. Panama came and I did counter-intelligence . . . then got called back off the reserves for Iraq One. Was a major in the MPs transferred to Ft. Meade and then the Pentagon security detail. That's how I came to 'Chocolate City,' when it was a lot more chocolate."

"W-what'd you want from me, man?"

"*Ma'rone*, fella," he mocks. "I'm gonna do right by you." He kisses his thumb. "Now, yes—Linda's done. Her kind is done before they even begin because the underlying power was never theirs. Viewing the world from the bottom, from the mud sill, I figured you would have realized that sooner. Notice I didn't call her a 'reformer' or social justice warrior. That's even more of a joke—and Linda's in on the joke, trust me. *She's* the damn racist!"

"But you're the empathic type, huh?" This bastard's sicker than Bracht.

"No, I'm practical. None of you read the stats: with all that 'community policing' and officer friendly bullshit her uniforms and detectives still put more niggers in the ground than the Klan, spareribs, and other niggers combined! "

He takes my squint for more hate. *Nah.* It's just that this motherfucker and Daddy'd get along sportingly. So I heave a load of real truth. "Uh-huh, Linda's a piece of shit who abused her authority. You, you're just another gangster, like your family."

He's storming right to me in a lather as if Stripe's not even there.

"You're the piece of shit! I was appointed to my responsibilities by the former *African American* chief of police . . . served him, a Latino and *two white female chiefs*, nothing *but* black mayors including a crackheaded commie in my tenure! Recruited by *ten* major cities to be chief yet never getting promoted to the top cop here. *Here, where it counts*! And *I'm* the frickin' ogre?"

My head's starting to clear despite my heart being split, roasted, wrung out. I try not to look at the table as I cough, mutter, "Again. I-I want amnesty for me, anyone connected to me. I want a settlement for this boy's f-family. And I'll let know you if I want your left nut, too . . . depending."

He laughs. "When I first saw you in that shithole apartment on Georgia Avenue, I couldn't quite believe the Feds' file when I checked up on you. Oh, not the same one Linda saw; I had to tickle my friends at Mar-a-Lago to get that. I bet Linda thought you'd be a wrecking crew on me, huh? That shit you pulled at the Carrollsburg, taking out my CI's . . . you're no joke when you're on point. Quite a change from when you're stuttering, vomiting, living in a tent with these crusty bitches Verna Leggett's got working that zoo."

"Evolution."

"*Intelligent design.* The Lord hewed a perfect storm from the firmament: your race's self-destructive cupidity for murder and rioting, hell-bent on taking us down the same hole . . . a germ invented by the Chinese comes to sap America's soul, our freedoms. And then our *real* President calls us to task."

"Legitimacy's overrated, yeah—you told me. So you were prolly geeking for the folk attacking the Capitol."

He sighs and grins. "That would be a breach of my oath."

"Being a pimp in blue . . . feeding molesters in suits. Rape, abuse. Your oath cover that?" Now he's the one squinting and I'm done with him running his spaghetti-hole. "*The girl.*"

"Ah yes. Your only card. Because I believe Linda has your phone . . . not this sparkly one here, but one that has certain info on it. Bless her I don't know how she pulled it off up there in Harrisburg when I have an army of allies there—but she really did me a favor."

"By taking the phone, knowing damn well it damages her, too? Or by not demanding a DNA test on that child . . . by stealing the her, hiding her six years ago, pretending to go after CiCi to bait you into protecting your . . . lover? Investment?"

"Cornish, I'm not a stupid man. You expect me to believe that you will just turn over this kid in return for all this amnesty bullshit. I'm an ogre, remember? I mean, if you're that ruthless I should run it up the flagpole about giving you a job, huh? Steady work . . . "

"You want her. That's what you mean by Linda doing you a favor. Croc was right."

"Who?"

"She can be a real daughter to you now, with all the black squeezed out, huh?"

"The scandal in my job, potential to explode in a chain reaction, destroying everything . . . was never as frightening to me as the scandal in my soul, we clear?"

I nod, trying not to look at Stripe's face just beyond Antonelli's chair. A pain hits my spine and it's almost as bad as being tased, I realize what's going to happen next. And not to me.

"Poor CiCi," I whisper.

"Excuse me?"

"You heard me. Not smart enough. The boys in the Crown Vic'll collecting her from the Suburban. Dumping here where: Blue Ridge Mountains, Chesapeake Bay?"

He just shrugs.

I look at Stripe's body. "I want the kid at juvie, street name 'Sweet Sunshine,' part of the deal. Prosecute Linda, whatever. But leave Verna and SFME be."

"Verna Leggett's a hero in this town. I'm shocked you'd insinuate any other treatment."

"Not running fade on you. I swear. Just want it done."

"So where's my kid?"

Okay . . . he really doesn't know . . .

"Before I say . . . you hip me to who among the Feds you got in your pocket? They gonna keep Verna clear? U.S. Attorney . . . Justice . . . FBI?"

He's waving his hands as if an annoyed housewife assuring an impatient tot. "I clean up my own garbage."

"You boasted about your pals . . . "

"Not playing games with you. And you got neither Linda's connections nor her Houdini-like knack for getting out of a bind, eh? I got Linda by her unshaven dyke curly ones this time."

"Al right man. You win. But I need . . . to check in with St. Jude's. That's where she is. Sanctuary. You just barging in demanding a thirteen-year-old runaway will rattle them. *And* the Diocese. They've *never* had this much cop muscle show up, have they?"

He doesn't ponder why I'm asking, just agrees. "Good point. I don't want to be denied the rites . . . *misericordia*."

So yeah, a buzzcut asshole in a gray suit, mustard-stained necktie hands me Katie's decorated phone. Says I can make one call, on speaker. Oh, and if I try to talk in some weird code, my ass gets tased again.

"*Weird code*?" I scoff. "Nah. I say it real. To your face."

He taps the number for me, holds the phone close, warns me again not to fuck around.

"Brother Karl-Maria," I say. "Yes, yours in Christ. Listen . . . Ernesto . . . he was . . . killed in a jail assault." I stare at Antonelli, who hits me back with a sneer, as if I insulted him. "No leads, according to the . . . corrections officers. Thank you, Brother."

"Wrap it up, Big Fella" Antonelli whispers. "It's cold down here and I want to see my little girl . . . "

"Police want to come from here at the CDF to do a welfare check . . . on the girl, Vickie. Hmmm . . . yeah. Hmmm . . . do you think they can have her ready, in chapel? Sanctuary? Look, these cops are special, like detectives, yeah, at the Daly Building, in charge, and they haven't been to the church before so maybe you could tell the residents that nobody's there to put a case on them. Hear me. You know how they be about po-po, right, especially Monica, yeah, Monica, she's crazy."

I swipe off the call. The SOD cop lets me keep the phone and immediately I get a text. They are all too busy glaring as

I bend to kiss Stripe's cold cheek. I whisper in his ear, "Me and my dad are the same, *m'hijo.*" I genuflect, kiss him again.

"I didn't want this, Cornish," the Deputy Chief shares, softly, as he watches me. "Nor did I want to be the keeper of men's vices. But we're at *war.* You do crappy things when you're at war. And a *secret* war at that. I'm sure Linda said the same thing."

"But y'all really *aren't* each other's enemies," I tell him as I wipe my eyes. "You're just opposite sides of the same shit-caked coin." I gesture to my poor Ernesto. "He's the enemy. I'm the enemy. Even CiCi. You don't hate us, man. You're *scared* of us."

"Yeah."

CHAPTER 30

"Everybody Dies"

THE SUBURBAN SLINGSHOTS AROUND RFK STADIUM almost in a full circle, then stops to pick up two more plainclothes. Now it's a party, as one of these motherfuckers—pale, ginger-haired orangutan has got Croc's erect dick of a dream gun, an HK MP7, slung under his gray suit jacket. Now I'm clocking him as one of the dudes from the Crown Vic. Trust, he probably was the one who dipped out Little, given his wolfish look.

So Woodman's driving, female cop up there with him, the orangutan and another plainclothes flanking me on the seat, two more back there with Antonelli. Nobody's masked because these types, they live forever, right?

Well, the Deputy Chief's fuming about something. Can't hear what as I strain the seatbelt. But then . . . "Oxidize the air. I can still smell the bitch's cigarettes!"

That's all he cared about CiCi . . . Agave. And now I think about Stripe, fending off blows, enduring that terror and agony. To keep him off balance and hold my rage down I say to him, sweet as pie, "I'm gonna call Ernesto's cousin. Make arrangements for his body . . . "

"You're kidding me, right?" Antonelli scoffs. "Johnnie find out what his malfunction is . . . "

"His family's gotta know if you are going to handle this right. Off the books."

When Woodman chuckles uh-huh I lose it a litte. *Okay a lot.* I tell him he's going to be on a slab next.

We're stopped at a light; Woodman turns and scowls at me, then begs Antonelli, "Chief, permission to tune up this big spook on general principle?"

I guess I do have him at-ease. "See, Johnnie? They can't help it. Must be some Mandingo versus Cormantine thing from Africa. Shocked they're still here, after rock, AIDS, COVID now clipping each other just to be on Instagram."

If that doesn't shame Woodman then he's all the way gone to these crackers. "Sorry, Chief."

All the way gone. Yep.

"Woodman, if you're gonna be Spec Ops, you know we do what we do based on the rules. And now our guest's agreed to abide, then go and sin no more, right . . . *Dickie*?"

"Till the day I die."

"*Hmph* . . . everybody dies." He looks out the window. "Make your call."

"*Hola, soy Ricardo Cornish...siento que Ernesto haya muerto. Sí . . . muy importanto.*"

"Wait," the orangutan with the heavy metal cuts me off. "English!"

"He doesn't know much." I cheese and keep going. " . . . *estamos llegando al lugar. Prepárate o yo también estaré muerto* . . . okay, I cry with you for ten minutes, that's all they will let me talk now . . . "

"Cute, Cornish. I told you we'd take care of the family so cut the crap. Mike, cuff him if he says another word. Call Sky Two. Just want some cover till we are out of here with the subject." He looks at me, smiles. "Her first ride with me might be in the chopper. Second gift after this teddy bear I got her. Someone stole it."

We're coming up on South Capitol now . . . and the very spot I first clocked Moses Roffe treating with this very Suburban.

"I tracked Roffe to you at the hotel here."

"So?" the Deputy Chief grunts. Roffe was just a wheel cog. Fungible, forgettable.

"Yo'" I call to Woodman. "We need to park over there. Figure you don't want this ops out in the open. It's still Linda's force."

"He's right," Antonelli barks. "Put us over here, by this lot."

Woodman's a shitty chauffeur but we are far enough away from the building for my purposes. Tall old elms and short cherry trees shade the church and SFME but not this crappy lot, and it's fitting Antonelli can't stand direct sun. He's frowning, sprouting droplets of sweat on his starched white shirt collar, mopping his face with his handkerchief as me and his squad climbs the granite steps to the church door.

"Sick irony," he muses. "That new wing, eh, Cornish? *K'ymira Thomas*? Jesus. I'll send another donation . . . "

The female plainclothes cautions before I pull open the double doors, "Be smart, Cornish. Hope you didn't signal a hundred homeless assholes to ambush us 'cause it won't go well."

"Prolly only ten, fifteen dudes up in there today."

"Pandemic," Antonelli adds. "Most would rather die in tents in our public parks and spaces than a proper shelter, with medical care. Aren't you glad you've bettered yourself?"

"Lotta folk died of the 'rona," I tell him. "The rest died of bad luck."

Once inside, Antonelli and I dip in the font, dab from the oil. Spread it to our lips and foreheads, as if that shit's going to mean anything when judgment comes. There's Brother Karl-Maria, another robed dude, a nun who's name I never got, all standing with a staffer jingling keys and a two-way.

"They're here to collect the young lady," I tell them. "Is she packed?"

Karl-Maria says, "In a minute." He eyes the HK dangling from a strap inside the ginger boy's jacket. "Remember where you are, officer."

Antonelli doesn't correct the orangutan. Rather, he laughs and observes, "This place is actually *very* pretty . . . all the time I'd be over at SFME and those simpering traphouse queens had their hands out I figured this was just a chapel for the bums and junkies . . . but this is a for-real church. Wow . . . "

"Took in homeless, wounded . . . when British burned the city in 1814," I school him. "You know the third verse of the "Star Spangled Banner" . . . about the 'hireling and slave?'"

"Yeah whatever." The heat in the nave's getting to him. The clergy offer ice water but he turns them down. "The kid," Antonelli then presses, "I won't have to spend a lot of time on any PTSD, bad dreams? I mean, Linda's patsies were cranks, but they weren't . . . child molesters?"

This guy's in another realm where the rest of us don't count. Yeah, Daddy—you'd be ace boon coons. "Why you asking me, Chief?"

"Your background, Cornish."

"She's tough. But, um, how gonna explain her to the world?"

"I got people who look after me and mine working on that. Need to know basis."

Karl-Maria quickly nods and says, "Verna's got her. Coming . . . soon."

That seems to put him off. "You want me to protect Miss Leggett and yet you drag her in deeper? Not very smart."

Fuck this bastard. "You saw shit about me in a file . . . about me and Jaime Bracht. Same file from the FBI and DHS Linda had?"

He smiles gleefully. "Bracht was a scumbag loose cannon. One think I bet Sleepy Joe wants to keep under wraps as well."

"So none of that scared you . . . about me?"

"He ain't shit, Chief," Woodman spits.

"What kind of *scooch* are you being now, Cornish? You using again?" Antonelli turns to his entourage. "Stay frosty . . . Detective Woodman, get out to the truck and call in some back-up, that nurse Roffe knew to keep the girl calm . . . and get Sky-Two's sit ref, okay? Chop-Chop!"

The bastard Woodman snickers at me, and yet his two-way crackling furiously as he hustles down the aisle past the empty pews. "Say again Sky-Two? Sky-Two that's not making sense . . . stand-by so I can get a better signal . . . "

He's out the oak doors. Hard to hear even the nasty traffic on South Capitol through those things.

And this asshole's not paying attention. "I want a place I can talk to her, in private," Antonelli declares. "Doesn't need to be in the Sanctuary, Father," he says. "Just don't want her to be around . . . you know . . . your flock. Homeless men and such."

"*Brother*, not Father," Karl-Maria huffs. "I'm sure the facility next door will accommodate you."

"Yeah," I add. "Better than the munie shelter."

"Watch your mouth, Cornish." Then Antonelli's mobile sounds. "*Ma'rone* . . . can you believe this? Code Seven text from Daly Building. Jesus." He swipes and answers the anticipated incoming call. He puts it on speaker . . .

. . . and swear God, I thinking Linda Figgis's been dying to do this to him . . . since I did it to her.

"*Look . . . outside . . . the window.*"

"Wait, is this you, Linda? Have you finally gone into uterine hysteria? Whadya mean 'look outside?' I got your *ass* Chief! You resign, then we think about keeping you out of prison! Linda? *Linda*?"

I'm smiling as the nun cranks one of the stained-glass windows open and the female SOD officer shouts at her to hold still. But then that chick gets an eyeful and gasps.

"Chief—*look*!"

He does. "*Christ Almighty.*"

I'm guessing lots of running lights flashing out there . . . and now the sirens that were coming in silent are blasting. The entourage pull their weapons, including that mean little machine pistol.

Brother Karl-Maria grabs a bug-eyed, mumbling Antonelli by his arm. "This is a church! Put away those firearms!"

A minion shoves the clerics away. Holds them in his gun sights. So much for pious patriots, protocol, rules. Legitimacy's overrated, remember?

And now the Deputy Chief's on me. Old white man's not intimidated by my height. Old white man's always gotten his way, always crushed and stomped so effortlessly, without having blood spatter his suits. "What'd you do? Answer me you mope, you *scimmie*!"

Be easy to beat him to death. But not in a church. "Wasn't speaking in weird code, just Spanish . . . to a lady named Abalos . . . know her?"

"Disloyal Fed?"

"Nah man, one of your own. Then I got a text on my sparkly phone that LaKeisha was okay. And LaKeisha, being in the artillery . . . sent a barrage of info Detective Abalos' way."

"What?"

Now I let the bullhorn—and the concurrent livestream image Antonelli's bringing up on his own phone screen—be my fists, my foot. Scream, motherfucker! Die!

"*Deputy Chief Antonelli . . . this is Commander Gates, Deputy Chief Patterson. I have stripped your ERT of duty so no Tac officers are out here but be advised we will fire upon provocation. So I want you and your officers to holster their weapons and come out, turn yourselves in to Internal Affairs personnel. Dante . . . don't make us come in there after you. Media's on its way and we want this clean an' done before you're a Twitter meme!*"

He's glowering me . . . his team murmurs and twists about like amateurs caught with their draws down. "Arrest Linda Figgis," he shouts into the phone and out the open window. "That's an order!"

"*Chief Figgis has already put in her resignation effective twenty-four hours from now. She here with us, cooperating. Accordingly, I act with her authority, as well as the U.S. Attorney and Justice Department.*"

"The Feds wouldn't countenance this farce, this . . . this *mutiny*!"

"*Fed's are finally cleaning house right now, too. Dante. Stand-down . . .* "

"Bullcrap! You call Ernie Chou and Tex Behan at the Bureau, Bob Silvestri at the U.S. Marshals . . . Peggy Hart at

DHS and they will vouch and stop this and . . . " He pauses, and it's like his horror movie face's coming to a horror movie end . . . almost melting . . . as he realizes what he's said and who he's exposed . . .

. . . so I hear feedback in the corridor connecting the nave to SFME. Twelve's coming for Twelve. There's a knock on the outer doors, too and hear they come, gats drawn on their blue brethren. Jesus, Mary and Joseph I'd love to put a clip of Croc's ACPs into their asses. But then I'd be the one in the prison infirmary or in Potter's Field with Al-Mayadeen and so many others.

"*Chief*?" the orangutan pleads to his Gruppen Fuhrer, anxious to use his toy.

But Antonelli's quietly depositing himself in a creaky pew. "How . . . how? You had nothing. Only the kid. That implicates Linda, and Linda knows it's *mutually assured destruction.* CiCi's done . . . "

"Chief don't say another word," another minion groans.

"You . . . a nigger druggie . . . retarded . . . you had nothing . . . " he repeats, bewildered. "This is a set-up . . . and I'll shake it. And what you saw before, will be a Carvel's Ice Cream Cake compared what you will suffer, Cornish."

I shrug. "Like a man told me, there's predators, prey . . . but I'm scavenger. We just pretend to be reckless to force the kill. Then we move in when no one's lookin'. These people around me. They ain't scum. And now you'll suffer like them, they get to watch."

The cops . . . I won't say "good" cops . . . aren't waiting for a surrender so they are moving in through the corridor and the front door, disarming and cuffing Dante's praetorian guard, and I swear I see the friars and nuns sigh in unison, clutch at each other. They went to the mat for me, and most don't even know me.

When I hit the exit from the connecting corridor, I see they're evacuating SFME—staff on street, kids, toward the new building. The K'ymira Thomas Building. There's Katie, fretful . . . and she's pointing to swaying, listless, pudgy black woman with big glasses on her face . . . who once told me in a library restroom that she was a blond who rode dragons. Tearfully, I mouth, "*Love ya gurl.*"

She mouths back "*See? One day I'd save you.*"

Abruptly I hear a ruckus back in the nave. Antonelli's voice, raspy and wet now.

"You ingrates. Feckless pussies. Figgis'd have your balls in a jar were it not for me. Savages are running amok in this city and you call *me* the menace? My friends got friends in Congress . . . they will cut your budget and sanction you *dickless*!"

The older light-skinned brass with the potbelly—Patterson—just nods. "Some of them're named in what this man over here collected, emailed. And I know Figgis is slick. Her story's gonna curl like a bag of snakes, and we just got word from the White House that her story's gonna be *the* story. So that's the end of *your* story, Dante."

He's got that empty look I saw on Roffe. The look someone who's used to fucking and laughing about it gets when suddenly they're fucked—and it's no joke no more.

"Can't prove you had *my boy* killed," I call him out. "But when the house cleaning comes to the CDF, we'll see who snitches on you. Then it's conspiracy to commit murder . . . or reckless homicide . . . abuse of process, wrongful arrest . . . all of the above, whatever."

"Back off Cornish," Patterson instructs. A jake—looks like one of the females Linda had in her army—yanks Antonelli out of the pew but gives him the seemingly official courtesy of an uncuffed walk to the open doors. And there, I see the sky's darkening . . . one of those bad-ass thunderstorms we get here in the Capital of the World after a gruesome summer day must be cranking.

Maybe that's why Antonelli's smiling. The burning sun's shrouded. Dark loves dark.

Guess so. For now I see him whip around on the jake, giving her a swat to her windpipe. He pulls her Glock and for a second, I figure I'm getting the bullet tickle.

He grins. "Yeah, *everybody dies.* This is the only sin I'll answer for."

And like this terrible ride began, it ends with a dude putting the spout between his teeth, pulling the trigger.

He doesn't even get to see Vickie. Maybe CiCi can describe her to him, wherever they share torment now.

I see Figgis surrounded by cops and suits. More cops and suits cut me off before I can get too close but she clears a path.

"The bullhorn . . . was my dying request, so to speak," she says, her eyes a brighter blue. She peers at Detective Abalos, who's directing the EMT's hovering over Antonelli's body. "You know . . . we never got to Monica. She would've made a great, great asset."

"Instead, she did her duty."

"Yeah, hon'. Um . . . I hear about Ernesto. CDF personnel, they'll be punished. And the whole department . . . and the city government. It will a be massacre. But like my daughter says, the dinosaurs had to go for mammals to rule."

"Stripe died for my mistakes. Don't you dare link him to a fucking thing about you. Caught feelings, Linda. *Bad.* Your wife, your girls—the Chimera's claimed them now, too."

She's weeping. Chief Patterson comes waddling over when he sees it, shoves me out of the way. An officer ushers Figgis into the back of unit, like a perp. The window's down however, and before the Ford roars off Figgis calls to me, "*That'll do, pig.*"

Fuck her.

Oh . . . and the rain starts, in curtains of water. I see a damn COVID mask and what's probably Boris Karloff's blood flush and splash and mingle with the other gutter flotsam. Yeah, the deluge will stop soon, after cooling everything off. Never washes away the filth, though. Never.

"I-I'll do better than, baby. You stay safe, ole gurl." Yet en I want to book, forget. Hell, I don't even know if Boston's l alive.

'm cringing for a different reason when Croc's wheeled ough the glass doors to the metal detector. Yet he passes, nehow. The gunsel decides to hang outdoors, of course, grab a half-smoke. I give him ten bucks to share food n Mary, and so I'm the fool pushing pushing Croc onto the ator like the brother on the old cop show, *Ironside.* Couldn't you the show's particulars as my meds are leveling me out. east Croc's behaving. The E. Barrett Prettyman Federal rthouse was the last place he'd clocked his parents des ago. Alive, wearing street clothes.

ne grand jury's on the second floor and we're in a sparse , no TV, nothing but potted plants, a vending machine s been shut down since the 'rona, a table with the *ington Post,* some old magazines and I'd haven't seen so printed news since the days I hunted it to sleep on.

tter of fact it's today's *Post,* opened to an old image of . . . as K'ymira . . . and columns of text. I'm squinting gh my old eyes and my appointment for specs isn't till week: "*Closed-door testimony continues in the vast MPD l. Witnesses include former Child and Family Services officials, fficers from at least four jurisdictions as well as U.S. Park SFME director Verna Leggett. Nine former officers and coms of the MPD Special Operations Division have already been , with another seventy-three members of the department sumired. No information regarding compensation of the victims.*"

na'll be okay," I counsel.

at'd you say under oath?" LaKeisha prods.

't say."

CHAPTER 31

Here I Am Again . . .

GET SO BUGGY IN THIS KIND of building . . . soulless, official. Always bad shit to deal with. Usually, my own: dropping civil commitment in return for me going into the Air Force, swopping out a general discharge for an honorable discharge when I left the Air Force, my only auntie getting me off Daddy's will because I lived in a canvas bag.

Or last week, obtaining Stripe's death certificate. Hope his cousin got Nimchuk's check.

But today, with my paper from the Daly Building, and good promise kept by a bad person, they are calling my name along with a couple of other folk who managed to put two large together. Mostly white men, of course, half who look like refugees MPD, others who are the stereotype of cybergeeks. One dude frescoed with skin ink. And in front of me a cute pinktoe, must be closer to my age judging from the wisps of gray in the flaxen hair . . . so this is definitely her third act. *G'head girl*!

The registration's with D.C.'s Department of Regulatory Affairs but a cop's giving the oath. Yeah, a *cop*, and that's mean shit these days, real live. This is some scrawny brother from the Public Affairs Division—the mugs tapdancing in about a dozen crazy press conferences around Linda Figgis and Dante Antonelli.

And the oath? Well, there are too many money launderers, hackers, corporate spies, henchmen for rich rapists or their sons in toney colleges out there, so the "Sandinistas" on the City Council reckoned. Now, as a formality to getting your final PI license, you got to recite an oath. I raise my right hand, I repeat what this skinny dude says. I look around and only the pinktoe seems as cised by this as me. I'm grinning like I won the lottery.

" . . . and though I am granted authority, I am also enjoined by duty, and shall never forget that I am part of the community in which I serve and apply my skills."

Almost all of these folks leave when the ceremony ends. The pinktoe's whole family, however, including a toddler granddaughter, remain to take pictures. Makes my eyes wet and maybe yeah, I've gone soft. Anyway, they don't seem to notice the big black man sneaking past them for the elevator down, and I like that.

In the lobby the guards are still doing temperature checks and enforcing masks but I'm on my way out.

I see Katie and LaKeisha, waiting where the Uber left us off.

Two former homeless women. Addled in some way, still. No one believes me when I say it was *they* who took out this whole horror show in the end. They, titans! Look at them!

But you know, it's better that everyone thinks it was me. Dante's secret pals in the Congress, in hayseed police forces all around . . . *fuck around and find out*!

"That was quick." Katie gushes. "May I see?"

I hand her the paper now stamped with some
and the wallet-sized ID card with a little badg
that's boss as fuck.

She passes it to LaKeisha, who just shr
that's Keesh.

"Okay," her tight little voice begins to wind
what happens next I think I'll be needing a jol
replace Stripe but I can kick in with my disabi

"Keesh . . . "

"See, you need a data person in this biz r
and with us as former homeless persons, y
addict and alcoholic, and me as mentally i
think of the diversity work we will get . . . u

I was going to say, let's just wait, see. In
Why not." I wink and it finally brings a sm

"Where's Croc?" I ask.

LaKeisha gestures. Croc's down the sidew
his phone. Him in a wheelchair's just wron
it lovingly as if an English matron—fuckin

Yeah, so we all join him, move to anotl
3rd and Constitution just across the
enter, I see a pair of dirty feet spring
ringing this place; possessions and two
small cardboard box.

"That's Mary, remember?" Katie wh
vetted, labelled acceptable, moved alo
Poor LaKeisha just folds her arms,
ries us with her eyes.

"Dickie?" Mary calls, fiddling wit
"Y'all want some . . . yer go home, wu
an' see me, huh?"

Croc smirks, tells her, "Leave him be, baby. Men keep heroes . . . but the Lord always be keepin'—"

"A ledger," I finish.

A red bulb flashes over the door, a tone sounds. Somebody's done, hopefully free to go. Relief floods and buoys me when a federal marshal escorts Verna into the waiting room then departs.

She's dressed in a blue pants suit and blouse, as if a tinier VP Kamala. Maybe it worked, because she's embracing the two women but not Croc, who just huffs, bites up a stick of gum.

I'm standing, awaiting my hug. I just get a shy smile.

"How's it looking?" I ask.

"I'm still here. Talk to my lawyer this evening. SFME will go on. My donors—I dunno."

"And Linda?"

"I-I have no idea. Maybe *you* do. Congratulations by the way. Fully licensed."

Croc finally speaks up, gruff and no gristle. "You ain't no ingénue, Miss Verna. Ev'ryone gets some kinda hook-up. Thas how D.C. works." You aren't allowed to use a mobile phone in the spot, but he opens his, shows a news brief of a rally somewhere across the river in Virginia, scheduled to turn in a march with the Washington Monument. Amid the flags, some of Dixie, banners, decorated cars and trucks and motorcycles, are placards pasted with huge pictures: "Faces of the Fallen." One such is of Dante Antonelli. "See? Even the Devil gets a parade . . . "

My dome and gut are quickly sore and sour and I need the men's room, some ice water. Uh-huh, Verna will or will not get through this, she will or will not join me for a sandwich tonight, a Rock Creek cola, on a bench overlooking the Potomac, watching the real people. Maybe a sandwich made by Raynata, now at a deli on U Street serving the hipsters and hustlers alike not far from the corner of Florida and Seventh where Al-Mayadeen first tracked me. Too bad the minimum wage won't pay enough for lawyers, so all she can do is see her son jointly with his other, newer, parents who took him, in the words of a judge, "in good faith." Again, I have no higher claim. I can't ever see Maximiliano until he's eighteen and ready for the truth. I'll probably be in a nursing home.

Eighteen. Stripe's age. Yeah in D.C., everyone gets some kind of hook-up . . . whether you want it or not.

So I excuse myself, cut down the hall, minding what the guards and marshals say about my route to the john and to wear a mask when in the common areas because there's a lot going on in the courthouse today.

Before I'm about to roll up in the shitter, I take out my phone, furtive and all secret I try to call the counselor handling Vittoria Sophia. Not cool, I know. Especially when the FBI dredged near Sandy Point, in Annapolis. Found her mother.

I swipe off. Best for all of us. But see, when I do this I just happened to notice, swear to God, one weird elevator down the corridor, all lit green and red, bristling with uniformed and plainclothes marshals. One dude's toting a shotgun.

I'm thinking maybe it's the ones the federal judges use, or maybe the really bad Dillinger and Hannibal Lechter motherfuckers in fetters and shackles.

Yet when the door opens out comes one of the U.S. Attorneys who interrogated me, and her boss from Justice who read me how the world was going to be . . . and to what

North Carolina barrier island Linda Figgis and her wife and her multicolor kids were relocating.

Another woman follows, teetering on high heels and in a dress that's stoplight red and frankly makes the two lawyers look like schoolgirls. Long mane of black hair, streaked with a bit of silver. Hips, breasts barely corralled by that . . . that dress . . . and . . . she's speaking to them . . .

. . . in . . . Spanish?

The wind's out my damn lungs, my feet seem glued to the marble floor and if I was going to vomit, piss my suit pants—I guess it would've, should've happened.

I call out, almost meekly, as if an elderly man. "*Esmeralda*?"

I hear the federal marshals shouting, yet all I see is her face, turning to meet my voice. Her anthracite black eyes widen. Lips redder than that dress part.

"*Mi amor.* You don't have much time . . . "

About the Author

Christopher Chambers is a crime novelist, lawyer, professor of media studies at Georgetown University, and International Fellow at International Conflict Resolution Center. His previous works include the first book in the Dickie Cornish detective series, *Scavenger*, as well as the novels *A Prayer for Deliverance* and *Sympathy for the Devil* (NAACP Image Award nominee); the graphic anthology (with Gary Phillips) *The Darker Mask*; and the PEN/Malamud honorable mention story "Leviathan." He was also a contributor to the Anthony award-winning anthology *The Obama Inheritance* and *Black Pulp 2* as well as *The Faking of the President*. Professor Chambers is also a regular commentator/contributor on media and culture issues on SiriusXM Radio, ABC News, HuffPost. He resides in his hometown of Washington, D.C. with his family and German Shepherd, Max.

RECENT AND FORTHCOMING BOOKS FROM THREE ROOMS PRESS

FICTION

Lucy Jane Bledsoe
No Stopping Us Now

Rishab Borah
The Door to Inferna

Meagan Brothers
Weird Girl and What's His Name

Christopher Chambers
Scavenger
Standalone

Ebele Chizea
Aquarian Dawn

Ron Dakron
Hello Devilfish!

Robert Duncan
Loudmouth

Michael T. Fournier
Hidden Wheel
Swing State

Aaron Hamburger
Nirvana Is Here

William Least Heat-Moon
Celestial Mechanics

Aimee Herman
Everything Grows

Kelly Ann Jacobson
Tink and Wendy

Jethro K. Lieberman
Everything Is Jake

Eamon Loingsigh
Light of the Diddicoy
Exile on Bridge Street

John Marshall
The Greenfather

Aram Saroyan
Still Night in L.A.

Robert Silverberg
The Face of the Waters

Stephen Spotte
Animal Wrongs

Richard Vetere
The Writers Afterlife
Champagne and Cocaine

Julia Watts
Quiver
Needlework

Gina Yates
Narcissus Nobody

MEMOIR & BIOGRAPHY

Nassrine Azimi and Michel Wasserman
Last Boat to Yokohama: The Life and Legacy of Beate Sirota Gordon

William S. Burroughs & Allen Ginsberg
Don't Hide the Madness: William S. Burroughs in Conversation with Allen Ginsberg edited by Steven Taylor

James Carr
BAD: The Autobiography of James Carr

Judy Gumbo
Yippie Girl: Exploits in Protest and Defeating the FBI

Judith Malina
Full Moon Stages: Personal Notes from 50 Years of The Living Theatre

Phil Marcade
Punk Avenue: Inside the New York City Underground, 1972–1982

Jililian Marshall
Japanthem: Counter-Cultural Experiences; Cross-Cultural Remixes

Alvin Orloff
Disasterama! Adventures in the Queer Underground 1977–1997

Nicca Ray
Ray by Ray: A Daughter's Take on the Legend of Nicholas Ray

Stephen Spotte
My Watery Self: Memoirs of a Marine Scientist

PHOTOGRAPHY-MEMOIR

Mike Watt
On & Off Bass

SHORT STORY ANTHOLOGIES

SINGLE AUTHOR

The Alien Archives: Stories
by Robert Silverberg

First-Person Singularities: Stories
by Robert Silverberg
with an introduction by John Scalzi

Tales from the Eternal Café: Stories
by Janet Hamill, with an introduction by Patti Smith

Time and Time Again: Sixteen Trips in Time
by Robert Silverberg

Voyagers: Twelve Journeys in Space and Time
by Robert Silverberg

MULTI-AUTHOR

Crime + Music: Twenty Stories of Music-Themed Noir
edited by Jim Fusilli

Dark City Lights: New York Stories
edited by Lawrence Block

The Faking of the President: Twenty Stories of White House Noir
edited by Peter Carlaftes

Florida Happens: Bouchercon 2018 Anthology
edited by Greg Herren

Have a NYC I, II & III: New York Short Stories;
edited by Peter Carlaftes & Kat Georges

Songs of My Selfie: An Anthology of Millennial Stories
edited by Constance Renfrow

The Obama Inheritance: 15 Stories of Conspiracy Noir
edited by Gary Phillips

This Way to the End Times: Classic and New Stories of the Apocalypse
edited by Robert Silverberg

MIXED MEDIA

John S. Paul
Sign Language: A Painter's Notebook (photography, poetry and prose)

DADA

Maintenant: A Journal of Contemporary Dada Writing & Art (Annual, since 2008)

HUMOR

Peter Carlaftes
A Year on Facebook

FILM & PLAYS

Israel Horovitz
My Old Lady: Complete Stage Play and Screenplay with an Essay on Adaptation

Peter Carlaftes
Triumph For Rent (3 Plays)
Teatrophy (3 More Plays)

Kat Georges
Three Somebodies: Plays about Notorious Dissidents

TRANSLATIONS

Thomas Bernhard
On Earth and in Hell
(poems of Thomas Bernhard with English translations by Peter Waugh)

Patrizia Gattaceca
Isula d'Anima / Soul Island
(poems by the author in Corsican with English translations)

César Vallejo | Gerard Malanga
Malanga Chasing Vallejo
(selected poems of César Vallejo with English translations and additional notes by Gerard Malanga)

George Wallace
EOS: Abductor of Men
(selected poems in Greek & English)

ESSAYS

Richard Katrovas
Raising Girls in Bohemia: Meditations of an American Father

Far Away From Close to Home
Vanessa Baden Kelly

Womentality: Thirteen Empowering Stories by Everyday Women Who Said Goodbye to the Workplace and Hello to Their Lives
edited by Erin Wildermuth

POETRY COLLECTIONS

Hala Alyan
Atrium

Peter Carlaftes
DrunkYard Dog
I Fold with the Hand I Was Dealt

Thomas Fucaloro
It Starts from the Belly and Blooms

Kat Georges
Our Lady of the Hunger

Robert Gibbons
Close to the Tree

Israel Horovitz
Heaven and Other Poems

David Lawton
Sharp Blue Stream

Jane LeCroy
Signature Play

Philip Meersman
This Is Belgian Chocolate

Jane Ormerod
Recreational Vehicles on Fire
Welcome to the Museum of Cattle

Lisa Panepinto
On This Borrowed Bike

George Wallace
Poppin' Johnny

Three Rooms Press | New York, NY | Current Catalog: www.threeroomspress.com

Three Rooms Press books are distributed by Publishers Group West: www.pgw.com